**Praise for the historical romances
of Patricia Ryan . . .**

The Sun and the Moon

"Never one to disappoint, Ms. Ryan has once again
delivered her readers a novel that packs a punch.
Just as we think we have the ending all figured out, she
hits us with an incredible twist."   —*The Literary Times*

"With each new medieval from Ms. Ryan, her
plotting and characters get better and better.
Filled with mystery, suspense, intrigue, and very
passionate romance. . . . I absolutely loved this story!"
    —*The Old Book Barn Gazette*

Silken Threads

"Patricia Ryan moves *Rear Window* to medieval
London, and does things Hitchcock never dreamed of!
Fresh, swift, and sexy."   —Mary Jo Putney

"*Silken Threads* resonates with the sounds, smells,
intrigues and passions of the Middle Ages. Add
engaging characters, authentic historical details and a
well-crafted mystery and you have a delectable
tapestry."   —*Romantic Times*

"A rich and rewarding book. The characters are
fully realized, the setting is impeccably accurate,
and the mystery kept me guessing. . . . *Silken Threads*
is romance at its best. This one goes on my keeper
shelf."   —*The Romance Reader* (Five stars)

continued on next page . . .

"Graeham and Joanna are an appealing pair."
—*Publishers Weekly*

"The conclusion has surprises and twists that would have had Hitchcock on his feet cheering. I know I was. . . . A keeper. . . ."
—Thea Brady, CompuServe Romance Reviews

Wild Wind

"A sensual, emotionally involving, and compelling story of forbidden love that readers will not soon forget."
—*Library Journal*

Secret Thunder

"A wonderful writer whose talent continues to enchant readers."
—*Romantic Times*

"A marvelous love story from the queen of medieval romance. . . . I will buy anything Patricia Ryan writes."
—*The Literary Times*

"Totally absorbing. . . . Full-bodied and rich, like vintage wine."
—*The Old Book Barn Gazette*

Heaven's Fire

"Lusty and exhilarating, this is medieval romance at its best. . . . A splendid tale!" —Particia Gaffney

"An intense tale of deception, religion, murder, and romance. Dramatic . . . a unique love story you will not soon forget." —*Rendezvous*

"Pure reading nirvana." —*Affaire de Coeur*

Falcon's Fire

"A richly textured pageant of passion. A grand adventure!" —Susan Wiggs

"A passionate tale of deception and forbidden love. Don't miss *Falcon's Fire*." Suzanne Barclay

"A powerful debut novel by an exciting new talent, *Falcon's Fire* will ignite your imagination and passion." —*Romantic Times*

More tales of medieval romance
by Patricia Ryan:

Falcon's Fire
Heaven's Fire
Secret Thunder
Wild Wind

And the story of how
Graeham and Joanna of Eastingham
meet and fall in love:
Silken Threads

The Sun and the Moon

Patricia Ryan

A SIGNET BOOK

SIGNET
Published by New American Library, a division of
Penguin Putnam Inc., 375 Hudson Street,
New York, New York 10014, U.S.A.
Penguin Books Ltd, 27 Wrights Lane,
London W8 5TZ, England
Penguin Books Australia Ltd,
Ringwood, Victoria, Australia
Penguin Books Canada Ltd, 10 Alcorn Avenue,
Toronto, Ontario, Canada M4V 3B2
Penguin Books (N.Z.) Ltd, 182–190 Wairau Road,
Auckland 10, New Zealand

Penguin Books Ltd, Registered Offices:
Harmondsworth, Middlesex, England

First published by Signet, an imprint of New American Library,
a division of Penguin Putnam Inc.

First Printing, June 2000
10 9 8 7 6 5 4 3 2 1

For Carol
I'll miss you

The alchemical operation consisted essentially in separating the prima materia, the so-called chaos, into the active principle, the soul, and the passive principle, the body, which were then reunited in personified form in the coniunctio or "chymical marriage" . . . the ritual cohabitation of Sol and Luna.

—Carl Jung, *Mysterium Coniunctionis, an Inquiry into the Separation and Synthesis of Psychic Opposites in Alchemy*

Chapter 1

June 1172, Oxford, England

"That's her," the young man whispered, pointing toward a bench in the rear of the candle-lit church, packed this evening with scholars listening intently as an earnest young lector held forth on the application of reason to faith. "That's the one you're looking for."

"Which one is she?" Hidden in the shadows of the nave, Hugh of Wexford squinted toward the bench, on which sat a handful of women amid a sea of males clad in identical black academic robes, most with tonsures shaved into the crowns of their heads, some in clerical skullcaps.

"The pretty one," said the young man, a mendicant scholar judging from the shabbiness of his black *cappa* and his eagerness to earn the tuppence Hugh had offered in exchange for pointing out his quarry. "The one without the veil."

Seven women occupied the bench. Four looked to be nuns, if their wimples and black tunics were any indication. Two, also veiled but not quite as severely attired, were probably local matrons whose husbands indulged them by allowing them access to Oxford's *studium generale,* a loose association of students and masters still in its infancy but already renowned throughout Europe for its enlightened scholarship.

Then there was the unveiled woman. "*That's* Phillipa de Paris?" Hugh frowned as he studied her. He'd been told she was five-and-twenty, but with her petite stature

and enormous dark eyes, she looked far younger. Clad
in an unadorned but well-made blue tunic, her black hair
plaited in two long braids falling over her chest, she
more closely resembled an unworldly young girl than a
self-sufficient, free-thinking woman scholar—or what
he'd imagined such a creature to look like, this being
his first encounter with the rare breed. The only real
indication of her scholastic calling was the document
case of tooled leather that hung from her girdle.

"Aye, that's her," the youth said. "She comes to most
of the arithmetic and geometry lectures, and all the *dis-
putationis* on logic. Sometimes she even gets up on her
bench and argues points along with the others. I've seen
it with my own two eyes!"

"Indeed." Hugh rubbed his jaw, coarse with nearly a
week's growth of beard. He'd expected her to be not
only older-looking, but plainer, perhaps even mannish,
given her immersion in the male domain of academia.
And, too, she defied convention by living so independently. For a maiden of noble birth to make her own
way in the world, with neither father nor husband nor
overlord to guide and protect her, was remarkable even
in broad-minded communities like Oxford. That this delicate waif had managed such a feat was downright
extraordinary.

It didn't sit right, his having been sent for the likes of
her. Still, he had an assignment to fulfill, and fulfill it
he would.

The boy's gaze lit on Hugh's unkempt, overgrown
hair, on the wineskin and worn leather satchel slung
across his chest, and finally on the sharply curved Turkish dagger sheathed in its ornate silver scabbard on his
hip. "You mind my asking what business you've got with
the lady Phillipa?"

"Nay." With his good left hand, Hugh dug two silver
pennies out of the kid purse hanging on his belt and
handed them over. "As long as you don't expect an
answer."

"It's just that . . . well, I don't often see your kind here in Oxford."

"Nor did you tonight," Hugh said, extracting two more pennies from his purse. Hugh gave the boy a meaningful look as he pressed the additional payment into his hand.

"Ah." The young scholar nodded nervously as he slid the coins into his own purse. "Right. Of course. I under—"

"Carry on," Hugh said dismissively, returning his attention to the woman on the bench.

"Aye, sir. Good night to you, sir."

Hugh lurked in the dimly lit nave until the young lector switched from Latin to French—proper Norman French, not the anglicized common tongue spoken in less rarified circles—to announce that he was done with his presentation and that anyone who cared to debate these matters was welcome to return for a *disputatio* at terce tomorrow. A drone of conversation filled St. Mary's Church as the scholars rose from their benches and filed out into the night.

Hugh ducked behind a pillar as the lady Phillipa passed by him, pinning a gray mantle over her shoulders as she chatted with two lanky young men about what they had just heard. "Ah, but is it really so critical to understand the nature of universals," she was saying in a soft, girlish voice, "if one accepts the nominalist position that universals are but one element in the realm of logic, which is really more about words, or how we express concepts, than about absolute reality, which is to say matters of metaphysic . . ."

"God's bones," Hugh muttered as he watched her leave the church. *Absolute reality* was finding yourself eyeball to eyeball with an infidel warrior screaming battle cries—and knowing that either his razor-edged *kilij* or your own sword would be sheathed in flesh before your next breath had filled your lungs.

Universals . . . nominalism . . . metaphysic. *Words within words within words.*

Hugh crept out of the church behind the last few stragglers. Just listening to such blather made his head thud. As harsh and brutal as his soldier's life had been, he thanked the saints he'd been spared the mewling, platitude-spouting life of a cleric.

Hugh stepped out onto Shidyerd Street, lined on either side with thatch-roofed shops and houses that sagged over the narrow dirt road, all but obliterating the meager moonlight that managed to penetrate the blanket of clouds overhead. The night air prickled with damp; it would rain this evening. He headed south, his predatory gaze fixed on the lady Phillipa and her companions.

He must get her alone. And soon, before it started raining.

At the corner, she turned left onto High Street, the main thoroughfare of the walled city of Oxford, waving good-bye to her friends, who went to the right. Hugh followed her at a discreet distance, keeping to the shadows to avoid being seen. Soft yellow lantern light spilled through the occasional window shutter; the only other source of illumination was that of a full moon shrouded by gathering clouds.

It struck him as odd to see this highborn girl roaming the city streets without an escort after dark. Only whores larked about on their own at this hour. Was it intellectual arrogance that gave Phillipa de Paris her illusion of invulnerability, or merely the lack of common sense so prevalent among women of her station?

She turned right at a corner, disappearing from sight. Hugh waited impatiently as a flock of scholars in disheveled cappas lurched past, braying with laughter. They weren't among those who'd attended the lecture at St. Mary's; they were coming from the wrong direction, and they reeked of ale.

When at last they had their backs to him, Hugh sprinted across the street, pausing to peer around the corner down which Lady Phillipa had turned. It was a cramped, winding lane, dark as hell save for the occasional dimly lit window.

Hugh made his way swiftly but stealthily down the lane—until at last he spied her, entering what appeared to be a small shop still open for business—one of Oxford's many booksellers, judging by the wooden sign above the door, which read ALFRED DE LENNE, VENDITOR LIBRORUM.

Hugh approached the shop cautiously to peer through its half-open window shutters. Dozens of wood-bound volumes were secured by chains to the massive reading tables crammed into the small space. The more valuable texts, most bound in deerskin or embroidered linen, were displayed in two iron cages against the back wall.

Despite the late hour, the proprietor, a scowling, jowly fellow whose great belly stretched the green wool of his tunic, was enjoying a brisk business. Five or six young scholars and an older man, all in cappas, leafed through the tethered books by the light of overhead lanterns, pondering which ones to rent for copying. Lady Phillipa, her back to Hugh, was perusing the volumes in one of the cages.

The portly bookseller approached her, his key ring jangling on his belt. "Evenin', Lady Phillipa."

She nodded in his direction. "Master Alfred."

"Anything in particular you'd like to see, milady?"

"That one." She pointed to a small volume covered in red-dyed deerskin. "The *Rhetorica ad Herennium*."

Master Alfred chose a key and twisted it in the lock. As he swung the cage open, Phillipa abruptly turned around, facing the front window—and Hugh.

He ducked out of sight, swearing under his breath. Damn, but it was a tiresome business, skulking about this way. He'd been trained to stand and fight, not slink through the shadows like a cat sniffing out a mouse. His instructions, however, had been explicit; he was to execute his mission with the utmost secrecy, lest the wrong people become privy to it.

Hugh allowed some moments to pass before he

chanced another wary glance into the shop. The customers still flipped through the chained books; the bookseller was returning the little red volume to its place in the cage.

But where was Phillipa?

Bloody hell.

Slamming the door open, Hugh strode into the bookshop. Heads turned. The proprietor paused in the act of relocking the cage to look him up and down, his scowl deepening.

"Where did she go?" Hugh demanded, his swift assessment of the little shop revealing two ways out aside from the front door—a corner ladder to the floor above and a door in the rear wall, between the cages.

"See here . . ." Master Alfred blocked the back door with his considerable bulk. "What would you be wantin' with the lady?"

Bungler, Hugh scolded himself. Not one minute ago, he'd been reflecting on the need for discretion, yet he'd bulled in here with the unthinking zeal of the soldier he'd once been, instantly rousing suspicion. The men in this shop might have little in the way of fighting skills; still, there were half a dozen of them and but one of him. If they wanted to detain him while the lady Phillipa got away, they could probably manage it.

Hugh would do well to remember that his livelihood these days depended more on cunning than brawn—cunning and a facility for fabrication, never a particular talent of his. "The lady, she . . . dropped something as she was leaving St. Mary's just now. I only wanted to return it to her."

"What did she drop, then?" demanded the bookseller, clearly dubious.

Hugh slid his leather satchel off his shoulder, thumped it on the nearest table, and withdrew from it the sealed document that he carried tucked among his clothes and gear. " 'Tis a letter, I reckon. Something's written on the outside." He frowned at the name inked on the folded sheet of parchment, as if he were incapable of deciphering it.

The older man, whom Hugh took to be a teacher, came closer to peer at the letter. "It's addressed to Lady Phillipa de Paris," he told the proprietor. "He's telling the truth. Let him go."

Master Alfred stepped aside with a grumpy sigh. "If you say so, magister."

Snatching up his satchel, Hugh muscled the stout bookseller aside, opened the door, and stepped out into a common rear croft shared by the surrounding buildings, from which the only outlet was a narrow gap between two stone town houses that faced the next street over. Clutching the letter in one hand and his satchel in the other, he strode swiftly down this alley, and was almost to the end of it when he paused, niggled by . . . something . . . a presence, a sense that he was not alone. He'd seen no one, heard nothing, yet he couldn't shake the impression that someone was lurking in the dark, watching him pass.

Turning, he looked back in the direction from which he had come. What had it been? A whisper of movement? An exhaled breath? The heat of another body?

"Who's there?" Was it her? Or perhaps some night-crawling cutpurse. Hugh tucked the letter under his belt and looped his satchel over his shoulder to free his hands. "Show yourself."

Silence.

There's no one there. 'Tis but a chimera, a fancy of the damp night air.

Still . . . His hand poised over the hilt of his *jambiya*, Hugh retraced his steps back up the alley, taking it slowly this time, peering this way and that into the darkness. He came upon a little alcove in the stone wall to the right and ducked into it, finding a wooden door; he jiggled its brass handle, but it was locked.

Stepping out of the niche, he saw something flutter in the shadows at the very edge of his vision. It was a hooded figure, slight and feminine, darting out of another recessed doorway farther up. *It's her.* Her footfalls receded swiftly as she sprinted away.

Hugh overtook her in three swift strides, seized her by the shoulders, spun her around. Her hood flew off.

"Get back!" Steel flashed in her hand. "Keep your hands where I can see them. Raise them in the air!"

"By the Rood, is that a dagger?" He chuckled. "You're a plucky little thing, I'll give you that."

"Get your hands up!" she commanded, with only the faintest hint of a tremor to belie her bravado. "I won't hesitate to use this."

"You do realize you'll have to go for the throat if you mean to do me any real harm with that thing." He took a lazy step toward her.

She took two awkward steps back to keep him at arm's length. *"Do it!"* An admirable display of ferocity, even if it was born of desperation. Knowing he could easily overtake her if she ran, she was forced to stand her ground, but what now? He almost felt sorry for her.

Almost.

Hugh rubbed his jaw as he leaned indolently against the stone wall to his right, uncorked his wineskin, and took a swallow. "It takes a fair measure of strength to plunge a dagger into a man's chest, or even his belly. Especially if you've got to get through something like this." He patted his heavy leathern tunic. "A wee thing like you, well . . . meaning no disrespect, my lady, but I don't quite think you're up to—"

"Hold your tongue and get your hands in the air!" She circled around to face him, just as he'd hoped. This was too easy.

"Now, a throat, on the other hand, can be opened up with surprising ease. A child could do it, provided he knew what he was doing." Hugh recorked the wineskin with care, so it wouldn't leak; he hated it when they leaked. "The trick is in placing the knife just so."

Unsheathing his *jambiya* in a blur, he lunged forward, forcing her to stagger backward. She hitched in a breath when she felt cold stone against her back, gasped "No!"

when he brought the edge of the broad, curved, keenly honed blade a hairsbreadth from her throat and held it there, arm outstretched. Her eyes grew huge as she gazed upon the lethal shimmer of steel in the darkness.

She met his gaze, motionless and alert, her own weapon quivering in her hand. Slowly she raised the aim of the dagger from his chest to his throat—a futile adjustment, inasmuch as it still missed contact with him by several inches. She *was* plucky, but not long on common sense, to have let herself fall into his hands like this. Now she would discover what came of such lack of foresight.

"I take it you're something of a novice at back-alley knife fights," Hugh said dryly. "Note the difference in the lengths of our arms. You could slash at me for hours without causing so much as a scratch, whereas I, simply by applying a bit of pressure and drawing the blade across, like so . . ."

He whipped the *jambiya* across her neck, purposefully but taking care not to cut her. Most men, when subject to this little demonstration of superior force, screamed and dropped their weapons. Lady Phillipa de Paris merely closed her eyes; her grip on the dagger never wavered.

"Is it silver you want?" she asked in a low, strained voice. Opening her eyes, she reached beneath her mantle with her free hand. "I have—"

"I don't want your silver."

Her eyes, when she looked up at him, put him in mind of some small, clever creature that's found itself cornered by something much larger and more powerful—yet loath to surrender to its fate, as others might, it persists in sorting frantically through its options. In the creature's wide-eyed stare, one can see not just fear, but the machinations of its busy little brain.

"What do you want," she asked, "if not money?"

Hugh allowed himself a smile. "Why does any man hold a woman at knife point in an alley at night?"

"I have powerful connections," she said quickly. "My

father, he's a great baron in Normandy. If you harm me, he'll see that you're hunted down and killed."

It was true that Lady Phillipa's father, Gui de Beauvais, was a baron of great influence and renown—although it was also true that he had sired Phillipa and her twin sister Ada on a Paris dressmaker rather than his lady wife. Nevertheless, from all accounts, he had lavished as much affection on Phillipa and Ada as on his legitimate offspring, even if he'd felt obliged to keep them tucked safely away in Paris, their existence unknown to his family in Beauvais. He most assuredly *would* have had his daughter's molester hunted down and exterminated . . . had he not died of old age some four years ago.

Interesting. Lady Phillipa looked Hugh straight in the eye as she spoke of Lord Gui seeking his revenge. It would seem she was a good deal more untroubled than he by bald-faced lying.

"It won't be a pleasant death," she continued desperately. "My father's men will make you suffer before you—"

"You're trying to puzzle a way out of this predicament," Hugh observed, grudgingly impressed with her coolheadedness. "You'd have done better to have avoided it in the first place. Any sensible person who was being followed—particularly a woman alone at night—would have steered well clear of her pursuer, not lurked in a secluded alley he was bound to pass through. 'Twas some inept attempt to shake me loose, I gather."

She lifted her chin, indignation flaring in her eyes. "I was going to follow you, see where you went, then report you to the sheriff's man so he could—"

With a bark of incredulous laughter, Hugh said, "You meant to follow *me*? Woman, you have no earthly idea who you're dealing with. You're a fool to have played this little game, and any harm that comes to you is harm you've brought down on your own head."

"Does it help you to justify your viciousness," she

asked quietly, "if you can blame your prey for having invited it?"

"Oh, you invited it, all right, wandering the streets alone at this hour as if you owned the world, smugly certain that you're too clever to ever fall victim to a blackguard like me."

"Too well armed, actually."

He snorted disparagingly. "If you were counting on that puny little weapon to protect you, you're suffering from some dangerous illusions."

"It's protected me in the past, and come away bloodied. I'm not afraid to use it, if that's what you're thinking. So don't be so sure you've got the upper hand here. I may be small, but I'm quick and agile, and I won't hesitate to defend myself by slicing whatever part of you happens to be closest to hand at the moment."

"Ah. Well, that won't do." Seizing Phillipa's weapon hand, Hugh twisted it, using just enough pressure to pry her fingers open without snapping any bones. She let out a furious little whimper as the dagger fell to the ground. "I'm rather fond of my body parts," he said as he kicked the weapon aside. "Wouldn't want any to come up missing." Any more than already had.

As Hugh's eyes grew accustomed to the dark, he could see her more clearly. By the rapid rise and fall of her chest, and the hint of panic that had crept into her eyes, he knew she was finally coming to terms with the futility of her situation.

Good.

"That dagger only made you more vulnerable, because it gave you the illusion of protection where none existed," Hugh said. "As you see, even unarmed, I would have bested you." He took a step toward her, bracing his left hand on the stone wall while his right still held the *jambiya* so its blade just barely kissed her throat; she shrank back from him, her expression grave. "I'm twice your size and far, far stronger, and very determined to get what I've come for."

She held his gaze steadfastly, although she shivered from head to toe.

"You've misjudged the situation badly," he said, lowering his voice to a menacingly intimate timbre as he leaned in closer. "A comely young thing like you should know better than to let yourself end up all alone with the likes of me in a dark, secluded place like this, with no room to maneuver and no one to help you . . . or to hear you if you scream. You're entirely at my mercy."

Hugh's gaze lit on her eyes, liquid-dark against creamy skin . . . on her mouth, as pink and precise as if it had been painted onto a statue. He shifted the *jambiya,* gliding its edge along her throat like a lover's caress.

With the tip of the blade he nudged her mantle aside, draping it over her shoulders. She sucked in a breath, closed her eyes. He appraised the rest of her as she stood flattened against the wall, her arms rigid at her sides. She was a delicate little thing, with fine bones and high, small breasts. The beaded girdle with which she'd cinched in her tunic pointed up the narrowness of her waist, the feminine swell of her hips.

He returned his gaze to her eyes, to find her regarding him with loathing . . . and surprising dispassion. "Get it over with, then."

Hugh pushed back from the door, studying her closely. "Just like that?"

"You're right—I'm outmatched," she said, exhibiting a remarkable degree of composure, under the circumstances. "I may not be able to walk away from here unscathed, but I do intend to walk away. I won't struggle, so long as you take that knife from my throat and just . . . do what you came for and be done with it."

"Indeed." With a smile of triumph, Hugh slipped the *jambiya* back in its sheath and reached toward his belt. "How very accommodating of you."

Chapter 2

Keep your wits about you, whatever you do. Panic is your worst enemy.

Phillipa closed her eyes and took a steadying breath as she pondered how best to incapacitate this mongrel and make her escape—for, although she *would* rather be ravished than have her throat slit, she would just as soon avoid either fate.

She'd managed to convince him that she was willing to submit, prompting him to let down his guard. With that bizarre knife of his stowed safely in its sheath, she might have a chance against him—but she must act swiftly and decisively.

"I want you to see this," he said. "Open your eyes." She did, at the same time raising both arms, one hand braced with the other. *Now. Hard.* She slammed her cocked wrist down toward the bridge of his nose—only, he saw the blow coming and dodged it, grunting when it caught him on the cheek.

"Well, I'll be damned . . ." His disbelieving chuckle turned to a groan of pain as she struck again, this time finding her mark squarely. The impact sent a jolt of pain up her arm. He swore rawly, something pale slipping out of his hand and falling lightly to the ground.

She brought a heel down on his instep, but it was heavily booted and she was in kid slippers; he didn't even seem to feel it. In desperation, she aimed a punch at his throat. He stumbled backward.

Run. Lifting her skirts, she turned to race up the alley, but he was on her in a heartbeat, his arms banding around her as they toppled together to the hard-packed dirt.

He twisted as they fell, landing on his back with her on top. Wrenching one arm free, she grabbed his right hand and groped for his thumb to yank it back . . . only to find it missing.

No thumb?

Taking advantage of her momentary bafflement, he pinioned her arms and rolled her facedown, immobilizing her with the solid weight of his body.

"Be still, for pity's sake," he said as she thrashed beneath him, or tried to, for struggling against him was like trying to budge granite.

She spat out a blistering oath—the first time such a word had ever passed her lips.

Again he laughed, a throaty chuckle that tickled her ear and shook his leather-clad chest against her back. "Shame on you, Lady Phillipa. I hardly think the good Canon Lotulf raised you to curse like a dockhand."

She stilled beneath him, contemplating this unexpected development. He knew her name.

Not only that, but he knew about her beloved uncle Lotulf, a canon of the Church who had brought her up, along with her sister, near the Cloister of Notre Dame in Paris. All anyone in Oxford knew about her was that she'd begun her studies at the University of Paris before moving here seven years ago. To have revealed that she'd been raised from birth in that city, rather than at her father's barony in Beauvais, would have raised prickly questions—questions she would just as soon avoid after a childhood of being called, even to her face, "Gui de Beauvais's Brilliant Little By-blow."

"How do you know me?" she demanded. "What is this about?"

"Perhaps this will help to explain things." Shifting on top of her, he reached on the ground behind them for the thing he had dropped, bringing it close to her face so that she could inspect it. It appeared to be a letter.

"It's addressed to you." Tucking the letter into her

hand, he levered himself off her and stood. "From Richard de Luci."

"Richard de . . ." Phillipa sat up, peering at the document in a vain attempt to make out the writing on the parchment or the image on the enormous seal. "The king's justiciar?"

"The same." He offered her his hand, but she rebuffed the gesture, coming as it did from a man who, just moments ago, had held a knife to her throat and threatened her virtue. Whether that threat still existed, if it ever had, remained to be seen; perhaps he'd just been having a bit of mean-spirited sport with her. In any event, attempting to run from him was clearly futile, so she may as well try and get to the bottom of this little mystery.

Gaining her feet unaided, Phillipa dusted off her tunic and mantle. "I don't believe this letter really is from Richard de Luci. I've never even met the man, and he has no idea who I am."

"You underestimate your notoriety," he said, amusement in his voice. It was a deep voice with a rusty edge to it and a certain quality that marked him, despite his disreputable appearance and bearing, as a man who had been born into the ranks of the English nobility. He had backed off from her a bit, she noticed—to put her at ease?—and was uncorking that wineskin again. "Care for some?" he asked, holding it out to her.

Ignoring him, she ran her fingers over the silken ribbons woven importantly through slits in the parchment and the huge dollop of lead that prevented their being tampered with. "What on earth would Richard de Luci want with me?" As Justicar of the Realm, Lord Richard served as King Henry's chief minister and *de facto* regent during the king's frequent travels.

"I've some notion, but I'm not yet privy to the details. Perhaps his lordship will enlighten you in the letter, but I doubt it. Most likely you'll have to wait until your audience with him at West Minster."

She blinked at him. "I have no audience with—"

"You do, actually. He's expecting you Thursday morning, in his chambers at the royal palace. I was sent to escort you there."

"Thursday . . ." Phillipa shook her head. "That's two days from now. West Minster's just outside London. It must be fifty miles from here."

"Sixty, more like. If we get an early start tomorrow and the weather holds up, we can make it there in two days. We can find accommodations at a monastery tomorrow night—there are lots of them on the way—and the following night we can stay with my sister and her—"

"I'm expected to travel with you? Share accommodations with you? This is outrageous!"

"Lord Richard needs to speak with you as soon as possible." Peering at the sky, he said, "We ought to get indoors before it starts raining. Perhaps we can find someplace where there's enough light to read by, and then you can see for yourself what he expects of—"

"I don't care what he expects of me, or who he is. Does he honestly think I'm going to drop everything and set off just like that, with . . . with . . . Who the devil are you, anyway?"

"Hugh of Wexford, at your service, my lady." Her assailant-turned-envoy executed a courtly little half-bow that she suspected he intended as a mockery. Straightening up, he raked his unkempt flaxen hair out of his face and squeezed some more wine into his mouth. He was a tall man, long of limb and square of shoulder, lean but sinewy.

There was something familiar about his name, but she would have remembered having met such an insufferable cur. "How do I know you?" she asked.

"You don't. That is, we've never met, but we do have a mutual acquaintance. Graeham of Eastingham is my brother by marriage."

"Graeham of . . . Graeham *Fox,* you mean?"

"Aye. He's lord of Eastingham now, and married to my sister. We'll be staying with them Wednesday night.

Eastingham's to the east of London and just a bit out of our way, but I think we'll both be more comfortable there than at an inn or monastery—and Graeham is eager to see you again."

Formerly her sire's most trusted serjant, Graeham Fox had at one time been promised to Phillipa, sight unseen, as a husband, but had become enamored of an Englishwoman named Joanna—presumably this Hugh of Wexford's sister—and had married her instead. It was a development that had troubled Phillipa little, since she had only agreed to the union for the Oxfordshire estate that went with it, an estate her doting papa deeded to her outright when Graeham declined the marriage.

Graeham's last duty for Lord Gui had been to escort Phillipa across the Channel and see her safely settled in Oxford. She got to know him well during those weeks, and came to like and admire him.

"I thought you were a mercenary knight," she said. "I seem to recall Graeham saying you fought for foreign princes in return for gold—that you were a master swordsman who could name his own price."

"My sword hand isn't what it used to be," Hugh said, his careless tone tainted by a hint of something . . . bitterness?

Phillipa's gaze sought out Hugh's right hand, but it was too dark to make out that missing thumb. "So now you're a member of Lord Richard's retinue. A sergeant-at-arms, something of that sort?"

"More of a . . . wraith," he said, shoving the cork back in the wineskin. "A thing you find creeping in the shadows when you turn around quickly."

"You're a spy," she concluded.

"Lord Richard simply calls me an agent of the crown. My duties are varied. They're generally investigative in nature, but anything that requires a quiet footstep and a sharp blade might fall into my lap."

"Do your duties include accosting innocent women in dark alleys and—"

"The dark alley was your idea," he said, taking a step

toward her as she automatically recoiled, "and not a particularly shrewd one. You allowed yourself to get trapped in a remote, confined space by an armed opponent of obviously superior strength."

"I had my dagger," she said, sounding callow even to herself, "and I was well hidden."

"I'm the type of man one should run from," he said soberly, "not hide from. Your instincts will have told you that, but you chose to ignore your gut and listen to that all-too-clever little brain of yours, which insisted that this"—he scooped her dagger off the ground and held it up—"would protect you."

Phillipa felt heat rise in her cheeks, and was grateful for the concealing dark; she hated to be seen blushing, especially by the person who had made her blush.

"But how could it protect you," he continued, "when you didn't even think to aim for the throat? You let me trick you into backing against the wall, which should have been the one thing you avoided at all cost, and then, of course, you had no idea how to keep from being disarmed."

"Perhaps not," she said testily, "but I was able to disarm *you,* or rather, convince you to disarm yourself."

"That you were." He inclined his head in a little show of concession. "You weren't entirely inept, and for the most part your missteps were merely due to inexperience—you're certainly intelligent enough."

"You were . . . you were testing me! You deliberately set out to terrify me just to see how I would react."

"Lord Richard will expect me to offer some sort of assessment of your strengths and weaknesses for this type of work."

"What type of work? What are you—"

"So, I suppose I *was* testing your mettle, trying to see what you're made of." He turned the dagger over in his hands, studying its jewel-encrusted handle. "You mucked it up in most respects, of course, although I have to admit you didn't succumb to panic, so there's hope for you yet. Keeping a cool head is half the battle in these situations—that's how you were able to trick me into putting my weapon away. And you seem to have keen powers of analysis, even if you rely too much on them and not enough on intuition. In short, you're trainable. Perhaps Lord Richard isn't entirely mad in wanting to recruit you."

"Recruit me for what? He can't seriously intend to use *me* as a spy!"

Hugh grimaced. " 'Spy' is such a lurid word, not to mention simplistic. But yes, it would seem Lord Richard does have you in mind for some sort of service of that nature to the crown. You really ought to read the letter before you start hammering me with questions." With a hint of impatience, he asked, "Isn't there *some* place we can go that will be lit at this time of night? Not the bookshop—a place where we can sit and talk. A public house of some sort?"

There was the Red Bull, right around the corner, but Phillipa hesitated to go there with him—to go anywhere with him. It was not that long ago that this man had been pressing a knife to her throat. Her wariness of him had eased in light of that business about testing her—and it certainly helped that he was Graeham Fox's brother-in-law—but it had not entirely abated. All she really knew about him, knew for sure, was that he was a dangerous man.

A very dangerous man.

Phillipa held out her hand and said, with as much authority as she could muster, "I'll take my dagger, if you don't mind."

"I shouldn't return it to you. 'Twill only continue to put you at risk."

" 'Twas a gift from my uncle Lotulf," she said archly. "For you to keep it would be steal—"

"But if it makes you feel safer in my company . . ." He handed her the dagger, which she slid back into its little sheath on her girdle. With a smile, he unfastened his own dagger from his belt, scabbard and all, and held it out to her as well. "Here. 'Twill double your false sense of security."

After a moment's nonplussed hesitation, she accepted the peace offering—if that was really what it was and not some trick or jest on his part. The scabbard was of heavy, ornately worked silver, and crescent-shaped, like the knife it held; she shoved it awkwardly beneath her girdle.

"Here it comes," Hugh said with a sigh.

She looked up to feel the sting of raindrops on her face. Thunder growled as the heavens opened up, saturating the thatched roofs all around them with a cold, steady hiss.

Phillipa hurriedly slipped the letter into her document case, next to her wax tablet and well-worn copies of Aristotle's *Logica Nova* and *Logica Vetus*. When she looked up, she found Hugh suddenly very close. He pulled her hood up as lightning flared, pulsing over the planes and ridges of his face, highlighting a broad forehead and well-hewn cheekbones, deepening the shallow cleft in his beard-darkened chin. His eyes looked almost gentle in the quiver of white light—an illusion, surely, but one that made it easier, when he reached for her hand, to let him take it.

"Come," he yelled over the droning rain as he urged her back up the alley, toward the bookshop.

"Nay. I know a better place." She pointed in the opposite direction. "This way."

They sprinted hand-in-hand down the alley, across the street and around the corner, rain drilling into them, thunder rumbling. His grip was unyielding, his strides lengthy—although it seemed he moderated his pace so as not to end up dragging her like a sack of turnips.

By the time they had reached their destination, an iron-banded door with the silhouette of a bull painted on it in red, Phillipa was drenched and shivering. "The tavern is downstairs," she told Hugh, who guided her with a hand on her back down a torchlit stairwell to a vaulted stone undercroft furnished with long tables and benches.

Around the largest table sat a dozen or so black-robed scholars, one of whom was reciting some bawdy verse that had been making the rounds in Oxford of late. Two townsmen talked quietly at another table; otherwise the tavern was empty save for its proprietress, the doughy, ruddy-faced Altheda.

"Got caught in the rain, did you, milady?" Ushering the couple to a quiet corner, Altheda appraised Hugh with a cursory flick of the eyes. "Oughtn't to let that happen," she scolded as she took Phillipa's sodden mantle, draping it over a peg in the stone wall. "You could catch a rheum of the chest and be gone just like that! You're that clever, Lady Phillipa, but you've got to stop thinkin' all them lofty thoughts and get yourself indoors when it looks like it's fixin' to pour."

"How very refreshing to encounter a bit of common sense in this city filled with deep thinkers." Hugh turned an engaging grin on Altheda as he raked his wet hair off his face. "I do love a woman who knows to come in out of the rain."

Altheda actually blushed; Phillipa smirked to herself as she sat at the scarred oaken table Altheda led them to.

Hugh of Wexford had the air of a man who'd always found it just a bit too easy to beguile the fairer sex. Phillipa supposed there were women who were all too susceptible to a head of tousled golden hair and a too-charming grin, especially when accompanied by a certain measure of height and brawn—but she'd never been one of them. It was those deep thinkers Hugh sneered at whom she admired, but she wouldn't expect a creature like Hugh of Wexford—part hired bully, part self-proclaimed "wraith"—to appreciate the appeal of intellect over muscle.

Taking a seat across from Phillipa, Hugh ordered a jug of claret, which Altheda brought promptly, along with two battered tin goblets, an oil lamp, and—bless her—an iron brazier filled with hot coals, which she set on the chalk floor next to Phillipa's feet.

"The proprietress knows you well," Hugh observed as he filled their goblets. "You must come here often. I've never known a lady of rank to set foot in such an establishment, much less make a regular practice of it."

"Frequently a *disputatio* will spill over into the alehouses and taverns," she said. " 'Twas the same in Paris. That's when I first realized that I must be willing to frequent such places if I intended to participate in the lively exchange of ideas that makes a university community so exciting."

He smiled crookedly. "You find Oxford exciting?"

Phillipa stiffened at his tone. "It may not be as thrilling as prowling dark alleys in search of innocent women to terrorize, but it suits me well enough."

Chuckling, he lifted his goblet to his mouth, his gaze all too direct—and amused—as he contemplated her over the rim.

His eyes were translucent in the muted amber glow of the oil lamp, reminding her of the costly glass that her uncle Lotulf had installed in the window of his study back in Paris. As a child, Phillipa used to like to sit on its deep sill while her uncle worked at his desk behind her, and observe the bustling street life of the Rue Saint-Christofle through the thick, bubbly panes of pale green glass. It was like gazing through seawater at another world, a world quite unlike the hushed scholastic haven that she and Ada inhabited, a world whose children scrambled about like puppies, working hard but playing harder, and laughing—always laughing.

"Is something wrong?" Hugh was frowning, his eyes searching hers.

Finding his candid scrutiny unnerving, Phillipa looked away, her gaze lighting on something glinting on his right earlobe . . . an *earring*?

Yes, and a rather curious one, a small gold loop engraved with a design that looked vaguely heathen. Phillipa had never seen a man wearing an earring before—no man of her own world, that was. Several times in Paris, and once in Oxford, she'd seen dark-skinned, exotically attired men wearing earrings like that.

When Hugh had lowered his goblet, Phillipa noticed that his nose was reddened and sported a slight bump about halfway down.

"Did I do that?" she asked, suddenly appalled. "I . . . I'm sorry for lashing out at you like that, but I thought—"

"Don't be sorry. 'Twas one of the few sensible things you did back there."

"Is . . . is it broken?"

"Aye, but don't flatter yourself into thinking you've got that good a punch. 'Twas Graeham Fox who did the honors, some six or seven years past, though he was only giving as good as he got. 'Twas a fairly savage pummeling we gave each other, as I recall."

"Why? I thought you two were mates." Phillipa took a sip of the claret, to which Altheda hadn't added nearly as much water as was her custom.

"We are. We just had a little . . . misunderstanding about my sister."

"A misunderstanding."

"We cleared it up."

"I don't suppose you could have cleared it up by discussing the situation like reasonable people."

Hugh quirked an eyebrow. "You don't know much about men, do you?"

Bristling at his condescension, she said, "On the contrary, I've been surrounded by scholars and clerics my entire life—nearly all of them men."

"Geldings, the lot of them. They know less of what it takes to be a man than you do."

"And what, pray, do you feel it takes to be a man? The ability to pummel another man savagely?"

"If I think he's hurt my sister—or anyone else I care about—absolutely. Without hesitation. Or if he's a threat to my kingdom, most certainly."

"Or if you're paid enough?" she asked acidly.

He took a slow sip of wine, again eyeing her over the rim—only this time he wasn't smiling. "You ought to read Lord Richard's letter, don't you think?"

Ah yes, the letter. Retrieving it from her document case, she squinted at the huge seal, which depicted a figure she took to be King Henry sitting on his throne, two unidentifiable objects in his outstretched hands. Inked on a corner of the missive were the words "Lady Phillipa de Paris, Oxford."

Phillipa broke the seal, pulled out the ribbons, and unfolded the sheet of thick, crackling parchment.

Chapter 3

Hugh propped his elbows on the table, nursing his wine as he watched Phillipa read Lord Richard's letter. He wondered how she would react when the justiciar revealed the truth about how she had come to his attention, and what this was really all about. Or perhaps his lordship would judge that information too sensitive to put in writing, and would expect Hugh to fill her in on the relevant background—including what they knew about her.

He would find out soon enough.

Her eyebrows had drawn together in concentration, producing a tiny furrow between the two graceful black ink strokes. She looked so serious, so intent, in striking contrast to her delicate features and girlishly exposed braids. Her hair, black and gleaming as a raven's wing, was parted down the middle with excruciating precision and snugly plaited. Hugh's gaze kept homing in on one lone wayward tendril, dampened by rain, that clung to the side of her face in a rather charming curlicue.

She looked up, noticed the direction of his gaze, and reached up to brush the curlicue away.

Hugh sighed.

"It's true," she said in a tone of wonderment, nodding toward the letter. "He has some sort of . . . espionage mission in mind for me."

Hugh couldn't help smiling. Despite Lady Phillipa's cool intellectuality, she had the most expressive, childlike eyes. No doubt she thought of herself as worldly—those with formidable educations tended to confuse book learning with actual experience—yet she was anything but. There was a lamblike innocence to her, no doubt the result of having spent her entire life in the sheltered embrace of academia. She thought she knew a great deal; in reality, she knew almost nothing of real import.

It was a dangerous state of mind for someone embarking on a clandestine mission for the crown, but Hugh knew better than to openly question the judgment of his immediate superior, who, as the king's justiciar, happened to be the second most important man in England. And although it had always rankled Hugh to be subject to the authority of others, fifteen years of military experience had accustomed him to heeding even those orders whose wisdom he doubted.

"How much do you know of what Lord Richard has planned for me?" Phillipa asked.

Hugh bought a moment by taking another swallow of the too-sweet claret. "What does he tell you in the letter?"

"Not much, only that he'd appreciate my accompanying you to West Minster for an audience with him on a matter of great urgency for the kingdom—a covert matter—but you'd already told me that."

"Hmm." So Hugh would have to brief her himself on the events leading up to this mysterious mission, including how Lord Richard had come to choose Phillipa for it.

"Lord Richard can't force me to come with you to West Minster," she said. "He acknowledges as much in the letter. And frankly, I can't see uprooting myself from my life here just like that and setting off on a two-day journey with . . ." She dropped her gaze, and Hugh wondered what expression she was hiding. Distaste? Fear? Something else?

"With the likes of me," he supplied.

"Quite. Lord Richard evidently anticipated my feelings on the matter, because the letter is mostly about you."

"Me?"

"I gather he was attempting to reassure me of your background and character, inasmuch as you're a complete stranger to me and I'm expected to cheerfully place myself in your keeping for the next two days."

And for some time after that, seeing as they would undoubtedly be working together, but Hugh decided that there would be plenty of time for her to discover that once she was in West Minster and committed to the enterprise.

"What did his lordship tell you about me?" Hugh asked.

Phillipa cast him an ominous look. "Nothing to offset your having held a knife to my throat and threatened to rape me."

Hugh let out an exasperated sigh. "We've gone over that. I was just—"

"You were just testing my mettle." She lifted her goblet, glaring at him as she took a drink. "How do you suppose Lord Richard would react if he knew how effectively your own actions had discredited every admirable thing he said about you?"

Not well. Hugh forced himself to smile carelessly as he redirected the conversation. "He said I was admirable?"

Consulting the letter, she said, "He writes that you're the eldest son of one of the most noble houses in England, and that your father, William of Wexford, groomed you from infancy to be"—she raised her eyes to his, her expression dubious—"the greatest knight in Christendom?"

Hugh drained his goblet and reached for the jug. "He failed."

Her gaze lit on his unshorn hair, his earring, his grimy leather tunic. "Yes, well . . . Lord Richard still appears to hold you in the highest regard. Let's see . . ." she mused, scanning the letter. "Here it is. 'By the time he was twelve, young Hugh of Wexford was widely renowned for his skill with the sword. He was dubbed at eighteen, whereupon he became a stipendiary knight, his swordsmanship legendary as he spent the next fifteen years engaged in foreign battles.' "

The fingers of Hugh's nearly useless right hand curled automatically around the bowl of his goblet, as it had done countless times around the silver-gilt pommel of the sword he no longer bothered to carry.

" 'Sir Hugh came into my service these two years past,' " Phillipa read, " 'through the recommendation of Richard de Clare, lord of Chepstow and earl of Pembroke, known also as Richard Strongbow, for whom Hugh had fought in Ireland. An injury he incurred while capturing Dublin had obliged Hugh to retire his sword' "—Phillipa glanced toward Hugh's mutilated hand as it cupped the goblet—" 'but Strongbow felt that a man of his backbone and valor might nonetheless prove of invaluable service to me. And so he has.' " Phillipa refolded the letter and slipped it back into her case. "I thought you only fought for foreign kings."

"I fought for whomever promised the most gold. Three years ago that happened to be Strongbow. He'd taken it into his head to reinstate the exiled king of Leinster, marry this fellow's daughter, and inherit his lands. Which he did, with my help and that of a good many other paid soldiers, only to end up having to surrender his nice new chunk of Ireland to King Henry and hold it as his vassal—which I knew all along was bound to happen."

"But you also knew you'd end up with a purse full of gold, and that was all that really mattered, wasn't it?"

Hugh would have taken more umbrage at her tone if the statement itself weren't, God help him, the plain and simple truth. Quietly he said, "Perhaps someday, when you've had more experience of the world, we can have this conversation. In the meantime, I'm afraid I haven't the patience for it."

She held his gaze for a long moment before dropping her eyes to her goblet. That thoughtful little crease reappeared between her brows. "Why did you become a stipendiary knight?" Looking up, she said, "You were dubbed by whom—your sire's overlord?"

"Aye, but I was made to pledge fealty to my father as well, and it was understood that I would remain at Wexford under his command, at least until he'd finished molding me into his vision of the ultimate chevalier." He raised his goblet to his mouth. "You ask too many questions."

" 'Tis the curse of the scholar." She leaned forward on her elbows. "So, you turned mercenary even though you were sworn to remain in your father's household and serve him?"

He nodded curtly. "The day after I was dubbed, I left Wexford for good."

"Do you mean you severed your ties with your family, just like that?"

"With my father. My sister was in London by then, or I wouldn't have left. And my mother had died after Joanna was born."

"But . . . aren't you heir to Wexford? What of your inheritance?"

"My father isn't lord of Wexford outright—he holds it for his overlord, who might or might not grant me its keeping when the time comes."

"But still . . . you'd sworn an oath of fealty. What of—"

"There comes a point," Hugh said, "when a man must decide whether he'll conform his life to the expectations of others, or carve his own path through the forest—and if that path involves a measure of sacrifice, well, it also yields the freedom to go one's own way, to be one's own master. I'm sure you understand what I'm saying, my lady, having carved out your own rather unique path in life."

"Yes," she said softly, her great brown eyes reflecting the dancing flame of the oil lamp. "Yes. I understand perfectly."

A weighty silence fell between them, punctured moments later when a group of scholars burst into the tavern, laughing uproariously and demanding wine—although most of them had clearly had their fill of it elsewhere. They took over a nearby table, upon which they proceeded to pound with their fists in an apparent attempt to hurry Altheda along.

Raising her voice to be heard above their rowdy neighbors, Phillipa said, "I'm afraid I couldn't possibly go with you to West Minster, Sir Hugh. Please tell Lord Richard that, whereas I appreciate his confidence in me, I must regrettably decline his request to—"

"Let's not discuss this here," Hugh said, with a glance at the table full of drunken scholars. " 'Twould be better to go outside, where no one can hear us, but if it's still raining—"

"It isn't, but there's nothing to talk about. My mind is made up."

And he had his orders; leaving Phillipa de Paris in Oxford was not an option. "How can you be so sure it's stopped raining?" he asked, the undercroft in which they sat being windowless and thick-walled.

"Their cappas are dry," she said, nodding toward the group who had just entered.

"So they are," Hugh murmured, impressed with her swift deduction. "Come, then." Rising from his bench, he extracted some pennies from his purse and tossed them on the table. "You keep a set of rooms here in town, I understand. Kibald Street, isn't it?"

She stood, scowling. "Just how much do you know about me?"

"Far too much to suit you, I'm sure." *Just wait till you tell her everything . . .*

Plucking her mantle off the peg, he helped her on with it, smoothing the damp wool over her shoulders, which felt fine-boned, almost fragile, beneath his hands.

Stiffly she said, "If you think I'm letting you into my flat—"

"My intent is merely to walk you home," he said mildly. "Think what you will of me in other respects, but I've never yet forced my way into a lady's chamber.

You may not credit that, after my little demonstration back there in the alley, but it's the plain truth. You're in no danger from me."

She looked away, adjusting her mantle. "Very well, then."

Not only had the rain ceased, but the clouds that brought it had dissolved in the storm, leaving the sky blessedly clear and the streets awash with moonlight. The night air was mild, and had that freshly scrubbed quality that sometimes lingers after a summer shower. It would have been the perfect June evening for a stroll had not the roads beneath their feet transformed during the storm into veritable rivers of mud.

"I assume you're aware," Hugh said, glancing around to make sure no one else was about, "that Queen Eleanor left England and the king's side two years ago, and now makes her home at her palace in Poitiers." It was her husband's public flaunting of his affair with Rosamund Clifford that had prompted the formidable Eleanor, Countess of Poitou, Duchess of Aquitaine, and Queen of England, to retire in fury and mortification to her ancestral city. There, in her balmy homeland in southwestern France, she established a new and distinctly distaff royal court presided over by her daughter, Marie de Champagne, where the Frankish *beau monde* mingled with poets and troubadours, philosophers and clerics.

"Yes, I've heard much of the court of Poitiers," Phillipa said, holding her skirts daintily off the ground as she picked her way around the worst of the puddles—a futile effort, inasmuch as the hem of her tunic was already soaked with mud. "They say Queen Eleanor and the Countess Marie have taken a keen interest in developing a code of manners that can be applied to . . . attachments between men and women. *'L'amour courtois,'* they call it. The idea is that love affairs should be conducted in accordance with certain rules of chivalry and courtliness."

"You do realize," Hugh said as they turned onto Kibald Street, "that this so-called 'courtly love,' for all its elaborate rules of conduct, embraces some fairly unorthodox ideas. Illicit love affairs are not only tolerated at the Poitiers court, but encouraged, because nothing must stand in the way of Cupid's arrow. Marriage is seen as stifling to true love, and seduction—especially of someone else's husband or wife—is considered something of an art form."

"Yes, I know." She laughed at his nonplussed expression. "Did you think such revelations would shock me? I've spent my life exchanging ideas with some of the most enlightened minds in the world. I've studied under more than one man who was excommunicated for heresy. Radical ideas don't frighten me, Sir Hugh. They invigorate me!"

The back of Hugh's neck prickled with a vague awareness, a presence—and then he heard it, a sound like an indrawn breath, coming from an alley just up ahead.

Pausing, Hugh raised a hand to silence Phillipa, who'd opened her mouth to speak.

There came a low grunt, followed by someone hissing, *"Shh!"* Hugh reached for his *jambiya,* but of course it wasn't there.

He wheeled around, seizing Phillipa by the waist and yanking the weapon out of its sheath. Pressing a finger to his lips, he cocked his head toward the alley.

She nodded, her eyes enormous.

He motioned her to back up to the corner and stay there. Creeping up to the mouth of the alley, he steeled himself and strode swiftly inside, *jambiya* outstretched.

A woman's startled laughter brought him up short— as did the sight of the buxom redhead braced against the alley wall with her skirts rucked up, her exposed legs—white as milk in the moonlight—clasped tightly around her companion's hips as he tupped her with abrupt, pounding strokes. Hugh couldn't see the fellow's face, because it was turned away, but he was tonsured and wore the cappa, albeit disheveled.

Hugh lowered the knife in his hand.

The wench met Hugh's eyes as she rocked against the wall, smiling with practiced seduction. She held his gaze, the tip of her tongue gliding over her rouged upper lip in a gesture of crude sexual promise. "You'll have to wait till I'm done with this one here, love," she said hoarsely, "and 'twill cost you three pennies."

The black-clad scholar whipped his head around, snarling, "Bugger off!" at Hugh. He was a spotty youth no more than sixteen.

"Certainly." Hugh backed up a step, inclining his head like a courtier exiting the royal presence. "Sorry for the intrusion."

"Tuppence, then!" The whore called out as her customer griped and swore. "You look like a man who could give a girl a tumble she'd not soon forget."

"And you're just the woman to inspire it," he said magnanimously. "But alas, I'm engaged elsewhere."

"So I see," the wench said, her gaze shifting to focus over Hugh's shoulder.

Turning around, Hugh saw Phillipa standing at the entrance to the alley, taking in the couple rutting against the wall with surprising equanimity. Hugh supposed she must have stumbled across many such back-alley assignations over the years, especially since she insisted upon walking the city streets alone at night. Still . . .

"Enjoy your . . . *engagement*." The whore returned her attention to her young customer, placating him with an ardent kiss as she moved against him in a carnal rhythm.

When Hugh turned back toward Phillipa, she was gone. He exited the alley, only to find her strolling along as if nothing untoward had occurred. As he came up alongside her, she handed him back his scabbard. "It's been digging into me—I'll have bruises tomorrow."

Refastening the scabbard to his belt, Hugh said, "I, uh . . . I'm sorry you had to see that . . . I mean, what was going on back there."

"That alley is popular with the ladies of the town." Her indifference seemed a bit forced. "Sometimes there's more than one couple in there, and once there were two women and . . . well . . ."

"Indeed."

"Not that I look," she said quickly. "I certainly don't peer in there every time I pass by."

"That's very circumspect of you," said Hugh, thinking, *I would look*.

They walked in awkward silence until Phillipa, having apparently resolved to steer the conversation back to its prior course, said, a bit too brightly, "Have you heard about the 'courts of love' that Queen Eleanor and her daughter are convening in Poitiers? 'Tis a rather fascinating custom from Gascony wherein the romantic dilemmas and grievances of lovers are argued before a panel of ladies—anonymously, through advocates, with the final judgment being delivered by the queen and her—"

"You can't be serious," Hugh interjected with a snort of laughter. "You find those ridiculous courts of love fascinating? And to think, I actually took you for a woman of some discernment!"

"Why should intimate relations between men and women be exempt from rules of civilized conduct?"

How careful should he be in choosing his words? Hugh wondered. The woman he was addressing, despite her aura of intellectual sophistication, was almost certainly a maiden. Most maidens were naturally ill at ease in regard to affairs of the flesh, yet Phillipa de Paris had not so much as blinked at that little alleyway tryst back there.

Opting for a middle ground in terms of frankness, he said, "What transpires between a man and a woman in bed, my lady, was never meant to be 'civilized.' 'Tis a time to give vent to one's animal nature, not stifle it."

She made a little sound of irritation. "I'm speaking as much about passion of the heart, Sir Hugh, as of the . . . loins."

"Passion springs from the loins, and there—if one has any sense at all—it remains."

"Do you mean to say that physical desire supersedes desire of the heart and mind—that the spiritual union of two lovers comes second to mere animal gratification?"

A gust of derisive laughter escaped him. "This 'spiritual union' you speak of, this courtly new notion of romantic love, is a pretty fabrication invented by the ladies of the Poitiers court for the purpose of emasculating any man foolish enough to take it seriously."

"Emasculating . . ." She laughed scornfully. "Really, Sir Hugh . . ."

"You haven't seen them, as I have, the young knights and princes who've been snared in the net of courtly love. They mince about with their long, flowing sleeves and pointed slippers, fawning over the ladies like eager little puppies. They don't hunt, they don't joust, they don't fly the falcons or throw the dice. All they do is recite vapid romantic verse about swooning larks and lighthearted starlings as they moon over their lady loves—a pathetic display."

"You've been to the Poitiers court?" she asked.

He nodded. "I spent three months there about a year and a half ago. 'Twas a novel experience. If you'd ever actually witnessed one of those courts of love, you'd not find them—"

"A year and a half ago . . ." Phillipa frowned as she stepped around a particularly bad patch of mud. "You were already working for Lord Richard by then. He had no objection to your spending three months away from—" She gasped and stopped in her tracks. "He sent you there! You were there as a spy! You were spying on the *queen*!"

Hugh paused long enough to uncork his wineskin and offer it to Phillipa, who shook her head. He had a squeeze, then continued walking. "This word 'spy' that you keep bandying about . . ."

"Lord Richard would only have sent you there at the behest of King Henry." She scurried to catch up to him, mud sucking at her slippers. "Her own husband was having her spied upon?"

"Her own *estranged* husband, who had heard certain disconcerting rumors while he was in Ireland bringing Strongbow back into the fold and laying claim to his new lands."

Phillipa took a second too long to respond, and when she did, her tone was just a bit too blasé. "Rumors?"

"Aye," he said, watching her closely out of the corner of his eye. " 'Twas whispered that the Poitiers court had become a hotbed of sedition, with the queen at the center of a disloyal coalition planning armed revolt against the king. You've heard naught of these matters?"

She looked up at him, and with impressively feigned sincerity, said, "Nay. Should I have?"

"Nay." But, of course, she had. Hugh sighed heavily, dismayed by her ability to lie right to his face even as he grudgingly admired it; perhaps espionage would come more easily to her than it had to him. "The major conspirators were said to be the king's own sons, the three eldest—Henry the younger, Richard, and Geoffrey."

" 'Tis a sad thing," she said, "for fathers and sons to become strangers to each other."

" 'Tisn't always easy," Hugh said grimly, "being the son of a powerful man with lofty ambitions. Especially when his plans for you aren't necessarily what you would choose for yourself."

She eyed him knowingly. "You're speaking from experience, I take it."

I'm speaking from idiocy. What was he thinking, scratching open old wounds for this woman he barely knew? What had transpired between Hugh and his sire had played itself out long ago; no use reliving it now. "Not only are the sons reputedly involved," Hugh continued, "but so is William, King of Scots, and Philip, Count of Flanders, as well as the Barons of Brittany, Aquitaine, and Anjou . . . and even, if one credits it, King Louis of France."

"Oh, dear."

Oh, dear, indeed. Louis Capet was the longtime enemy of Henry Plantagenet—King of England, Duke of Normandy, and Count of Anjou in his own right, as well as being Duke of Aquitaine and Count of Poitou by virtue of marriage. King Louis was Eleanor of Aquitaine's first husband, having divorced her after siring two daughters on her, the eldest of whom was Marie de Champagne.

"If the queen really is plotting rebellion," Hugh said, "she's keeping it well under wraps. She's a brilliant woman, fully capable of nurturing this scheme in complete secrecy. I certainly learned nothing of value during my visit to Poitiers." Possibly only because Hugh was more suited to open confrontation than slippery intrigue—especially at the time, when he was fresh off the battlefield. But then, Lord Richard's various other operatives had unearthed no more than he.

"So, as far as the king is concerned," she said, perhaps a bit uneasily, "the rumors are just that—unsubstantiated hearsay."

"Aye, which puts him in an awkward position in terms of defending himself. How can he take action against his own wife—his own sons—without proof? He's unpopular enough of late, what with the outrage over Becket's death, and now this business with Rosamund Clifford. He betrayed his wife, and openly, which garnered great public sympathy for her. If he now takes her into custody without cause, he'll be vilified. He can't afford to act hastily, or with too few facts."

After a moment of strained silence, Phillipa said, "This . . . service Lord Richard wants me to perform . . . it has something to do with these rumors, I take it."

"Aye. King Henry is in Normandy at present. Recently the Count of Toulouse came to him privily, warning him that treason is, indeed, being hatched in Poitiers. All the king needs is proof of this treachery, and then he can take action against it. That, I believe, is where you come in, although I'm at a loss as to what Lord Richard means to do with you."

"As am I." Phillipa paused in front of a shuttered shopfront with a sign shaped like a boot hanging over the front door. "This is where I live—in two rooms upstairs."

Hugh regarded the modest abode with bemusement; a baron's daughter, living above a cobbler's shop.

"This conversation has changed nothing," Phillipa said. "I have no intention of accompanying you to West Minster. I am curious, however, as to how his lordship came to enlist my aid. And please don't tell me again that it was my notoriety as a scholar. Even in the unlikely event that the king's justiciar has heard of me, he'd have no reason to call upon my help with these matters. What makes him think I have any interest in them—or that my interests mesh with his? In fact, he took quite a risk, trying to recruit me. What if my sympathies lie with Queen Eleanor?"

"I suppose they might." Hugh allowed himself a slow smile as he leaned against her front door and squeezed a long stream of wine into his mouth. "But they don't."

She folded her arms across her chest. "You have no way of knowing that."

"Ah, but I do—and so does Lord Richard." Hugh worked the cork carefully back into the mouth of the wineskin. "For some time now, he's had me intercepting the correspondence of . . . certain parties as it crosses the English Channel."

Her face, luminous in the quicksilver moonlight, grew even paler. "Certain parties . . ."

"Certain parties suspected of harboring ill-will toward the king of the English . . . parties such as Lotulf de Beauvais, canon of Notre Dame and longtime advisor to the tediously pious King Louis."

"Uncle Lotulf?" Unfolding her arms, she took a step toward Hugh. "You've been . . . you've been reading my uncle's letters?"

"Aye. The young acolyte he uses as a courier has a weakness for silver, I discovered, so 'twas a simple matter to—"

"All of them?"

Soberly, Hugh said, "Yes, my lady. We have every

letter he's written to you for the past two years—or rather, copies of them. The originals were sent on to you, of course."

He saw, again, that cornered look in her eyes, that furious sorting through of the situation, the weighing of possibilities and options. "But . . . I would have known. Those letters were bound and . . . and sealed . . ."

He smiled indulgently. " 'Tis no great challenge to re-seal a letter so that it looks as if it's never been opened. There are little tricks—"

"Of course you would have your little tricks," she muttered, turning away from him and rubbing her temples with quivering fists. "So I suppose you know . . . you know . . ."

"That your uncle, being an intimate of King Louis, has surmised that a plot is underway to dethrone King Henry? Yes, and I must say, it was damnably indiscreet of him to share this conjecture with you in writing. And even more ill advised to state outright that he's all in favor of this insurrection, Henry Plantagenet being a—how did he put it?— 'wife-stealing, archbishop-murdering, fornicating minion of Lucifer,' while his darling Louis Capet is all but canonized already. We know everything, my lady. Every last damning detail."

"Damning it may be, in your eyes and Lord Richard's," Phillipa said in a quavering voice, "but you'll do well to remember that my uncle is a subject of France, and as such you've no right to . . . to punish him, or . . ." Her gaze traveled to the *jambiya*, now sheathed once more on Hugh's hip.

"I'm not an assassin, my lady," he said quietly. Before she could savor her relief, he added, "The crown does, however, employ other men for that purpose, men with venom in their veins who kill for sport—and who don't give a fig whether or not they've got the 'right' to do it."

"Oh, God," she murmured, looking suddenly very young and very lost. Perversely, Hugh's instinct was to gather her up and reassure her that Lord Richard's threat to her uncle was an empty one—if, indeed, it was—but duty kept him leaning insolently against this door as she wrung her hands and fretted. He'd been charged with delivering Phillipa de Paris to the lord justiciar at West Minster Palace Thursday morning, and if that required him to fill her with terror for her uncle's well-being, so be it. It was her own fault, for being so mulish and uncooperative. He didn't feel sorry for her.

He shouldn't feel sorry for her.

Hugh sighed in disgust. "You should know," he said, "that we intercepted your letters as well—those to your uncle, that is, or most of them."

"Of course," she murmured, nodding distractedly. "Of course."

"That's how we know that your sympathies lie, not with Queen Eleanor and her sedition, but with King Henry. In one recent letter, if you recall, you told your uncle that after seven years in Oxford, you considered yourself more English than French, and felt a certain allegiance to the English king. You repeatedly attempted to dissuade Canon Lotulf from getting involved in any 'ill-conceived mischief' King Louis might be cooking up with Queen Eleanor—to no avail, of course. Methinks your uncle is as stubborn as you are."

"My uncle is a good man," she said with heartbreaking earnestness, those great, dark eyes of hers shimmering wetly. "He . . . he took us in as his wards, my sister and I, when the typhoid killed our mother. We were just two little children he'd never laid eyes on before, four years old—"

"My lady . . ." Pushing away from the door, Hugh took a step toward her.

This time she didn't recoil from him, but actually reached out and laid a hand on his chest—very lightly, yet he fancied he felt her touch all the way through his thick leather tunic and shirt. It felt like a hand reaching inside him to gently squeeze his heart.

"And he took us in," Phillipa continued desperately, her gaze never leaving his, "and brought us up, as a kindness to my father—or so I thought for years, but once, right before I left Paris for Oxford, he told me the truth."

"My lady." Hugh closed his hand—his good left hand—over hers. "Please . . ."

"He said he'd told my father he wouldn't be able to live with two little girls underfoot, that he was too busy with church business to be responsible for us, and that Papa should ship us off to a convent school . . . but then he met us. Once he saw us, with our dolls clutched to our chests and our faces streaked with tears, he couldn't send us away. He said he might not have loved us instantly, but he knew without a doubt that he would grow to love us as he loved life itself. He raised us, Sir Hugh, not like mere wards, but as if we were his own daughters—although he gave us as much freedom as if we were sons. He gave me everything, let me study under the greatest teachers in Paris, taught me how to think independently—"

"My lady, please listen to me," Hugh implored, squeezing her hand, which shivered beneath his.

"He may be misguided about King Henry," she said in a thin, wavering voice, "but that's just because of his regard for Louis Capet. He's an old man, very obstinate at times, but very devout and very good at heart. He's a wonderful man, Sir Hugh, and . . ." Her voice snagged. "And if any harm came to him, I think it would kill me."

Tears trembled in her eyes, on the verge of spilling over, as she continued to hold Hugh captive to her imploring gaze.

Hugh felt curiously starved for air. "I . . . he doesn't have to come to any harm, your uncle."

"Nay?" She blinked, and wet rivulets coursed down her face.

Hugh released her hand to wipe away the tears. They were hot to the touch, her cheeks warm and soft as a babe's.

"He . . . he's nobody, really," Hugh heard himself saying, "just a tame old churchman, not an actual conspirator. It needn't be necessary to . . . that is . . ." *Don't*

let her tears sway you, Hugh rebuked himself, abashed
to have let her get to him this way. *Remember your
objective.*

Her eyes grew wide as that busy little mind of hers
sorted through what Hugh was too flummoxed to say
outright. "You mean it needn't be necessary to have
him . . ." Her gaze traveled to the *jambiya,* then back
to his face. She retreated a step, breaking contact with
him. "As long as I cooperate, is that it?"

Hugh drew in a fortifying breath. "Let's put it this
way—I can't vouch for what will happen if you *don't*
work with us. But if you do, I can't conceive that Lord
Richard would allow your uncle to be . . . penalized for
harboring a few eccentric notions. He *is* an old man,
after all, and we're civilized—"

"Please, *please* don't tell me how civilized you are,"
she said shakily, "mere moments after threatening, if
only implicitly, to have a harmless old man murdered."

Hugh held his tongue while she turned her back on
him, rubbing her forehead. Facing down *kilij*-wielding
Turks was child's play compared to this.

"So, that's it then," she said dispiritedly. "I balked at
shoving my entire life aside to serve the justiciar of England in some capacity that is, as yet, a complete mystery
to me, so now you're blackmailing me. If I want my
uncle to stay safe and sound, I must let you drag me
away to play the spy for Lord Richard."

"All that's really expected of you at this point," Hugh
said evenly, "is that you allow me to escort you to West
Minster for the audience with Lord Richard. He'll tell
you then what he has in mind for you. If, after hearing
him out, you still want no part of it"—he shrugged—
"you'll be free to return to Oxford, confident that your
uncle will be left in peace."

She turned back around, searched his eyes. "Verily?"

"Verily. But I hope his lordship can convince you to
aid us in our cause. After all, it's a cause you believe
in—the right of the duly crowned king of the English,
Henry Plantagenet, to remain on the throne. And

mayhap . . ." Hugh hesitated, but then plunged on ahead. "Mayhap 'twill do you some good, getting away from Oxford for a while and seeing a bit of the real world."

She arched an eloquent brow. "You think I'm that sheltered?"

With a chuckle, he said, "I *know* you're that sheltered, my lady. 'Twill be interesting to see how you equip yourself when you've got more than docile little clerics and scholars to deal with."

"Is that a dare, Sir Hugh?"

"Absolutely," he said with a grin, thinking this was a person who prided herself on rising to challenges. "I'll leave you now so you can get some sleep—we've got an exhausting journey ahead of us. We'll need to get an early start, so I'll come round for you at sunrise."

"Where are you staying?" she asked. "The inn outside Eastgate?"

He shook his head. "That Augustinian priory against the city wall to the south."

"St. Frideswide's? That's where I keep my mare, Fritzi. Don't come by for me. I'll meet you there, in the stables, when the bells ring prime."

"All right, then. Oh—pack lightly. I've got no packhorse."

"That won't be a problem," she said with a wry little smile. "I've only got one other tunic."

A baron's daughter with two gowns to her name, Hugh mused as he retraced his steps along Kibald Street on his way to St. Frideswide's. Yet somehow he wasn't surprised. Phillipa de Paris was a rather singular entity, to be sure, but the disparate halves of her—the guileless noble maiden and the urbane Oxford scholar—seemed to fuse together in a way that made a curious sort of sense. There was a certain logic to her, and by extension a certain predictability.

If he'd thought about it, he would have guessed she only owned two tunics.

Hugh slowed down when he spied a figure loitering

on the corner of Kibald and Grope Lane, picking up his
pace when he determined that it was just a woman, and
a smallish one at that.

When she saw him, she called out, "Evenin', sir," in
a voice so high and reedy it might have belonged to a
child. In fact, as Hugh got closer, it became increasingly
apparent that she was little more than that, despite her
face paint and scarlet kirtle. With her black-dyed braids,
big eyes, and delicate build, she looked unnervingly like
a younger, tartier version of the lady Phillipa.

"Are you lonely, then?" she asked with a coy smile.

Why, Hugh wondered, did they always want to know
if you were lonely? When he was lonely, he sought out
his mates for a bit of rowdy companionship. It was at
times like this, when he'd gone just a bit too long without a woman, that he went on the prowl for an obliging
wench, and he didn't mind paying if that's what it took—
unless she'd just crawled out from under some other
fellow. Hugh liked to be a whore's first customer of the
evening; that way, he didn't have to wonder what poxy
bastard had just shared the same accommodations.

"Are you with child?" he asked, noticing a bulge beneath her kirtle, a substantial one, that its clever folds
couldn't completely disguise.

"It won't get in the way," she promised, patting her
round stomach. "You can have me on me hands and
knees, and you'll never even know it was there. I'll
charge you only a penny if it bothers you. Usually I
get twice that, but it's been a slow night—you're my
first bloke."

"How old are you?" he asked.

She hesitated, then gave him that coquettish smile
again. "How old do you want me to be?"

He regarded her balefully.

The girl rolled her eyes dramatically. "Fourteen."
There came that smile again, evidently the only one in
her repertoire.

Hugh raised a skeptical eyebrow.

"Almost. Come on, then, sir. There's a place down

the street where we can go. I'll make you so happy—
and you'll only be out a penny."

Ah, happiness. A presumed cure for loneliness.

Hugh reached into his purse.

"You're wastin' your time, Mae," said another, older
woman as she sauntered out of the darkness; it was the
red-haired wench from the alley. "This one's already had
it off tonight, courtesy of *her ladyship*." She held her
hand up, little finger raised, as if waiting for a courtly
chevalier to escort her on a stroll around the castle
gardens.

Did she think he'd bedded the lady Phillipa? Incredulous laughter burst from Hugh as he scooped silver pennies out of the little kidskin sack.

"You're wrong, Gildy." Mae pointed to Hugh's outstretched hand with an air of triumph. "He's fixin'
to . . ." She trailed off, gaping at the coins in Hugh's
hand.

"Here." Taking the girl's hand, Hugh turned it palm
up, filled it with the pennies—two shillings' worth, perhaps—and closed her fingers around them. "There's a
convent to the south of here—St. Ermengild's. I've
heard the abbess will take in women in need for a modest donation. Go there before your baby is due." Eyeing
her swollen belly, he added, "I wouldn't waste any time
if I were you."

Mae stared unblinkingly at the coins in her hand.
"Sir . . . I . . ." She shook her head in disbelief.

"Quite the gallant gentleman, ain't he?" Gildy said.
"See, Mae? I told you he wouldn't be wantin' no tumble
from the likes of you. Not when he's got *her ladyship*
liftin' her skirts for him."

"Where on earth did you get that idea?" he asked,
cinching his purse closed.

"Ooh, you *are* the gallant one, aren't you?" Gildy
laughed harshly. "She ain't got no reputation to protect,
that one, so don't be wastin' your breath. Everyone in
Oxford knows about the lady Phillipa."

"Knows what?" Hugh asked.

"She's one of them free-thinkers, one of them women what thinks they have as much of a right to bed sport as any man. They say she don't even believe in marriage."

What had she said? *Radical ideas don't frighten me, Sir Hugh. They invigorate me!*

With a snort, the whore added, "That one spreads her legs as easily as I do, I'll wager, only she don't take no silver for it. And they say *she's* the clever one!" The wench howled with laughter.

" 'Tis the truth, sir," said the young Mae as she filled her little purse with the coins. "She takes lovers as freely as any man—them fellows in the black robes, mostly. Brings 'em right into her house, just as bold as you please. I seen it with my own two eyes."

"And the men she shares her bed with," Gildy said, "they don't keep it no secret. They even brag about it while they're diddlin' *me!*"

"Indeed." Hugh rasped a hand over his jaw, not quite sure what to make of this remarkable claim. Phillipa did hold progressive views, and she greatly prized her freedom and independence. And she'd be attractive to men, certainly. She was pretty enough—but not in the way he normally associated with loose women.

Was it possible that there were brazen appetites hidden beneath Phillipa de Paris's innocently studious facade? Hugh's gut told him it wasn't . . . but, although his gut had served him admirably for the most part, it had also been known to lead him far afield from time to time.

Could he have been that grossly mistaken about the woman's character? It was dismaying, on the one hand, to think so—but it was also, he had to admit, somewhat intriguing.

Actually, very intriguing.

"Sorry if you didn't know," offered Mae.

Hugh smiled negligently. " 'Tis of no import. You'd best be heading home now. In the morning you can pay a carter traveling south to give you a ride to St. Ermengild's."

"I'll do that, sir," she promised, rising on tiptoe to give him a kiss on the cheek. "Thank you," she called over her shoulder as she walked away. "I won't never forget this."

Gildy surveyed Hugh up and down as if he were something hanging by a hook in the window of a butcher shop. "Her ladyship's a fool if she goes back to those soft-bellied scholars after havin' a taste of you. But if you ask me, any wench what gives it away for free is a fool." With a careless shrug, she turned and sauntered back into the night.

Chapter 4

The manor of Eastingham, two days later

"Hugh," Graeham shouted, "stop kicking your sister!"

Shielding her eyes against a feverish sunset, Phillipa scanned the open meadow where Graeham Fox was overseeing a game of sport among his son and the sons of his villeins—a nightly summer tradition at Eastingham, judging from the way the twenty or so boys had converged on the meadow after supper, equipped with their flat, oddly carved sticks and leather-covered balls. An audience of high-spirited girls, including the eldest of Joanna and Graeham's three children, six-year-old Cateryn, sat like a row of chittering sparrows on the low stone fence that bordered the meadow. Phillipa and a heavily pregnant Joanna also sat on the fence, but some distance away from the girls so as to be able to hold a conversation in relative peace. In the grass at Joanna's feet lay an old black-and-white tomcat and a three-legged spaniel that seemed to follow her wherever she went.

"I said stop it!" Graeham admonished five-year-old Hugh of Eastingham as he strode across the meadow.

"I didn't kick her hard," claimed the boy as he held his stick out of reach of his three-year-old sister, Nell, who had toddled onto the playing field in the middle of the game.

"Let me see!" pleaded the little girl in the voluminous white tunic as she reached for the stick with plump, straining arms. "Let me see!"

"Here we go again," Joanna chuckled. Cupping her hands to her mouth, she called out, "I'm sorry, Graeham. You know how she is—she just won't stay put."

From across the meadow, Graeham speared his wife with an exaggerated scowl. She answered him with a look of mock terror. During supper, Graeham had described Joanna as being one of those women whose beauty is only enhanced by pregnancy. Indeed, with her ruddy cheeks and sparkling eyes, she glowed as if lit from within.

"She won't leave me be!" Hugh backed up from Nell, glaring at her as he held the stick overhead.

"Let me see!" Nell wailed plaintively.

"That's no reason for you to kick her," scolded Graeham as he scooped up his daughter, who nearly pitched herself out of his arms in her zeal to grab the stick.

"Let me see!"

" 'Tis the same every night," Hugh griped. "She barges onto the field like a wild pig, squealing and ruining every—"

"As did you when you were her age," Graeham said as he carried a frantically writhing Nell toward her mother. There could be no doubt that these two were father and daughter, with their luminous blue eyes and reddish-brown hair that gleamed like fire in the setting sun. Cateryn had her mother's bronze mane, while young Hugh, with his hair like ripened wheat, took after the uncle for whom he'd been named.

Graeham handed little Nell over to her mother, who set aside her embroidery hoop to take the child onto her diminished lap. Issuing a stern command to "Stay with your mum this time," Graeham kissed his daughter on the nose and his wife on the mouth, blowing another kiss to Cateryn as he loped back onto the field. "All right, boys, let's finish this up while there's still light to see by."

"Let me see! I want to see!" Nell twisted and bucked on Joanna's lap, struggling to get down.

"Nell, be still," Joanna said over the shouts of the

boys in the meadow and the laughter of the girls. "I've got a baby in my tummy, remember? You'll upset him if you keep on that way."

Phillipa found herself holding out her arms. "Give her to me."

"Are you sure? She's quite a handful."

"Oh, I think I can manage." How great a challenge could it be to hold a child on one's lap?

It was like holding a sack filled with forty pounds of thrashing snakes. The child was much stronger than Phillipa had anticipated, and very determined to break free and run back into the meadow—which she did almost instantly.

"You've got to hold her a bit more firmly than that," Joanna called out as Phillipa sprinted after the child.

"I was afraid of hurting her." Phillipa made an unsuccessful grab for the child, who writhed out of her clutches and raced off, shrieking excitedly.

Joanna laughed. "You can't hurt her just by holding her. Have you never held a child?"

"Nay." Phillipa wrapped her arms around the wriggling little girl and half-dragged, half-carried her back to the stone fence.

"Never?" Joanna laughed incredulously.

For some idiotic reason, Phillipa felt her face grow warm as she settled back down on the fence, her arms locked stiffly around the squirming Nell. "I . . . I've never really been around any children . . ." Even when she was young herself, the only other child she'd had any contact with was her sister Ada.

"I'm sorry." Joanna rested a hand on her arm. "It's just that your life is so much different than mine, I hardly know what to make of it."

"Few people do." Phillipa adopted a studiously indifferent smile as Nell kicked and whined in her arms. "It matters not. My life suits me, and that's the important thing." She'd said the same thing to Hugh two nights ago in Oxford . . . *my life suits me well enough.* Never before had she been made to feel so defensive about her solitary existence. That was because, until now, she'd been surrounded by other academics, who understood how difficult it was to maintain both a life of the mind and a family life. In fact, those who'd taken minor orders in the church would lose much of their status, including their teaching privileges, if they married—and marriage was now forbidden altogether for deacons and priests.

"Of course your life suits you." Joanna resumed her embroidery, a complicated design on blue silk involving peacocks and interwoven vines. "I would never suggest otherwise."

Your brother is not so tactful, Phillipa thought, remembering their conversations about Oxford and academia during their two-day journey here, and his conviction that she'd wrapped herself up in "a safe, snug little cocoon of book-learning," where she could neither see nor hear nor feel the world around her.

As if Joanna had sensed that Phillipa was thinking about Hugh, she said, "I wish my brother hadn't disappeared like that after supper. Nell settles down with her uncle Hugh. He's the only one who can control her."

The little girl stilled at the mention of her uncle. "Where Unca Hugh?" she asked, looking around. She'd latched on to him the moment he and Phillipa had arrived at Eastingham that afternoon, even going so far as to sit on his lap all during supper, which he'd tolerated with surprising equanimity, feeding her bits of meat from his own trencher as if she were a lady he was wooing. Hugh was obviously a frequent visitor to his sister's home, and Nell's favorite human being in the world.

Glancing up from her needlework, Joanna asked Phillipa, "Did he tell you where he was going when he took off after supper?"

"He said he needed to wash off the dust of the journey."

"Ah, yes. There's a stream in the south woods. He likes to bathe there."

"Want Unca Hugh!" Nell mewed, kicking her chubby legs.

"Uncle Hugh is meeting with an important man to-morrow," Joanna told her daughter. "He wants to be nice and clean."

According to Hugh, Joanna and Graeham were the only two people in England—aside from King Henry and his justiciar—who knew about his clandestine work for the crown. As far as his casual acquaintances were concerned, he was just a rather amiable nobleman with a bit too much time and money on his hands—another firstborn son frittering away the years until he became lord of the manor. Few people knew he'd spent fifteen years as a paid soldier; if they noticed his missing thumb, they were, like Phillipa, too polite to ask about it. It was also not generally known that Hugh had been estranged from his father for his entire adult life, as had his sister; who knew whether he would even be appointed lord of Wexford when Lord William passed from the world.

"You can bathe, too, if you'd like," Joanna told Phillipa, "and you needn't resort to the stream. We've got a perfectly good tub, and I'll be happy to have it brought up to your chamber and filled with hot water if you'd like a nice bath before bed."

"That would be lovely. You've been most hospitable."

"Your room is to your liking, I hope. I can move you to another if—"

"Nay, it's fine—perfect." Phillipa held on tight to Nell, who'd begun fidgeting distractedly, although she was no longer laboring to get down.

"It's rather small, I know. When Graeham built the new wing, he was trying to fit as many private chambers in it as possible, but some of them are no larger than garderobes."

"Perhaps, but those big windows make up for it." Phillipa's gaze sought out the stone manor house beyond the meadow, a massive edifice comprised of an older, L-shaped section housing the original hall, solar, and chapel, and the newly constructed wing with its many individual chambers.

"The first thing Graeham did when we married and

settled in here," Joanna said, "was to start building that new section. We'd agreed we were going to fill our house with children, but he didn't want them to have to bunk down with the servants in the great hall. You see, he'd spent his own childhood sleeping in the dorter of Holy Trinity with a hundred other boys, and then it was the barracks at your father's castle in Beauvais, so privacy has always been—"

"Mummy," Nell said, wriggling agitatedly on Phillipa's lap, "I need to pee. *Now.*"

Now? Phillipa thought. *This very instant?*

"Lady Nellwyn," Joanna intoned without missing a stitch, "what have I told you about not waiting until the last minute?"

Bobbing up and down on Phillipa's lap, her expression pained, the child said, "I need the privy, Mummy."

"She . . . she needs the privy," Phillipa repeated inanely, thinking the gray gown she had on was the cleanest of her two tunics, the blue one being mud-stained from that rainstorm the night before she left Oxford, and that if this child were to actually—Dear God—to actually *urinate* on her, she would have nothing decent to wear to her audience with Lord Richard tomorrow morning.

"Can you hold it in for a bit?" Joanna asked the child.

"Perhaps," Phillipa said, lifting Nell beneath the arms in order to set her on the ground, "I should get her off my—"

"Nay, don't let her go, whatever you do. She'll run off and we'll never catch her."

"Oh." Phillipa set the child back down on her lap, reflecting that the business of looking after one three-year-old was a good deal more complicated than she would have anticipated.

With a sigh, Joanna called out, "Cat, I need you!"

Her older daughter, sitting much farther down the fence with her friends, yelled, "What is it, Mum?"

"Don't ask me what it is. Just come here!"

And do hurry, Phillipa silently begged as Cateryn came toward them with grudgingly slow footsteps.

"I want you to take Nell into the house to use the garderobe," Joanna instructed her older daughter. "And get her ready for bed while you're at it."

"But Mum," Cateryn lamented, "the game's not over."

" 'Twill be over very soon, and you know your brother's team is going to win."

Oh, for pity's sake! Phillipa thought, expecting at any moment to feel a dreaded dampness through her tunic. "I'll take her."

"Nay, thank you anyway," said Joanna, "but Cateryn must learn to do as she's told. *Now,* Cat."

Pulling a face, the girl reached for Nell and hauled her off a grateful Phillipa's lap. "Come on, you pesky thing. Let's go." She planted a kiss on her sister's head and led her by her hand toward the house.

Phillipa breathed a monumental sigh of relief.

Joanna smiled at Phillipa before returning her attention to her embroidery. "I can't get over how much you look like your sister Ada. I became friends with her while she was living in London, you know. Of course, she was very ill then."

"Yes, she told me you took wonderful care of her. She's so grateful for it—for everything you and Graeham did for her. As am I."

"Is she still abroad?" Joanna asked. Ada, although never as studious as her sister, had taken an interest in medicine while she was regaining her health at London's St. Bartholemew's hospital. Upon her return to Paris, she'd talked Lord Gui into sending her to study the diseases of women at the great medical school in Salerno, where scholars of both sexes could learn the healing arts.

"Ah, you don't know," Phillipa said with a smile. "Yes, she's still in Salerno, and there she will remain. She got married in March."

"Married!"

"To another physician, an Italian named Tommaso

Salernus. She writes that he's very clever and completely devoted to her, and that he's tall and has black curly hair and looks like a Roman god.''

"A Roman god!" Joanna exclaimed laughingly. "She must be in love!"

"I'm sure she wrote to you about her marriage, but it can take so long for letters to get here from Italy. She's very happy there. She says the climate is temperate, and she adores her work almost as much as she adores her husband. She claims she can't wait to start having children, but . . ."

Joanna glanced up from her needlework. "But?"

Phillipa squinted at the boys in the meadow, backlit by the blazing sky. "She takes great satisfaction in being a physician. I worry that if she has children, she won't be as free to practice medicine."

"She won't." Joanna looked toward the meadow somewhat wistfully; Phillipa knew she was gazing at her son. "But there will be rewards enough to compensate."

Phillipa shook her head fervently. "Nothing is worth the loss of one's liberty, even a small part of it."

Joanna smiled as she passed her needle in and out of the sky-blue silk. "My brother is much like you."

"Hugh?" Dubious laughter burst from Phillipa. "You must be joking."

"Not at all. He's fanatically self-sufficient, insists on living by his own rules. You and he have that in common, I think."

"Aye, well, that's all we have in common," Phillipa said. "He's not much for thinking things through, your brother. I've only known him two days, but not once has he bothered to sit down and analyze a situation thoughtfully, or plan a course of action and carry it through. Instead, he just sort of . . . well, for instance, around this time yesterday evening, when we were halfway here and should have been finding a place to spend the night, Hugh passed up a perfectly suitable monastery simply because there was no room for us in the prior's lodge and we would have had to sleep in the guest house with the indigent travelers. I didn't mind, but he was insistent that we carry on. We finally ended up in the prior's lodge at Chertsey, but it was well after dark by the time we got there, and Fritzi and I were both exhausted. If it had been up to me, I'd have arranged our accommodations in advance, and then we wouldn't have been at the mercy of . . ." Phillipa realized that Joanna's mouth was curving into a lopsided smile reminiscent of her brother's. "What's so funny?"

"My dear Phillipa . . . I've never known my brother to arrange anything in advance, or analyze any situation, thoughtfully or otherwise. He prefers to simply . . . deal with circumstances as they arise."

"Not very judicious," Phillipa sniffed, thinking, *How priggish I must sound; I must try to remember that I'm not in Oxford anymore.* The undiluted opinions that were encouraged and expected in a university community, Uncle Lotulf used to counsel her, should be suppressed in the wider world, where diplomacy was prized over frankness. "What I mean is, considering the responsibility that Lord Richard has invested in him—"

"Yes, I know," Joanna said, "yet somehow everything always turns out all right with Hugh. Think about it— he *did* find you accommodations last night, and I'll wager you slept better at Chertsey, where you presumably had your own bedchambers, than if you'd had to burrow into the straw in some monastic guest house amid strangers. And by covering so much ground yesterday, you arrived here all the earlier today and had more time to rest and refresh yourself before your meeting with Lord Richard tomorrow."

"Hmph."

"My brother may be brash and he may be impulsive— maddeningly so at times—but he's not stupid."

"I didn't mean to imply that he was," Phillipa said quickly. "In fact, I suppose he has a great deal of . . . native intelligence. A man can't be entirely witless and survive fifteen years of warfare." Still, as a soldier, Hugh of Wexford's cognitive abilities would be limited to those applications that were useful on the battlefield—such as improvising strategies as he went along, his apparent specialty. Most knights couldn't even write their own name.

A roar of boyish whoops and hollers erupted in the meadow.

"Well done!" Joanna called out.

"What happened?" Phillipa asked.

"It's over. Haven't you been paying attention?"

Paying attention? Having little interest in games of sport and no inkling as to how this particular one was played, Phillipa had pretty much ignored it. That Joanna had managed to follow its progress while talking to Phillipa and doing her needlework was quite remarkable.

Joanna called out her congratulations to her son as he ran to her, grinning broadly. Laying her embroidery on the fence next to her, she wrapped him up in a hug as he hurtled himself into her arms.

Joanna's enthusiasm—and that of Graeham, when he joined them and the other boys on young Hugh's team—took Phillipa somewhat aback. It was only a game, after all, the manipulation of a little leather ball for the amusement of children. She felt that sense of detachment that often ambushed her when she ventured out of her academic refuge and into the greater world—the sense that, on the one hand, she had so much more perspective and insight than those around her, and on the other, that they all shared in a vast and mysterious store of common knowledge that she would never be privy to.

"Did you enjoy the game, Lady Phillipa?" Sending his son back to the house with an affectionate smack on the rump, Graeham straddled the fence to the other side of his wife.

"I . . . 'twas . . ."

"She had no idea what was going on." Joanna squeezed Phillipa's hand. "I wish you could spend the summer here with us. You could use some color in your cheeks. I could set up a net in the meadow and teach you to play *jeu de paume*."

Graeham smoothed a hand over Joanna's prodigious belly, smiling indulgently. "I don't think you'll be playing *jeu de paume* this year, lady wife."

"Nay . . . I suppose not." Sighing, Joanna closed her hand over his. "Why am I so often big with child in the summer, when I just want to frolic in the sun with everyone else?"

With an intimate chuckle, Graeham said, "Because in the winter, you just want to curl up in some warm, snug place . . ." He lowered his voice, both arms encircling his wife. "With your husband."

Graeham whispered something in Joanna's ear, prompting soft laughter from her. They kissed. Phillipa looked away, feeling uncomfortably like a voyeur . . . worse, an interloper.

Feigning an air of nonchalance, she rose from the fence, smoothing down her tunic. "I think I'd like to take a little walk before the sun sets completely. After two days in the saddle, 'twould be good to stretch my legs."

"Would you like us to come with you?" Graeham asked, although Phillipa sensed he was asking just to be polite. "We could give you a proper tour of—"

"If it's all the same to you, I wouldn't mind being alone for a bit—that's another thing I haven't had quite enough of lately."

Graeham smiled. "I can certainly understand that. Enjoy your walk."

'Twill be a quick walk, she thought as she turned and wandered away from them, across a grassy field riffled by a warm, sweet-scented breeze. *There's not much light left in the day.* Sprawling sheep pastures and cultivated fields formed a haphazard patchwork on the undulating land. To her right, in a sort of shallow valley, she could see the thatched rooftops of the village of Eastingham, painted gold by the setting sun. Just ahead of her was what looked to be an orchard, although she couldn't say

what kind; she'd never been good at identifying trees. Beyond the orchard was a fish pond, and beyond that, dense woods.

Phillipa was an urban creature at heart, despite Linleigh, the Oxfordshire estate her sire had been generous enough to grant her seven years ago. She appreciated her holding for the income it produced, which allowed her the indulgence of collecting the books stacked from floor to ceiling in her little Oxford flat. Nevertheless, she rarely visited Linleigh, leaving its administration in the hands of her trusted bailiff. As beautiful as the countryside could be, pastoral pursuits bored her; they always had.

The orchard drew her, perhaps because of the tidy rows in which the tall, mature trees had been planted, which appealed to her sense of precision and orderliness. She strolled down a tree-lined aisle, breathing in the earthy scents and listening to a soft, summer-evening refrain of chirps and trills from within the leafy canopy overhead. The sun, hovering low on the horizon, shot its dying rays through the rows of trees, casting the orchard into streaks of light and shadow.

Several yards into the orchard, she turned and looked back the way she had come. Off in the distance she could see Joanna and Graeham facing each other on the fence—alone, all the villagers having gone home at the end of the game. Joanna took Graeham's hand and placed it on her belly.

Phillipa stepped behind a tree, lest one of them glance this way and find her watching them.

Presently, Graeham started—at a movement of the baby's? He laughed and said something to Joanna. She laughed too.

Their foreheads touched. Graeham's free hand rose to curl around her neck. He spoke to her. She nodded, smiling.

Phillipa drew in a deep breath, which caught in her throat.

It could be her, sitting on that fence, her fourth child curled up in her belly while her husband marveled at the wonderment of it, of them. Had things transpired as planned seven years ago, had Graeham not chosen Joanna over her, that husband would have been him. At the time, Phillipa had felt nothing but relief, even gratitude—she would get Linleigh and the chance to pursue her studies in Oxford, fast becoming the most forward-thinking center of learning in Europe, but without the burden of a husband. She would enjoy a life of extraordinary autonomy, the kind of life most women could only dream of, even women of her rank—*especially* women of her rank, who, bred to be marriage prizes, were discouraged from any pursuit more ambitious than fancy needlework. And, of course, she'd felt nothing for Graeham, whom she'd just met. Nor did she harbor any feelings for him now other than friendship, but she had to admit no woman could ask for a more attentive husband or devoted father. Fortune had smiled on Joanna when Graeham Fox had sacrificed everything—or been willing to—in order to marry her.

Graeham gathered Joanna in his arms and kissed her again, only this time he didn't stop. They kissed endlessly, while Phillipa watched, ashamed to be compromising their privacy this way, but strangely incapable of looking away.

Of course, Phillipa had been as fortunate as Joanna, but in a different way. Some women were meant for marriage and children, some for . . . greater things?

They still hadn't stopped kissing.

Different things.

"Shame on you, Lady Phillipa," came a man's soft, amused voice from behind her.

Chapter 5

Phillipa whipped around with a harsh little intake of breath to find Hugh of Wexford standing in the shadows not two yards behind her. He looked different this evening, with a long shirt hanging loosely over gray chausses, his damp hair neatly combed away from his face and . . . there was something else that she couldn't quite place. As always, he had his leather satchel slung over one shoulder and that ubiquitous wineskin looped across his chest, but he was beltless this evening, and therefore without that odd heathen dagger.

Summoning her self-composure, Phillipa said, "You shouldn't sneak up behind a person that way."

"How else to discover people's secret foibles?" Grinning, he dumped his satchel on the ground and uncorked the wineskin. "I wouldn't have taken you for the type to skulk about, spying on people unawares."

With a huff of scornful laughter, she said, "You're a fine one to talk!"

"I skulk for the good of the realm."

"For the good of your purse, you mean."

She heard him sigh. He took a step toward her, into a band of sunlight that glinted off his earring and turned his shirt of bleached linen blinding white. Holding the wineskin out to her, he said, "I don't suppose there'd be any point to offering you some of this."

Phillipa's instinct was to automatically shake her head—as he well knew, after two days in her company. Instead, she braced herself—against what?—and closed the distance between them, reaching for the wineskin.

With a surprised little quirk of the eyebrows, he pulled it off and handed it to her.

He stared at her as she drank, his gaze lighting on her mouth, her throat. His eyes were crystalline in the waning sun, his gaze unnervingly intent as always.

She saw what it was that was different about him, and realized with dismay that she'd been staring at him, too. Handing back the wineskin, she said, "You shaved."

He ran a hand over his now-smooth jaw and that sturdy chin with its slight cleft—a feature he shared with his sister. " 'Twouldn't do to show up at West Minster Palace looking like a raker."

Phillipa smiled inwardly to think of insolent, arrogant Hugh of Wexford cleaning streets and emptying privies.

"You managed to shave at a stream in the middle of the woods?" she asked.

"A soldier learns to shave anywhere, sleep anywhere, and eat anything." His gaze focused over her shoulder; turning, she saw that he was looking at Joanna and Graeham, still embracing on the fence, although they were talking now rather than kissing. "Is it true you don't believe in marriage?" he asked.

She looked at him sharply, vexed at how much he knew about her—or thought he did. "Where did you hear that?"

He shifted his gaze to her. " 'Twas a . . ." Seemingly discomfited, he looked away. "Someone in Oxford told me. Is it true?"

Phillipa wondered what else he'd been told, and was all too sure she knew. " 'Tisn't as simple as . . . just not believing in marriage. I don't suppose there's anything wrong with it in theory, but in practice it can be stifling, especially to pursuits of the mind. There's a reason clerics are discouraged from marrying."

"You're not a cleric."

"Only because I'm a woman. All serious scholars take minor orders sooner or later. If I were a man, I'd have been tonsured years ago."

"Had you ever considered taking the veil?"

She choked on a mouthful of wine. "I didn't mean I had any inclination to bury myself away in some convent! Only that marriage and academics don't seem to mix very well."

"Nor marriage and true love, if one believes in that *amour courtois* drivel—as you seem to."

"I never said I believed in it," she said, thrusting the wineskin into his hand. "Precisely. That is, I have no reason to disbelieve it . . ."

"Have you experienced it yourself, this thunderbolt of love they blather on about in Poitiers?" he asked, shrugging the wineskin back over his chest. "Dear God, you have, haven't you? You've imagined yourself smitten by true love, helpless in the wake of its—"

"Certainly not!" she said with a bit too much conviction. "I . . . I just find it . . . intriguing."

He chuckled and shook his head. "How any thinking person could find it anything other than the most fatuous, sentimental, self-serving—"

"Sentimental!" Heat rose up her throat. "You're saying I'm sentimental?"

He laughed outright at her indignation. "I think you're susceptible to sentimentality, despite that image of cool intellectuality you like to project. How else to explain your being hoodwinked by this nonsense?"

"I can explain my interest in courtly love," she said. "And it has nothing to do with sentimentality. I don't suppose you've heard of a woman named Héloïse. She became notorious some fifty years ago in Paris for her love affair with a great philosopher and teacher named Peter Abelard—although she was famously brilliant in her own right."

Hugh leaned against one of the trees, eyeing her with an inscrutable expression as he raised the wineskin to his mouth. "Indeed."

"I'd taken an interest in Héloïse even as a young child," Phillipa said, "because I knew she'd been brought up, like me, by an uncle serving as a canon of Notre Dame—Fulbert was his name. Regardless of your

contempt for the notion of a spiritual union, Sir Hugh,
Abelard and Héloïse shared a passion that was truly of
the heart and mind. All of Paris celebrated their love,
even though, as a cleric and teacher, Abelard was expected to be chaste."

"And he wasn't?" Hugh's smile struck her as just a bit
too knowing. "So their union was more than spiritual."

Unaccountably flustered, she said, "I never said it was
a platonic union—they even had a child, a son. Still,
Héloïse resisted Fulbert's demand that she marry Abelard and salvage her reputation. She felt Abelard was
the greatest thinker in Europe—as he was—and that
marriage would destroy him as a teacher. In the end . . ."
Phillipa sighed heavily. "It got complicated."

"Everything always does," Hugh murmured, sounding
almost melancholy.

"Héloïse let Abelard talk her into marrying him, but
in secret, which only further enraged Fulbert. He had
Abelard . . ." She glanced uncomfortably at Hugh, who
was watching her with that merciless intensity of his.
"He had him . . . castrated. Abelard became a monk,
Héloïse a nun—but she was never a bride of Christ, not
really. She belonged, heart and soul, to Peter Abelard,
until the day she died."

"You can't possibly know that."

"But I do. I met her when I was fourteen, three years
before her death. My uncle Lotulf took me to the convent of the Paraclete, where she was abbess. I thought
her the most remarkable person I'd ever met. She crackled with intelligence, yet she was also so witty, so warm-
hearted—and still so deeply in love with Abelard, even
though he'd been gone for twenty years and she'd not
seen him for many years before that. All I could think
was that I wanted to be just like her—except, of course,
for taking the veil. All that spirit, all that radiance, cloistered away in a convent for a lifetime. The tragedy of
it . . ."

"You realize, of course, that this idol of yours, this
Héloïse, was destroyed by the very same romantic pas-

sion that you find so inexplicably intriguing—as was Abelard."

"They were destroyed by the notion that their passion was shameful unless it existed within the bonds of holy matrimony," she corrected archly. "Abelard doomed them both when he coerced her into becoming his wife."

"Are you saying they should have lived openly in sin? I can't think Fulbert would have tolerated that for very long."

"They could have left Paris, run away together—perhaps to Oxford, where there aren't so many rigid expectations."

Hugh took his time shoving the cork back in the wineskin, his expression thoughtful. "Lord Richard tells me you had your share of suitors in Paris, young noblemen studying at the university, but not so many since you came to Oxford."

A little groan of exasperation rose in her throat. "Is there anything you don't know about me?"

"There are things I don't know for sure." Before she could ask him what he meant by that, he said, "I assume you've avoided matrimony because of what happened to Héloïse."

" 'Twould have been shamefully naive of me—especially after meeting Héloïse—to think that I could have the life of the mind and the life of a wife and mother." She turned away from him, chafing her arms as the ribbons of sunlight faded and twilight cloaked the orchard in a cool purplish veil.

She hadn't thought of them in some time, those misguided young men with their earnest proposals. She'd never encouraged them—indeed, she'd actively avoided them—yet still they'd sought her out, and once they latched on to her, they were damnably difficult to shake. All of them expected her to cheerfully give up her studies—and of course, her freedom—once she was wed, or at least once she started producing heirs for them.

Then a curious thing happened shortly after she'd settled in Oxford. Her first unsolicited suitor there, Walter

Colrede, on learning of her adulation for Héloïse, concluded—erroneously but conveniently—that Phillipa was as unfettered as her idol in regard to matters of the flesh.

In fact, Phillipa had never so much as kissed a man, much less bedded one. It was one thing, she'd found, to admire and even espouse the free expression of physical passion, but quite another to practice it. The act of copulation struck her as grossly undignified and fraught with risk. Perhaps if she'd ever been in love, as Héloïse had been . . . but even the most ardent of her suitors had inspired no feelings in her stronger than sisterly affection.

Walter had informed Phillipa that marriage was now impossible. A member of the so-called secular clergy—excluding any man who had taken major orders through ordination as a deacon or priest—might marry if he was willing to sacrifice certain clerical privileges, but he was strictly forbidden to marry more than once, and his bride must be a maiden. And so was born the solution to the problem of Phillipa's troublesome suitors—all of whom, being scholars, were in minor orders. When Walter had chivalrously promised her that he would reveal her licentiousness to no one, she assured him that such discretion was unnecessary. She cared not if the unenlightened judged her harshly; she was unashamed of her convictions and, like Héloïse, disdainful of marriage. In the years since then, this subterfuge had served its purpose in keeping her from being hounded by marriage-minded young men.

From behind her, Hugh asked quietly, "What is it like, this life of the mind for which you've sacrificed so much? What do you do with your days?"

Reaching up, she snapped a twig off the tree nearest her. "I study."

A moment passed. When he spoke again, he was right behind her, although she hadn't heard his footsteps. "That's all?"

She shrugged and stepped away from him, turning to

lean against the trunk of the tree. "There are monks and nuns who do naught but pray all day."

Through the gathering darkness, she saw him smile. "You've already established what you think of cloistered life. I take it you're not particularly devout."

"Not unthinkingly so," she said, sliding the twig's smooth little leaves one by one between her fingers. "Abelard said, 'By doubting we come to inquiry. By inquiry, we come to truth.' As for dedicating my life to study, by doing so I'm at the very least improving my mind. The same cannot be said of those monks and nuns who spend their days in incessant prayer behind convent walls."

He stalked lazily toward her, prompting her to instinctively flatten her back against the tree. "Perhaps they're improving the world."

"Perhaps they're simply hiding from the world."

"Are you not doing much the same thing?" he asked, suddenly right in front of her, very close. "You hide away in your comfortable little scholastic refuge, never thinking to get out in the world and apply that formidable brain of yours to any real purpose. You've learned much, but what good does that knowledge do if it just stays locked up in here?" He stroked her forehead, very softly, his coarse fingertips sending a breathless tickle down deep into her chest. The twig slipped from her fingers and fell silently to the ground.

She wanted to answer his accusation with some clever rebuttal, but the air seemed to have left her lungs.

"You really are just hiding away in a cocoon," he said, his voice dropping almost to a whisper as he lightly caressed her face.

Her chest ached. She closed her eyes, stunned that such a storm of sensation could be provoked by something as simple as callused fingertips grazing her temple, her cheek, the curve of her jaw. She breathed in the warmth of Hugh's skin mingled with a trace of Castile soap and the grassy scent of his clean linen shirt, and felt strangely lightheaded.

"I wonder," he murmured, turning his hand to trail his knuckles down her throat, skimming his fingers along the neck of her tunic, "what will become of you."

She opened her eyes and met his gaze, luminous in the dusky half-light. There was something almost tender in his expression, or perhaps she was merely seeing what she wanted to see.

"Caterpillars do turn into butterflies," he said, "but first they have to want to. They have to break free of that nice, familiar little cocoon. They must give up the only sanctuary they've ever known before they can be part of the greater world."

He gently cupped her chin, tilted it up.

She sucked in a breath, dissolving the spell he'd woven around her. Wresting her head to the side, she said, "Why are you doing this?"

There came a pause, and then he said, "Must I have a reason?"

"Everything that happens has a reason." She sidestepped him and backed away, wrapping her arms tightly around herself.

He regarded her in silence for a moment, a speculative glint in his eyes, as if he were trying to puzzle something out. "Does it bother you when I touch you?"

Bother her? It roused her blood, stole the breath from her lungs. What would she do, she wondered, if she were a different kind of woman, the kind everyone in Oxford thought she was? How would she respond to Hugh's mesmerizing touch if she really were like Héloïse, and not just pretending?

"It . . . doesn't bother me," she lied. "I just don't quite see the point of . . . of . . ."

"Point?" he chuckled. Propping a shoulder against the same tree trunk she'd just abandoned, Hugh folded his arms. "Do the beasts of the forest have a point when they nuzzle and lick each other just for the pleasure of it, or when they curl up together at night . . . or when they mate?"

Was he deliberately trying to disconcert her? "We

aren't animals," she pointed out, hating how prim she sounded.

"People crave each other's touch just as animals do, whether it's simple comfort they seek, or warmth, or carnal release." He seemed to be watching her closely . . . for her reaction? "The mistake is in complicating an elemental human drive, such as that for sex, by wrapping it up in this spurious notion of romantic love."

"Well, then," she began, hoping she didn't sound as rattled as she felt; surely it wouldn't have troubled Héloïse to hear a man speak of "carnal release" and "sex." "Do you believe in marriage?"

He ran a hand absently over his jaw. "Marriage is useful for legitimizing children and ensuring that property passes down properly, but that's the extent of it."

"Then I take it you do plan to marry once you're lord of Wexford."

With a bemused laugh, he said, "What on earth makes you think I'll be lord of Wexford?"

"I know there's a chance your father's overlord won't grant it to you—"

"And if he does, I'll turn it down."

Phillipa was dumbfounded that he would reject his birthright so summarily. "You would turn down one of the finest holdings in England?"

Even in this dim light, she could see the muscles of his jaw clench. "The most miserable years of my life were spent at Wexford. I've no desire to ever set foot there again."

"But you're the firstborn son—the only son. Isn't it your duty to keep Wexford in the family? And as for marriage, don't you feel you have an obligation to perpetuate the—"

"Obligation!" He pushed abruptly away from the tree. "Who the hell are you to lecture me on my obligations?"

"I only meant—"

"For your information, my lady—not that it's any of your concern, but that's unlikely to stop you from your ceaseless interrogations—my obligations begin and end"—he slammed a fist on his chest—"with me. Wexford Castle can crumble to ruins as far as I care. That being the case, I need never face the unsavory prospect of binding myself in matrimony to one woman for the rest of my life, thank the saints."

"So, you've as little use for marriage as for romance." Not wanting him to think his candid references to sex had shocked her, she said, "I take it, then, that you . . . couple like an animal, for simple physical pleasure."

He shrugged. "You profess to have no use for marriage either, and I seem to recall you saying you'd never been in love. So isn't that why you couple? For pleasure?"

Isn't that why you couple . . . ? So . . . he *had* heard all there was to hear, and he believed what he'd been told. Either that, or . . . yes, she could see it in his eyes. He didn't believe it, or rather, he didn't know what to believe, because the whispers about her contradicted his image of her as a bookish prude. He was testing her—goading her to see whether she'd blush and stammer and frantically defend her reputation. Resolving not to give him that satisfaction, she said, "I asked you first, Sir Hugh. Why do you couple? Is it simply for physical pleasure?"

Silence descended between them as he digested what she'd said—or rather, hadn't said, the denials she hadn't offered. She wished she could see his expression a little better, but it was almost completely dark now.

Presently he said, "If you think there's something simple about physical pleasure, my lady, then I think you've been seeking it with the wrong men."

"Indeed," she said through a ripple of nervous laughter.

"Indeed." He closed the distance between them before she could think what to say next. "Even something as simple as a kiss need not feel simple . . ." He wrapped his big hands around her head, raising her face to his. "Not if it's done right."

No sooner had she drawn in a breath to object than

he closed his mouth over hers, firmly, gripping her head to still it, ignoring the involuntary little whimper that rose in her throat.

His lips felt warm and slightly damp, and much softer than she'd imagined a man's lips might feel against hers. She pushed against his shoulders, feeling hard, unyielding muscles through the thin linen of his shirt, but he paid her no heed.

His mouth moved over hers, possessively, hungrily, but slowly, so slowly, as if he were savoring the taste and feel of her, despite her futile struggles. As he lingered over the kiss, Phillipa felt as if she were caught up in a dream . . . a fever dream, delirious and intoxicating.

He cupped the back of her head with one hand, his other arm banding around her, drawing her close, nearly lifting her off her feet as he prolonged the kiss, coaxing her into returning it. She clutched handfuls of his shirt, her heart thundering in her ears.

Heat flooded her, like a thousand tiny flames licking her from within, kindling a strange, drunken pleasure she'd never felt before. *I'm mad,* she thought giddily. *He's stolen my senses with one kiss.*

His hands roamed over her, warm and bewitchingly insistent through her woolen tunic. He caressed her arms, the slope of her back, the curve of her waist, his touch growing ever more purposeful as he molded her to him.

There was a sense of desperation, in the way he seized her hips, pulling her toward him. Something dug into her lower belly, making her gasp—that strange dagger of his, she thought, but then she remembered he wasn't wearing it. He rubbed against her, pressing the solid ridge between her legs, stroking her with it, and she felt its shape and heat through their clothes and realized what it must be.

Jesu! She broke the kiss, jolted out of her sensual reverie. "Sir Hugh . . ."

"Don't worry," he said breathlessly, gathering up her skirt with unsteady hands. "No one can see us here."

" 'Tisn't that." She grabbed his wrists, but her strength was no match for his, and her skirt continued to rise. "Stop, Hugh. Please . . ."

"I'll lay my shirt on the ground for you to lie upon so your tunic won't get—"

"I said stop!"

"Or perhaps I can bring you back to my chamber without anyone seeing." He slid a hand beneath her bunched-up skirt and over her bare bottom.

"Stop!" Hauling back, she struck his face as hard as she could.

His head whipped back.

Her hand stung.

He released her skirt. She scrambled away from him, reflexively yanking her dagger out of its sheath, her gaze trained on his shadowy form.

For several long moments, he just stared at her, his eyes half-hidden by strands of damp hair that quivered with every breath he took. His gaze lit on the dagger in her trembling hand. Over her own harsh breathing, she heard his grim little huff of laughter. "Don't forget to aim for the throat."

He turned his back to her, taking his weight carelessly on one hip as he combed his hair off his face with his fingers. Only a long, tremulous exhalation betrayed his true state of mind.

"If I were the kind of man to take a woman by force," he said, his voice low and raw, "that thing wouldn't help you. I should think our little adventure in that alley in Oxford would have taught you that much."

She slid the dagger back into its sheath and willed steadiness into her voice. "I did tell you to stop."

"Yes, well . . ." Still facing away from her, he kneaded the side of his face where she had slapped him. "I thought you were trying to protect your tunic. 'Twas my understanding your virtue is past redeeming."

Her cheeks stung furiously; the contemptible dog! "That's the only reason you . . . mauled me that way—

because of what you've heard about me. It didn't have anything to do with me, just . . . physical gratification."

"The gratification would have been mutual, I assure you." He popped the cork out of his wineskin. "What happened to those exalted notions of sexual freedom you're reputed to embrace?"

"Free doesn't mean undiscriminating."

There came a moment's frigid silence as he absorbed that, the wineskin halfway to his mouth. He replaced the cork without taking a drink, and turned to face her, his expression black.

"Forgive me, my lady," he said icily, offering one of those taunting little bows of his. "I should have known better than to think you'd grant your favors to the likes of me when you could have your pick of all those worthy Oxford scholars with their cultivated minds and soft white hands."

Phillipa bit back the urge to tell him that wasn't what she'd meant, not quite, that she'd been speaking generally and had intended no insult to him personally. After all, she should be trying to discourage him, not mollify him. Experience had taught her to use any means at her disposal to defuse the amorous attentions of men—and never had she felt more threatened by those attentions than she did right now.

Because you're in his thrall. Because you feel it, too, the heat, the longing . . .

Hugh *was* unworthy of her, she told herself. He was a charming libertine, accustomed to effortless seductions. He only wanted to use her; he'd admitted as much, with no shame or hesitation. That she embraced, theoretically, the free expression of sexual desire, was irrelevant. To give herself to such a man would demean her utterly; it made her cringe inside to think that she'd succumbed to his kiss even momentarily.

"As long as we understand each other," she said thinly.

Did he smile? It was dark; perhaps it was a grimace. "I wouldn't say I understand you, my lady." Crossing to his satchel, he scooped it off the ground and slung it over his back. "But at least now I won't waste any more time trying to."

He turned and stalked back to the house.

Chapter 6

"I don't like it." Hugh stood at a window in Richard de Luci's chamber at the royal palace, looking down upon a courtyard flooded with morning sunlight. On a stone bench at the far end sat Phillipa de Paris, her nose in one of the little books she lugged about in that tooled leather case hanging from her girdle, biding her time until the justiciar was ready to see her.

Lord Richard had called Hugh in first in order to debrief him—about his trip to Oxford, his impressions of the lady Phillipa and her suitability for espionage work—and to sketchily outline in advance the assignment he'd mapped out for them. Upon hearing what his lordship had in mind, Hugh almost wished he'd left Phillipa back in Oxford.

"I wouldn't ask this of a wedded woman," said Lord Richard from his desk behind Hugh, "or, God knows, a maiden. But as you reported yourself, Lady Phillipa is known to be . . . rather unhampered by convention in her relations with men."

A fact that his lordship had clearly known before sending Hugh to Oxford, but had failed to mention. Had he deliberately withheld the information just to see whether Hugh would uncover it himself?

"Damned convenient for us, her being so free with her favors," said Lord Richard, "especially since we know her sympathies lie with the king. And, of course, there's her history with the fellow we're going after. She couldn't be more perfect for this mission."

"I still don't like it," Hugh said, watching the subject of their conversation look up from her reading to observe two deerhound pups cavorting on the stone court nearby. Her smile made her look very young and very sweet. Was this really the same woman who'd returned his kiss with such heated abandon last night . . . only to cut him down to size when he sought to take their passion to its logical conclusion?

"I don't much like it myself," the justiciar admitted with a sigh. "The point, however, is not whether the plan is *likable,* but whether it will work. I believe it will. And I believe it to be our best hope for exposing the queen's sedition while there's still time to do something about it."

Turning away from the window, Hugh found Lord Richard perched on the edge of his desk, a thick slab of age-polished oak the size of a small room, yet dwarfed by the capacious grandeur of the surrounding chamber, with its high ceiling and spectacularly painted walls. The justiciar crossed his arms, scrutinizing Hugh with those scalding blue eyes of his. He cut an even more imposing figure than usual today, in a gold-trimmed black tunic, his silver-white hair combed back to expose the prodigious forehead reputed to be a sign of his whipcrack intelligence.

"What if she won't do it?" Hugh asked.

"I'll dare her. Didn't you just tell me she can't resist rising to a challenge?"

Indeed he had, damn it all.

Lord Richard called in one of the manservants waiting outside the door and sent him down to the courtyard to fetch Phillipa. "You're clearly ambivalent about this mission, Hugh. That's fine—I don't expect mindless compliance from a man like you. However, I do expect you to execute your orders to the best of your ability, regardless of how they sit with you."

"Have I ever done otherwise?"

"Not to my knowledge, but you seem particularly ill at ease about the lady Phillipa's involvement this time round."

"It's one thing," Hugh said, a bit too stridently, "for her to take lovers of her choosing because of her intellectual convictions. It's quite another to expect her to . . . to . . ."

"If her participation weren't critical to our cause, I would never presume to ask such a thing of her, regardless of her reputation—she is, after all, a lady of rank, not a common trollop. But, Hugh, there is simply no one who can take her place if she refuses to cooperate with us. I wish to God you hadn't told her she had a choice in the matter. You wasted the threat about her uncle by telling her 'twas just to get her to West Minster and then she could decide for herself. You should have let her think we'd have the old man eviscerated and quartered if she didn't participate."

"Every so often," Hugh gritted out, "even I reach a threshold as to how much of a bastard I can be."

"Really?" the justiciar said with a mild smile. "I wouldn't have thought it." More soberly he said, "All I ask—or shall I say, demand—is that you say nothing during this meeting to discourage her from helping us. After all, if she does agree to it, then obviously her sensibilities cannot have been all that bruised."

Obviously? Hugh turned back to the window to find the bench at the edge of the courtyard empty. There was nothing obvious about it, or about her, nothing conventional or logical, and certainly nothing predictable, despite what he'd briefly thought . . . nothing that made any real sense whatsoever. She was a complete enigma to him, this delicate little creature in her silken cocoon who claimed to be so conversant in the ways of the world.

"Lady Phillipa de Paris," intoned the manservant as he escorted Phillipa through the door. Lord Richard approached her and introduced himself, all charm and wit, the consummate diplomatist. Hugh merely nodded to her from his place by the window.

Sending the servant away with instructions to bring wine, the justiciar guided Phillipa toward a group of high-backed, intricately carved chairs clustered near an arched fireplace neatly stacked with unlit logs. Her eyes widened as she took in the colossal jewel-toned depiction of the Seven Ages of Man painted on the smoothly whitewashed wall directly across from her. Twisting in her chair, she inspected the equally grandiose Twelve Labors of the Months behind her and the circular Map of the World over the fireplace. The rear wall, because of its many windows, had merely been painted green with hundreds of little gold stars and crescents.

"I've a weakness for pictorial decoration," his lordship explained as he gestured her into a chair and took a seat opposite her. "My one real indulgence."

"Ah. Yes . . ."

"What do you think of the paintings?"

Phillipa blinked, and in that moment, Hugh knew exactly what she thought of them, which was pretty much what he thought—that, as the saying went, too much of anything is nothing.

"I . . ." she began. "That is, to be perfectly honest, my lord . . ."

From across the room, Hugh caught her eye and shook his head infinitesimally, mouthing, "remarkable."

She glanced away, her mouth twitching. Looking the justiciar straight in the eye, she said, "I think they're remarkable, sire."

He beamed. "I'm thinking of having something done on the ceiling. What think you, Lady Phillipa—the Vices and Virtues, or perhaps an immense Wheel of Fortune?"

She glanced at Hugh, who cocked an eyebrow and shrugged.

"Er . . . the Vices and Virtues, I should think. Ever so much more . . . instructive."

"Yes!" His lordship seemed pleased. "That it would be."

The servant arrived with a tray of wine and fruit, which he set on a little table before leaving. Lord Richard leaned back in his chair, his legs crossed, his cup cradled in his hand. After thanking Phillipa for coming all the way to West Minster from Oxford on such short notice, he called Hugh over, gesturing him into the chair next to his and diagonally across from Phillipa's.

"My lady," the justiciar began, "do you recall, from Paris, a man by the name of Aldous Ewing? You would have known him when you were sixteen or seventeen— he was three or four years older."

Phillipa frowned. "I knew an Aldous of Tettenham— an Englishman."

"That's the fellow." Turning to Hugh, who knew only the man's name and none of the particulars, Lord Richard said, "Younger son of a Middlesex baron. Entered minor orders at fourteen, moved to Paris a year later to study canon law. Erudite, charming . . ." He glanced at Phillipa. "And quite handsome, I understand."

Phillipa met his gaze steadily. "He certainly seemed to think so."

"Rather an avid suitor of yours, was he not?"

"Not through any encouragement of mine."

Lord Richard brought his cup to his lips, his searing gaze never leaving Phillipa. "Absolutely smitten with you, by all accounts. Begged you to marry him, despite . . . the circumstances of your birth, and even though it would have stymied his Church career by preventing him from taking major orders. I understand he was devastated when you refused."

Phillipa cast a speculative look toward Hugh, who dropped his gaze to the rush-covered floor.

"He's a lawyer now," his lordship continued, "and a deacon of the Church."

"Really." Phillipa looked surprised. "So he took major orders after all."

"It would seem since he couldn't have you, he decided to settle for power and prestige. I don't know what he was like in Paris, but my reports indicate that he's become the quintessential canon lawyer—politically astute, self-serving, devious, and most of all rabidly ambitious. And like most of his breed, he hasn't let his ordination to the diaconate keep him from living a dissolute, even worldly, existence. He's had numerous lemans over the years, although he's taken great pains to be discreet about them. Deacons who flaunt their mistresses don't earn appointments to the archdeaconry, and that's something he wants desperately."

"Where does he live?" Hugh asked. "London?"

"Aye, when he's not abroad. He built a house across the river in Southwark."

"Southwark?" Phillipa interjected.

Hugh knew why she was surprised. The London suburb was notorious for its public inns and bathhouses, many of which were little more than glorified brothels. He said, "There's more to Southwark of late than the stews, my lady. In fact, more and more noblemen are building their London town houses there rather than within the city walls. It's become as stylish as it is disreputable."

"And Aldous Ewing is nothing if not stylish," the justiciar commented. "They say he imports the finest wool from Sicily and silks from Florence for his clerical robes."

"He was . . . different in Paris," Phillipa said pensively. "Not that he didn't have his vices. He was self-centered even then, and vain, and far from chaste if you believed the idle talk—but so were many of the well-born young scholars who came there to study, regardless of whether they wore the tonsure. He was like the rest of them in that he never understood my interest in academics. I always thought of Aldous simply as young and"—she shrugged—"innocuous."

"Innocuous . . ." Lord Richard shook his head disgustedly and drained his cup. "Would that he were still innocuous, and I'd not have had to summon you from Oxford, my lady."

"What has he done?" Phillipa asked.

Grimacing in a preoccupied way, Lord Richard reached out to set his empty cup on the table. "That's what I'm hoping you'll be able to find out."

Phillipa's gaze flicked from the justiciar to Hugh and back again. "Is he involved in the queen's rebellion?"

"If such rebellion truly exists, aye—we think so. He's been critical of King Henry ever since that business with Thomas Becket over curbing the powers of the Church. And since poor Becket's death, he's disparaged the king openly, even going so far as to say he ought to be charged with murder."

"Many others have said the same thing," Hugh pointed out. "What evidence is there that he's one of the conspirators?"

Lord Richard sat back and steepled his hands. "Here's what we know. Aldous Ewing is ostensibly attached to St. Paul's in London, but his father's donations to the Church have bought him the freedom to do as he pleases—and what he pleases is to spend most of his time abroad. He travels frequently to Paris, and is known to be a favorite in King Louis's court. He was there at Eastertime, when there was reputed to be a great deal of seditious activity there. On the very same day he left Paris to return to England, his sister left Poitiers . . . but I'm getting ahead of myself. He has an older sister—"

"Aye," Phillipa said. "Clare of Halthorpe. I met her briefly when she came to visit Aldous in Paris. Squabbled with her brother constantly, as I recall. Made quite sure I knew she was a confidante of Queen Eleanor's."

"Aye, that sounds like the lady Clare." To Hugh, the justiciar said, "She's the wife of Baron Bertram of Halthorpe, but she's been a fixture in the queen's circle for years."

"When I met her in Paris," Phillipa said, "she told me she hadn't seen England or her husband in over a year and didn't miss either."

"Lady Clare is known to utterly despise England," said Lord Richard. "Finds the climate cold and dismal and the people narrow-minded compared to the Continent—'drearily moralistic' is how she put it in a letter to her sister."

Hugh saw Phillipa's mouth tighten at Lord Richard's casual reference to intercepting correspondence, but she kept her counsel.

"She especially loathes Halthorpe," the justiciar continued, "Could never stand being there. In fact, for the past two years, she's made her home at the queen's palace in Poitiers."

"I recall a lady Clare from Poitiers." Hugh scratched his chin. "Fair-skinned, jet black hair, coldly beautiful eyes."

"That's her," Phillipa said. "She made me think of a marble statue that's been polished just a bit too hard."

"She was always whispering in the corner with one of the young cavaliers," Hugh said.

Lord Richard nodded. "She's been at the center of a number of romantic intrigues. At Christmastide she wrote to her sister that Poitiers was 'a haven of warmth, elegance and delicious dissipation,' and that she'd rather have her eyes put out by red-hot pokers than ever leave it."

"And yet, she did," Phillipa noted.

"Aye, and her departure was quite abrupt, though there's no evidence that she'd fallen out of favor with the queen—on the contrary, they seemed especially inseparable right before she left. They say her husband, Lord Bertram, barely recognized her when she showed up at Halthorpe Castle with her retinue, it had been so long since he'd seen her. He immediately departed for the Continent with his mistress and servants, although he left all his soldiers behind."

"And Aldous Ewing left Paris at the same time?" Hugh asked.

"Aye, but he wasn't alone. He had a dozen armed men with him whom we took to be retainers of King Louis, and two carts filled with casks and chests, although we have no idea what was in them. A week later, they delivered this mysterious cargo into Lady Clare's safekeeping at Halthorpe Castle. Aldous Ewing immediately returned to his home in Southwark, but the men-at-arms remained at Halthorpe."

Hugh leaned back in his chair and clasped his hands over his stomach. "Pretty fishy goings-on."

"That they are," the justiciar concurred. "I wish I knew what was in those two carts."

"Why don't you just send a contingent of men to search Halthorpe Castle?" Phillipa suggested.

Lord Richard shook his head. "They would meet resistance from King Louis's men and possibly also from Lord Bertram's soldiers, who we understand are quite numerous. Meanwhile, any incriminating items would be destroyed or moved elsewhere before we could get our hands on them. But more importantly, the king is loath to go barging into an English castle with soldiers until he has proof that treason is underfoot. He wants the matter investigated, but with the utmost discretion, and he wants solid, unimpeachable evidence of the queen's sedition." To Phillipa he said, "That, my lady, is where you come in."

Warily Phillipa said, "You want me to . . . reestablish my acquaintance with Aldous?"

"That and . . ." Averting his gaze, Lord Richard flicked a speck of lint from his tunic. "Ideally . . . insinuate yourself into his household, and possibly Halthorpe Castle as well."

Phillipa compelled the justiciar with the intensity of her gaze to look at her. "And how, my lord," she asked tightly, "do you propose I do that?"

Lord Richard's expression betrayed both his embarrassment at having to spell it out and his irritation at being forced to. "At one time Aldous Ewing was very much enamored of you, my lady. He was willing to sacrifice a Church career to be your husband. If fate were to throw you in his path again, and if you were to encourage him this time, well . . . I daresay he would jump at the chance to have now what he could not have in Paris."

"He can't marry now that he's a deacon." Holding the justiciar's gaze resolutely, Phillipa said, "Can I assume you're asking me to become his leman?"

Again, his lordship seemed unable to look Phillipa in the eye. "I . . . would never ask a woman to . . . violate her principles." Which didn't, of course, answer the question, especially given Phillipa's rather iconoclastic "principles." He picked up his cup and, finding it empty, set it down again with a frown.

"Principles aside," Phillipa said, "it confounds me why men always assume that if a woman wants something, her sexual favors are her only means of acquiring it. Do I seem incapable of using my wits to ferret out the information you seek?"

Ever the cagey diplomat, Lord Richard said, "The extent of your acquaintance with the man is up to you, of course. I will say that the more . . . intimate your relationship with him, the more he will want you about and the more you will learn."

"His lordship is right," Hugh said. "Keen though your wits may be, my lady, a beautiful woman's most potent weapon is not, I'm afraid, that which lies between her ears."

Phillipa shot him a look of distaste.

Lord Richard glanced at him with a baleful expression as he poured Phillipa a cup of wine. "I can't emphasize enough how critical your cooperation is, and how grateful King Henry will be." He set the wine cup back down when she refused to take it. "He would reward you most handsomely, my lady. He would make you a very wealthy—"

" 'Twasn't insulting enough to ask me to bed this man for his secrets," Phillipa snapped, "you now propose to *pay* me, as if I were some street-corner tart? What will it be—tuppence every time I lie down and spread my legs for him?"

Hugh couldn't help admiring her outburst—and chuckling inwardly at Lord Richard's obvious discomfiture.

Gravely the justiciar said, "I meant no disrespect, my lady. It's just that I'm desperate, as is the king. We both remember all too well the struggle between King Stephen and Matilda Empress that ravaged England thirty years ago—the years of chaos and devastation. Another civil war could destroy England. With your help, we can keep that from happening."

Hugh's chest grew tight as he studied Phillipa, waiting for her response. *Don't do it,* he thought, and then silently chided himself. Why should it trouble him for her to play the whore for the good of the realm? She'd done it often enough for less noble reasons.

Except, of course, for last night, when she'd made it all too clear that she did, after all, have her standards.

She looked at Hugh, clearly unsettled; he pointedly looked away.

"You're the ideal person to infiltrate Aldous and Clare's inner circle and bring back proof of what they're up to," the justiciar told Phillipa. "Given your past with Aldous and your innate cleverness, you could have him confiding in you in no time. And as for ferreting out secrets, Hugh tells me your analytical skills are second to—"

"Save your flattery, my lord. I'm not susceptible to it."

"Are you susceptible to begging?" he asked. "If I plead with you to help us, because you're the only person we can turn to—"

"My lord, I . . . I know you're desperate, but I . . ." She shook her head. "You don't understand. I can't . . ."

"You don't think you're up to it." Lord Richard leaned forward, his elbows resting on his knees. "I can't say as I blame you for your lack of confidence."

"I didn't say I wasn't *confident,*" Phillipa corrected.

You sly dog, Hugh thought. Changing tack yet again, Lord Richard meant to ensnare her precisely as he'd said he would—by issuing a dare.

"Nay, it's understandable for you to be intimidated by a mission of this sort," said the justiciar. "You've led a rather sheltered life, after all, and—"

"Why does everyone think I've been sheltered merely because I've been educated?"

"Yes, well . . . my point is, I understand why you feel overwhelmed at the prospect of an espionage mission, although I was hoping you'd consider it"—Lord Richard shrugged—"a challenge of sorts. As well as being an opportunity to experience a bit of the larger world beyond the walls of Oxford."

Phillipa sank back into her chair, chewing her lip. Meeting Hugh's gaze squarely for the first time that morning, she asked, "What do you think I should do?"

So taken by surprise was Hugh that she'd asked his advice that he found himself momentarily speechless. She looked so dazed, so torn, that he couldn't help feeling sorry for her—damned inconvenient, inasmuch as Lord Richard had made him promise not to dissuade her from agreeing to this rather ignominious mission.

But wherefore should he pity her, when she viewed him with such contempt? Last night she'd told him the story of Abelard and Héloïse as if he'd spent his life in a cave and had no idea who they were—before informing him that she was too "discriminating" to tup him as she'd tupped half of Oxford. Just how ignorant, how pathetically unworthy of her, did she think he was?

In the final analysis, did it really matter how he advised her? The decision lay with her, and she did not strike him as the type of woman to be easily swayed; she would accept or reject the mission not on Hugh's say-so, but in accordance with her own sense of what was right. And as for prostituting herself for the crown, what was it his lordship had said earlier? *If she does agree to it, then obviously her sensibilities cannot have been all that bruised.*

She was watching him, waiting for him to counsel her; so was Lord Richard, to whom Hugh owed his allegiance . . . and his obedience.

Hugh snatched his cup off the table and tossed the wine down in one gulp. " 'Twouldn't be the first time you've had a skullcap hanging on your bedpost, my lady. At least this time, some good may come of it."

Bright color stained Phillipa's cheeks. "I'll do it."

Heat seethed in Hugh's belly as he pictured Phillipa and this Aldous Ewing locked together in amorous embrace. Grinding his jaw, he silently cursed himself, Phillipa, Lord Richard, the king, his headstrong queen, her damnable sons, and this whole blasted business.

Lord Richard sagged into his chair with relief. "You won't regret this, my lady."

"You think not?" Hugh refilled his cup and sat back in his chair to sip it. "Just wait till you tell her the rest of it."

Chapter 7

London

Would she have agreed to this mission, Phillipa wondered as she strolled arm-in-arm with Hugh across London Bridge, if she'd known the two of them would have
to execute it posing as man and wife?

My dear lady, Lord Richard had said when she'd protested the arrangement during their meeting last week,
*you don't think I'd send you into such a situation all
alone, a defenseless woman with no man along for protection should something go amiss? And, too, for all your
cleverness, you're a novice at investigative work, whereas
Hugh is, if not my most experienced man, certainly my
most dependable.*

"This is a good spot," Hugh said as they approached
the southern end of the decrepit old wooden structure,
which connected London proper with Southwark and
everything else on the other side of the Thames. Guiding
her with a hand on her back, he led her through the
cacophonous swarm of pedestrians to the western edge
of the bridge. They braced their elbows on the weath-
ered oak rail, looking out over the great sun-spangled
river and the vessels gliding along it this fine afternoon
or lying at anchor—longboats, little two-man merchant
boats, tall-masted ships with foreign banners snapping,
and even a strange, rotund ship with castles at bow
and stern.

"That's Southwark?" Phillipa asked, surveying the
rather unprepossessing cluster of thatched and tiled roof-

tops on the near shore to the south. "Doesn't look much like a haven of sin."

"And what, pray, did you expect? Naked wenches dancing in the streets?" Hugh chuckled rustily. "You really must get out of Oxford more often, my lady."

"I'm here, aren't I?" And glad of it, despite the circumstances. There was something about being in London, with its raucous sights and sounds and smells, not to mention being a part of this clandestine mission, that sent the blood racing through her veins as never before.

"Try to face north," Hugh said, "toward the city. That way, when Aldous passes by, he'll be more likely to recognize you."

He was right; after all, the point of lingering here was to "accidentally" bump into Aldous Ewing, who would presumably cross the bridge sometime before nightfall on his way home from St. Paul's Cathedral, where he went through the motions of performing his diaconal duties when he was in town. She and Hugh had spent all of yesterday loitering outside the cathedral itself, to no avail; he hadn't passed by them, or if he had, he hadn't noticed them—or rather, her. With any luck, he would not only see them this afternoon, but end up offering them the hospitality of his Southwark town house; with a bit more, they might eventually see the inside of Halthorpe Castle, about eight miles northeast of London.

Turning, Phillipa gazed across the river at the mile or so of bustling waterfront along the city's south side, delimited on the west by Baynard's Castle and on the east by the much larger and spectacularly whitewashed Tower of London. A light breeze, redolent of the river, wafted the veil of whisper-sheer samite that floated over her braids, secured by a circlet of silver filigree.

"I still think it most ill-advised for us to pose as man and wife," Phillipa said, "given that our intent is for Aldous to pursue me. I can't believe it wouldn't discourage him to have you hanging about watching me flirt with him."

Hugh shrugged. "Like his sister—and you, for that

matter—he seems to be entirely taken in by this *amour courtois* nonsense. Matrimony is no impediment to seduction for the likes of him, particularly if the lady's husband seems inclined to turn a blind eye. It appears, my lady, that you can embrace the concept intellectually more easily than you can put it into practice—a common shortcoming among those who spend too much time reading about life and not enough living it."

Ignoring the gibe, she said, "It's just all so foreign to me. When Lord Richard said that Aldous seemed particularly drawn to married women, you nodded as if you understood perfectly, but I can't for the life of me conceive why someone would welcome a situation that just makes things that much more complicated."

"Because," Hugh said, his tone only slightly patronizing, "it can actually make things that much simpler. Wedded ladies tend to expect very little from a man beyond a certain measure of prowess in the sport of love. It can be damnably refreshing not to have to feign infatuation in exchange for a friendly tumble or two."

"Need it always be feigned?" She turned to look up at him, cursing the note of wistfulness in her voice. "Have you never had real feelings for a woman?"

For one startling moment, his eyes, greener and deeper than the water surrounding them, seemed to look right inside her, seeing everything—her very soul laid bare. He took her chin in his hand, his fingers so rough and hot that they made her heart flutter crazily. *He's going to kiss me again,* she thought, *and I'm going to let him. I'm going to kiss him back.*

But he didn't kiss her. Instead, he said, "Keep looking north," and turned her face once more in that direction, his fingertips slowly grazing the edge of her jaw before he withdrew his hand.

Leaning on the rail next to her, he slid an arm around her waist, as if they were a devoted married couple out for a summer afternoon's stroll, and not two agents for the crown who had nothing in common save a zealous desire for autonomy—yet who, in some cosmic jest, had been forced to spend every waking hour together for the next few weeks.

And presumably, if all went as planned, every sleeping hour. Phillipa rubbed her arms, although the breeze was mild.

"Nervous?" Hugh gently kneaded her back, his palm warm through the thin silk of her tunic—pink shot with silver threads—and the linen kirtle beneath it, one of a wardrobe of luxurious costumes that Lord Richard had commissioned for her from the royal dressmakers after their meeting in West Minster. On the justiciar's instructions, the gowns had been cut in the provocative new Parisian fashion, with necklines that displayed a generous expanse of bosom and bodices that fit snugly by means of smocking, elaborate tucks, and tight lacings.

He'd provided her with suitable accessories as well— exquisite girdles, slippers, necklaces, earrings, brooches, and of course a wedding ring, all studded with smoothly polished gemstones. The clothes and jewels were hers to keep—along with a little ivory-inlaid casket filled with Spanish gold coins—not only as recompense for her services to the crown, but in order to equip her for her role. *You need to look prosperous and elegant,* the justiciar had decreed. *Both of you.*

Hugh was outfitted this morning in a finely made deep purple tunic and black chausses, his face cleanly shaven, his hair smoothed into a tidy queue at the nape of his neck. He still wore that curious earring, and that infidel dagger hung from his belt in lieu of a knight's customary sword; otherwise he was the very picture of a debonair young nobleman, and an extremely handsome one, that slight bump on his nose imparting a rugged note to what might otherwise have been too beautiful a face.

"I'm not . . . nervous, exactly," Phillipa said as she tried to disregard the paths of heat that lingered on her back wherever Hugh stroked her. She'd been doing a great deal of that these past few days, purposefully ignoring the exhilarating hum of awareness generated by his casual caresses, his careless smiles, his very presence.

Recognizing that awareness for what it was—sexual attraction—both chagrined and intrigued her. Of all the men to induce in her, for the first time, such unruly desires, why did it have to be cocky, dangerous Hugh of Wexford? Why not a more deserving man, a creature of the mind, one of those deep thinkers she'd always held in such high esteem?

Because Hugh was different, of course, nothing like the tame scholars and clerics with whom she had been surrounded the first five-and-twenty years of her life. They *were* admirable men, most of them—astute, thoughtful, civilized. She respected them, often even liked them. But never once, even with the most attractive of her erstwhile suitors, had she lain awake at night imagining the heat and strength of his body against hers, wondering how it would feel to be possessed by him, completely . . . to experience the physical act of love about which she'd heard so much.

Enthralled as she was by these heady new yearnings, Phillipa cautioned herself to remember that they were spawned by nothing weightier than the simple novelty of Hugh of Wexford. He seemed exotic, and therefore desirable, only because he was everything she was unused to—virile, impulsive, and sexually aggressive. In a company of soldiers, his demeanor would not stand out. There was nothing special about him, not really, nothing to inspire any feelings more profound than carnal hunger—a hunger he evidently shared, judging from the incident in the orchard. Not that she was the exclusive object of his lust, of course, soldiers being accustomed to taking their ease with any accommodating woman.

She shouldn't read too much into his little attentions— the frequency with which he touched her, the quiet intensity in his gaze when, from time to time, she turned and found him looking at her. Such gestures meant nothing to a man like him. Indeed, she would do well to remember his taunt about skullcaps hanging from her bedpost.

The image invoked uneasy thoughts of Aldous Ewing.

Bedding him was, of course, out of the question; it was also, as she'd tried in vain to explain to both Lord Richard and Hugh last week, completely unnecessary. They'd paid her no heed, and rather than belabor the point, she'd let them believe what they wanted—that she was willing to become Aldous's leman—although she meant to coax his secrets from him using her wits, not her body. Not that she wouldn't have to entice him—she must lead Aldous on, make him think she was ripe for seduction— but surely she could finesse the information out of him without having to actually follow through.

"Phillipa? Lady Phillipa?" It was a man's voice, but not Hugh's.

Rousing from her reverie, Phillipa looked around. A tall, arrestingly handsome, dark-haired man dressed all in black, a cleric, was bearing down on her through the crowd of pedestrians.

"Aldous," she said, a dull panic seizing her.

Hugh's hand tightened briefly on her waist. He turned her purposefully away from the rail, toward Aldous, and, standing behind her, squeezed her hand reassuringly. Leaning in close to her, he whispered, "You can do this, Phillipa. I'm right here with you," adding, "Smile," as Aldous approached with outstretched arms.

She smiled. "Aldous. Is that really you?"

"Phillipa! My God!" Seizing her by the shoulders, Aldous kissed her soundly on each cheek. "Look at you!" He surveyed her from head to toe, his appreciation obvious. "You're more ravishing than ever. When was the last time I saw you?"

Swallowing down her trepidation, she said, " 'Twould have to have been Paris—seven years ago, perhaps eight."

"Yes, of course. Paris." Aldous's gaze shifted to Hugh, his smile growing just a bit more subdued as he took in their hands still clasped together.

"Er, Aldous," Phillipa said, "this is . . . my husband, Hugh of Oxford. Hugh, this is an old friend of mine from Paris, Aldous of Tettenham."

"Ah." Aldous's expressive brown eyes flickered, just momentarily, with surprise . . . and dismay. "So. You married after all."

Back when Aldous had been wooing her so ardently, she'd told him what she'd told all her suitors—that she would never marry, lest it destroy her. At the time, she'd believed it.

Don't you still?

"You're a fortunate man, Hugh of Oxford." Fixing a polite smile on his face, Aldous offered Hugh a perfunctory little bow.

"Well I know it," Hugh replied with a tilt of his head. He squeezed Phillipa's hand again as his other arm curled around her waist—a possessive gesture that surprised her, inasmuch as his role in their little masquerade was to be that of the willing cuckold. As if the same thought had occurred to him, he released her and stepped away to the side, standing farther away from her than Aldous did.

"By the way," Aldous said, "I've been known as Aldous Ewing since my ordination to the diaconate."

"You're a deacon!" Phillipa exclaimed. "I thought you had no interest in major orders."

With sudden gravity, Aldous said, "It seems we've both taken roads we once forswore." He abruptly smiled again. "But such is life, eh? Things change. You've certainly changed." Again he appraised her up and down, his attention lingering this time on the feminine contours revealed by her sleekly stylish gown. When he met her eyes again, there was a frank interest in his gaze that he made no effort to disguise. "I see you've given up on those shapeless wool tunics—and that ghastly document case as well. Traded away those precious books of yours for silken gowns and fancy baubles, have you?"

"Er . . ."

"As a matter of fact, she's traded away nothing," Hugh said, coming to her rescue. "Phillipa still loves her books, only I've managed to talk her out of lugging them around with her. She's far too beautiful to be going about looking like a cross between a nun and a letter courier, wouldn't you agree?''

"I would indeed,'' Aldous murmured, giving her, just briefly, a look that made her feel as if she were standing naked before him . . . or that he wished she were. "So, what brings you two to London?'' he asked. "Or do you live here?''

"Nay, we're just visiting from Oxford,'' said Phillipa, exhorting herself to look Aldous squarely in the eye as she presented the story she and Hugh had agreed upon—a pastiche of truths and fabrications. If one was obliged to lie, one might as well do it credibly. "We've been staying at Wexford Castle with Hugh's father, but they've never gotten on that well, and the visit has become''—she hesitated as if leery of being indiscreet—"a bit tiresome, so we've decided to look for an inn in Southwark. Just for tonight. We'll be heading back to Oxford tomorrow.''

Aldous studied Hugh as if taking his measure. "You're William of Wexford's son?''

"I am.''

"Not the one who turned mercenary.''

"He only has one.''

Aldous smiled slowly, his gaze traveling from Hugh's earring to the dagger sheathed on his belt. "An artfully vague answer. Interesting. Your father and my father used to go hawking together quite a bit, I believe.''

This was news to Phillipa, and apparently to Hugh, who hesitated before saying, "Is that so? I had no idea. Did you join them?''

"Once or twice. It never held much appeal for me. My sister used to go along—she has an affinity for birds of prey.''

"Then she must have gotten along well with my sire.''

"Indeed she did,'' Aldous said with a dry little smile. "I must say I'm curious as to how a fellow with . . . your sort of background ended up united in matrimony with a lady scholar from Paris.''

"I met her in Oxford, actually,'' Hugh said.

"I left Paris not long after you did, seven years ago," Phillipa told Aldous, "thinking to pursue my studies in Oxford. 'Twas the following year, at Christmastime, that I met Hugh. I'd gone to Oxford Castle to pay my respects to Queen Eleanor, who'd retired there to give birth to her son John. She was . . . well, she was in a melancholic humor at the time. Her physician attributed it to the presence of black bile in her veins."

Hugh grimaced convincingly. "More likely 'twas the presence of her husband's whore at Woodstock," he said, referring to Queen Eleanor's having stumbled upon Rosamund Clifford several weeks earlier, ensconced at the queen's most beloved residence.

"Aye, I heard about that," Aldous muttered. Of course he had; all of England and France had heard about it.

"I spent a great deal of time at Oxford Castle that Christmas season," Phillipa said, "trying to liven the queen's spirits. 'Twas there that I met Hugh. He'd been summoned by the queen, along with some other trusted knights, to counsel her on a certain matter, and—"

"My dear." Hugh reached out and gripped her arm, scowling at her as if she'd spoken recklessly. "Your friend isn't interested in every tiny detail." Turning to Aldous, he said, "Suffice it to say I was enamored of the lady Phillipa from the moment we met."

"As was I. I was smitten by the thunderbolt of true love," Phillipa said. From the corner of her eye, she saw Hugh's mouth quiver. "Although I refused to wed him until he'd forsaken the life of a mercenary."

"You're confidants of the queen's, then," said Aldous, sounding slightly awed.

"Would that I could make such a claim," Hugh said modestly. "I've been in her company only once in recent years, during a visit to Poitiers, and we didn't speak. I doubt she even remembers me from Oxford, she was so preoccupied then."

"Nor me," said Phillipa. "Not that I don't think of her—and pray for her—every day. Especially now, with the way her husband has humiliated her and disgraced the throne—"

"Phillipa . . ." Hugh scolded under his breath.

"Please." Aldous held up a hand. "You needn't be circumspect on my account. I assure you I'm in complete sympathy with your views."

"Oh, I knew it!" Taking a step toward Aldous, Phillipa reached out and grasped both of his hands. "You were always so discerning, so perceptive. You always knew right from wrong and were never afraid to take a stand. How I admired that about you."

In truth, she was astounded that Aldous had been so easily hoodwinked into thinking they shared his disloyalty toward the king—subterfuge that Lord Richard felt was critical if Aldous was to let down his guard around them.

He was snapping at the bait; now to reel him in. Judging from his moonstruck expression as she gazed into his eyes, it wouldn't be difficult—not that that absolved her from a certain measure of contrition to be playing him along like this. To look a man in the eye and lie to him was bad enough; to toy with his affections as she did so was all but inexcusable. If Phillipa were a more pious sort, she'd find a parish priest and confess this duplicity, regardless that it was for the good of the realm; perhaps she would, anyway.

"I do wish we didn't have to go back to Oxford tomorrow, especially now that I know you're here." She caressed Aldous's palms with her fingers, her voice dropping to a slightly huskier register. "I've missed you so much over the years. I have . . ." She lowered her voice, as if wary of Hugh's overhearing. "Certain regrets. So often I've wished I could see you again and perhaps"— she dropped her gaze, hoping she wasn't overdoing it—"make up, in some small way, for having been so . . . unappreciative of you."

"Yes," he said hoarsely. Clearing his throat, he said, "I mean, yes, I . . . I'd love to see more of you." His gaze lowered to her breasts and then shot back up. "That is . . . I meant . . ."

"I think I know what you meant," she murmured silkily, "and I'd like that, too. Or . . . I *would* have liked it, if only—"

"Darling, we really should be getting along," Hugh interrupted, coming up behind her and laying a hand on her shoulder; she dropped Aldous's hands with guilty speed. "We need to find an inn and get our horses and luggage brought there before nightfall. And you need to unwind if you're going to get a good night's sleep before our journey tomorrow."

"Do you . . . do you *have* to go back to Oxford?" Aldous asked.

She nodded. "I don't think I could bear a public inn for more than one night."

"You shouldn't have to stay in such a place for even one night."

"We tried the local monasteries. There were no suitable accommodations for us, although they did let us leave our mounts and belongings at Holy Trinity. If only we knew someone in the city—"

"You know me. Not that I live in the city proper. I live over in Southwark, but my house is quite large, and you're more than welcome to stay there."

"Oh, Aldous," she said, "We couldn't possibly impose—"

" 'Twould be no imposition," he said earnestly. "You could stay as long as you like—weeks, months . . ."

"That's awfully generous of you, Aldous," said Hugh. "What think you, Phillipa? We can have our holiday after all."

"Say yes," Aldous implored. "I'd love to have you."

"Do you hear that, darling?" Hugh closed his big hands over Phillipa's shoulders and massaged them lightly. "He'd love to have you."

"*Both* of you," Aldous quickly amended. "And I'll give you the largest guest chamber. It's got a feather bed and its own fireplace."

"Sounds mighty cozy, doesn't it?" Hugh murmured into Phillipa's ear.

Too cozy, Phillipa thought, wondering what, exactly, she'd gotten herself into.

Chapter 8

Southwark

Hugh heard the muffled laughter as soon as he walked through the front door of Aldous's house—low, intimate laughter. Hers . . . and his.

He drew in a deep, unsteady breath, let it out slowly.

A little marble font of holy water stood off to the side of the small entrance hall, one of that bastard's many sanctimonious affectations. Hugh normally walked right past it, but this evening he felt compelled to dip in his fingers and cross himself, thinking, *Help me to bear this. Help me not to care.*

The laughter was emanating from the second-floor *salle* that served as a combination sitting and dining room in Aldous's massive, ostentatious stone house. Hugh climbed the stairs slowly, his gaze trained on the leather-curtained doorway to the *salle,* his tread silent despite the wooden-soled riding boots he'd worn for his trip to West Minster this afternoon.

It had been his first progress report to Lord Richard since he and Phillipa had moved into Aldous's house a week ago . . .

"Any luck getting him to talk about a plot against the king?" the justiciar had asked.

"Nay, although every time we hint at the subject, I sense he's hiding something."

"Aye, well, brilliant though your intuition is, King Henry will need more than that before he can move against the queen."

"We *have* been able to do some snooping about during the day, while Aldous is at St. Paul's. We found a
recent letter from his sister, the lady Clare, about some
important personage whose arrival they're awaiting—a
foreigner, I gather. Evidently Aldous is expected to escort this fellow to Halthorpe Castle as soon as he gets
to London. I have a copy," he said, handing the document to Lord Richard. It was Phillipa who'd penned the
duplicate, taking the task on herself without consulting
Hugh. She assumed he was illiterate, of course.

"Good work," Lord Richard praised. "As for the lady
Phillipa, she's the one I'm expecting to extract the truth
from Aldous. Has she added his skullcap to her collection yet?"

Hugh had gritted his teeth until they throbbed. "Nay,
but she's working up to it . . ."

Standing on the second-floor landing, Hugh edged
aside the leather curtain a bit and saw them, standing
very close together on the narrow balcony overlooking
the Thames at the far end of the lamplit *salle*. Phillipa,
dressed in a gown of ivory damask that bared her shoulders and the soft upper swells of her breasts, her inky
hair in a pearl-wrapped coil at the nape of her neck,
looked ethereally lovely against the dusky sky.

This was the first time Hugh had seen Aldous in anything other than black clerical garb. He'd shed his long
robe and skullcap this evening—because he knew he'd
be alone with Phillipa?—and wore instead a snowy,
crisply pleated shirt over black chausses. When he
turned his head, Hugh could see the small tonsure neatly
shaved into the deacon's thick, dark hair. He towered
over Phillipa, being nearly as tall as Hugh. Despite his
vocation, he looked to be fit, and judging from the way
most women blushed and stammered in his presence—
from highborn ladies to his many maidservants—Hugh
knew they found him handsome.

Not that Phillipa reacted that way to him. Even at her
most flirtatious, she maintained a certain cool dignity
that Hugh—and apparently, Aldous—found oddly fetch-

ing. But then, Phillipa was the last woman Hugh would expect to lose her composure over a man. Hugh suspected, for example, that she was as drawn to him, on a purely sexual level, as he was to her; it was evident in the way she'd responded to his kiss in the orchard before reining him in, and there were other things, little looks, gestures, comments . . .

But these were subtle things, hints and implications. It was clear that she meant to appear unmoved by him, and for the most part, she succeeded. Despite his displeasure at being deemed unworthy of her, part of him admired her for not surrendering to him as easily as did most women he set his sights on.

"Would you care for another?" Aldous asked.

"*Mm* . . . please."

The deacon had a silver bowl in his hand, Hugh saw, and now he reached into it, producing a dainty strawberry on a long stem, which he held toward Phillipa's mouth. She closed her lips over the ripe fruit and bit it off the stem, never losing eye contact with Aldous.

Hugh let out a pent-up breath, wondering why it troubled him so much to watch her bewitch Aldous Ewing this way. That Hugh hungered himself for the favors that she would eventually yield to Aldous should be of no import. Often in the past, Hugh had shared women with other men, even women he'd taken quite a fancy to, like that voluptuous silver-blond laundress who'd followed them about during the Finnish campaign. If it hadn't bothered him for Ingebord to tup half the fellows in his regiment, why should it bother him for Phillipa to be planning on tupping Aldous? Hugh hadn't even bedded her, nor was he likely to, given her "discriminating" tastes. He had no claim on her, no right to feel incensed at the prospect of her lying with Aldous.

And yet he did.

"When do you expect your husband to return from the horse fair?" Aldous asked.

Phillipa raised her shoulders in a gracefully indifferent shrug and reached into the bowl Aldous held. "Hugh comes and goes as he pleases. He's a hard man to keep track of—and God forbid I should try to."

She fed the berry to Aldous, who covered her hand with his as he plucked it off the stem.

"Can I surmise that the 'thunderbolt of love' with which you were once smitten has faded over time?" he asked.

" 'Tisn't easy to maintain that sort of passion over the course of a marriage. And, too, Hugh is . . . a hard man to love. He's something of a loner at heart. Fiercely independent, loathes having to answer to anybody."

All of which, Hugh reflected, was entirely accurate. They'd gotten into the habit, in their dealings with Aldous, of feeding him verifiable facts whenever possible, not only because it was easier to tell the truth than to lie, but as a safety precaution in case he took it into his head to check up on them.

"I think," Phillipa continued, "that's why Hugh turned mercenary—better to fight for a series of foreign princes as a paid soldier, free to leave at any time, than answer to one man for the rest of his life. And I think perhaps that's why he forswears the sort of blind, unthinking allegiance to King Henry that afflicts so many of his subjects. Hugh offers his fealty to those he finds deserving of it—like Queen Eleanor and her sons."

You shrewd little thing, Hugh thought, admiring how neatly she'd twisted the conversation around to politics. But his hopes that Aldous would rise to the bait were dashed when the deacon asked, "And what of Hugh's feelings for you? Have they diminished as well?"

Phillipa hid her disappointment well, plucking another berry out of the bowl and twirling it by its stem. "You're assuming he ever had real feelings for me."

"Are you saying he never loved you?" Aldous asked incredulously. "I can't imagine knowing a woman like you, being with her, and not falling helplessly in love. He must have a stone for a heart. He's incapable of love."

Phillipa shook her head, looking, if Hugh was not mistaken, genuinely sad. " 'Tisn't that he *can't* love. He *won't* love. I think he's afraid that if he lets a woman into his heart, even . . . even me, he'll be in her power, subject to her expectations. He's afraid he'll lose that precious independence of his."

It was uncanny, Hugh thought, how well she'd pegged him, even if it vexed him to hear her dissect his character for the benefit of this self-important, hypocritical whoreson. That she was only doing it to make Aldous think their marriage had lost its spark—which would presumably pave the way for him to seduce her—didn't do much to take the sting out of it.

"Why did he marry you, then?" Aldous asked.

"He wanted to possess me." Phillipa ate the berry and dropped the stem into the bowl, then lifted one of two blue glass goblets from the balcony's stone railing and took a sip. "Once he did, he lost interest."

Hugh was impressed—and somewhat abashed—at how well she seemed to have puzzled him out, for of course, such had been his pattern since he'd first started wenching at fifteen. He became fixated on a woman and had to have her, at all cost—but from the moment she lay down beneath him, the spell was broken. Not that he wouldn't bed her again, especially if she were exceptionally desirable, like Ingebord, but he would never again feel that driving compulsion to possess her . . . and only her.

For, when he was in the grip of such a sexual obsession, no substitute would satisfy him; surrogate couplings with whores and the like were always vaguely pathetic, and no more gratifying than self-abuse. He'd learned over the years not even to bother to seek out other women until the object of his passion had yielded to him.

It was for this reason that he hadn't relieved his lust through a visit to one of Southwark's many stews this past week, although he'd considered it. Night after night he lay next to Phillipa on the big feather bed they shared, feeling her heat, breathing in her warm, womanly scent, watching the rise and fall of her breasts beneath those damnably modest night shifts she wore.

Lying there in the dark, painfully stiff beneath his drawers, he would soak the sheets with sweat as he tried not to think of Phillipa sitting up in bed and pulling that shift over her head . . . Phillipa warm and soft and naked in his arms, Phillipa moaning as he drove into her, her body pumping all the aching hunger from his and leaving him sated, at last, so that he no longer dreamed of her every night and thought about her every day, so that he no longer cared and was no longer in her thrall.

Most nights it got to be too much. If he hadn't succumbed to sleep by the time the bells of nearby St. Mary Overie rang matins, he arose from bed—silently, so as not to wake Phillipa—got dressed, saddled up Odin, and rode as hard as he could along one of the thoroughfares leading south. By the time he returned, brushed down his weary mount, and slipped back into bed, he was generally exhausted enough to sleep.

If he could have Phillipa, just once—if she would deign to give him that much—then he would be free of this maddening lust that held him in its grip. If not for the low regard in which she held him, she might already have submitted to him—but there was naught he could do about that. He was who he was, a soldier at heart, a creature of the body. Phillipa de Paris, on the other hand, was a creature of the mind inclined to seek out her own kind.

Like Aldous Ewing, who even now was trailing the back of his hand down Phillipa's face and gazing deeply into her eyes. "If I were your husband," he said quietly, "I'd not tire of you, not ever. You would be all I ever needed, all I ever wanted."

If Phillipa shared Hugh's doubt on that matter, she didn't show it. Indeed, she met his gaze and held it raptly, as if she were just as caught up in the moment as he. In fact, last night she had told Hugh that this was, for her, the hardest part of their mission—leading Aldous to believe she was losing her heart to him.

"You would have been a good husband," she said. "I

know that now. Forgive me for having rebuffed you as
I did."

"Forgive *me*," he murmured, setting the silver bowl
on the railing, "for not having fought harder for you. If
I'd known how deeply enamored of you I would remain
all these years later, I would never have let you go."

He took Phillipa's face between his hands, lowering his
head. She stared at him unblinkingly as he prepared to kiss
her, the wineglass quivering in her white-knuckled grip.

"Here you are!" Sweeping the leather curtain aside,
Hugh strode into the *salle*.

There came a burst of shattering glass as Aldous and
Phillipa abruptly parted.

"Oh." Phillipa, parchment-pale save for two bright
spots on her cheeks, looked from Hugh to the shards of
blue glass at her feet. The balcony's stone floor and the
skirt of her ivory tunic were spattered with crimson.
"Oh, Aldous, your goblet! 'Twas Venetian glass—it must
have been very dear."

"I care naught for the goblet," Aldous said. "That
exquisite gown is ruined now."

"Not if I can get some salt on it right away."

"I'll get someone to help you." Crossing the *salle*
without so much as looking in Hugh's direction, Aldous
plucked a little bronze bell off a corner cabinet filled
with reliquaries and rang it.

Phillipa, stepping into the *salle* from the balcony,
looked toward Hugh with bleak discomfiture, as if she
were ashamed at having been caught in midseduction,
but there was something else in her eyes that he recognized as puzzlement. She was wondering why Hugh had
interrupted the cozy little tryst, inasmuch as she was
under a mandate to become Aldous Ewing's leman.

Hugh was wondering the same thing.

A trio of maids—young and comely, like all of Aldous's female servants—flurried into the room to do his
bidding. Blythe, *tsking* over Phillipa's gown, led her
away to clean it. Claennis set about tidying up the mess
on the balcony. Hugh halted Elthia as she was leaving

the *salle,* the silver bowl in one hand and Aldous's goblet in the other, and chose a strawberry from the bowl.

Unsheathing his *jambiya,* he severed the berry from its stem, catching it on the tip of the lethally sharp blade and popping it in his mouth. He tossed the stem back in the bowl and sent the wench on her way, then wiped the juice-stained blade on his grimy riding chausses. The fruit was perfectly ripe and sweet as honey.

"I've never seen a dagger quite like that," said Aldous, standing some distance away with a pensive scowl. "Where did it come from?"

"I took it off a dead Turk nine years ago in a place called Tripoli," Hugh said, twirling the blade slowly to savor the silvery ripple of watered steel adorned with elaborate gold-inlayed infidel inscriptions. "He'd probably taken it off some other poor dead son of a bitch from God knows where, who'd taken it off someone else, and so on. This particular *jambiya* is very old. No telling where it originally came from. It could have been anywhere in Byzantium, or perhaps Anatolia, or Syria, or even Egypt."

"Very impressive."

Hugh slid the knife into its sheath. "You think I carry it as an affectation."

"Nay, I—"

Aldous sucked in his breath as Hugh unsheathed the jambiya with blinding speed. "This"—he said, whipping the blade through the air so fast it whistled—"is why the *jambiya* has become my weapon of choice."

"Because . . . you can wield it so well?" Aldous ventured.

"Because I can wield it at all." Hugh held up the weapon with his mutilated right hand to show how well he could grip its odd, anvil-shaped hilt of walrus ivory with just four fingers. "A man needs a thumb to handle a sword, but with this, I can still disembowel a fellow pretty cleanly." Crossing to Aldous in two strides, he simulated an upward thrust to the belly that left the deacon stumbling backward. "Or open his throat, or

puncture his heart . . ." He shrugged negligently. "It's
come in handy on a number of occasions."

Aldous stood against the wall, regarding him grimly.

"Do you suppose there's anything left over from supper?" Hugh asked as he casually resheathed the *jambiya*.
"I haven't eaten for hours."

"If you go out back to the kitchen," Aldous said woodenly, "I'm sure the cook can find something for you."

Hugh nodded his thanks and left, thinking, *You idiot!
You fool!* To have barged in just as Aldous was making
his move was foolish enough, but then to have staged
that menacing little demonstration . . . What had he been
thinking of?

He hadn't been thinking. He'd been reacting on instinct—taking a stand as any male animal did when another male encroached on what was his. Which would
have been fine, except that not only was Phillipa far
from "his," but his role in this little mystery play was to
turn a blind eye to his wife's indiscretions, not thwart
them with implicit threats of disembowelment.

He really was a soldier at heart, with a soldier's predis-
position for forthright confrontation. The subtleties of
spying—the playacting and prevarications—were so utterly foreign to his nature that it was a wonder he managed it at all. Phillipa, with her innate cleverness, her
composure, and her knack for acting her part was really
much more adept at this sort of work than he was.

Perhaps Lord Richard *should* have let her conduct this
mission on her own. All Hugh seemed to be good at
was mucking things up.

Lying in bed that night, Phillipa heard the distant
pealing of church bells and knew it was matins. She lay
perfectly still, feigning sleep, until she heard the bed
ropes creak and the curtains being parted, accompanied
by Hugh's weight shifting on the feather mattress; then
she opened her eyes.

By the watery moonlight that illuminated their sizable
chamber, she saw him sitting on the edge of the bed

with his back to her, framed by the open bed curtains, his head bowed, his elbows resting on his knees. His shirt, damp with sweat, clung to the shifting muscles of his shoulders and arms as he dragged his hands through his hair.

He always strove to be quiet when he arose during the night, apparently unaware that she, too, was lying awake in the dark, struggling for a few meager hours of sleep. That first night, she'd ascribed her wakefulness to being unused to sharing a bed, but as the long, restive nights wore on, she had to admit that it was Hugh himself keeping her awake—his nearness, his heat, the memory of what had transpired in the orchard and the knowledge that she had but to reach for him, and he would eagerly take now what she had denied him then.

Sighing raggedly, Hugh reached for something on the floor—one of the pair of brown chausses he'd peeled off at bedtime. Gathering up the woolen stocking, he leaned over to tug it over a foot and up his leg, lifting his long shirt to fasten it by means of an attached leather strip to his linen underdrawers. How, precisely, the strip connected to the drawers was a mystery to Phillipa, inasmuch as he kept his back to her every night when he was readying himself for one of these mysterious nocturnal jaunts.

Until she'd begun sharing this room with Hugh a week ago, Phillipa had never even seen a man in his underclothes, much less slept next to one. When he had set about undressing for bed that first night, she'd wondered how much he would take off, since she'd been given to understand that most men slept without a stitch on, especially in warm weather. She'd been relieved when he'd left on his shirt and drawers, but part of her had also been just the tiniest bit disappointed.

The closest she'd ever come to viewing an unclothed man was the occasional water carrier or dockworker who, on an especially sweltering day, would toil in naught but a loincloth or short breeches. Her impression of what a man might look like wearing nothing at all had been formed as a child when she and Ada had jimmied open a locked cabinet in Uncle Lotulf's study and found a book that featured an illustration of Adam and Eve before the Fall. The picture was notable for the couple's utter nakedness, which had both scandalized and fascinated the little girls. It was Adam, of course, who had most intrigued them. His body was as smooth and hairless as Eve's, only he had no breasts, his stomach was flatter, and between his legs there sprouted a curious wormlike appendage no larger than a man's little finger.

Ada and Phillipa had ruminated at length over that appendage, speculating on its possible functions. Over time, from analyzing overheard ribald jests and songs, they surmised that it came into play during lewd goings-on with women of base character. It was through the writings of Trotula of Salerno and two or three other Italian women physicians that the sisters, by then nearly grown, came to understand, if only nominally, what was involved in the coital act and that its purpose was procreation.

Trotula and her colleagues also enumerated various techniques for preventing conception, to Phillipa's bewilderment. Much as she championed free sexual expression, it had always secretly confounded her why any woman would engage in such an act unless the point was to get pregnant—for, although she would never admit it openly, the idea of letting a man shove that little worm between her legs and discharge his seed in her had always struck her as not only undignified, but downright repulsive.

Until now.

Thinking back to the orchard, she recalled her shock when Hugh had pulled her toward him, letting her feel his vital part, which had been many times larger than that of the man in the picture. She'd realized that the organ must stiffen somewhat to allow for entrance into the womanly chamber, but for it to distend to such proportions! She'd been astounded.

Wouldn't it hurt terribly to have one's body invaded by something so thick and hard? From things she'd heard, she was fairly certain that losing one's maidenhood was, indeed, a painful ordeal. But afterward? Upon reflection, Phillipa concluded that the sensation of being penetrated so fully, once one was used to it, might afford a certain measure of primal satisfaction that could be interpreted as pleasurable.

In fact, it had been Ada's hypothesis that women were capable of a physical release similar to a man's ejaculation. This Phillipa doubted, although she had come to accept that women could experience a certain degree of carnal arousal. She'd felt it herself this past week as she'd lain in bed next to Hugh with her imagination running riot. The contemplation of fleshly matters, she had found, produced a strange lassitude of the senses, as well as a certain excruciating emptiness in her womanly parts that felt akin to both pleasure and pain. It was as if she had an exceptionally maddening itch and no way to scratch it.

Hugh donned the other legging and his riding boots. Standing, he plucked his belt off its hook and buckled it—along with the attached purse and heathen dagger—over his shirt.

Phillipa closed her eyes again in case Hugh looked in her direction as he stole silently from their chamber, then rose from bed and crossed to the window, which overlooked the stableyard. Hidden behind the half-open shutter, she watched him leave the house by the back door and enter the stable, as he did every night. Soon came a faint glimmer of light as he lit the horn lantern hanging from the rafters above Odin's stall; in a few minutes, he would emerge on the back of his huge dun stallion and tear off down Tooley Street.

Normally she watched at the window until he rode away, then returned to bed and drifted into a fitful slumber, from which she would awaken later in the night as Hugh slipped back under the covers. Within minutes she would hear his breathing take on the deep, steady cadence of sleep. After that, she generally lay awake for some time, wondering where he'd gone, and what he'd done, that he should return so depleted. Throwing the dice in some alehouse, perhaps? Or, more likely, disporting himself in some wench's bed. Perhaps he had a leman nearby; it stood to reason that a man like Hugh of Wexford would keep a woman handy to see to his needs.

Try as she might, Phillipa couldn't erase from her mind the image of Hugh lying between this faceless woman's legs, pushing himself into her, filling her with his seed. There was something unaccountably distressing about the notion of him easing himself with someone else.

Someone else? What a fool she was, to feel jealous over some anonymous mistress of Hugh's, when she herself had made it clear enough to him that his advances were unwelcome.

What if she hadn't? What if she'd let him spread his shirt on the ground that evening in the orchard and lain down on it and opened her arms to him? What if she'd let him take his pleasure with her in the cool, dreamy twilight? *The gratification would have been mutual, I assure you . . .* What if she'd cast aside her fears and misgivings and let herself be in the world, and of it, for one brief, enchanted interlude?

He would merely have been using her, of course, as he had used a hundred women before her. Sex was no more meaningful to him than any other bodily function, if a bit more diverting. During that encounter in the orchard, when he'd disarmed her with his kisses only to take such astounding liberties with her, she'd been repulsed to think of giving herself to a man whose only interest in her was as a recipient of his lust. Since then, however, as she'd lain next to him night after night, her body thrumming with desire, she'd had occasion to rethink the matter.

Héloïse had been but eighteen when she'd lost her innocence, and according to Abelard in his widely circulated account of their doomed affair, she'd relished their lovemaking as much as he. It hadn't been physical passion that had destroyed Héloïse, but the passion that burned in her heart. As fascinating as Phillipa found the concept of romantic love, she was not at risk of falling prey to it; not only was she far too cerebral to let herself get carried away like that, but Héloïse's unhappy destiny was a powerful deterrent to such folly.

Phillipa had always known that she must avoid infatuation at all cost. At one time she'd been content as well to shun the pleasures of the flesh, thinking it no great loss. But of late . . .

Of late it had come to seem a very great loss indeed.

Caterpillars do turn into butterflies, but first they have to want to. They have to break free of that nice, familiar little cocoon . . .

Snatching her new black, sable-lined mantle off its peg, Phillipa pinned it over her night shift and made her way on silent, bare feet down the service stairwell and outside to the stableyard.

Chapter 9

Phillipa hesitated in the doorway of the stable, an immense ragstone-and-timber structure capable of accommodating many times more horses than Aldous would ever house in it. Her resolve faltered when she saw the yellowish lamplight spilling out of Odin's stall at the far end of the long central aisle and heard the snap of leather as Hugh buckled the beast into his saddle.

Steeling herself, she tidied the loose hair that hung in disorderly tendrils to her hips and walked slowly down the aisle, straw crackling underfoot. The sounds from within the stall ceased.

She stilled, holding her breath.

Hugh stepped out into the aisle, a bridle dangling from his hand as he regarded her with quiet surprise.

She licked her dry lips; his gaze lit on her mouth, then her eyes.

He said her name, very softly, and then, "What are you doing here?"

Phillipa took a deep breath, but it did little to calm her. "Every night, when you leave to share some other woman's bed, I lie there thinking . . ." She looked down, her heart hammering, her voice so soft and tremulous she could barely hear it herself. "Wishing . . . you would stay in my bed."

She swallowed hard, thinking, *There—I've said it,* and then, in the roaring silence that ensued, *Oh, God, what have I said?*

"This was a mistake." Clutching her mantle around herself, she turned to leave.

He dropped the bridle. "Phillipa!"

But she was running back down the aisle now, on quaking legs, blood rushing in a wave of mortification to her face.

Footsteps crunched in the straw behind her as she neared the doorway. He seized her by the shoulders, spun her around.

"Please . . ." She tried to wrest herself from his grip, but he backed her against a massive oak support beam and held her there.

" 'Twas no mistake," he said hoarsely, framing her face with unsteady hands. He kissed her roughly, desperately, shoving his fingers through her hair to tilt her head up, the fine stubble on his jaw chafing her face.

Reeling, she returned the kiss, her arms encircling his back, taut with muscle. His mouth plundered hers almost painfully, but she welcomed the assault. *Take me,* she thought. *Free me . . .*

Hugh kissed her jaw, her cheek, her forehead, his chest heaving. "There is no other woman," he murmured breathlessly against her hair. "There's only you."

Pushing aside her fur-lined mantle, he closed both hands over her breasts, capturing her startled cry in his mouth. He kneaded the tender flesh with impassioned urgency, his callused fingers scraping her nipples through her night shift. It should have hurt, but instead it made her moan in shameless pleasure.

He deepened the kiss, forsaking her breasts to caress her restlessly wherever he could reach—her arms, the curve of her waist, the flare of her hips, even—

She drew in a breath, her fingers digging into his shoulders, as he molded a hand to the aching flesh between her thighs, stroking her so purposefully through her shift that she knew he could feel her heat, her need . . .

"I've been going mad from wanting you," Hugh rasped as he unbuckled his belt and flung it aside. He whipped up the skirt of her shift and lifted her against the post, wrapping her legs around his waist. Claiming her mouth again, he ground his hips against her where she was most inflamed, his own desire evident as a rock-hard column beneath his shirt and drawers.

He tugged his shirt up, yanking at the cord that secured his drawers. In her mind's eye, Phillipa saw the red-haired whore who tupped her customers against the wall in that alley off Kibald Street in Oxford. Wrenching her head to the side, she broke the kiss. "Not here," she said. "Not like this."

Hugh set her on the ground, but if she'd thought he was going to take her back to their chamber and that nice, soft feather bed, she was sorely mistaken. He pulled her into the adjacent stall, lowering her into a pile of fresh straw.

She started to sit up, opening her mouth to say that this wasn't what she'd had in mind either, but he was on her in a heartbeat, pressing her into fur and straw with the weight of his body as he silenced her protestations with another searing kiss.

Raising her skirt, he levered her thighs open and reached between them to untie his drawers.

Her heart thudded painfully in her chest. This was all happening so fast; she felt as if she'd been caught in a raging tempest with no place to take shelter.

She gasped when she felt something hard and warm prod the soft flesh of her inner thigh. It felt unnervingly large, a hot column of satin-smooth steel, its tip slickly damp; she hadn't expected that.

Scooping his hands beneath her bottom to lift her, he reared over her, positioning himself.

This will hurt.

"Hugh, wait," she pleaded, clutching at his shirt.

"I can't wait." He flexed his hips, nudging her open.

"We need to talk."

"Afterward." The cords in his neck bulged with strain as he prepared to drive himself into her.

"Hugh, just . . . not so fast."

"Why? What's the matter?" He trembled as he arched over her, his hair hanging down, his face darkly flushed.

"It's my first time."

"*What?*"

"It's . . . it's my first time, and I thought if you could slow down a bit, it wouldn't be so—"

"Your first time?" He looked at her as if she were mad. "You can't be serious. Do you mean *our* first time?"

"I'm . . . a virgin, Hugh. I am."

He stared at her in absolute astonishment, then closed his eyes and swore softly under his breath.

"Hugh . . . I was going to tell you, but it all happened so—"

"I should have known." Pushing himself off her, he turned his back to her as he retied his drawers. "I did know."

"Hugh?" Sitting up, Phillipa smoothed her skirt back over her legs. "I didn't mean we couldn't . . ." She laid a tentative hand on his shoulder. "I just meant perhaps you could take things a bit more slowly."

"I certainly would have," he said, turning to face her, "if I'd known. Why on earth do you let people think you're . . ." He shook his head. *"Why?"*

Averting her gaze, she wrapped her arms around her upraised knees. " 'Twas the best way to make myself seem unsuitable for marriage."

"Unsuitable . . . of course." From the corner of her eye, she saw him rub the back of his neck. "It makes a certain preposterous sense. But . . . you've been seen bringing men into your home. And they talk about you, the men you've . . . the men you're supposed to have . . . been with. They brag of having bedded you."

She lifted her shoulders. "I've invited other scholars into my home if we were engaged in a particularly interesting conversation and I didn't want it to end. If some of them misrepresented the visit afterward, well . . . men are known to lie about such things."

"And you welcomed those lies because they bolstered your image as an intellectual libertine." He raked his hair off his face with both hands. "It doesn't make sense, though. If you were so determined to have a tarnished reputation, why didn't you just"—he shrugged—"tarnish it fair and square? One may as well *be* wanton if it's what everyone is going to think anyway."

"The truth is, I never really wanted to . . . do the things that would earn that sort of reputation." She stole an uneasy glance at him. "Perhaps if I'd ever been in love, but . . ."

"Ah, love." With a wry grin, he said, "The reason you've never been struck by Cupid's arrow, my lady, is that his quiver is, in fact, quite empty. If you mean to wait for true love, I'm afraid you'll be a maiden forever."

"I know that. And I don't want to grow old and die without ever having . . ." She bit her lip, as reticent to say it as she'd always been to do it. "That's why I . . ."

"God's bones. That's what this is all about. You were hoping I'd rid you of your tiresome maidenhead."

" 'Twasn't like that," she said. " 'Twasn't some . . . cold-blooded plan."

"Well, that's something," he said bitingly.

"I wanted it." She twisted around in the heap of straw to face him. "I wanted *you*. And I know you wanted me—not because you have . . . feelings for me, of course, but because . . . well, I suppose because a man simply has certain . . . animal needs."

He was studying her, his expression unreadable in the dim stall.

"And that's fine," she said quickly. "That's good. It's perfect, in fact, because I don't want any . . . emotional complications. I just want to experience"—she looked away, pulling her mantle around herself like a cocoon—"a bit more of life. Isn't that what you've been saying I ought to do?"

"Aye, but the way you're proposing to do it—"

"What I'm proposing," she said, "is a very simple arrangement—a liaison, if you will, but of the most rudimentary sort, purely physical."

"I thought you said your plan wasn't cold-blooded."

"If I were as dispassionate about all this as you seem

to think I am, I'd have lost my innocence to someone else long before this. I told you I wanted you, and I meant it." *Careful.* A man like Hugh of Wexford, for whom seduction was merely another pastime, would surely laugh if he knew she'd been lying awake night after night in a fever of desire for him. "The thing is, I want no attachments, but neither do you. Once this mission is concluded, we'll never see each other again. Really, the circumstances are most advantageous."

"Advantageous circumstances," Hugh muttered with a bitter little laugh. "Well, I suppose that's better than if you prattled on about larks and starlings and the rest of that maudlin drivel."

"Then you're . . . amenable to . . . to . . ."

"Nay." He stood, leaning over to swipe bits of straw off his chausses.

"But . . ."

"My . . . *animal needs* notwithstanding," he said drolly, "I hardly think the way to satisfy them is by ruining maidens."

"Ruining . . . oh, for pity's sake." She awkwardly gained her feet, accepting the hand he offered. "You wouldn't be *ruining* me. My reputation is past salvaging, and as for my virtue, I've little use for it. If anything, it's become a burden to me."

"You say that now, but how will you feel on the morrow?"

"Relieved."

"Possibly. Or you might discover, in the light of day, that you've squandered something precious . . ." He paused, adding soberly, ". . . on someone who didn't appreciate it. I've never relished the role of debaucher, Phillipa. I don't want to be the man a woman can't bear to look at the next day when she realizes it really was just about sex."

"But it *is* just about sex. I'm no lovesick young girl, Hugh, and I mean it when I say I want no attachments. If you're worried that I'll pester you with unwanted attention afterward, rest assured I've no interest of that sort in you. You're the last man I would lose my heart to."

Hugh's expression darkened as he absorbed that. She could see his jaw shift as he gritted his teeth. "Thank you for the clarification, my lady, but it was hardly necessary. I'm quite well aware of my many shortcomings."

"I . . . that didn't come out—"

"It came out just fine." Stalking into the aisle, he bent to retrieve his belt, which he buckled over his hips with swift, efficient movements. "I know how hard it is for you to feign tact, but you needn't go to the trouble on my account."

"Hugh . . ."

"Since we're being honest," he said acidly, "you might as well know that I'm not quite as noble as I've been letting on. 'Tis true I've no taste for deflowering maidens, but not just because I'm too chivalrous to ruin them. The fact is, it's a tedious business, initiating a virgin. I prefer an experienced woman who knows what she's doing."

Phillipa's cheeks burned with anger and humiliation as she watched Hugh turn and walk back down the aisle, only to pause in the entrance to Odin's stall, one hand clawing through his hair. "There's something I don't understand." With a caustic little grunt, he added, "Quite a few things, actually, but . . ." Looking at her over his shoulder, he asked, "Given your . . . inexperience, why did you agree to this mission, knowing that it would entail sleeping with Aldous Ewing?"

"I told you in the beginning," she said testily, "you and Lord Richard, that there are more ways to get what one wants from a man than to barter one's body for it."

Sighing, he bent over to retrieve the bridle from where he'd dropped it in the straw. "You really are very naive, my lady."

"*Me*—naive?"

He turned to face her. "And as certain as ever that that all-too-clever little brain of yours will solve any problem and get you out of any fix. Only, it's not your brain Aldous is so enamored of. I heard you trying to tease information out of him tonight, to no avail. But give him a taste of that for which he hungers so ardently"—Hugh's gaze raked her head to toe—"and I daresay he'll be far more malleable."

"Nonsense," Phillipa said, but her protest rang hollow even to her ears. More and more over the past week, as Aldous had deflected her every attempt to cajole his secrets from him, she'd come to suspect that her efforts were entirely futile. "The problem is that Aldous isn't stupid. To declare that he's in sympathy with the queen is one thing. To admit his involvement in a plot against the king is treason. I've got to outwit him, not bed him."

"If you bed him," Hugh said wearily, "you'll be able to outwit him. This isn't something I'd expect you to know, my lady, but men get stupid in bed—stupid and trusting and gullible. A man will confide far more to his mistress than he will to a woman who simply lets him feed her strawberries. Lord Richard knows this. That is why he expects you to become Aldous Ewing's leman— as does Aldous by now. It *is* naive to think that you could entice a man like him indefinitely without delivering. Sooner or later he'll get fed up with your little games and send you packing, and then where will we be?"

Phillipa wished to God that he didn't make so much excellent sense. She loathed being caught in a web of logic, that being her particular intellectual domain; that Hugh of Wexford had managed the feat only made it worse. "If I have to . . . deliver, I will," she claimed, surprised that she more or less meant it.

Why shouldn't she bed Aldous Ewing, if it would help to keep England from another devastating civil war? Perhaps if some other man had a claim on her . . . but the only man in her life was standing right in front of her, and he seemed to harbor no feelings for her whatsoever—save perhaps for a mild contempt at her naïveté. Hugh certainly wouldn't mind if she took Aldous into her bed; indeed, he was pushing her in that direction just moments after his own aborted tryst with her.

In addition to the other sensible reasons for bedding Aldous, there was the fact that Richard de Luci, Justiciar of the Realm, had gone to considerable effort and expense to recruit her, costume her for her part, and install her in Aldous's home. She shuddered to think what his lordship's reaction might be if she quit the mission at this point over an aspect of it that he'd been completely frank about from the beginning—the expectation that she would become Aldous Ewing's mistress.

"You don't mean that," Hugh said, watching her closely. "You've no intention of letting Aldous seduce you."

"It's just sex," she said, trying to sound more indifferent than she felt, trying to believe it meant nothing, that she could do it for the good of the kingdom. "It did bother me before, to think of giving myself to a man I didn't love, but as tonight will have proven, I no longer harbor such qualms."

Hugh searched her eyes, his consternation obvious—*interesting*—until he gathered himself and schooled his expression. "Nay, you're bluffing. Surely you realize that Aldous will know you're a virgin the first time he beds you. How would you manage to explain that, given that you and I are supposedly married?"

There he went again, snaring her in another galling web of logic. She smiled slowly as it came to her how she could extricate herself from this one. "I never told Aldous in so many words that our marriage was consummated."

"Why would it not have been consummated?"

She shrugged. "Perhaps I'll tell him you have the pox and I don't want to catch it."

"The *pox*." He held up a hand. "Now, wait just a—"

"Or I can say you're incapable of performing," she suggested, nonchalantly plucking pieces of straw off her mantle.

"Incapable of . . . ! You bloody well will *not* tell him
I'm—"

"Or—I know! I'll tell him you prefer men, and
that—"

"What?"

"And that the marriage is just for appearances." Spinning around, she headed for the door.

"Damn it, Phillipa—"

"There are a hundred ways to explain it," she said
lightly, pausing in the doorway to glance back at him,
standing there with his face turning purple and the har-
ness quivering in his fist. "My all-too-clever little brain
will come up with something."

Chapter 10

"Your move." Hugh sat back in his chair and reached for his wine as Phillipa studied the chess set laid out this evening on the little stone table on the balcony. She tended to take a great deal of time pondering her next move—unlike Hugh, whose decisions were a good deal more spontaneous—and she had a habit of chewing on her lower lip as she did so, which made her look deceptively childlike.

Or was it deceptive? Now that Hugh knew she was not quite the worldly creature she'd pretended to be, she was less of an enigma . . . but just as fascinating. And, God help him, just as alluring.

Laced this evening into a gown of blood-red satin, the pink-stained sky infusing her with a feverish blush, she put him in mind of some delicate little fruit just ripe for picking. Her hair had been plaited into four long braids which had then been wrapped together in pairs with intricately woven gold ribbons; around her head she wore a circlet of hammered gold. As she leaned over the chessboard, her bosom swelled above the jewel-encrusted gold band that trimmed the tunic's neckline, cut deliberately low to reveal a tantalizing little frill of sheer white silken kirtle.

All through supper, as he'd watched her flirt with Aldous, Hugh couldn't stop imagining her in that kirtle and nothing else, her hair loose about her shoulders, her arms open for him.

Not for Aldous. For him.

He shouldn't indulge in such fancies, he knew, not after their disheartening little encounter in the stable last night. After she'd gone back into the house, he'd ridden like a demon and collapsed in bed just before dawn, despising her for the contempt in which she held him and determined to put her out of his mind.

Yet he'd awakened this morning with his loins on fire from having dreamed of her yet again and cursing himself for not having taken what she'd so freely offered the night before. At least he would have cured himself of this insatiable hunger that afflicted him. Instead, after washing his hands of her last night, he was as much in her thrall as ever today. Joanna had always said he could never hold a grudge.

Perhaps he'd better learn to. It was troubling enough to lust so singlemindedly after Phillipa, but to feel so possessive of her, so protective, to crave her company as he did, to find himself thinking that she was the most remarkable woman he'd ever known, to wonder, God help him, if she felt as drawn to him as he did to her . . .

And, of course, to feel such white-hot fury at the thought of her giving herself to Aldous Ewing . . .

To succumb to this type of infatuation was not only foolhardy but dangerous. When a man tethered himself to a woman, he never again had complete autonomy over his life, which was why Hugh had spent most of his five-and-thirty years avoiding such attachments. He'd learned how to keep his feelings in check while indulging the needs of his body. Although he'd liked most of the women who'd shared his bed over the years, and been genuinely fond of many of them, never once had he felt in danger of losing his heart.

Until now.

From below the balcony came the clopping of hooves on flagstone and the voices of men speaking a foreign tongue. Phillipa met Hugh's gaze for a brief moment before leaping up from the table, as did Hugh, to peer over the railing.

Advancing into the courtyard through Aldous Ewing's front gate were two men on mules, a pair of heavily laden packhorses bringing up the rear. The man in front, dressed in a long, outmoded tunic crisscrossed with satchels and document cases, was lean to the point of being bony, with silver-threaded black hair puffing out from beneath a snug felt cap tied loosely beneath his chin. His humbly dressed companion was also black-haired, but very stout and with swarthier skin.

They reined in their mules and dismounted, the older one saying something in a language that sounded familiar to Hugh, although he recognized only about every other word.

"It's one of the Italian dialects," he told Phillipa, "but not the one I know."

She glanced at him curiously, as if surprised that he spoke a foreign tongue; if she had known how many he spoke, after having fought alongside foreigners in every corner of the world, she would have been stunned.

Footsteps raced up the stairs; Hugh and Phillipa turned to find Claennis, one of Aldous's pretty little maidservants, bursting into the *salle.* "Master Aldous! He's here, the gentleman from . . ." She looked around anxiously before spying Hugh and Phillipa on the balcony. "Beg pardon, but do you know where I can find Master Aldous?"

"We haven't seen him since supper," Hugh said as they entered the *salle.*

"Oh." Claennis wrung her hands. "There's two gentlemen downstairs, and I think one of them's that Orlando Storzi Master Aldous has been waiting for. He'd wanted to greet him himself, but—"

"Orlando Storzi!" Phillipa exclaimed, although the name meant naught to Hugh.

"Aye, he's come all the way from Rome, and Master Aldous—"

"We'll find Master Aldous," Phillipa told Claennis. "You go downstairs and welcome his guests—and fetch the stableboy to see to their mounts."

"Yes, milady."

Hugh turned to Phillipa as the girl was sprinting back down the stairs. "And Orlando Storzi would be . . . ?"

"A very renowned scientist and metaphysician," she said. "He wrote a famous treatise on the two essential forces of nature, dissolution and coagulation. He's also well known for his research into Eastern scientific advances."

"*Mm-hm* . . . fascinating." Taking Phillipa's arm, Hugh led her out of the *salle*. "Any clever ideas as to where Aldous might be?"

"Didn't he ask Elthia to bring him a headache powder as supper was ending? Perhaps he's lying down."

At Aldous's bedchamber door, Hugh raised a hand to knock, but stilled at the sound of the deacon's voice from within, low and breathless. "Yes . . . oh . . ."

Frowning in bafflement, Phillipa whispered, "I thought he was lying down."

"I imagine he is." A devilish impulse made Hugh grab the door's handle and swing it open. "Aldous, are you—"

"*Jesu!*" Aldous sat on the edge of his bed—above which hung an enormous wooden crucifix—with his robes bunched up, grasping fistfuls of Elthia's blond hair as she knelt between his legs.

"Sorry to disturb you, Aldous," Hugh said as if naught were amiss, "but *Signore* Orlando has arrived." Closing the door, he led a nonplussed Phillipa away by the elbow. "It seems he wasn't lying down after all. Shall we go downstairs and greet Aldous's guests? The good deacon seems to have more pressing matters to attend to."

Phillipa turned to look over her shoulder at the door to Aldous's chamber as Hugh guided her toward the stairwell. "What were they . . . I mean . . ." Slanting a speculative look at Hugh as they descended the stairs, she said, "She can't have been . . . that can't have been what it looked like."

"What did it look like?" he asked with studied innocence.

She made a kittenish little growl of exasperation. "Just *please* tell me what they were doing."

"Why don't you set your all-too-clever little brain to sorting it out?"

He guided a scowling Phillipa into the ground floor entrance hall, where they found Claennis ushering the two Italians through the front door.

"*Signore* Orlando!" Aldous came pounding down the stairs, furiously straightening his robes, his face flushed, his hair unkempt. His skullcap flew off, but he didn't seem to notice. "I'm Aldous Ewing. So sorry I didn't come out to greet you. I was"—he glanced toward Phillipa in apparent mortification—"occupied with . . . church business."

"Encouraging one of your servants in prayer, weren't you?" Hugh asked. In response to Aldous's red-faced glare, he added, "I saw someone on her knees. I just assumed—"

"*Signore* Orlando," Phillipa said quickly, " 'tis an honor to meet you. I'm Phillipa of Oxford, and this is my husband, Hugh. I've read your *Chemicum Philosophorum*—most enlightening."

Aldous gaped at her.

"You know my work?" Orlando asked in heavily accented French as he reached for Phillipa's hands, clasping them tightly in his. "A beautiful woman who read the *metafisica*! Istagio!" he cried, turning to his companion. "Did I not tell you I would love England?"

"*Sì, signore,*" replied Istagio, leering at the shapely Claennis. "Is very beautiful country."

"*Signore* Orlando," Aldous said, "I'm sure you could use some refreshments after such a grueling journey. Claennis, would you bring some spiced wine and almond cakes to the *salle*? Oh, and take the *signore*'s servant out to the kitchen for a bite of—"

"Istagio is not my servant," Orlando corrected. "He . . . how do you say . . . he make the bells."

Hugh and Phillipa exchanged a look. *He make the bells?*

"Yes, quite . . ." Aldous, looking rather baffled himself, spread his hands and shrugged. "If *Signore* . . . Istagio, is it? . . . would like to join us upstairs—"

"If I could please to see my *laboratorio* first," Orlando said, "so that I can unpack my equipment . . ."

"Your lab—"

"The place where I am to work on the—"

"Oh!" With a jittery little laugh, Aldous said, "No, no, no. That won't take place here, Master Orlando. My sister should have been clearer when she wrote to you. First thing tomorrow morning, I'll escort you and Istagio to Halthorpe Castle, which is northeast of London. That's where you'll be staying and, er . . ." He glanced furtively toward Hugh and Phillipa. "My sister has set aside a place for you, in the cellar, I believe, where you can"—he cleared his throat—"unpack your equipment."

"Ah." Orlando smiled apologetically. "Lady Clare, she write to me in the Frankish tongue, which I am so poor to understand. My fault entirely. *Sono spiacente.* Please forgive."

"Not at all," Aldous said.

Phillipa said, "You might have quite a bit of trouble with the anglicized French we speak here in England, *signore*. Would you prefer to converse in Latin?" Although normally reserved for academic and religious discourse, Latin was a language that educated people everywhere were well acquainted with.

"*Grazie*, but no," Orlando said. "I am eager to make bigger my mind by speaking in your native tongue. Also, we must think of Istagio—he has very little Latin."

"As you wish." Aldous waved Orlando and Istagio up the stairs, saying, "It's the door to the right. We'll join you in a moment." To Hugh and Phillipa—but mostly to Phillipa—he said, "Of course you know that you're more than welcome to remain here until I get back from Halthorpe. I shouldn't be long—I'm only planning on staying over one night." He sounded guarded and subdued, as well he might, after the unseemly little encounter they'd just witnessed.

Phillipa darted a troubled glance in Hugh's direction. He knew what she was thinking: that they could ill afford

to be left behind in Southwark while the situation they
were investigating unfolded at Halthorpe.

"Say, Aldous," Hugh ventured, "you don't suppose
Phillipa and I could go along with you tomorrow?"

"To Halthorpe?" Aldous frowned. "Why?"

Hugh shrugged. " 'Twould be a change of scenery.
I've heard it's lovely there."

Aldous let out a scornful little laugh. "You've been
misinformed, then. 'Tis a great, gloomy old pile of rocks.
Ugliest castle in England."

"Well, I *am* eager to see your sister again. I remember
her well from Poitiers."

"You can't remember her that well," Aldous muttered, "if you're eager to see her again." With a firm
shake of his head, he said, "Nay, you'd just be miserable
if you came along, and there'd hardly be any point, since
I'll be returning immediately."

Hugh cursed inwardly, knowing there was nothing to
be gained by pressing the point; Aldous seemed unshak-
able.

"After you." Aldous stepped aside so that Hugh could
go on ahead of him. As he turned to climb the stairs,
Hugh noticed the deacon reaching out to restrain Phillipa with a hand on her arm.

"I'll be back as soon as I can," Aldous promised her
in a voice barely higher than a whisper.

Hugh thought she might press Aldous for an invitation
to Halthorpe, futile though that effort would probably
be. Instead, she said, in a tone of cool reserve, "I won't
be here, Aldous. I think it best that Hugh and I return
to Oxford as soon as possible."

Aldous whispered her name like an anguished plea,
and then Hugh heard the soft rustle of silk.

From the top step, he turned to see Aldous guiding
Phillipa through the leather curtain hanging across the
door to the pantry, directly off the entrance hall. A
glance into the *salle* revealed Orlando and Istagio on the
balcony, chatting in their native tongue as they gazed
across the Thames at the sun setting on London.

Hugh stole back down the stairs and up to the leather-curtained doorway without making a sound.

" . . . sorry, so sorry," Aldous was saying in a tone of abject contrition. "You're the one I want, the only one. I only turned to Elthia because you have me so mad with desire."

"When I saw you with her, like that," Phillipa said, "it felt as if a knife had pierced my very heart."

"Imagine how I feel," Aldous said unsteadily, "knowing you belong to another, that you share his bed every night while I lie there in a torment of longing . . ."

"Aldous . . ."

"Come to my room tonight," he begged, "after Hugh is asleep."

Hugh's hands curled into fists. By Corpus, the lecherous bastard was so determined to have her that he'd risk Hugh's wrath even after yesterday's little demonstration with the *jambiya*.

Not that Hugh could blame him.

"No, Aldous."

"I didn't . . . I didn't finish with Elthia. Please, Phillipa, I need you. And you need me, although you may not realize it."

"Ah, but I do," she said softly. "I need you desperately. I can scarcely think of anything else."

"My God, then why won't you come to me? He doesn't love you—you told me so yourself. He doesn't deserve your fidelity."

"I know that, it's just . . ."

"Yes?"

"I can't bring myself to betray him while he sleeps beneath the same roof."

There came a moment of silence as Aldous thought that over. *Oh, you* are *a clever little thing,* Hugh thought grimly. *Too damned clever.*

"If we were somewhere else," she said, "anywhere but here, with Hugh so close at hand, I wouldn't hesitate to . . . to be with you. What I wouldn't give for the chance to make amends for how I acted toward you in

Paris. I withheld so much from you then. How I ache to give myself to you, body and soul, to lose my senses in your embrace. When I think of how it could be between us, how passionate, how utterly abandoned . . ."

"Come with me to Halthorpe," Aldous said abruptly. "Just you."

She was ingenious, all right; she'd laid her trap and Aldous had tumbled unwittingly into it.

Part of Hugh wished he hadn't.

"Just me?" she asked. "But . . . what will we tell Hugh?"

"Tell him . . . I don't know, tell him . . ." Aldous let out a little groan of frustration. "Christ, surely we can think of something!"

"I know . . ."

Hugh raised his gaze to the heavens; of course she knew.

"Hugh has promised his sister that he'll spend some time with her while we're in this part of England," she said conspiratorially. "We've been putting it off because she and I don't get along, but Hugh's been chafing at the bit to see her. I could tell him that I'd talked you into letting me stay at Halthorpe while he visits her alone. That way he could spend as long as he likes there without having to listen to me gripe and complain the whole time."

"Yes! Yes!"

"Of course, you'd have to extend your visit to Halthorpe," she said. "That is, *our* visit. If it was just overnight, we couldn't make this work. But if it were a matter of several weeks—"

"Oh, what I'd give to spend that long with you! I'd consign my soul to the Devil himself for that privilege."

Hugh rolled his eyes.

"As would I," she said softly. "I can't wait to share your bed."

Hugh wished to God she wasn't a damned good actress. He'd been secretly relieved when she'd revealed her intention to extract Aldous's secrets without bedding him.

Now that she'd abandoned that naive but comforting notion, Hugh hardly knew how to feel.

He should rejoice at her decision, because it would advance their mission and possibly save England from another ruinous civil war. Yet, when he imagined her in Aldous Ewing's bed, taking him into her arms . . . and her body . . . his gut twisted in helpless rage.

Hugh wasn't used to being at the mercy of his emotions, and he didn't care for the feeling one bit. He mustn't let himself imagine that he had some sort of claim on Phillipa de Paris. If she was willing to play the role of Aldous Ewing's leman, he should encourage her, not just for the good of the realm, but for the sake of his own precious freedom. Indeed, he should be eager for her to sleep with Aldous, for if anything could extinguish his own ungovernable passion for her, it would surely be the knowledge that she was another man's mistress.

"Starting tomorrow night," Aldous said, "you *will* be sharing my bed. I'll have Clare put us in connecting chambers."

Hugh rubbed his pulsing forehead.

"It sounds like a dream," Phillipa said.

Or a nightmare, Hugh thought, depending on one's point of view. Lord Richard would undoubtedly welcome Phillipa's decision to hie off with Aldous on the morrow, given that it seemed to be the only way either one of them were going to see the inside of Halthorpe Castle and sort through the gathering intrigue, and regardless of the fact that Hugh would not be available for Phillipa's protection, should she need it. Despite her razor-sharp wits and consummate acting skills, she would be more vulnerable without him. And, too, for all her deductive brilliance, he was far more experienced than she at this type of work.

Aye, but that's not why you wish she wouldn't go.

"I want you to know," Aldous said with unctuous sincerity, "that from now on, there will be only you, no . . . Elthias. That's a solemn promise."

"Thank you, Aldous. That means a great deal to me."

There came a lengthy silence. Were they kissing?

Hugh found the fingers of his mangled right hand curling reflexively around the walrus-ivory hilt of his *jambiya.*

He squeezed his eyes shut, summoning all the strength at his disposal. *Don't think about it. Put it out of your mind. Rise above it . . .*

"Sir Hugh?"

He opened his eyes to discover Claennis standing at the foot of the stairs holding a tray laden with almond cakes, goblets, and a clay jug of warm, exotically fragrant spiced wine.

"Is something wrong?" she asked.

"Nay, nothing. I just . . ." He shook his head, rubbing the back of his neck.

"Do you have a headache? I can bring you—"

"I'm fine," he said brusquely, sweeping past her to climb the stairs two at a time. "I don't need anything. Nothing at all."

"That's it, then, milady," announced Blythe, the maid-servant Aldous had assigned to attend to Phillipa's needs during her visit to Southwark. Closing the lid of the big, iron-banded trunk that held most of Phillipa's clothes, she said, "You're all packed for tomorrow morning. I hope you have a good visit. I've heard Halthorpe's one of the oldest stone castles in England, and huge—almost too huge. They say you can get lost in it if you're not careful."

"I'm sure I'll enjoy my stay," Phillipa said as she stood at the open window, gazing out at the night sky and thinking, *What am I doing? I must be mad.*

"Let's get you ready for bed, then." Blythe removed the circlet from Phillipa's head, as well as her rings and garnet earrings, stowing them in the enameled chest that held her valuables. Standing behind Phillipa, she unwrapped the golden ribbons from around her two pairs of braids.

There came a knock at the door, and then Hugh's

muffled voice: " 'Tis I." He always knocked first, in case Phillipa was bathing or dressing. By the time he came to bed every evening, she was in her night shift and under the covers, with the oil lamps extinguished, but because of the time she'd spent packing tonight, she was late in retiring.

"Shall I send him away, milady?" Blythe asked as she fetched Phillipa's oxhorn-handled hairbrush from the wash stand.

"Nay, let him in." Phillipa hadn't had the chance to speak privately to Hugh since the arrival of Orlando and Istagio.

The maid opened the door for Hugh, who drew up short when he saw that Phillipa was still fully clothed. "Sorry—I thought you'd be . . ." Turning, he said, "I'll come back later."

"No, stay. Blythe, you can leave now. I'll attend to myself." She held her hand out for the brush, which Blythe gave her.

After Blythe had departed, closing the door behind her, Hugh and Phillipa regarded each other from across the room in awful silence. He was wearing the most dignified of his new tunics—deep blue with black trim, and his hair was pulled back, the way she liked it. He looked unbearably handsome in the golden lamplight . . . but also rather distant, perhaps even sad, just as he'd seemed all evening. She wasn't used to this quiet, sober side of him, and she found she preferred the old, insolent, cocksure Hugh much better.

Wanting something to do with her hands, Phillipa started unraveling one of her braids and brushing it out. "You didn't seem surprised," she said without looking up, "when Aldous told Orlando and Istagio that I'd be coming along to Halthorpe tomorrow."

"I overheard you cooking up your little scheme with Aldous."

She winced involuntarily, abashed that he'd been privy to that appalling little scene, heard the things she'd said . . . *How I ache to give myself to you, body and soul, to lose my senses in your embrace . . .*

"Did you kiss him?" Hugh asked.

She looked up, startled not just by the question but by the pained way he'd asked it, and shook her head. Hugh seemed relieved until she said, "He kissed *me.*" She recalled her distaste as Aldous's mouth had ground against hers, her revulsion when he'd tried to worm his tongue between her lips. She'd pushed him away then, saying she was afraid someone would walk in on them. It was then that she realized how wretched it would be to lose her virginity to such a man.

Hugh looked away, his hands on his hips, his jaw clenching in that way that meant he was grinding his teeth. "I hope you know what you're getting yourself into. There's no talking your way out of his bed now— not if you go with him to Halthorpe."

"I know that," she said, with just a hint of a tremor to betray the fear clutching at her stomach.

He nodded, his gaze on the floor of ornately painted tiles. "I won't be there to protect you if something goes wrong."

"I've got my wits to protect me."

She thought he'd make a jest out of that, but he merely met her gaze and said, softly and earnestly, "Be careful, Phillipa."

Her throat tightened around the reckless words she longed to say: *Ask me to stay . . . beg me not to go. Please, Hugh, tell me you don't want me to be with him, that you couldn't bear it, that it would kill you.*

She turned to look out the window, thinking, *I'm doomed if I say those things,* and telling herself she shouldn't have to, that he *would* beg her to stay if he cared enough, if he cared at all . . .

If he cared the way she did . . . and wished to God she didn't.

Quietly he asked, "Are you sure you're ready to go through with this?"

That wasn't the same as asking her not to. Without

turning around, she said, "Can I sleep with a man I can barely stand for the good of the realm? I think so. I just—" The words caught in her throat. Taking a deep breath to fortify herself, she added, "I just don't want him to be the first."

Keeping her back to him, she closed her eyes, waiting for his response, dreading what it would be . . . *I've no taste for deflowering maidens . . . it's a tedious business . . .*

Unable to hear a thing over the blood roaring in her ears, she wondered if he was even in the room or if he'd left, laughing to himself—

She hitched in a breath when his arms encircled her from behind. He pulled her back against him, nuzzling the top of her head; even through all their layers of clothes, she could feel his heart hammering as wildly as hers.

There came a hot tickle in her hair as he whispered gruffly, "Neither do I."

Chapter 11

"Don't let me do this unless you're sure," he murmured into her hair.

"I'm sure." She'd never been so sure of anything in her life.

He loosened one arm from around her, reached out, and closed the window shutters, sliding the wooden pin across to latch them. Taking her by the shoulders, he turned her around so that she was facing him and gathered her in his arms—gently, as if she were breakable. Still gripping the hairbrush, she returned the embrace, her face in the crook of his neck, breathing in the warmth of his skin, savoring the strength of his arms around her, the rightness of this, of him being the first . . .

If only there could never be another.

He kissed the top of her head, saying, "I just don't want you to end up regretting this."

"I won't. But . . ."

"Yes?"

"I'm afraid you might already regret it."

"Me? I've wanted this desperately, almost from the moment I met you."

"But . . . those things you said last night, about . . . preferring experienced women . . ."

From deep in his throat there rose a little sound like a cross between a chuckle and a groan. "You must never believe anything a man says when he's angry at a woman."

Drawing back from her a bit, he touched his lips to her forehead, very softly, and then to her eyelids, her temple, the crest of her cheek, the tip of her nose . . .

He lifted her chin with his fingertips, whispering, "Are you nervous?"

"A little."

"Me, too." His mouth was warm against hers, the kiss sweet and soft and perfect.

She was astounded at his tenderness, which was the last thing she would have expected after their encounters in the orchard and the stable. He'd been so unrestrained then, ravenous in his passion. Tonight he seemed determined to hold back, for her, and she found herself deeply moved by that.

When at last the kiss ended, he said, "Your hair needs brushing out. Let me do it."

The request surprised her, but she merely handed him the hairbrush, whereupon he led her by the hand to their big bed, shoving the bed curtains aside so that she could sit on the edge of the feather mattress, made up with embroidered linen sheets and a white silken counterpane. He sat next to her, turning her so that she faced the foot of the bed and he was behind her, and proceeded to unplait the braid she'd started on. When he finished that one, he did the rest, then drew the brush slowly through the unbound tresses, over and over again, the stiff boar bristles grazing her scalp in a most deliciously soothing manner. She closed her eyes, relishing the sensation.

He took his time at this task, brushing her hair until it crackled. She felt luxuriously tranquil, as if she were floating on the surface of a warm, calm lake, with no obligations, no expectations, just pure gratification of the senses.

Setting aside the brush, Hugh gathered her hair over one shoulder so that it pooled in a silken mass in her lap. A moment passed, and then she felt his lips, hot and soft, on the back of her neck. And again. And again.

The sensuous daze he'd induced in her only heightened the pleasure of his kisses. She felt their heat, their promise, deep down to the very core of her being. They kindled something in her, a yawning hunger that had lain dormant too long, and that would now be appeased.

Her heart quickened when she felt him tug at the golden cord that laced her tunic up the back, untying its knot and pulling it through its eyelets. The gown's once-snug bodice loosened and hung slack over the kirtle of gossamer, crinkled silk that she wore beneath it. Phillipa could breathe freely for the first time all day.

He reached around her to untie the ribbon that secured the kirtle's low, gathered neckline, clearly intending to remove it as well, but she closed a hand over his, stilling him.

"Could I . . . leave the kirtle on?" she asked, turning to look at him over her shoulder.

She'd half-expected him to argue with her, or perhaps chuckle at her squeamishness, but there was no hint of displeasure or even condescension in his tone when he said, "Of course. I'm too impatient." He gave her another gentle, lingering kiss, then asked, "Would you like me to put out the oil lamps?"

Touched by his solicitude, she said, "Perhaps all but one."

Rising from the bed, Hugh extinguished two of the three lamps, immersing the chamber in a soft amber twilight. He took off his belt and tunic and untied the leather thong that bound his hair. The top few ties of his shirt were open, revealing a smoothly muscled chest lightly furred with golden hair. He sat on the edge of the bed to pull off his shoes and chausses.

Standing, Phillipa shucked off her red silken gown and hung it up, letting some of her hip-length hair fall to the front for modesty, since her kirtle was filmy enough to see through. She kicked off her gold-dyed kidskin slippers and pulled back the bedcovers.

"You don't go to bed in your stockings, do you?"

She turned to find him standing behind her in naught but his shirt and drawers, smiling at her.

"N-nay." But neither did she go to bed in her kirtle;

tonight her customary bedtime routine didn't apply, but she wasn't quite sure what should take its place.

"Allow me." Kneeling at her feet, Hugh reached beneath the floor-length hem of the kirtle and glided his hands up a stockinged leg, making her breath catch in her throat. He removed her garter and unrolled the black silken stocking with an ease born, no doubt, of years of practice, but Phillipa didn't let herself dwell on all the women who'd shared his bed. Tonight he would share hers, and that was all that mattered.

When he'd stripped off both stockings, Phillipa reclined against the pillows heaped against the headboard and pulled the covers up to her waist, taking care that her hair still cloaked her. It was foolish, she knew, to worry about her sheer kirtle, considering what would soon take place between her and Hugh, but in her entire life no one, not even Ada, had ever seen her unclothed.

Joining her under the covers, Hugh braced himself on an elbow while lightly stroking her face and throat with his left hand, contemplating her with drowsy-eyed intensity, as if he might be content to do this for hours. It had never occurred to Phillipa that sex might involve much touching other than that necessary for the act itself. How long would they be engaged in these preliminaries, she wondered, before he climbed on top of her and finished things? Would he want her to touch him? Would it hurt much when he pushed into her? She assumed ejaculation was instantaneous; if not, she would be at a complete loss as to how to proceed.

She was at a complete loss in any event.

"I wish I *were* more experienced," she admitted. "I'd know what to do then, and it would be better for you."

He smiled as if at a misguided child. "It's never been better for me than it is right now. You're doing fine."

Phillipa licked her lips anxiously. "I wouldn't want to become pregnant. I understand there are ways—"

"I'll pull out."

She studied the Saracen rug hanging on the opposite wall as she tried to make sense of that. The methods recommended by Trotula and her colleagues to keep from quickening with child involved wearing certain items around the neck or placing them in the entrance to the womb. If by "pulling out," Hugh meant that he would withdraw his member from her body before releasing his seed, then the act must take longer than she'd thought.

Hugh rubbed a finger between her eyebrows. "You get a little crease right here when you're fretting about something. It's actually rather appealing in most situations—but not this one."

She let out a pent-up sigh.

"How much do you know of what men and women do together in bed?" he asked.

"Apparently less than I'd thought."

He chuckled as he smoothed his palm down the center of her chest, letting it rest warmly between her breasts. His smile faded. "Your heart is racing. You're afraid."

"A bit."

"Of what? Pain?"

"Partly. And partly of my own ignorance. I'm not sure *what* to expect, aside from the pain. I'm afraid I'll do the wrong things, or not do the things you're used to. I'm afraid I'll disappoint you."

"You couldn't possibly disappoint me."

"I already have, by not taking off my kirtle. An experienced woman wouldn't be ashamed to be naked in bed with a man."

"I'm not going to pretend that I wouldn't love for you to take that kirtle off. A thousand times I've imagined what you look like without your clothes on. Every night, I dream of holding you naked in my arms." He grinned. "But the cleverest women know that a man is sometimes more enticed by that which is hidden from view"—he slid his hand beneath her concealing blanket of hair, lightly shaping a breast through her kirtle—"than by that which is openly flaunted."

His hand felt so warm through the finely creased silk, his touch so soothing and yet so seductive.

"I'll tell you what to do, if it's important," he promised as he prolonged the caress, creating a maddeningly subtle friction that made her nipple as tight and hard as a pebble. "And I'll tell you what to expect so nothing will alarm you. As for pain . . ." His expression sobered. "I can't promise you that there will be none. But I'll do everything I can to ensure that your pleasure overshadows it."

"Is that possible?" she asked dubiously.

He smiled and gently thumbed her nipple, igniting a little thrill of sensation that snaked deep inside her, making her gasp with startled pleasure.

"I don't think it will be a problem," he said smugly as he treated her other breast to the same delicate torment.

"It's just that I hadn't realized, until recently . . ." Warmth swept up her throat as she pondered how to express it. "That is, I used to think that a man's . . . the part of him that . . ." Her gaze dropped automatically toward the covers bunched around his hips.

"The part that enters a woman," he supplied without, thank God, smiling.

Drawing in a breath, she said, "I saw a picture once, when I was young, a picture of Adam, and his . . . his part, it looked, well, very small and very . . ." She shrugged. "Not like anything that could cause a woman any real discomfort."

"Or any real pleasure," he said wryly. "I know that type of picture, and it's . . . a bit misleading. You've gathered as much, and now you're more apprehensive than ever because you've no idea what to expect. There's a simple remedy for that." Pushing the bedcovers down, he reached beneath his shirt for the drawstring to his drawers.

"Oh." Phillipa sat up. "No, please don't—not yet." She buried her scalding face in her hands. "God, you must think me the most priggish, childish little—"

"Not at all." Sitting up, he enfolded her in his arms. "I'm just rushing things again. Of course you need time."

"Oh, God," she said plaintively, "it *is* tedious, initiating a virgin, isn't it?"

"Being here like this with you," he whispered into her hair, "and knowing that I'm the only man you've ever given yourself to, is the most astonishing and beautiful and thrilling thing that's ever happened to me in bed. Don't doubt that. Not for a moment."

She looked up and searched his gaze, finding it entirely free of guile and filled with tenderness, and felt something unfurl dizzily inside her.

No, she thought. *'Tisn't real, what I'm feeling, 'tisn't to be trusted.* The prospect of making love for the first time was wreaking havoc with her emotions. She didn't harbor such feelings for Hugh.

She couldn't harbor them. She wouldn't.

" 'Twould be better for you, though," Hugh said, "if you didn't fear me."

"I don't—"

"You fear that part of me you won't let me uncover."

"Ah."

"Here." Hugh urged her to lie down on her side, with him facing her, pulled the covers back up to his waist, and raised his shirt. "Give me your hand." When she hesitated, knowing what he intended, he said, "I'll leave my drawers on if it will help. I won't untie them until you're ready. In fact, you'll have to untie them yourself—I solemnly vow not to touch them. How's that?"

"Most reassuring." She couldn't help smiling at his efforts to put her at ease, although she was still absurdly reticent to play along.

With a crooked smile, he added, "The . . . part in question is fairly quiescent at present, not the sort of thing to make a lady swoon in terror."

With a roll of the eyes, she presented her hand, which he directed under the covers and pressed, gently but firmly, between his legs. Through the finely woven linen of his drawers she felt a warm mass a good deal longer and thicker than "Adam's" minuscule instrument, but fairly pliant to the touch. Common sense and her memories of what she'd felt against her thigh last night suggested that it would not remain so.

He guided her hand farther down. Her bewilderment must have been obvious, because he said, "Adam's anatomy was incomplete, I gather."

"Evidently."

Hugh drew her hand up, molding her fingers to the shaft beneath his drawers, which seemed to have swelled somewhat.

"How does it feel," she asked, "when that happens? When it gets . . ."

"It always feels good," he said, releasing her hand, "like heat gathering in my loins. But tonight it feels extraordinary, because you're the one making it happen."

She explored him tentatively through the loose linen as he grew, it seemed, heavier in her hand. He watched her quietly, his gaze losing focus as she lightly stroked the length of him. She marveled as his flesh stiffened to her touch, but withdrew her hand abruptly when it twitched and began to rise.

"Don't stop," he implored, putting her hand back where it had been. He kissed her as she fondled him, his hands in her hair, his breathing becoming faster.

Hugh deepened the kiss, his tongue flirting with hers. Pulling her great mass of hair behind her, he let his hands wander over her in a slow, mesmerizing dance that filled her with a quivery warmth.

With her free hand, she caressed his chest and back and shoulders through his shirt, feeling his muscles tighten as his arousal escalated. He moved his hips, thrusting against her hand, the linen of his drawers taut over his straining organ.

"If . . . if you're ready," she said, "you may as well go ahead and . . ."

"You haven't untied my drawers." He smiled into her eyes.

"Ah." He really did mean to make her do it. She reached for the drawstring but couldn't quite bring herself to pull it.

"You're hesitating because *you're* not ready."

Steeling herself, she said, "Yes, I am."

Phillipa tensed when he pulled the skirt of her kirtle up over her hip, although the sheet and counterpane still covered her. A soft little cry escaped her when he touched her where no man had ever touched her—where she'd never even touched herself. He investigated her gently, parting, probing . . .

She squeezed her eyes shut at the tempest of sensation generated by callused fingertips on her most sensitive flesh.

"You're not ready, not quite," he said. " 'Twill be better for you if you're wet when I enter you."

Wet? "Ah, yes. Of course."

"I want you to . . . finish, even though it's your first time."

Good Lord, she thought, was Ada right? Could women really . . .

He smiled as he rubbed at that spot between her eyebrows. "You don't have any idea what I mean, do you?"

She shook her head in frustration. "I wish I weren't so ignorant about . . . matters of the flesh."

"I'm glad you are." He rolled her onto her back, bracing himself over her as he lowered his mouth to hers. "It means I get to be with you the first time you reach the height of passion." He kissed her softly. "I can look upon your face when you come apart . . ." Another kiss. "Perhaps even be inside you. Close your eyes," he murmured as he threaded his fingers through her hair, fanning it over the pillows.

She did, trying not to think about how much of her he could see in this translucent kirtle without her hair to shield her.

"You're so beautiful," he whispered as he swept his fingertips over her throat, her breasts, her stomach . . . Her eyes flew open when he reached beneath her rucked-up kirtle, but he kissed them closed again. "Relax," he breathed against her eyelids as he slid his hand upward. "Think of it as a journey to a place you've never been before. Let me take you there."

His hand closed over her breast, flesh against flesh, so hot and astonishing that it sucked the breath from her lungs. He rubbed her nipples with his fingertips, coaxing little sighs of pleasure from her. When at last he smoothed his hand downward, over her belly, to rest it lightly at the juncture of her thighs, she was trembling in anticipation. "Part your legs a bit," he whispered.

She sighed helplessly at the first feathery brush of his fingertip. He kissed her as he gradually intensified the caress, his clever fingers stroking and teasing until her hips flexed shamelessly and she moaned into his mouth.

Her back arched off the bed when he pushed a finger inside her, although it met resistance before it could penetrate very far. "You're tight," he whispered, inserting a second finger—to stretch her?—before renewing the intimate caress with fingertips that were now extraordinarily slippery.

The delicious frustration she'd felt all those nights she'd lain in bed next to him, imagining this moment, were naught to the hunger gathering up in her now. It was a hunger Hugh shared, judging from his ragged breathing and the way his entire body seemed to quiver, like a bowstring drawn taut.

There was only one way to appease this hunger, this terrible emptiness. Reaching down, Phillipa untied Hugh's drawers, eliciting an ardent, almost painful kiss from him.

"Tell me what to do," she pleaded. "Do I . . . just lie here, or . . ."

He shook his head. "We should start with you on top." Scooping her up, he rolled onto his back. "Put your legs on either side of me, like so."

"What? No!" She found herself sitting astride him, her kirtle and his roomy shirt blanketing them, although their most intimate parts were in direct contact. "I can't be on top, Hugh. I don't know what to do."

"Yes, you do." Curling a hand around her neck, he

lowered her face to his and kissed her deeply. "You just don't realize it yet."

"Hugh . . ."

"It's best this way. You're so small and tight, and your maidenhead is intact. And I'm so . . . so close, so eager. I'm afraid I'll end up hurting you if I'm on top. This way, you can take me in at your own pace."

"But . . ."

"Trust me, love." Hugh reached up to stroke her cheek, his gaze heartbreakingly earnest. " 'Twill pain you less this way. I don't want to hurt you. Here." Gripping her hip with one hand, he slid the other beneath her kirtle. "Raise yourself up a bit." She felt a slick, hard pressure as he pushed himself into her, just the tip, although it felt like a fist stretching her open.

"Oh, God, stop," she gasped.

"I'm stopping." He let go of her, lowering his hands to his sides. "I'm stopping. I'll do nothing more. It's all up to you now."

Phillipa almost wished he hadn't left it up to her. As much as she wanted him fully inside her, she couldn't imagine how he would ever fit—how she would make him fit.

"Just lower yourself slowly," he said. "Try it."

She did, biting her lip, and felt him meet the barrier of her virginity. "How will you break through?"

"I don't have to. You'll stretch to accommodate me if you go slowly enough. The pain is less that way."

She pressed down again, grimacing as he slowly impaled her. *This* was the less painful route?

"Take it slowly," he reminded her. "And if you want to stop at any time, I mean stop for good and not go on, that's all right—you can." He met her gaze reassuringly, looking boyishly handsome lying back against the mountain of pillows, his eyes heavy-lidded, his flaxen hair disheveled, that exotic earring glinting in golden halflight.

"Wouldn't you be . . . frustrated," she asked, "if I chose not to go on?"

"A man learns to live with such frustrations. Either

that, or he finds ways to force himself on unwilling women—and I meant it when I said I'm no debaucher. Of course, if you're going to put a stop to things, I'd prefer you didn't wait until the very last—"

"I'm not going to put a stop to things. I daresay I want this even more than you do."

"I highly doubt that," he said with a chuckle that she felt in her very womb.

Closing her eyes, she bore down again, making minimal progress, although her flesh burned from the strain.

"Lift yourself up a little," he suggested, "and then down again."

She did, and found that this greatly facilitated his passage into her body. Keeping her eyes closed, she continued this up-and-down movement, easing him into her by small increments. Presently the discomfort diminished, eclipsed, as Hugh had predicted, by pleasure. The sense of being steadily filled by him reignited her arousal, which swiftly escalated to its former intensity. An exquisite tension gripped her, especially where her body joined with his. Her movements took on a kind of desperate abandon as she strove to take him fully into her.

She heard Hugh's breathing grow erratic, felt a quivering strain in his hips as he penetrated her inch by inch. When at last he was fully buried within her, Phillipa opened her eyes to find him clutching the pillow beneath his head in his effort not to touch her, his face flushed, his eyes glittering as if he were reeling drunk.

"Are you all right?" he asked in a low, rusty voice.

She nodded. "It feels . . ." There were no words for the excruciating pleasure of being so intimately connected to him. She felt him throb inside her and instinctively thrust her hips, letting him slide out a bit and then in, moaning at the sensation of being stroked from within; he moaned, too. Surrendering to her body's driving need, she thrust again, and again, feeling the strange tension in her mount with trembling inevitability toward . . . something . . .

Her heart raced with the panic of an impending crisis.

Torn between her spiraling pleasure and fear of the unknown, she stilled. "I . . . I can't . . ."

"You can." Releasing the pillow, Hugh closed his hands around her hips and rocked them slowly, flexing upward to meet her thrusts. "It's supposed to happen. Let it happen."

Their sinuous movements made her feel as if she were being caressed, deeply and slowly, where she was most inflamed. Grasping handfuls of his shirt, she writhed in breathless delirium as the crisis approached. She heard her own ragged cry as it overtook her, roaring through her like a thunderclap, sudden and convulsive.

Abruptly Hugh pulled her to him and rolled them over so that he was on top. He drove into her hard; she bit her lip to stifle a whimper of pain. There came another fierce thrust, and another, and then he paused and, with a strangled groan of effort, wrenched himself out of her.

He held her so tightly it hurt, shuddering as something hot pulsed between them. With a ragged sigh, he sank onto her, his arms trembling as they held her. "I'm sorry," he said shakily. "I hurt you."

"Shh." She wrapped her arms around him, under his bunched-up shirt. "It's all right. I'm all right. 'Twas wonderful."

"You're wonderful," he murmured, his heart pounding against her chest. "You were . . . God, it was . . ." He emitted a masculine little growl of gratification. "Thank you." He lifted his head to bestow a breathless kiss on her forehead, then slumped down on her again. "Am I too heavy?"

"Nay, stay right here," she said, loving the weight of him on top of her. She caressed his bare back beneath his shirt, her hands stilling as they encountered an irregularity on the surface of his skin.

He seemed to stop breathing as she lightly traced the ridge of scar tissue, obviously old and well healed, from the small of his back up to his right shoulder. There were other ridges, she realized, crisscrossing each other randomly, but all more or less vertical.

Phillipa did not need to be told that these were whip marks. What crime could Hugh of Wexford have committed to earn what must have been an exceptionally savage flogging—or several of them? Were these awful scars the reason he always wore a shirt to bed? She turned toward Hugh to find him watching her with those fathomless sea-green eyes of his. Before she could ask him about the scars, he kissed her on the mouth and raised himself up, taking his weight on his elbows. "I *am* heavy."

"Hugh . . ."

Not unkindly, he said, "I'd rather not have this conversation, if it's all the same to you." Pulling the covers back up, he managed to ease off her and retie his drawers without compromising her modesty—a touching effort on his part, especially given that he'd just claimed her virginity.

He got out of bed to dampen a cloth in the wash basin.

"Hugh," she said, "your shirt." It was torn down the front seam. "How did that happen?"

"Actually you tore it when you, uh . . . at the end."

She gaped at the rent garment. "I . . . I'm sorry!"

He grinned crookedly. "I'm not." Returning to bed, he wiped the damp cloth across her belly, then rinsed it out and passed it under the covers and between her legs, very gently; it felt cool and soothing on her traumatized flesh. He withdrew the cloth, frowning at the pinkish bloodstain on it. Dropping it back in the wash basin, he extinguished the oil lamp, plunging the chamber into complete darkness, and returned to bed, gathering Phillipa in his arms.

"I hope that wasn't too much of an ordeal for you," he said. "I tried to make it . . . I wanted it to be . . ."

" 'Twas everything I could have wanted it to be," she assured him with a kiss. "Thank you for giving that to me."

"I'm so grateful you asked me. I just wish . . ."

"Yes?"

He answered her with a long, unsteady sigh. "The second time won't hurt as much."

The second time. With Aldous. *God, what have I done?*

Hugh seemed about to say something, but he stilled his tongue. After a long, ponderous silence, he kissed her on the forehead, very softly. "Sleep well, Phillipa."

There was little chance of that, she thought, considering what she had to face tomorrow.

Chapter 12

West Minster

"Any idea how long he'll keep her at Halthorpe?" asked Lord Richard.

Hugh, standing at the window gazing upon the empty bench in the courtyard of the royal palace, sighed heavily. "I really couldn't say."

"How long does it take to tire of a woman like Phillipa de Paris, do you suppose?"

A lifetime. Two lifetimes. Hugh closed and rubbed the back of his neck, fighting back a tapestry of images from last night . . . Phillipa, untouched and innocent in that alluring scarlet gown, imploring him with those great, liquid brown eyes . . . *I just don't want him to be the first . . .*

He smiled to himself, remembering how she'd hidden her face in her hands rather than look upon his privy parts . . .

Only to surrender herself to erotic abandon once he was inside her. He savored the memory of her exquisite little body barely visible through that sheer silken kirtle, of her writhing in delirious ecstasy, crying out in astonishment as she tumbled over the edge for the very first time . . .

God's bones, she'd torn his shirt right down the middle. Who would have guessed at the hidden depths of passion lurking beneath that prim exterior?

It was he who had been the instrument of her pleasure, he, Hugh of Wexford, who had driven her over that edge, who had awakened her sensual nature . . .

Only to hand her over to Aldous Ewing for his carnal amusement until, as Lord Richard pointed out, he tired of her and tossed her aside.

In the meantime, would she unearth the deacon's secrets and save England from civil war? Did Hugh even care anymore?

"You're to be commended for infiltrating Aldous's home so successfully without being found out," Lord Richard was saying, "you and Lady Phillipa both. And for her to have talked him into taking her along to Halthorpe . . ."

When Hugh had awakened this morning to find that Phillipa had already left for Halthorpe, along with Aldous and the Italians, he'd felt, quite literally, as if his guts had been ripped right out of his belly. It was only through the most profound effort of will that he'd come here to make a full report of this development to Lord Richard, as was his duty, rather than ride off to Halthorpe and drag Phillipa out of Aldous's clutches, as was his desire.

Clearly Phillipa hadn't wanted to say goodbye to Hugh, or she would have awakened him. Instead, she'd somehow managed to dress and haul her luggage out of the chamber without disturbing his sleep. Hugh had felt utterly bereft from the moment he realized she was gone, and maddened at the prospect of her sharing Aldous's bed tonight and for the next . . . how many weeks?

He'd ridden here this morning in a daze of anguish, rage . . . and bewilderment. Always, in the past, his fixation on a woman had dissipated after he'd bedded her. He'd expected that to happen with Phillipa, had hoped and prayed for this wild desire to be swept away, replaced by cool disregard. Yet this morning, when he'd found the bed empty and her things gone, he'd felt only the most abject sense of loss.

She'd taken everything with her, even the clothes

she'd been wearing yesterday and the hairbrush with which he'd soothed her nerves last night. The only evidence of her that remained was a whispery hint of her scent on the bed pillows and a minuscule streak of her virgin's blood on the bottom sheet.

"King Henry will be pleased with your progress, I'm sure. He's most anxious to confirm the queen's sedition . . ."

Aldous wouldn't be careful with her. He wouldn't know it was only her second time, and that it could still hurt. She would try to keep from crying out, so as not to make him suspicious. Perhaps she'd weep afterward, when she was alone . . .

Hugh ground a fist against his forehead. Halthorpe wasn't far away, although it was on the other side of London from West Minster. As long as Lord Richard didn't keep him here all day, he could make it there by nightfall. He'd need some reason. He could say his sister lived close by—as, indeed, she did, Eastingham being not far to the west of Halthorpe—and that he'd decided to visit with her during the day while spending his nights at Halthorpe with his lady wife . . .

"Hugh? Did you hear me?"

Turning, Hugh found Lord Richard sitting on the edge of his desk, as was his habit, and glowering; he was not a man to tolerate being ignored. Hugh leaned back against the windowsill and crossed his arms. "Sorry, I . . ."

"I said I'm sending you across the Channel to Normandy."

"Normandy . . ." Hugh closed his eyes briefly, cursing the fates. He couldn't go to Normandy *and* Halthorpe.

"Rouen. King Henry is there, and he's requested a meeting with you so that you can fill him in on your progress in exposing the plot against him. Given the nature of your mission, I was going to write and ask him if he couldn't wait a few weeks for your report, but since you're available now . . ." The justiciar shrugged.

"Why must I go at all? Can't we just send an envoy with an encrypted message?"

Lord Richard shook his head. "He insists upon meeting with you personally."

Hugh groaned in exasperation. "I *am* still engaged in an ongoing mission, at least perfunctorily. What if I'm needed here while I'm in Rouen? What if Lady Phillipa finds herself—"

"There's more than one reason the king wants to meet with you, Hugh."

"What do you mean?"

Lord Richard leveled his fiery blue eyes on Hugh. "You did not hear this from me, but King Henry is considering naming you Sheriff of London."

Hugh cocked his head, automatically assuming he'd heard wrong. London's two sheriffs, responsible for keeping the king's peace in the great city and the surrounding shire of Middlesex, were among the most powerful and influential men in the realm. Formerly elected by the citizenry of London, they were now directly appointed by the king from among the landed nobility.

"But . . ." Hugh shook his head as if that would resolve his confusion. "London already has two sheriffs."

"John of Hilton will be vacating his post as of September. Seems his gout's getting the better of him. That leaves old Martin Fitz William. King Henry wants to team him up with someone who's actually got some experience in investigating crimes and enforcing justice, and who's also young enough to handle the demands of the office—although of course you'll have undersheriffs to do most of the legwork. Commanding them will be one of your two primary duties. The other will be to preside over the sheriff's court, which will be located in your home—"

"I don't have a home." Hugh lived with Joanna and Graeham when he was in the London area, and wherever fate landed him when he was on an assignment.

"You'll have one if you're appointed to the sheriffship. Part of your remuneration will be a fine town house in the city, as befitting your position. You'll report to the justiciar of London, who answers directly to the king, and is a good, just man. You'll get along well with him."

"You speak as if I've already been appointed."

"The king thinks very highly of you, Hugh. He wants to meet with you in part to take your measure and assure himself that you're the man for the job. If he decides in your favor, he'll probably offer it to you on the spot, knowing him. I'd be careful to try and impress him if I were you. Dress like a gentleman, for God's sake, not in that bloody awful leathern tunic, and show the proper deference. Remember, he's the king."

Hugh almost laughed. "You're assuming I *want* to be sheriff of London."

Lord Richard blinked at him. "Of *course* you want to be sheriff of London. It's the chance of a lifetime."

"For a man who doesn't mind being tied down to one place and one master forever, perhaps."

"But you love London—you've told me so often. And as for having a 'master,' you'll really be fairly autonomous."

Hugh quirked an eyebrow.

"To a point," Lord Richard conceded. "Listen, Hugh, I know how you hate to have to answer to anyone, even me, but—"

"I don't want it," Hugh said resolutely. "If he offers it to me, I'll turn it down. That being the case, I respectfully request that I be relieved from having to travel all the way to Rouen."

"Oh, you're going to Rouen," Lord Richard said coolly. "If only to tell the king to his face what you've just told me—if you've got the stones for it—but you're going."

Hugh slammed his hands on the windowsill, growling out a raw oath.

"What's troubling you, Hugh?" asked Lord Richard, his voice gentling but his gaze as unnervingly astute as ever.

"Nothing," Hugh said quickly, his eyes lighting on the Map of the World over the justiciar's shoulder.

"You really must learn how to lie more credibly than that," Lord Richard observed mildly. "Looking elsewhere will give you away every time."

Hugh just sighed and kneaded the bridge of his nose.

"Is it the girl?" his lordship asked.

"Nay, I—"

"You're worried about her."

Hugh exhaled harshly. "Yes." It was the truth—or part of it.

"Don't be. She's smarter than either one of us—resourceful, ingenious, analytical. She was born for this type of work."

"I know, but—"

"She'll be fine. And your presence is required in Rouen."

"Lord Richard . . ."

"It's a royal summons, Hugh," Lord Richard said quietly. "You have no choice."

He didn't, of course. His jaw set, Hugh said, "Very well."

"I suggest you leave at once." Sitting at his desk and sorting through a stack of documents, Lord Richard said, "I have some items for you to deliver to the king, if you don't mind."

"Not at all." Turning back to the window, Hugh closed his eyes and did some quick mental calculations. Assuming no delays on the road to Hastings, clear weather across the Channel and a trouble-free ride from Fécamp to Rouen, it would take Hugh, at best, four days there and four days back—but probably more. And he must add to that however long the king kept him waiting at the ducal palace before their audience . . . if he was even there, Henry Plantagenet not being known for lingering in one place very long. Hugh might end up having to chase the man halfway across France . . .

By the time he returned to England and made his way to Halthorpe Castle, eight or nine days at least would have passed—probably a fortnight or more—and Phillipa . . .

Hugh opened his eyes, his gaze seeking out the stone bench at the far end of the courtyard, still empty.

Phillipa would be Aldous Ewing's leman.

Chapter 13

"Milady . . ." the young maid said hesitantly as she lowered the sleek white shift over Phillipa's head, "are you sure you want to be doin' this?"

Phillipa couldn't imagine anything less appealing than stealing into Aldous Ewing's bedchamber tonight all oiled and perfumed and bedecked in a slippery little film of silk, but she merely said, "Yes, Edmee, quite sure."

Edmee smoothed down and adjusted the low-cut, sleeveless nightgown, frowning at its scandalous design. It was slashed wide open on both sides down to the hips, with lacings to pull the fabric snug, like the newest style in ladies' tunics—however, instead of displaying a coy little glimpse of kirtle beneath, the two side slits revealed a generous and tantalizing expanse of flesh. It was a garment whose sole purpose was to incite a man's lust.

And Edmee obviously didn't approve. One of a handful of servants whom Lady Clare had brought with her from Poitiers to Halthorpe, Edmee was, in fact, a simple Poitevan peasant, and a pious one at that, judging from the crude wooden cross around her neck. Tall and buxom in the sturdy manner of a farmwife, with straw-colored hair peeking out from her kerchief and a broad, freckle-spattered face, Edmee was Phillipa's antithesis both physically and temperamentally. Nevertheless, she was one of the few Halthorpe denizens with whom Phillipa felt truly at ease—one of two, actually, Orlando

Storzi, who shared an intellectual rapport with her, being the other.

Clare had other guests, a coterie of posturing poets and decadent Frankish nobles who'd followed her here from Poitiers over the past few weeks. Despite Phillipa's tolerance for radical ideas, their careless amorality repulsed her. Perhaps that was why the like-minded Edmee had gravitated to her upon her arrival at Halthorpe, prompting Phillipa to request Edmee as her personal maid during her stay here—although, as Castle Halthorpe was somewhat understaffed, Phillipa had to share her with Clare and Clare's friend and confidante, Marguerite du Roche.

But now that affinity would be compromised. For, after a full week of deflecting Aldous's amorous advances by claiming it was an inconvenient time of the month, Phillipa had no choice but to offer the sexual favors she had managed with such effort to withhold thus far. Edmee was clearly disappointed by her mistress's fall from grace.

"Lift your arm, milady." Lacing up the left side of the provocative shift with work-roughened fingers, Edmee said, "You'll pardon my asking, but . . . does your husband . . . Hugh of Oxford, is it?"

"Aye."

"Does Sir Hugh know about you and Master Aldous?"

Phillipa drew in a steadying breath and let it out. "Aye."

Edmee glanced at Phillipa as she tied off the cord, her eyebrows rising in disapproval. "I never will understand you highborn folk," she said in a provincial blend of Norman French and her rustic ancestral dialect. "The priests say as how adultery is a grievous sin. Don't none of you fear the torments of Hell?"

"It's . . . complicated," Phillipa murmured as she studied the stone wall that separated her room from Aldous's. The connecting chambers he'd promised her were unavailable, all of them being occupied, it turned

out, by Clare's other house guests, most of whom had
arrived after Aldous's last visit here, and none of whom
Clare was willing to displace for the sake of a younger
brother she seemed barely to tolerate. Pleased though
Aldous had been to find the castle filled with people—
they would provide a human buffer between himself and
his sister, he'd explained—he was infuriated at having to
make do with chambers that did not share an adjoining
door. What would become of his coveted promotion to
archdeacon, he'd demanded of his sister, if someone saw
him entering Phillipa's chamber, or her entering his? In
his own home, he needn't fret overmuch about discretion, but among strangers, he must be vigilant, lest his
Church career end up in ashes.

As a sop, Clare had let him prowl Halthorpe Castle,
a rabbit warren the size of a small city, and choose two
adjacent chambers that would be as remotely situated as
possible. He'd picked a pair of dismal, empty little
ground-floor cells at the far end of the oldest wing and
had fresh rushes and furnishings brought in. Despite
their relative isolation, Aldous never visited Phillipa in
her chamber, lest Edmee see him there and gossip to
the other servants, and Phillipa had found excuses not
to visit him in his. During the past week, he had kissed
her only once—thank God!—and had rarely even spoken to her privately. Instead, he conducted his more intimate communications by means of notes passed by his
sister, who seemed to view the whole business as border-
ing on hilarious. No doubt she giggled with the others
about Aldous's absurd machinations behind his back.

In any event, such machinations were unlikely to fool
anyone. As if it weren't telling enough that he'd brought
Phillipa with him from Southwark and installed her in
the chamber next to his, there were his constant little
attentions . . . his habit of whispering in her ear during
dinner, the way he'd caress her arm as if by accident,
the many times she'd turn and find him gazing at her
like a moonstruck schoolboy without seeming to realize
it. He appeared to lose perspective where she was con-

cerned. She encouraged him, of course—although it still made her queasy to do so—but thus far she'd had no luck in coaxing his secrets out of him.

Nor had Orlando been forthcoming about his mysterious activities in the cellar, which kept him and Istagio occupied most days until suppertime and sometimes, as tonight, quite a bit later. Despite the camaraderie of the mind that Orlando shared with Phillipa, he sidestepped her inquiries with the air of a man who'd been sworn to secrecy. Her discreet questioning of the other guests had been fruitless; they were not only ignorant of the goings-on in the cellar, but apathetic as well, being too caught up in themselves and their various romantic entanglements to care about much else.

"Lift the other arm, milady." Circling around her, Edmee laced up her right side. " 'Tis a good thing I served at the queen's palace in Poitiers, or I don't know what I'd think of Halthorpe! My poor mother would keel over from shock if she knew how Lady Clare carried on—or that Marguerite du Roche . . ." Edmee shuddered as she tied off the cord. "Some of the things I've seen, serving them . . ."

Ah, yes, the libidinous Lady Marguerite, with her cat-like eyes and blazing red hair—which she always wore loose and uncovered, although it was rumored she had a husband somewhere. The most sexually predatory creature Phillipa had ever encountered, Marguerite embraced seduction like a blood sport.

"Is it true," Edmee asked, "about the list?"

Phillipa sighed. "It's true." Upon her arrival at Halthorpe, Clare's friend Marguerite had drawn up a list of twenty men she intended to tup before the summer was over. The candidates were most of the male guests and the handsomest of King Louis's men-at-arms, who were quartered along with Lord Bertram's soldiers in the sprawling barracks located in the outer bailey. That Marguerite had set her sights on the latter only served to point up her own depravity, for Louis's men were a brutal lot whose pastimes included boar-baiting, vicious kick-fighting, and if the rumors could be credited, the occasional rape. "They say she bedded all but three within a fortnight."

"Even Nicolas Capellanus?" Edmee asked, referring to the bald-head, taciturn priest who served in the thankless role of Halthorpe's chaplain. Formerly attached to the court of pious King Louis in Paris, he tolerated the ungodly atmosphere at Halthorpe with grim-faced disapproval.

"I understand Father Nicolas was one of the three who refused her, along with Turstin de Ver and Raoul d'Argentan." Turstin, Clare's pet troubadour, turned out to fancy the charms of his own sex; Raoul was, to everyone's amusement, too embarrassingly besotted with his wife, the lovely but troublesome Isabelle, to dally with Marguerite.

"If this is the way you lords and ladies conduct yourselves," Edmee proclaimed as she brushed out Phillipa's hair, "I don't want none of it."

Neither do I, Phillipa thought, reflecting that romantic love as it existed at Halthorpe, with its sordid little intrigues and aura of depravity, was far from her idealistic vision of *l'amour courtois*.

Was Hugh right? Was it all just fatuous, self-serving drivel? Was there nothing more to relations between the sexes than the propitious alignment of body parts?

No. She knew it wasn't that simple. After having given herself to Hugh, having united herself with him and felt the power and beauty of it deep in her soul, she knew it wasn't just about bodies.

Something happened that night, something she couldn't help but think of as profound, even sacred. She'd ceased to be just Phillipa, and Hugh had ceased to be just Hugh. They had connected on a higher level, a level quite apart from the realm of the flesh. Phillipa found this realization both humbling and exhilarating.

And, of course, absolutely terrifying.

Her first day or two at Halthorpe, Phillipa had half-expected Hugh to show up there on some pretext and either spirit her away or get himself invited to stay on. Hugh's presence here would give her the excuse she needed to avoid sleeping with Aldous, which she found she could no longer bear to face.

Making love to Hugh had been transcendent. Going through the motions of it with Aldous would be unendurable. She'd thought she could do it, but that was before Hugh had awakened her, with such compelling tenderness, to the mysteries of physical passion. How could she sully what she'd shared with Hugh by lying down beneath Aldous and spreading her legs like some two-penny whore?

She'd couldn't, hence her claim that she was suffering her monthly flux, but seven days had been as long as she could stretch out that particular ploy. All week, she'd secretly prayed for Hugh to ride up on Odin and rescue her from her fate as Aldous's leman.

But he hadn't. Nor had he tried to stop her from coming here. Indeed, he'd encouraged her. *A man will confide far more to his mistress than he will to a woman who simply lets him feed her strawberries . . .*

Despair smoldered like a coal in her stomach. *Oh, Hugh . . . Why did you let me go? Why haven't you come for me?*

She felt a searing burst of rage at him, as she always did when her thoughts traveled down this particular path. He didn't care for her, he couldn't, to have forsaken her this way.

Closing her eyes, she pictured him as he'd looked that night, lying beneath her, dreamy-eyed and beautiful in the wavering lamplight. The anger faded, replaced by a yearning so keen that it pierced her like a knife.

Come for me, Hugh. Please . . .

A knock sounded on her chamber door, followed by a woman's silky-smooth voice. "Phillipa? It's Clare."

"Shall I tell her you've retired for the night?" whispered Edmee, who knew how little Phillipa cared for her hostess, an antipathy that appeared to be quite mutual.

Phillipa was about to tell Edmee to do just that, when

Clare added, in a slightly amused conspiratorial tone, "I've got something for you. The gentleman in question will be most put out if I don't deliver it immediately."

Phillipa groaned inwardly. Another note from Aldous. She'd best have a look at it. "Let her in," she told Edmee with a weary sigh.

But as Edmee was reaching for the handle of the door, it swung open and in strode Clare, to the jangling of the chatelaine's keys she wore on a long gold chain around her neck. Halthorpe's mistress was as pale and polished as ever in a sumptuous tunic of midnight blue satin slashed all over the bodice and sleeves to show the kirtle beneath, her black wig fastidiously styled, sapphires winking on every finger and thumb—of her right hand. Her left was encased in its ubiquitous leather gauntlet, to protect it from the talons of the hooded kestrel tethered to it. Clare was training the young hawk to hunt, Aldous had explained; she carried it about with her to help accustom it to the company of humans.

"Ah, you *are* in, dear." Clare's rouged lips curved slyly upward as she took in Phillipa's elegant dishabille, while not so much as looking in Edmee's direction; she and Marguerite both treated the maid with utter contempt. "And dressed for bed—my brother's, from the look of it. It's about time. His ballocks must be damn near ready to explode by now."

Phillipa held Clare's gaze steadily, but from the corner of her eye, she saw poor Edmee's jaw drop.

"He's sent another note?" Phillipa asked.

"Aye. He's most distraught that you haven't answered the one I gave you this morning."

"I didn't realize he expected me to write him back."

"He's just overexcited at the impending consummation of your grand passion," Clare said aridly.

To she whom I most desire, this morning's note had read, *to she whose voice is as sweet as that of the wild nightingale, whose limbs I long to feel twining round me like tender honeysuckle shoots. From your poor, lovesick Aldous, who is enslaved by your beauty, captivated by your charms. How I yearn for the solace of your embrace, dear lady. Come to me tonight and let me love you. You are the angel of my heart, the dove of my soul, my earthly delight and my heavenly inspiration . . .*

But it was his closing lines that she had read over and over as an idea gradually took shape in her mind. *Remember that there is you and only you. My love stays pure for you, my body chaste . . . until the blissful hour of our union. It is with a trembling heart that I await your visit to me tonight. Don't knock. Don't speak. Just join me in my bed and let us surrender ourselves to each other.*

"Here's the new note." Slipping two fingers between her ample and well-powdered breasts, Clare produced from the snug bodice of her gown a tightly folded little sheet of parchment, which she handed to Phillipa. "I told him I would only play the go-between in this tiresome little farce for just so long."

Sauntering around the chamber, Clare inspected the tattered old wall hangings and ancient furnishings with her perpetually bored expression. Straw crackled when she poked at the fur-draped mattress on the uncurtained bed. The bed in Aldous's chamber, Phillipa had noticed, was twice the size of hers, fancily carved and painted, with fringed white curtains held back by tassled satin ties. Phillipa would bet anything the mattress was filled with goose down.

She unfolded the note Clare had just handed her. *Pray, come to me tonight,* it began without preamble, *as I so fervently entreated you in my earlier missive. I won't rest until I reach the peak of joy of your arms . . .*

"Not much here, is there?"

Looking up from the note, Phillipa saw Clare standing at the wash stand, apathetically sorting through the neatly laid-out toiletries. Edmee, who was hanging up the tunic Phillipa had worn that day, glanced toward Clare and then quickly away, as if afraid her distaste would show on her face.

"Your complexion could use some evening out." One-handed, Clare popped the glass stopper out of a vial and sniffed it. "There's an apothecary in Paris who makes a mixture of fine white lead and rose water that works wonders for me. You should try it." With a frosty little chuckle, she added, "You don't want to look like Gui de Beauvais's Brilliant Little By-blow forever, do you?" She inserted the stopper back in the vial and replaced it on the wash stand, then leaned forward to inspect her lip rouge in the little steel looking glass mounted on the wall above.

As Phillipa was summoning up a retort that wouldn't be too scathing, a muffled *boom* reverberated through the castle.

The kestrel screamed and pumped its wings, straining against the thong attached to its legs. "There, there, Salome," Clare soothed, lightly stroking its feathers. " 'Tis only a wine barrel rolling off its stack." It was the same thing she had told Phillipa the first time that sound had emanated from the cellar beneath the great hall, where Orlando and Istagio were carrying out their mysterious undertaking. Had the noise come from outside, rather than downstairs, Phillipa would have taken it for thunder; what else could produce such a violent roar?

"Those must be heavy barrels," Phillipa said.

"I suppose they must be," Clare said, idly fingering her collection of keys, an occasional nervous habit of hers and the only indication to Phillipa that she was ever anything less than coolly serene.

How Phillipa wished she could get her hands on those keys. She had naturally tried to investigate the cellar, but there was a heavy oak door at the top of the stairwell that led to it from the great hall, and it was always locked. Every morning, Clare unlocked it for Orlando and Istagio, who apparently bolted it from the inside after they closed it behind them, for it was immovable during the day. When they emerged in the evening after completing their day's work, one of them always immediately went and fetched Clare, who locked the door for the night.

"I'll send some of that white lead compound over to you on the morrow," Clare said as she crossed to the door. "In the meantime, Aldous is alone in his chamber and waiting for you. Do pry open those dainty little legs of yours and treat him to a proper tupping so he'll cease his bloody whining. I'm sick to death of it."

After the door had slammed behind Clare, Edmee crossed herself. "Jesus have mercy. I never thought to hear a lady of rank say such things."

"One would think you'd be used to Lady Clare's ways by now," Phillipa said. "You've been with her since Poitiers, yes?"

"Only since right before she left there. Her own lady's maid took sick with an ague that wouldn't go away, so I was asked if I wouldn't like to take over. I knew it would mean comin' to England, but it sounded like an adventure, and there weren't nothing to keep me in Poitiers—the fellow I was sweet on had just married someone else, and . . ." She shook her head sadly. "Perhaps I should have stayed anyway."

Phillipa patted her arm. "I'm glad you didn't."

"You're kind to say so." Edmee smiled at her as she began turning down the fur throws on Phillipa's bed.

Phillipa nibbled on her bottom lip. "I wouldn't mind knowing what's really making those sounds."

"You don't think it's wine barrels falling over?"

"Does it sound like wine barrels falling over?"

Edmee shrugged. "You and Master Orlando seem friendly enough. Have you asked him?"

"Aye. He says it's wine barrels."

"Then perhaps it is."

Phillipa paced the length of the chamber, and back again. "You're friendly with Istagio."

Edmee snorted as she plumped up the pillows. "He's friendly with *me,* you mean—the lecherous cur."

Orlando's rotund and bumbling assistant had latched on to Edmee with a zeal and tenacity that did have a somewhat canine quality to it, although the lewd glint in his eyes when he leered at her struck Phillipa as more reptilian than doglike. In truth, he looked at most women that way, even Phillipa when he didn't think she noticed, but for some reason he concentrated his inept efforts at seduction on Edmee. At first, Phillipa couldn't understand it; Edmee was likable enough, but with her thick bones and small, close-set eyes, she wasn't what you'd call pretty. She did have that pale blond hair, though, and a rather prodigious bosom; perhaps those were the qualities that had so entranced Istagio.

"He's always trying to impress you," Phillipa observed. "Yesterday I heard him bragging about his family's bell foundry in Italy and how many generations—"

"He shouldn't be tellin' me these things," Edmee declared, seeming genuinely distressed. "He shouldn't . . ." She looked away abruptly. "I . . . I don't want him tryin' to impress me. I don't want him hoverin' over me and . . . and *lookin'* at me like that. 'Tisn't as if I give him any reason to think I want that sort of attention."

"That doesn't stop some men."

"Then how can I make him leave me be?" she asked plaintively.

"Perhaps you shouldn't," Phillipa replied. "At least . . . not right away."

Edmee stared at her for a moment and then blinked. "You want me to ask him what's goin' on in the cellar."

"Well . . . perhaps you can . . . charm the information out of him," Phillipa suggested with a smile. "Lead him on a bit—just a bit. Let him think that you're perhaps just a *wee* bit interested, ask him a few leading questions . . ."

Edmee shook her head. "If I do that, milady, he'll never leave me alone again!"

"But at least we'll find out what's happening in the cellar."

" 'Tisn't worth it," Edmee said resolutely.

She had a point; the only way she could shake Istagio loose was by ignoring him, not interrogating him about his work. Not that Phillipa wasn't still tempted to try and talk her into it, her mission being more important than Edmee's romantic complications, but all she would accomplish by pressing the point would be to make Edmee suspicious of her motives.

"You're right, of course," Phillipa said with forced nonchalance. " 'Twouldn't do to make Istagio even more of a pest just to satisfy our idle curiosity."

Of course, she'd done that and more with Aldous, she thought. She'd let him kiss her; she'd promised to sleep with him. He was waiting for her right now, wondering how long it would take her to send Edmee away and come to him.

It's time, she thought. *Time to play out the rest of it.* "I don't think I need anything else tonight, Edmee. Why don't you go now and see if Lady Clare or Lady Marguerite can use—"

"Milady . . ." Edmee regarded Phillipa's risqué silken shift with a pained expression. "Are you sure you should . . ."

"Edmee, please."

"Think of your husband," she implored. "Think of Sir Hugh."

Would that I could think of anything else. "I'll see you in the morning, Edmee."

With an air of grave resignation, the maid murmured, "Yes, milady," and left.

Aldous is alone in his chamber and waiting for you . . .

Phillipa immediately crossed to one of the three arrow slits on the back wall that served in lieu of windows and stood with her ear to it. She closed her eyes, listening for sounds from Aldous's chamber, but all she could hear was the indolent grunting of frogs in the moat and muffled laughter from the great hall, where Clare's guests always caroused late into the night. Sometimes they sang or danced. Three times this past week, Clare had convened courts of love to arbitrate the disputes of paramours, with herself sitting in sole judgment of her guests' romantic squabbles. These had been utter farces, just as Hugh had claimed, but not half as disturbing as the little game Clare had presided over two nights ago,

which involved pairing up couples based on throws of
the dice, confiscating every stitch of their clothing, and
locking them in a bedchamber together until dawn.

With a sigh of exasperation—Phillipa *had* to know
whether Aldous was still alone or not—she went to the
door and eased it open. Finding the dark stone corridor
empty, she crept to his chamber door and pressed her
ear to it. For a minute she heard nothing, and then came
a sort of melodic mumbling. She recognized the tune as
that of a drinking song Turstin de Ver had taught Clare's
guests after supper last night. Aldous was half-humming
and half-singing it in that indifferent way people do
when they're alone.

So. She wasn't there yet.

Returning to her own chamber, Phillipa blew out the
candles and opened the door a crack—just enough so
that she could see the area outside Aldous's chamber
without drawing attention to herself.

And then she waited.

Aldous Ewing, freshly bathed and reclining on his soft
down bed in naught but his underdrawers and shirt—
silky Egyptian cotton, the very best—started growing
hard at the first muted creak of the door.

At last. All those months in Paris when he'd hungered
for her and made do with whores instead, all those years
afterward of wondering what it would have been like if
she'd only said, *Yes, Aldous, take me. I'm yours to use
as you will . . .*

A thousand times, awake and in his dreams, he'd
imagined what it would be like to fuck the cool and
lovely Phillipa de Paris.

Now he would find out.

The door opened with a slow squeak of old leather
hinges. Reaching down, Aldous adjusted his cock through
his drawers as he grew fully erect.

He smiled when he saw her, cloaked in a hooded mantle of black satin. She paused for a moment, a spectral
figure in the dusky corridor, before stepping over the

threshold of Aldous's chamber. He'd lit it with a dozen candles for the occasion, strewn mint among the rushes, tied the bed curtains back, and sprinkled the purple counterpane with sprigs of rosemary and lavender.

Soon . . .

His smile waned when she turned to close the door behind her. Phillipa wasn't that tall—was she?

She lowered the hood as she faced him. He just about swallowed his tongue when he saw the fiery gleam of her red hair in the candlelight.

"L-lady Marguerite?"

Marguerite du Roche's delicately plucked eyebrows arched upward. "I understood we weren't to speak," she said in that cat's-purr voice of hers. "Or was that just to be me?"

"I . . . I beg your—"

"If there are to be rules of play, they ought to be clearly stated and strictly enforced, don't you think?" She unpinned her mantle and let it drop.

This time he did swallow his tongue.

She was naked. Well, not entirely. She had on a pair of black-and-gold beaded slippers and black silk stockings gartered above the knee. But other than that, she was thoroughly, voluptuously, astoundingly naked. Her body was as milky-pale as her face, the hair of her sex as bright as that which cascaded over her like rippling snakes. She had tits as hard and round as apples, and her nipples . . .

They'd been rouged, he realized, painted with something to redden them. This discovery sent a sharp surge of arousal straight to his groin.

"Shall we clarify the rules?" In her hand Marguerite held a short whip with a cluster of lashes on the end, such as those used by Camaldolian hermits to flagellate themselves. The sight of this weapon of punishment sparked another hot little spasm of lust.

"The . . . the rules?" he stammered. "I don't—"

"They're your rules." Coming around to the side of the bed, she lifted a stockinged leg and draped it across his lap, right over his throbbing tool, which she could surely feel against her calf. There was something tucked into the garter—a folded-up slip of parchment. She plucked it out, unfolded it, and read, " 'Don't knock. Don't speak. Just join me in my bed and let us surrender ourselves to each other.' "

She handed him the note, which he stared at incredulously. "Where did you g-get—"

"Somebody slipped it under my door this morning. I assumed it was you."

He shook his head. " 'Twas intended for the lady . . . for someone else. M-my sister, she was supposed to give it directly to—"

Marguerite laughed. "And she tucked it under my door instead. That sounds like something Clare might do."

It did, Aldous realized with a groan. Clare seemed to delight in orchestrating the erotic intrigues of those around her.

"It seems we've been snared in her little trap, you and I. The question," Marguerite purred as she rubbed her leg back and forth over Aldous's erection, drawing a carnal little whimper from him, "is what we're going to do about it."

Do about it . . . ? Aldous struggled to think this out rationally despite the maddening friction of her firm calf against his cock. Clare had obviously never given the first note to Phillipa, thinking it some great jest to misdirect it to Marguerite, so it stood to reason she would have withheld the second, as well. Phillipa had no idea he'd been expecting her tonight. She wouldn't come.

Marguerite had come instead.

"Well?" Her icy green eyes locked with his, Marguerite trailed the lashes of the whip over her breasts, causing her nipples to tighten into crimson-stained buds. Lowering the instrument, she slowly stroked its leather-wrapped handle between her legs.

Aldous's fist snapped shut, crushing the sheet of

parchment in his hand. He hurled it aside and reached for her.

"Not so fast." She treated his hand to a stinging crack of the whip; he recoiled with a cry that sounded humiliatingly girlish. "We haven't clarified the rules."

"The . . . the . . ."

" 'Don't speak,' " she mused. "I like that one. But I'd like it better if I could talk and you were the one who had to hold his tongue. What do you think?"

"Uh, well . . ."

"Shh!" Leaning forward, she prodded the handle of the whip between his lips and into his mouth; Aldous tasted her on the leather. "Don't speak. You may think whatever thoughts you like, but keep them to yourself. Or else"—she drew the whip handle almost completely out of his mouth, then shoved it back in even deeper, nudging the back of his throat—"I'll be forced to gag you. You wouldn't want that, would you? You may nod or shake your head."

Aldous, his eyes stinging as his throat convulsed, managed to shake his head.

She slid the handle out. The air left his lungs in a gush of relief. A tear slid from one eye. He went to wipe it away, but she said, "Nay, leave it. I love the sight of tears on a man's cheeks."

He dutifully lowered his hands.

"I liked the part about surrendering, too," she said, "only, as you've probably already guessed, I would prefer that you submit to me than the other way round."

Aldous nodded, stunned not just by her treatment of him, but by his own reaction to it. He was so hard it actually hurt.

"Move down, off the pillows," she commanded, "so you're lying flat. Good. Now lift your shirt and open your drawers."

After a moment's nonplussed hesitation, he did as she instructed, shaken by his sense of vulnerability as he lay there exposed to her critical scrutiny.

" 'Twill have to do." She shoved the pointed toe of her slipper into his hip, making him wince. "Roll over."

He rolled facedown on the purple counterpane, which felt slick and cool against his pulsing-hot cock, but . . .

"Er . . . the herbs I scattered about," he said, "they're digging into me."

"Excellent." Marguerite climbed over him with feline grace, a slow pounce that left her straddling his legs. Abruptly she yanked his drawers down to his thighs.

"That pretty white bum of yours would look quite fetching laced with nice red lash marks, don't you think?" When he hesitated in responding, she grabbed a handful of his hair and jerked his head back. "Don't you?"

He nodded frantically. She released his hair and reached behind her for something. Craning his neck, he saw her untying the thick satin cord that gathered the curtains to the post at the bottom right corner of the bed. She pulled it away, letting the curtains unfurl, then released the other three cords as well, enclosing the bed on all four sides, as if they were in a tent of white damask.

From the tangle of cords she'd amassed, she chose one and wrapped it several times around Aldous's right wrist. Bending his right leg back, she said, "Grab your foot," and lashed his ankle tight with the same length of cord.

He watched in titillated fascination as she extracted another cord from the pile and repeated the process with his left wrist and ankle, leaving him bound hand and foot like a hog at butchering time. His heart pounded at the intoxicating sense of powerlessness.

"That's better," she murmured, brushing the whip's lashes in circles over his bare buttocks as his flesh erupted in goose bumps. "You like handing over the reins, don't you?" Sliding a hand between his legs, she cradled his turgid flesh; he moaned pitifully, thrusting against her cool, soft palm. "Aye, you like it," she said soothingly. "But you must stop moving like that, because it isn't time for you to come yet. If I let you come at all, 'twill be much later.''

Dazed with lust and close, so close, he shook his head and pressed harder, harder . . .

A sharp, slicing pain jolted him out of his sensual delirium. She'd whipped him across his buttocks, and hard. "How dare you try to exert your will over mine?"

He groaned helplessly as she struck him again, and again, and again . . . Pain merged with pleasure to form an excruciating ecstasy Aldous had never experienced before. If she kept this up, he would go off far too soon.

Dimly he was aware of the creak of wood, the squeak of leather. *The door* . . . ?

Footsteps rustled in the rushes.

"Stop!" he gasped as Marguerite raised the whip high.

"Aldous?" It was a woman's voice, sweet and soft.

Phillipa! She did come! She was in the room—*merciful God!*—though she couldn't see him—*them*—through the curtains that enveloped the bed.

"Nay," he begged as the whip descended, crying out raggedly when it connected, harder than ever.

"Aldous . . ." Phillipa's voice was closer now. "Are you all—?"

"No!" he cried, writhing against his bindings. "Yes! Go! For God's sake—"

The curtain whipped aside and she stood there, angelic and bewitching in the most extraordinary little slip of white satin, her hair a silken black cascade, those huge, dark eyes lighting first on him, hogtied with his drawers shoved down, then on a giggling Marguerite, and finally—*Strike me dead now, Lord, please, NOW!*—on the whip lightly tickling his exposed and smarting arse.

Eyes wide with shock, Phillipa opened her mouth as if to speak, but nothing came out.

"Care to take a crack at him yourself?" Marguerite held the whip toward Phillipa, handle first.

She flinched and backed up, letting the curtain fall

closed. The rushes crackled beneath her rapidly re-treating footsteps.

"Phillipa!" Aldous screamed as the door slammed. *"Phillipa! Come ba—"* Jesu, no! *"Phillipa! Phillipa!"* Thrashing against his bindings, he howled, *"I'm sorry, Phillipa! Phillipa! This means nothing! You're the one, the only one!"*

"Well," Marguerite sniffed as she lifted one of the two remaining satin cords and wadded it up, "not quite, obviously, or you wouldn't be here with me, would you?"

"Nay! You don't understand! *She* doesn't under-stand!"

"Much as I'd love to hear how you're going to explain it to her—I really would—I did clearly instruct you not to speak."

Pressing a knee into his back to subdue him, she pried his mouth open and stuffed the wadded-up cord into it, passing the fourth and last cord between his lips and tying it behind his head to hold the gag in place.

Tears of futility and shame pricked his eyes; he blinked them back.

"Let them flow," Marguerite softly urged as she reached once more for the whip. "There will be many more before this night is over."

Chapter 14

It was nearly a week later, as Phillipa and the rest of Clare's guests were enjoying an open-air Midsummer's Eve feast at trestle tables in Halthorpe Castle's outer bailey, that Clare caught the eye of Marguerite du Roche and said, "What do you know . . . a real man, coming here to Halthorpe. Must be some sort of mistake."

Clare nodded toward something over Phillipa's shoulder. Marguerite, raising a hand to shade her eyes against the low, early evening sun, smiled slowly. "Perhaps he's lost."

"I feel certain," Clare said silkily, "that I could help him to find his way."

Phillipa turned and tracked their gazes to the drawbridge that spanned the moat outside the castle's high stone curtain wall. Squinting, she made out the silhouette of a tall, broad-shouldered man on horseback riding through the double-towered gatehouse. When he emerged from the shadows of the gatehouse and into the sun, her heart skittered in her chest.

He came.

Hugh looked much the same this evening as when she'd first met him, his golden hair disheveled, his jaw dark with stubble, and that intriguing glimmer of gold on his right earlobe. He was dressed the same, too, in the grubby leathern soldier's tunic that he preferred for long rides. Were it not for his magnificent dun stallion—a nobleman's mount—one might almost think him a freebooter come to rob and pillage. There was an aura of savage masculinity to him, especially as compared to the other men at Halthorpe, with their fanciful costumes and affected manners—except, of course, for King Louis's twelve brutal men-at-arms and Lord Bertram's soldiers, but they kept to their barracks, rarely even venturing into the inner bailey. No wonder Clare was so entranced by Hugh.

Even at this distance, Phillipa could see Hugh's eyes, translucent as glass, focus in on her and hold her gaze. She smiled almost timidly, remembering the last time she'd seen him, fast asleep in their bed at Aldous's house, his mouth slightly parted, a lock of hair across his eyes, looking like a young boy in the silvery dawn light. It had taken every bit of strength she'd possessed to leave him there.

He nodded to her, not smiling exactly, but looking at her so intently that she felt a shivery warmth all up and down her spine, as if he were stroking her there with his big, callused hand.

"I saw him first," Clare told her friend. "You may have at him when I'm done."

"Must we take turns?" asked Marguerite. "He looks as if he could take us both on together without too much trouble."

"I'd ask to join in the revelry, *midons*," said the troubadour Turstin de Ver, seated in his usual spot at Clare's right hand, between his patroness and Marguerite, "but I suspect that's one boy who prefers to play with girls." Turstin was the type of older man who had managed, over time, to grow into the awkward features with which he'd been cursed at birth—in his case, an oversized nose and equally conspicuous ears. Lean and somewhat craggy, with sandy hair turning to silver and a perpetually amused glint in his eyes, he struck Phillipa as oddly handsome.

Aldous turned to see what everyone was looking at. "Oh, for God's sake," he growled.

"Do you know that man?" Clare asked.

"Yes, damn it all. He's Phillipa's husband." Aldous muttered something under his breath that sounded downright sacrilegious, in contrast to his saintly black clerical garb and skullcap. No wonder he was vexed. His relationship with Phillipa had been strained enough since the night she'd walked in on him with Marguerite. Hugh's presence here would only serve to chill it further.

The morning after that sordid little incident, Aldous had sought her out and offered a litany of contrite apologies, explaining that Clare had played a trick on him by delivering to Marguerite the notes he'd written to Phillipa, and that he was just a man, after all, with any man's base drives, but that he adored her and was immeasurably sorry for what she'd seen. What she'd seen had, in fact, so bewildered and shocked her that she couldn't even manage the display of outrage she'd so carefully rehearsed in her mind . . . *Aldous, how could you? You said your love would stay pure for me, your body chaste* . . . Instead, after gaping at them like a carp in a barrel, she'd turned and fled, with the image seared in her mind of Aldous and Marguerite engaged in some form of carnal congress so deviant that Phillipa simply couldn't fathom it—and didn't care to.

Claiming to be hurt and humiliated by Aldous's faithlessness, Phillipa informed him that he would have to work hard at wooing her back into his good graces—not to mention his bed. He had done just that this past week, smothering her with amorous attention even in front of the others—his concern for discretion evidently less critical than his need to win her back—and meekly accepting it when she refused his kisses. As a result, she got to remain at Halthorpe and continue her investigation, fruitless though it had been so far, but without the burden of sharing Aldous Ewing's bed—although she was still obliged to encourage his pursuit of her. If he knew she had no intention of bedding him, ever, he would cast her off instantly.

Interestingly, last night, unable to sleep because of the heat, Phillipa had risen from bed to stand in front of one of the arrow loops in the hope of catching a stray breeze. What she caught instead were sounds from Aldous's chamber next door—a low, masculine groan that trailed off into a kind of sob, then a woman's voice—Marguerite's voice—soft, cajoling, a little breathless. ". . . don't tighten up like that . . . that's right . . . give in to it and it won't hurt so much . . . I know you like it . . ." It would be unwise, Phillipa had decided, to let Aldous know she'd caught wind of his ongoing liaison with Marguerite. Any self-respecting woman would walk away from a man who treated her so shabbily, and walking away from Aldous right now was not an option.

It was a credit either to Phillipa's shrewdness or Aldous's gullibility—or perhaps both—that he never suspected that it was, in fact, she who had slipped the first note under Marguerite's chamber door that morning. He blamed himself entirely—himself and Clare, who naturally denied having passed the note to Marguerite, although she said she wished she'd thought of it. Aldous didn't believe her, of course, and their relations since then had been testier than ever.

Ogling Hugh as he dismounted by the stables, Marguerite said, "*He's* married to the Brilliant Little Byblow?" She exchanged a look of amused astonishment with Clare.

"How absolutely extraordinary!" Clare exclaimed. "What fun this will be! And just when you were all starting to bore me witless."

Edmee, assisting the other house servants this evening in serving a monumental mince and pigeon pie, the seventh of the twenty courses that Clare's Poitevan cooks were busily concocting in the nearby cookhouse, looked from Hugh to Phillipa, her expression pensive. Was she thinking about Phillipa's supposed love affair with Aldous Ewing?

Aldous, on Clare's left, leaned toward his sister, hissing, "Send him away."

Orlando paused in the act of lifting his silver wine cup to scowl at Aldous. "Why you wanta send him away? Sir Hugh, he is the lady Phillipa's *marito,* her husband. She want him here, no?" Because he spent his days and most of his nights closeted in the cellar, Orlando was relatively oblivious to the tangle of romantic intrigues at Halthorpe, including Aldous's ongoing campaign to seduce Phillipa.

Ignoring Orlando, Aldous told Clare, "I want him out of here! Do whatever you must to get rid of him."

"You are mad as a ferret," Clare spat out, pinning her brother with a fixed glare that made her look like one of her birds of prey, "if you think I'm going to turn a man like that out of my home just because he happens to be married to the woman you're trying to fuck."

Orlando frowned in evident puzzlement. "*Sono spiacente,* but my speaking of your language is so poor. What means this word . . ."

Istagio, sitting next to Orlando, let go of Edmee's skirt, which he had grabbed as she walked past, to whisper in the older man's ear. Orlando's eyes widened and then narrowed on Aldous. "But you are . . . how you say . . . a man of the cloth, no? And she is wedded lady. For shame."

Well, at least one person at Halthorpe still knows what shame is, thought Phillipa. Loath for Orlando to think so poorly of her—aside from Edmee, he was the only person at Halthorpe she could really talk to—she said, " 'Tisn't what you think, Orlando."

"Yes it is!" Grasping Phillipa's hand too tightly, Aldous said, "*You* don't want him here, do you?"

"I . . ." Everyone at the table turned to stare at her.

"But you see, Aldous," Clare said with weary impatience, "it really doesn't matter what she wants. I'm mistress of Halthorpe, and I want him to stay. So, stay he will."

Marguerite pressed a finger to her crimson lips. "He's coming."

Phillipa turned on her bench to find Hugh striding toward them across the lawn of cropped grass. She tried to extract her hand from Aldous's, but he held on tight.

Pausing, Hugh inclined his head to her. "My lady."

"My lord husband."

Hugh's gaze lit on Aldous's hand clutching hers. His eyes turned opaque, the set of his jaw rigid, although Phillipa doubted anyone else noticed. Turning, he aimed a courtly little bow in Clare's direction. "Lady Clare, I presume."

"Clare," Phillipa said, "This is my husband, Hugh of Oxford. Hugh, I'd like you to meet Clare of Halthorpe."

Clare surveyed him from head to toe, and back again. "Now that you're close up, I can't help but think that I've seen you somewhere before."

"Poitiers," Hugh said. "I was there about a year and a half ago."

"Verily?" She leveled her cool, heavy-lidded gaze on him and smiled. "Then you should fit right in here at Halthorpe."

"The gentleman to Clare's right," Phillipa told Hugh, "is Turstin de Ver, who writes verse for her, and next to him is Clare's friend Marguerite du Roche. You know the *signores* Orlando and Istagio, and then we have Father Nicolas Capellanus—"

"Hugh?" Raoul d'Argentan rose and came forward, arms outspread. "It *is* you! Good Lord, man! How long has it been?"

"Raoul? Is this what you look like off the battlefield?" Hugh and Raoul exchanged a hug and a battery of backslaps. "You're pretty enough to kiss!"

"*Damn,* but it's good to see you, Hugh!" Raoul was a robust, dark-haired fellow with a hearty manner unlike that of most of the other men at Halthorpe.

"Same here, Raoul, but what the devil happened to you? Where's that beard? You used to look like a bear and smell like a boar, but now . . ." With a lopsided grin, Hugh lifted the long, trailing sleeve of Raoul's opulent tunic and let it fall, then ruffled his carefully coifed hair.

Raoul rolled his eyes, his ears pinkening.

"He's been domesticated by marriage," said Turstin with a dry chuckle. "True love tends to tame the most feral of men." This observation was greeted with knowing laughter by the assembled guests.

Hugh wasn't smiling anymore. "You're married?"

Raoul introduced Hugh to Isabelle, his pretty little chestnut-haired wife. She gave Hugh a cursory smile, then lowered her voice and said, "Raoul, your hair."

"What's that, lamb?"

"Your hair. Fix your hair. He's messed it all up."

"Ah." Finger-combing his hair back into place, Raoul said, "Darling, you've heard me speak of Hugh. This is the fellow I met in Milan when we were fighting Frederick Barbarossa, before Strongbow recruited us for the Irish campaign."

"Oh!" Isabelle's gaze fastened on Hugh's right hand. "The one who left his thumb in Ireland."

Silence enveloped the gathering as everyone stared at the puckered wound on Hugh's right hand.

"How did you lose it?" asked Marguerite, her voice as husky as if she were inquiring about someone's first sexual exploit.

"Ireland's very big and very wild," Hugh said lightly. "It's easy to lose things there."

Amid the chuckles that greeted this statement, Clare said, "Aldous, why don't you move and let Hugh sit next to his wife?"

And next to you as well, thought Phillipa, feeling a little twist of jealousy tighten her stomach. Was this the way Hugh felt about her and Aldous? Did he assume she was his leman by now? Did it trouble him or was he just relieved?

"Perhaps Hugh would rather sit with his friend." Aldous stabbed his sister with a look that oozed venom.

"Excellent idea." Hugh took a seat on the bench next to Raoul. " 'Twill give me a chance to relive old battles."

"Speaking of old battles," said Turstin, leaning on his elbows, "How *did* you lose that thumb? Or is it too grisly a tale for the ladies' ears?"

"Too boring, actually." Hugh accepted a cup of wine from Edmee, but waved away her offer of pigeon pie.

"Boring!" Raoul exclaimed. "I was there, and I'd hardly call it—"

"You were there?" Marguerite sat forward, eyes glittering.

Clare turned her cool, imperious gaze on Raoul. "Tell us."

Yanking her hand out of Aldous's grip, Phillipa said, "I don't think Hugh wants the story told."

Hugh raised his cup to his mouth, meeting Phillipa's gaze over the rim. She saw something in his eyes that she fancied was gratitude, but it vanished when Aldous draped his arm familiarly around her shoulders. She shrugged him off.

"*Lady Clare* wants the story told," said Isabelle. "Tell it, Raoul."

"But . . ." Raoul glanced uneasily at Hugh, grimly sipping his wine.

"Tell it," Isabelle ordered in an exasperated whisper.

Phillipa was about to object again when Hugh caught her eye and, grimacing, shook his head fractionally. Clearly, he would rather grit this out than let her antagonize Clare, the right decision if their priority was to be their mission.

Raoul sighed heavily. "Yes, well. Let's see . . . 'twas three years ago that we went to Ireland with Strongbow." He frowned. "But no, the story begins long before that. Hugh, when was it that you fought for Donaghy Nels? 'Twas your first campaign as a mercenary, was it not, so you would have been . . . eighteen?"

"I was never that young." Hugh signaled a serving wench for a refill of his cup.

With a roll of his eyes, Raoul said, " 'Twas his first campaign, at any rate. He went to Ireland with a company of Scots and Northmen from the Hebrides to fight for a chieftain from Meath named Donaghy Nels. Something to do with Donaghy's kin having some claim on his holdings, wasn't it, Hugh? Or was it stolen cattle?"

Hugh shrugged as he brought his cup to his lips. "It's your story, Raoul. Tell it however you like."

"In any event," Raoul continued, seeming to warm to his recitation now that he had a rapt audience hanging on his every word, "after Hugh was finished winning back the land or cattle or whatever it was, Donaghy paid him and sent him on his way, but not before making him swear on the relic in the hilt of his sword that he would never take up arms against him, Donaghy, for the rest of his life. Because he knew, of course, that a mercenary will fight for whoever pays him the most, and he was always battling one of the other chieftains over something. What was it in that hilt, Hugh? A bit of the baby Jesus's manger hay, wasn't it?"

"Sounds good." Hugh swallowed down some more wine.

"After that," Raoul said, "Hugh headed north and helped take Finland for Eric of Sweden. Then it was . . . Kiev? Nay, the Elbe-Oder campaign, then Kiev, then the Holy Land, Egypt, Saxony . . . That's where I met him, about five or six years ago, fighting for Milan and the cities of North Italy. When we were done there, we heard Richard Strongbow was gathering mercenaries to go to Ireland on behalf of the king of Leinster, a fellow named Dermot Mac Murrough, who'd been exiled by the high-king, Rory O Connor of Connacht. Strongbow was offering more gold than either one of us had ever been paid, so we went."

Hugh was staring at nothing, Phillipa saw, his gaze unfocused and a little melancholy. She wondered what he was seeing.

"We reinstated Dermot," Raoul said, "which was no easy task, let me tell you. Rory had some of the most ferocious chieftains in Ireland fighting for him—they've got swarms of them there, each with his own little kingdom. We captured Waterford before moving on to Dublin. 'Twas during the fighting round Dublin that Hugh realized one of the war-bands allied with Rory O Connor was headed up by none other than Donaghy Nels. In other words, Hugh was wielding his sword against the very man he'd vowed never to take up arms against."

After a moment of dense silence, Turstin asked, "What did he do?"

Hugh spoke up before Raoul could. "I did what any man would do who knew all that really mattered was a purse full of gold." He met Phillipa's gaze fleetingly before tossing down some more wine. She had said that to him at the Red Bull the night they'd met in Oxford. Those had been her words, her smug, glibly self-righteous words of condemnation. She wished she could take them back.

"Hugh did what any soldier worth his salt would do when he was expected to stand and fight," Raoul said heatedly. "He stood and fought. He'd have you think 'twas an act of dishonor for him to have done battle with Donaghy Nels—"

"Once I knew he was the man I was fighting, it damn well was. But I was so used to taking the money and unsheathing my sword that . . ." Swearing under his breath, Hugh lifted his cup. "It's your story, Raoul. You tell it."

"It happened that some of us got taken hostage during the battle for Dublin, including me and Hugh. We weren't worried, because we knew we'd be exchanged for cattle if our captors won, and released outright if they lost. But when Donaghy heard that Hugh was one of the captured enemy, he came to the keep where we were being held and . . ." Raoul glanced at Hugh, who was gesturing for more wine.

"What happened?" Turstin asked.

"Donaghy said he wanted to make sure, since Hugh of Wexford didn't keep to his oaths, that he would never hold a sword again. He brought in a chopping block and an axe and told some of his men to hold Hugh down so he could hack off his thumb."

Raoul, who appeared suddenly sobered, paused to take a breath. Crickets sang in the grass as twilight descended; otherwise, not a sound could be heard.

Phillipa's gaze was riveted on Hugh, who was studying the wine in his cup as he slowly twirled it.

"Hugh said he didn't need to be held down—he'd betrayed his oath and 'twas only right that he pay the price of that. He placed his hand on the block as calmly as you please and nodded to Donaghy to go ahead and lower the axe. Didn't make a sound when the thumb came off, or even when they cauterized the wound with the red-hot tip of his own sword. Went a little pale, mind you."

There came a murmur or two of nervous laughter, some soft exclamations. Phillipa, still watching Hugh, felt a pressure in her chest so heavy it almost brought tears to her eyes.

Raoul shook his head pensively. " 'Twas the damnedest thing I ever saw in all my years of fighting. Hugh always said you could cast pain away if you really wanted to, that you could—how did he put it?—rise above it." Whacking Hugh on the back, he said, "I never believed it till I saw him lose that thumb."

"What an inspiring tale," Clare said softly, eyeing Hugh in a way that made Phillipa want to douse her in wine.

"We took Dublin and were released," Raoul said, "and that's the last I saw of Hugh. 'Twas two years ago. What have you been doing since then, my friend?"

Hugh smiled as if it were an effort, which it undoubtedly was. "Keeping a close guard on my other body parts."

Marguerite chuckled throatily. "Perhaps some of us could help you with that."

Over a smattering of snickers, Hugh said, "I shall bear that in mind."

"So, Sir Hugh," began Turstin as the servants brought out the next course—trenchers of crustless white bread heaped with mussel stew. "What brings you to Castle Halthorpe this fine evening?"

What, indeed, Phillipa wondered. Had he come just to check up on her meager progress, or was there another reason? A trencher of stew was placed in front of her. She pushed it away, too preoccupied by Hugh's presence here to eat.

"I've been visiting my sister," Hugh replied, refusing the trencher that a wench tried to set in front of him. "But after a fortnight without my lady wife, I found that I missed her company."

"How very touching," Clare said smoothly.

Aldous rested a hand on Phillipa's leg. She lifted it off.

Raoul's look of anticipation as he was served a trencher of stew turned forlorn when Isabelle had it taken away, whispering, "Onions and leeks . . . you know what they do to you."

Marguerite smiled at Hugh as she speared a mussel on the tip of her gold-handled eating knife, a diabolical little glint in her eyes. "Did you come here because you were worried that your bookish little wife might succumb to . . . temptations of the flesh, surrounded by reprobates like us?"

"Nay, I'm not much prone to jealousy." Hugh averted his gaze the way he always did when he lied. *Interesting . . .* With a careless shrug, he said, "In truth, 'twas simple restlessness that brought me here more than anything else."

"You're restless?" Marguerite brought the mussel to her mouth and touched the tip of her pointed tongue to it. "Methinks you've come to the right place. And I must say it's fortuitous that you're not the jealous type, because we tend to share rather freely at Halthorpe." She glanced at Aldous and Phillipa as she slid the mussel between her lips, seeming to swallow it whole. "In fact, one night last week, while the good deacon here was entertaining me in his bedchamber, who should walk in—without knocking, mind you—but Lady By-blow herself, looking like a Venice courtesan and smelling like the perfume district in Paris. If I told you what she was wearing—or rather, *not* wearing . . ."

Phillipa's gaze shot to Hugh. He abruptly looked away, his jaw clenching.

"Mother of God," Aldous muttered under his breath, lifting his cup to drain it.

" 'Twas obvious why she was there," Marguerite continued implacably. "But I couldn't very well just get up and walk away after I'd gotten Aldous all trussed up like a roasted swan."

Guffaws burst forth from the listeners, except for Aldous, who choked on his wine, Father Nicolas, who muttered disapprovingly and crossed himself, and the clearly mystified Orlando. Edmee, serving the table next to theirs, looked toward Phillipa in horrified puzzlement.

Phillipa closed her eyes briefly. *Just help me to get through this . . .*

As the hilarity was subsiding, Turstin said, "From the blackness of your expression, Sir Hugh, one might almost think you *were* subject to jealousy."

"One would be wrong," he said tightly. "If I seem out of sorts, 'tis simply because I'm fatigued from my journey."

" 'Tis a precept of *l'amour courtois*," said the troubadour as he tore off a bit of his trencher to dip in the stew, "that true love is impossible without jealousy. What think you of this theory, Sir Hugh?"

Clare and Marguerite awaited Hugh's answer with predatory smiles. He'd just maintained that Aldous's having presumably bedded his wife didn't make him jealous. If he were to defend the principles of courtly love just to avoid conflict, it would be tantamount to admitting that he felt no love for her.

"To be perfectly honest," he said, "I'm not really very keen on *l'amour courtois*. This whole notion of a spiritual dimension to love strikes me as wishful thinking, at best. The fiction of romantic love is naught but the same fleshly hunger even the dumbest beast feels."

"Mm . . ." Marguerite purred, shivering delicately. "Fleshly hunger . . ."

So, thought Phillipa. Hugh had opted for the truth, but the outcome was the same, a public admission that he felt nothing for her—aside, perhaps, for a measure of animal lust. But in the wake of their rapturous love-making, Phillipa knew that her own hunger for Hugh was as much of the spirit as of the flesh.

Turstin chuckled. "So you're immune to love regardless of whether it can exist without jealousy."

"That must be how you managed to escape its civilizing influence," Clare observed as she licked the broth from the stew off her fingertips.

"You realize," Turstin said around a mouthful of broth-soaked bread, "that *l'amour courtois* isn't simply an idle fancy dreamed up by the ladies of the Poitiers court. 'Twas derived from the romantic writings of a man named Ovid, who was a great Roman poet from the first century before the birth of—"

"I know who Ovid was," Hugh said evenly. "Is it his *Ars Amatoria* you're referring to, or the *Remedia Amoris*?"

Phillipa gaped at Hugh, along with Turstin.

"Er . . . the *Ars Amatoria,*" said Turstin, regarding Hugh with seemingly newfound esteem.

"Ah, yes." Hugh nodded as he raised his cup. "His treatise on the art of loving. Have you read it?"

"Of course," Turstin said irately, adding a bit more sheepishly, "in part."

"A more comprehensive reading," Hugh said, "would reveal that the whole thing is an elaborate jest, meant to ridicule illicit love affairs by setting forth the rules of seduction in a tone of the utmost gravity. But the gravity is all pretense, as are the rules. 'Twas meant to be funny, for pity's sake. Ovid would howl with laughter if he knew it had been adopted as the basis of a whole new philosophy of romance."

In the silence that followed this impromptu dissertation, Phillipa felt her face heat slowly from within. Good Lord, all this time she'd assumed he couldn't even read . . .

"You must excuse my surprise at your scholarship," said Turstin. " 'Twas my understanding that knights are trained in the arts of war and little else."

"That's true for the most part," Hugh replied, "but my sire felt that the consummate knight's mind should be as finely honed as his sword. From when I was four till I was dubbed at eighteen, he hired a series of learned clerics from Paris and Oxford to teach me at night after my military training was done."

"At night?" Raoul asked.

Hugh nodded. "Till the chapel bell rang matins."

"Matins." Raoul shook his head in disbelief. "And you were up before dawn for your training, if your master at arms was anything like the rest of them. That didn't allow a great deal of time for sleep."

Aldous, evidently recovered from Marguerite's ribald little anecdote, snorted as he picked among the mussels on his trencher with his eating knife. "From what I know of William of Wexford, I'm surprised he allowed any."

"William of Wexford?" Clare sat forward abruptly, showing more animation than Phillipa had ever seen her display. "You're William of Wexford's son?"

"I am."

She smiled almost softly. "Lord William is a remarkable man. If it was his intent to mold you in his own image, you couldn't have had a better exemplar. No wonder you're so"—her tone turned coquettish—"exceptional, in so many ways."

"Not so exceptional," Marguerite ventured, "that a woman's influence might not do you some good. I'm familiar with Ovid, too. That, and my complete moral dissolution are what came of a grueling convent education. I can't argue with your interpretation of the *Ars Amatoria,* but I can tell you that in Ovid's romantic vision, as in that of most men, 'tis the man who schemes and seduces, and the woman who submits."

It rankled Phillipa, for some reason, to discover that the loathsome, wanton Marguerite du Roche was not only well read, but articulate about what she knew.

"In the world of *l'amour courtois,*" Marguerite continued, "woman is more than merely a vessel for a man's lust—or, as the Church would have it, the Devil's handmaiden." She smirked in the direction of Father Nicolas, who was known for his low opinion of the fair sex. "At Poitiers, men have been lured away from their hunting and whoring and taught to embrace a more refined and elegant and, yes, feminine form of society. A better form, where women are revered, adulated."

"And presumably obeyed," Hugh said.

Marguerite smiled a secret sort of smile and lifted her shoulders. "Obedience is a natural consequence of reverence."

"Can there not be a middle ground," Hugh asked, "with both parties equal—at least in matters of the heart?"

"Matters of the heart?" Turstin chortled. "You can't mean 'the fiction of romantic love.'" There was some appreciative laughter.

"Matters of the flesh, then," Hugh amended. "Surely men and women can be on an equal footing in bed."

"Someone must take the whip hand." Marguerite stabbed another mussel. "Why not the woman?"

Aldous knocked over his cup, soaking his trencher with wine and spilling it in a crimson flood across the table. "Sorry . . . sorry," he muttered, dabbing at it with his napkin. In a sudden outburst, he roared at the closest maidservant, who happened to be Edmee, "What are you waiting for? Come over here and clean up this bloody mess!"

Edmee scurried to do as she was told. Phillipa directed a sympathetic look at her; she managed a tentative smile.

"I still think Ovid had a great deal to say that's of worth," said Turstin. "Abbé Bernard and Peter Abelard both quoted from the *Ars Amatoria* in their teachings."

"Abelard was a brilliant man," Hugh said, "but he was just a man. He admitted himself in his *Historica Calamitatum* that he'd originally set out simply to seduce Héloïse, employing guile and subterfuge of the type Ovid had described. This leads me to think his reading of the *Ars Amatoria* might have lacked the academic detachment required for a truly critical analysis. And as for Bernard . . ."

Groaning inwardly, Phillipa closed her eyes again, remembering her self-important little lecture in the orchard of Eastingham that evening . . . *I don't suppose you've heard of a woman named Héloïse. She became notorious some fifty years ago in Paris for her love affair with a great philosopher and teacher named Peter Abelard . . .*

Phillipa had been trying to explain her interest in courtly love; Hugh must have thought her utterly puerile—and not just because she had assumed complete ignorance on his part. For Phillipa knew now that romantic love as it was envisioned at Poitiers—and Halthorpe—had nothing in common with the intense and abiding passion shared by Abelard and Héloïse.

She had wanted to understand that all-consuming passion. Now, at last, she did understand it, because, God help her, she felt it herself—for Hugh.

But there was a difference. Abelard had loved Héloïse back. The ardor that had burned in the great woman's heart was reciprocated in full measure, yet still it had destroyed her. How much more damage could Phillipa's love for Hugh unleash, given that his interest in her didn't surpass the realm of "fleshly hunger"? The lovemaking that had so transported her had been a mere diversion for him; as heartbreakingly tender and passionate as he'd been, she was, in the final analysis, just another in a series of women who had come apart in the arms of Hugh of Wexford.

The problem did not exist, Uncle Lotulf used to say, that could not be dissected and dealt with, if only one analyzed it logically without surrendering to murky emotion. Phillipa's problem was that her love for Hugh, if she indulged it, could tear her apart. The logical solution: Don't indulge it. Fight it. Sweep it aside.

But how to lessen the pain, how to make it bearable? By remembering, of course, that the object of her ardor did not care for her as she cared for him. Hugh of Wexford was a man with some fine qualities, or else she would not have lost her heart to him as she had, but he was also a man who had passed her off to another man as one would pass off a choice horse or hunting dog.

That he had been able to do that, even at Sir Richard's behest, stung every time she thought about it. Whether it was easy or hard for him mattered not; he could have changed his mind, asked her not to go, but he didn't. She should savor the pain that had caused her, nourish it within her until it drove out her ruinous love for him.

And until her unruly feelings diminished, she must keep them to herself. Sharing them with a man who didn't return them would only worsen the pain by coupling it with humiliation.

Let him think you are *sleeping with Aldous, and that it matters naught to you, or he'll know how much you care.*

What if he wanted to make love again? Much as the admission shamed her, she ached to feel his arms around her once more, to yield to the sweet invasion of her body by his, to experience that shuddering ecstasy she'd never even known existed. But if her intent was to steal her heart back from him, should she continue to give him her body? *Could* she, without falling even more deeply under his spell?

"Is something wrong?"

She opened her eyes to find Aldous regarding her with an expression of unctuous sincerity.

"Nay, nothing, I'm just . . . nothing's wrong."

Leaning in close, Aldous said, "It's infuriating to have that bastard show up uninvited like this, and just when I thought . . . perhaps you were ready to forgive me and . . ."

"I'd planned on coming to you tonight," she said, hoping she sounded convincing.

"Did you? Jesu, this is driving me mad! Come to me anyway."

"I can't, Aldous. Not while he's sharing my bed."

"He doesn't care, he said so himself."

From the corner of her eye, she saw Hugh watching them over the rim of his cup, looking as if he cared very much, indeed. But by what right did he feel possessive of her, after handing her over to Aldous?

"I still can't do it. I'm sorry."

"Do you think you could talk him into going back to his sister's house?"

"I'll try," she lied.

"Try hard, my love. Remember, you're the one—the only one."

When he reached for her hand, she let him take it.

Chapter 15

Hugh gritted his teeth when he noticed Lady Clare strolling toward him out of the darkness. He shouldn't have let himself get so sotted; enacting his role in this strange little drama was challenging enough sober.

As the final courses of supper were being served—to the others, for Hugh had no stomach for food tonight—Halthorpe's villeins had built an enormous Midsummer's Eve bonfire in the middle of the outer bailey. Breaking out reed flutes and cowbells, they had danced around it in holiday celebration as Lady Clare's guests, including Phillipa and Aldous, gathered to clap and sing—except for Hugh, who sat by himself at the table, watching from a distance as he emptied a jug of wine and started in on another.

A while ago, the music had taken on a more measured, haunting cadence, and Marguerite du Roche had stepped into the circle of onlookers, moving in a slow, sinuous, overtly seductive manner that had prompted the few remaining villeins to fall away. She had been performing this trancelike dance since. She swiveled her hips, caressed her breasts, whipped her hair like a fiery banner. In a trailing silken gown the color of fresh rust, with flames roaring behind her, her slit-eyed gaze lighting on one man after another, she might have been a succubus from the netherworld out to seduce their very souls.

"Marguerite's like that in the bedchamber, as well," Clare observed as she sat next to Hugh on the bench, her keys rattling, her right side snugged up against him although she was facing the other way; a kestrel now clung to her gloved left fist. "Completely loses herself in sensual abandonment."

Hugh did not bother asking her how she knew this.

Leaning back against the table, her arms outstretched on it, Clare smiled at him the way whores did, the sexual promise crudely obvious. She was one of those women who strikes you as dramatically beautiful until you get close and realize that the hair is a bit too flatly black, the skin too marble-white—save for a bright pink smudge on each cheek. Phillipa, who'd been born with the coloring Clare emulated through artifice, had skin as translucent as oiled parchment, revealing the occasional little blue vein beneath; Hugh loved making her blush and watching hot color bloom within her cheeks.

Right now, Phillipa was standing with her back to him, hand-in-hand with Aldous as they watched Marguerite dance. In that lovely ivory tunic that bared her shoulders, her hair in a pearl-wrapped chignon, she was as angelic a vision as Marguerite was demonic.

Clare said, "Father and I used to fly the hawks with your sire—did you know that?"

"Aldous told me," Hugh said thickly. Damn, but he wished he hadn't drunk so much.

"I knew Lord William had a son two or three years younger than me, but you never came hawking with us."

"My father didn't permit any activities that would take time away from my training."

Her smile deepened. "We were almost betrothed, you and I."

God's bones. The thought of being bound in matrimony to this woman was too grotesque to contemplate.

"Father tried to arrange it," she said, "but Lord William refused."

"Because he thought you were too old for me?" Hugh lifted his cup to his mouth.

She shook her head. "Probably because he was sleeping with me."

Hugh managed not to pass the wine through his nose.

"I was thirteen when he took my maidenhead," she said conversationally. "He was just a little older than you are now, and the handsomest, most commanding man I'd ever known. And perceptive—he'd noticed me mooning over him. One morning while we were hawking, he got me away from the others on some pretext and took me into the woods and laid his mantle on the ground. I asked him what he was doing. He said he was tired and needed to lie down, and asked if I wasn't tired, as well. 'Twas a warm day, so he took off his tunic and said perhaps I would be more comfortable without my—"

"Yes, I get the idea," Hugh ground out, feeling an unexpected burst of sympathy for her—or rather, for the young girl whose childish infatuation his father had so thoughtlessly exploited. This was the same man who used to lecture Hugh so ceaselessly on matters of chivalry and honor. He hadn't thought his loathing for his sire could deepen any further; he'd been wrong.

"I've never met a man like him since," Clare said wistfully. "Although I must say, you come close. I think I remember you from Poitiers." An impish spark lit her eyes as she raised his cup to her lips and took a sip. "Didn't you tup me in the arse one night while I took Roger de la Foret in my mouth?"

Hugh suddenly wished he were a good deal drunker. "I don't believe so."

"Aye, 'twas in the barn," she continued blithely. "You brought in one of the stablehands then—that strapping brute with red hair, remember? You two cheered him on while he had a go at me."

"I think I would recall such a . . . romantic interlude."

"You know, I think you're right. I'm getting you mixed up with Roger's cousin, Guillaume—he was fair-haired, like you. Men do tend to merge together in one's memory."

Hugh could recall every woman he'd ever tupped, down to the smallest detail. "I kept pretty much to myself during my stay at Poitiers," he said.

"Did you?" A spark of recognition lit her eyes. "Ah! Now I remember you. Yes, of course. You caught my eye because you were so handsome, but there was a spectral quality to you—always appearing and disappearing in the shadows . . . watching, listening, but never very much a part of things. You didn't seem to have any interest in the ladies of the court—although I did hear two of the kitchen wenches whispering about you once when they didn't know I was behind them."

Ah, yes, thought Hugh. *Those pretty little kitchen wenches.*

Clare smiled. "I seem to recall them comparing you to a stallion." Before Hugh realized what she was doing, she'd snaked one hand beneath his leathern tunic and seized him through his drawers. "Ah, yes, that must have been you," she said, fondling him purposefully—as if he could ever rouse to the likes of her. "If you can slip away from that prissy little wife of yours tonight, why don't you join me in my chamber? Marguerite will be there, too."

"Perhaps some other time." He pried her hand off his cock, which she was wringing like a washrag. Best not to reject her outright; if she felt spurned, she might turn him away from Halthorpe, and Phillipa along with him. "I'm afraid I've drunk far more wine tonight than I should have. Bewitching though you both are, I fear I would be unequal to the challenge."

This was not entirely true, of course, Hugh having never been too drunk to perform if the wench was inspiring enough. But he knew enough about women to steer well clear of both Clare and Marguerite even if he weren't still firmly in Phillipa's thrall. Clare, although she fancied herself quite the siren, was far too hard and opaque to be alluring—not to mention that her oily-sweet perfume made his nostrils flare. And as for Marguerite, Hugh had learned long ago to avoid the type of bed sport from which one might come away clawed.

"I hope you're not refusing me out of misguided devotion to your lady wife," Clare said as she caressed the fidgety kestrel. "You do know how she's been carrying on with my brother. I mean, look at them."

Hugh did, and saw Aldous leaning down to whisper in Phillipa's ear, one arm curling possessively around her waist.

"We're neither of us hamstrung by archaic notions of fidelity," he said, his hand twitching with the urge to unsheathe his *jambiya*.

"Then, perhaps I can talk you into going hawking with me tomorrow. I've got a huge, particularly vicious gyrfalcon I'll bet you could handle just fine. What say you?" She smiled. "You can bring a mantle in case we get tired and need to lie down."

"It sounds . . ." *Intolerable*. "Enchanting. Unfortunately, one needs a functioning right hand for falconry." The gauntlets were all made for the left hand, the right being employed for a multitude of tasks that required a thumb. Thank the saints.

"What a pity," Clare said with a pout. "Outdoor sport can be so stimulating." Rising from the bench, she bent to whisper in his ear, "Never fear—I'll get my talons in you sooner or later." She turned and sauntered away, the absurdly long train of her emerald silk gown dragging through the grass like a lizard's tail. "Edmee," she shouted to the sturdily built wench passing by with an armload of wine jugs, "come get me ready for bed."

Hugh gulped down the remainder of his wine, eyeing Phillipa and Aldous and trying not to think of him in bed with her, on top of her . . .

Did she leave her shift on with him, or had he talked her out of it? Did she undress while he watched? Did he get to hold her naked in his arms? Did she moan when he was inside her?

"Christ." The thought of her going willingly to Aldous's bed after that night with him was agonizing. A feverish tide of anger rose within him, anger both at himself, for having let her do this, and at her, for not puzzling a way out of it. She was clever enough; she could have thought of something.

She'd wanted *to use her wits instead of her body. You told her it wouldn't work.*

Hugh scrubbed his hands over his face, trying to wade through his hazy, wine-induced rage toward rational thought. He reminded himself that he had no claim on her. Phillipa had only asked Hugh to bed her so that Aldous wouldn't be the first. She had made herself clear enough that night in Southwark when she'd followed him into the stable, telling him that her virtue had become a burden to her but that he, Hugh, was the last man she would lose her heart to.

It was a good thing she was sleeping with Aldous, if only for the sake of the mission, and a *damned* good thing she didn't fancy herself in love with Hugh, because he didn't need that kind of trouble on top of his own ungovernable feelings.

Given a bit of encouragement, he was all too afraid he could imagine those feelings to be something more than they were and end up playing the deferential husband for the rest of his life instead of just for a few weeks. He would then be tied to someone else for eternity, fettered by her needs and expectations, something he'd vowed to himself when he broke free of his father's dominion seventeen years ago would never happen to him. He'd resolved with the utmost conviction to make his way alone, unbridled forever by the demands of overlord, sire, wife, or family. He would go where he pleased, fighting for the highest bidder and partaking of his wenches and his wine and his dice as he saw fit, with no one to rein him in or tie him down, no one to flog the spirit out of him or tame his soul, until the day he passed from this earth.

True love tends to tame the most feral of men, Turstin de Ver had said of Raoul, once a man's man and a damned good soldier and now his wife's groveling little lap dog. If Turstin was right, and Hugh was immune to love, then he should be safe from any risk of suffering the same fate.

He didn't feel safe.

Looking up, he saw Phillipa walking toward him, ghostly and radiant against the curtain of leaping flames. Behind her, Aldous looked away from Marguerite's performance to follow her with his eyes, scowling. Pausing on the other side of the table, she said, "Hello, Hugh." They hadn't spoke privily since he'd arrived.

"Phillipa."

Her expression guarded, she said, "It's gotten late. I'll be going to bed now."

Hugh cocked his head toward Aldous. "With him, or . . ."

"N-nay, in my own chamber—our chamber now, I suppose. When you're ready, it's at the very end of the east wing, on the ground floor."

"I'll fetch my things and be along shortly."

"Very well."

After collecting his satchel and saddlebags from the stable, Hugh made his way unsteadily—*damn, but I wish I hadn't drunk so much*—across the drawbridge to the inner bailey. His drinking, normally fairly steady, had escalated dramatically during his two-week sojourn to Rouen for his meeting with King Henry—during which he had, indeed, been offered the sheriffship of London, which he'd declined. The king had been dismayed by this turn of events, and asked Hugh to reconsider, but Hugh had been too haunted by thoughts of Phillipa in Aldous's bed to concentrate on much else. He'd striven to drown his misery in wine, which had succeeded only in making him grow more choleric day by day, as if his nerves could not stop twitching.

It was with some effort that he negotiated his way through the labyrinthine castle to the crumbling old east wing and down the dank corridor that ran the length of it to the door at the end. He almost knocked, as had been his habit in Southwark, but on an impulse driven by his smoldering frustration, he merely yanked the door open and walked in.

Phillipa looked up sharply from where she sat on the edge of a fur-draped, uncurtained bed, still in her ivory tunic, unwrapping the rope of pearls from around the hair coiled at her nape. "Hugh."

With a curt nod, he dumped his baggage into the rushes that blanketed the floor of this surprisingly modest and ill-furnished little room. "Why did you end up in this part of the castle? Are any of the other guests housed down here?"

She hesitated, glancing away as she freed the pearls from her hair and laid them on the bed next to her. "Just Aldous. He's got the chamber next door."

Of course. With a bitter little exhalation, Hugh raked a hand through his hair. "You needn't stay here on my account. I mean, I assume you've been sleeping in his bed—this one is just barely big enough for—"

"Are you drunk?"

"Not nearly drunk enough."

"Given the circumstances," she said as she slid silver hairpins out of her chignon and set them aside, "don't you think you should try to keep your wits about you?"

"Given the circumstances," he snarled as he strode toward her, "I think I should drink myself into a blind fucking stupor. Just because you find this situation easy to stomach doesn't mean I do."

"You're wrong, Hugh." She pulled out the last pin; her hair uncoiled in a serpentine black river down her back.

"Am I?" He loomed over her, fists quivering. *Don't do this. Deal with it, rise above it.* But then he pictured her, writhing and crying out as Aldous Ewing rutted away on top of her, and the pain of it boiled red-hot in his veins. "You seem to have fallen rather smoothly into the role of Aldous Ewing's whore."

Her eyes darkened with outrage. "Isn't that what you wanted?" she demanded in a voice that quivered with anger. "Isn't that why you sent me here?"

"Christ!" Hugh wheeled around and paced away, grinding his fists against his temples. She would drive him mad if he let her.

"Hugh," she said quietly. He heard the soft whisper of her damask gown and knew that she was standing. "I . . ." She sighed. " 'Tisn't as if I have any feelings for Aldous."

With a bitter little chuckle, he turned back to face her. "Oh, I don't flatter myself that you need to have feelings for a man to spread your legs for him."

Her gentleness turned to ire. "Perhaps I've simply come to share your views about sex—that it's naught but animal gratification. You've made it clear enough you don't attach any emotions to the act—why should I?"

"You're already thinking like a whore," he ground out. "That being the case, you won't mind servicing me now, I trust."

She hitched in an indignant little breath as he unbuckled his belt and flung it off. "I most certainly would!"

"Be a sport." He stalked toward her, whipping his leathern tunic over his head. "I've been a fortnight without having it off. I could use a quick tumble."

Turning her back to him, she fetched her pearls and hairpins off the bed. "I'm going to find someplace else to sleep."

He seized her bare shoulders from behind. "I'll be damned if I'm going to let you spend tonight in his bed."

"I didn't mean his—" Her words ended with a gasp as Hugh wrapped his arms around her, grabbing a breast with one hand while the other gathered up the skirt of her tunic. The pearls and pins fell into the rushes.

"I don't care what you do tomorrow night," he said gruffly, although it was a lie, "or any night thereafter, but tonight you're mine. You'll stay in this bed if I have to chain you to it."

"Hugh—" Her gasp was more like a whimper as he slid a finger into her snug little sex. She tightened reflexively, sending heat pumping into his groin.

"Do you feel this?" He rubbed himself against her from behind as he thrust his finger in and out of her, deep, deeper . . . "Every night I lie awake like this, remembering how it felt to be inside you, how wild you

went at the end, how it drove me right to the edge—
and wondering if I'll ever see you like that again, if I'll
ever make it happen again. You've wondered the same
thing. You've wanted this, too, haven't you?"

"I wish I hadn't."

Hugh yanked on the wide, scooping neckline of her
tunic and the kirtle beneath, baring one breast, which
he kneaded as he caressed her intimately. "Does he
touch you like this? Do you come with him?"

"N-nay . . . he doesn't . . . we don't . . ."

"That's something, anyway." He squeezed her nipple
rhythmically, drawing a tremulous little gasp from her
as it stiffened. "Do you have any idea what torture it is
to know that you share his bed, that he gets to lie with
you night after night?"

"Hugh . . ."

"God, Phillipa . . . I can't bear this." If only he didn't
feel this mad, unrelenting need for her. If only he could
stop caring. If only he could stop thinking about her for
one bloody minute out of the day . . .

She breathed his name on a trembling moan. He
moaned, too, when he felt her grow wet. She was as
breathless as he was, he realized, her body swaying lan-
guorously, her head falling back against his chest.

Reaching between them, he untied his drawers. She
tried to turn around, thinking no doubt that he meant
to lay her on the bed, but he took her by the shoulders
and made her face the bed again. "Kneel." Pushing her
onto her knees in the rushes, he guided her head down
so that her cheek rested on the rough fur throw covering
the bed. Her hair had fallen across her face; he left it
there.

Shaken by the tumult of unwanted feelings roiling inside him, the last thing he wanted was to look upon her
face as he took her, to gaze into those big, liquid brown
eyes and feel his heart catch tight in his chest. Let this
be a hard, mindless fuck to drive the demons out of his
soul, he thought as he flipped her skirt up and seized

her hips. Let this be about bodies, about coming. Let this be about anything but love.

He rammed into her with a growl of effort. *Still so tight, so excruciatingly tight . . .*

She groaned hoarsely, clutching handfuls of fur. "Oh, God, Hugh . . ."

He reached around her as he pounded into her, stroking her where they were joined, wanting her to come, needing to claim her in a way that *he* hadn't, to make her surrender herself in a tempest of sensation.

The bed ropes groaned with each savage thrust, the straw in the mattress crushing faster, faster . . . Her entire body went rigid; she tore the fur off the bed, crying out rawly as her climax overtook her.

Hugh arched over her, erupting with shocking suddenness as she shuddered beneath him, around him. He heard himself shout as his pleasure was wrenched from him. It crashed through him in wave after heartstopping wave, until he collapsed spent and trembling on top of her, murmuring her name over and over again.

She was shaking, he realized, with her face buried in the bunched-up fur, which she still clutched tightly in her fists.

"Phillipa?" he whispered unsteadily.

Her response was so muffled that he couldn't make it out, but it had a damp, choked sound to it.

Jesu. He shouldn't have done this, not . . . not like this. He'd never even treated a whore this way. This had been a barbarous act, a form of retribution. He hadn't even had the presence of mind to withdraw, something he never failed to do.

And now look at her, bent over this bed, weeping silently in the wake of her ravishment.

With a muttered curse, he pulled out of her. She flinched and cried out in obvious pain.

"Phillipa?"

Shoving her skirt back down, she braced her hands on the bed as if to rise, but he caught her around the waist. "Phillipa, did I hurt you?"

She sank into the rushes and curled up with her hair cloaking her like a mantle, strands of it sticking to her wet face. She was shivering. "You said the . . . the second time it wouldn't—" Her voice caught. "It wouldn't hurt so much."

Second time? Feeling suddenly all too sober, he stared at her in incomprehension. "But . . . you and Aldous . . ."

She shook her head, tears trickling down her cheeks. "Never. I couldn't. Not after . . ." She lowered her face to her updrawn knees. "Not after you and I . . ." A little sob rose in her throat. "I couldn't."

"Oh, God, Phillipa." It *had* meant something to her, she *had* cared. He gathered her in his arms, pulled her onto his lap, buried his face in her hair. "Oh, God. I'm sorry. I'm sorry. Did I hurt you badly? Are you all—"

"I'm all right. I'm fine. Just . . ." She shook her head.

Just shaken that he would treat her so shabbily. He cupped her head to his chest. "Phillipa, how did you manage . . . I mean, Aldous brought you here to . . ."

"Lies, trickery . . . I've been stalling him, but he still thinks I meant to . . . to sleep with him." She rubbed at her tears as fresh ones welled in her eyes. "I knew I couldn't, though—not after being with you. 'Twas . . . so . . ."

So perfect. Sweet and fiery and passionate and perfect—an exquisite memory that he'd tainted forever by using her so ill tonight. "I shouldn't have done this."

In a voice hoarse with tears, she said, "I shouldn't have wanted you to."

Hugh dabbed at her tears with the hem of his shirt as she wept. His throat tightened as if it were being squeezed in a fist. *Rise above it.* He hadn't shed tears since his first flogging at the age of seven; to do so now would just make this situation that much more wretched.

Softly, haltingly, she said, "I told you once that I would never lose my heart to you. I was wrong."

Oh, God. He closed his eyes and held her tight, struggling against the urge to blurt out what was in his own heart. All that he was, all that he ever wanted to be, depended on his being alone, apart . . . free. He'd spent seventeen years undoing the damage wrought by the first eighteen, molding himself into *his* image of who he wanted to be—a man who wrote his own rules and answered to nobody but himself, a man who would be destroyed by an attachment to anyone.

Even Phillipa.

"I wasn't going to tell you how I felt," she said. "I wanted to deny it, to sweep it aside—but it's no good. I can't fight it."

"Perhaps," he said gently, "you should try."

Phillipa gazed morosely across the room. "You don't feel it. I was hoping perhaps . . ." She drew in a shuddery breath. "But I can't fault you. You never led me to think you really cared."

"You shouldn't want me to." He threaded her hair off her face. "What about Héloïse?"

"I was wrong to let what happened to her fill me with fear. I'm not Héloïse." Phillipa looked up at him with her heartbreakingly tearstained face. "And you're not Abelard. It needn't destroy me just because I feel—"

"But it would," Hugh said, knowing that it was he who was being called on to be strong, he who must transcend his unruly desires and put a stop to this before it was too late. He could do it. He'd been trained since infancy to seal himself off to his feelings, and especially to pain. It was what he knew; he was good at it. He would draw on that strength now, for both of them. " 'Twould destroy me, too," he added, "if I . . ." *If I gave in to my feelings for you, if I admitted what you meant to me.* "If I felt the same thing."

Phillipa closed her eyes, her chin quivering. She nodded.

Hugh kissed her hair. " 'Twould be best if we had never . . ." His gaze took in her rumpled tunic, the bed with its fur throws askew. "This has made things . . . more complicated between us." Loathing himself for laying this all at her feet, but knowing it was for the best, he said, "It's made you imagine more between us than really exists."

Meeting his gaze, she asked quietly, "Is it really only my imagination, Hugh?"

He looked away abruptly, hearing Lord Richard's voice. *Looking elsewhere will give you away every time.* "I'm afraid so. 'Tis only natural, of course, for a woman to indulge in such fancies about the first man she lies with. Over time, the feelings will diminish and you'll see them for what they are. In the meantime, because things have gotten so out of hand . . ." He rubbed the back of his neck, hating this. " 'Tis best, I think, if we don't sleep together."

Her brows knitted, carving that inexplicably beguiling little furrow between them. "But there's only the one bed. Won't they be suspicious if we ask for another?"

He gritted his teeth. "Perhaps you should just sleep in Aldous's bed from now on. This castle is like a brothel—no one will look askance."

"But Aldous and I . . . we don't—"

"You should," he managed. "For the good of the mission."

She pushed away from him, her expression grim. "I already told him I wouldn't share his bed while you're here."

Stealing himself, Hugh said, "Then I'll leave on the morrow."

"No!" She shook her head frantically. "No, Hugh. I told him . . . he thinks . . . if you leave, I'll *have* to sleep with him. Please, Hugh, I can't." Fresh tears swam in her eyes. "I can't!"

"Even for the good of the mission?"

"That's just it!" she said, reminding him once again of a small, cornered creature drawing upon its wits to extract itself from danger. "It's for the good of the mission that you must stay here. I need you to help in the investigation. I've made very little progress on my own."

"Only because you won't bed Aldous. If you were his mistress, he'd tell you everything you wanted to know."

"There are other ways. Please, Hugh," she implored, grasping his shirt. "I can't . . . I can't be with him like that. I can't."

Hugh wiped her tears away, gathered her in his arms. "All right," he said, "I'll stay."

She sagged against him in relief.

"I'll sleep on the floor," he said.

"Nonsense. You'll sleep in the bed, with me." She glanced up at him, her expression lightening. "Are you afraid I'll ravish you in the middle of the night?"

He smiled at the notion of guileless little Phillipa de Paris turning sexually aggressive. It felt good to smile, after what had just transpired between them. "Phillipa, I *am* sorry for . . . using you as I did just now. Terribly sorry. You don't deserve such treatment."

"You were provoked."

"I was a monster. Tell me how to make it up to you."

She sighed and settled against him. "You can make it up to me by forgetting it happened. If we're not to . . . be together like that anymore, if we're not to make love, then I want to remember how it was in Southwark, that first time."

He nodded, kissed her head, held her close. "So do I."

"You're not a monster," she said softly. "You're a good man making do under trying circumstances. Knowing you has been . . ." She shook her head against his chest. "It's opened up a whole new world, it's changed me."

"It's changed me, too."

"I don't want to squander this . . . connection between us, just because . . . just because we can't be lovers. I haven't had very many friends in my life. Except for Ada, I haven't had anyone who was truly a friend of my heart, someone I could let down my guard with, and talk to, and . . ."

"If you'd let me be your friend—a real friend—after everything that's happened between us, I would be immeasurably grateful. 'Twould mean more to me than you can imagine."

She looked up at him and smiled a watery little smile. "Let's be friends, then."

He kissed her forehead, held her tight. "Friends."

Chapter 16

Hugh drifted out of another dream about Phillipa to feel her fingers, cool and soft, stroking his face. "Hugh . . ."

"Mmm . . ." Covering her hand with his, he rubbed his beard-roughened jaw against her palm. Half-asleep, he could still see her, sitting up in bed and pulling her shift over her head, the moonlight kissing her naked flesh . . .

With wakefulness stealing upon him, he knew it was just a dream—that's what came of sharing this bed with her every night as "friends"—but the arousal coursing through him was very real.

"Hugh, wake up."

He slitted his eyes open, expecting to find the room awash in morning sunlight, only to discover that it was still nighttime. The chamber was dark, save for a candle guttering on the little writing table next to the bed. Phillipa, in her voluminous linen sleeping shift, sat cross-legged on the bed next to him holding a sheaf of parchment pages with ink-stained fingers.

"I've done it," she said, spreading the pages out on her lap.

He rubbed his eyes. "What have you done, love?"

She glanced up from the pages, then quickly down again. The endearment had slipped out only because he was bleary from having just awakened. While he was pondering whether to explain that, she said, "I've deciphered the code."

He stared at her. "You haven't."

She smiled winsomely. "You know how I am about challenges."

During the four days he'd been at Halthorpe, Hugh and Phillipa had explored the castle and questioned its residents, with meager results—until this afternoon, when Phillipa had asked Clare to take her and Aldous hawking in order to get them out of the way while Hugh searched their bedchambers. Aldous now slept in a richly appointed chamber above the great hall, where he'd re-located when it became clear that he had no chance of bedding Phillipa while Hugh was at Halthorpe. Hugh found nothing of interest there save a book identified on its tooled-leather cover as *Prayers for the Canonical Hours,* but which actually contained a collection of grossly obscene verses and pictures.

He had better luck in Clare's room, where he pulled aside a tapestry to find an almost invisible gap between two stones in the wall. Tucked into it, folded up small, was a sheet of thin, velvety-soft calf parchment heavily inked in Hebrew, which was a language Hugh could read passably well, along with Latin, French, and Greek. But when he tried to read it, he realized that it was gibberish.

Increasingly, sensitive communiqués were being trans-lated into code; obviously this was just such an encrypted message. Hugh painstakingly re-searched Clare's and Al-dous's chambers for the key with which to decipher this code—a table or grid of some sort—but with no success. Clare had probably hidden it somewhere else, as a safe-guard. Given the size and complexity of this castle, Hugh despaired of ever finding it. Nevertheless, he penned a duplicate and returned the original to its hiding place.

It wasn't until they were ready to retire for the night that Hugh had the chance to show the document to Phil-lipa, who maintained that, given enough time, she could unravel the code—even though she didn't know Hebrew, a gap in her scholarship that Hugh was ashamed to find immensely pleasing. At her request, Hugh wrote out the twenty-six letters of the Hebrew alphabet before talking her into coming to bed so that she could tackle the job with a fresh mind on the morrow—although he cautioned her against getting her hopes up. Codes could be devilishly tricky to crack, he told her; he'd long ago given up trying. There was a lay brother at Bermondsey Abbey who used to decipher intercepted dispatches for Lord Richard—curious, since the fellow was otherwise so feebleminded that he could barely speak or feed himself—but he died last year of a stomach ailment.

Phillipa *had* come to bed with him, but apparently she had arisen during the night to work on untangling the code.

"What time is it?" Hugh asked around a yawn.

"Well past matins. Look!" she said excitedly, holding up a sheet of parchment inked in her elegantly tidy hand.

"What's that?" He punched up the pillow under his head.

"The document you found, decoded into Latin."

"You mean you really did it? How on earth . . ."

" 'Twasn't that hard," she said. "Just time-consuming."

"But you don't even know Hebrew!"

"I didn't need to know the language, just the alphabet. You see, I assumed that the Hebrew letters were just symbols for Latin or French letters—probably Latin, since it's mostly clerics who devise these codes." She was speaking very rapidly, and with a childlike zeal that he found greatly endearing. "Any sort of symbol might have been chosen to stand in for the plaintext."

"Plaintext?"

"That's the actual message, the words that are being encoded. The code needn't have been in Hebrew letters—in fact, it's usually Latin. But to make it more difficult to decode, Greek letters are sometimes used, or numbers, or signs of the zodiac . . . but the person who encrypted this probably wanted it to look like an ordinary letter written in Hebrew. Not that Hebrew is often used for correspondence, but that would be just the point, wouldn't it? The casual observer might recognize the language, so it would look like a real letter, but most people, even learned people, can't read Hebrew. With the occasional remarkable exception."

Phillipa punctuated that compliment by reaching out to touch his arm through the rolled-up sleeve of his shirt, just briefly, before continuing with her discourse. She went on to discuss the method by which she had puzzled out this code, which involved constructing "frequency tables" of the most common Latin letters and arrangements of letters and using them to detect patterns in the cipher, from which she picked out words by trial and error until a message materialized out of the chaos . . .

There was rather more to it, but much of her explanation was lost on Hugh, not only because he was groggy from being roused from slumber to listen to this incomprehensible decryption analysis, but because she had touched his arm and said something about him being a remarkable exception, and when she'd done that, something welled up in his chest and crept into his throat and stole his senses and made him realize—oh, God—that this was it, this was what those fools meant when they wrote about larks and starlings, only they shouldn't have been writing about larks and starlings, they should have been writing about a small, exhilarated woman sitting cross-legged in her nightclothes reaching out to touch a man's arm.

". . . so once I had my final draft of the alphabet circle . . ." She sorted through the pages on her lap to produce one on which she had drawn a circle inscribed around the inner edge with Hebrew letters and around the outer with Latin. "I had my key and could simply transpose each letter of the message until I had translated it completely."

Hugh took the page from her to blink dazedly at the "alphabet circle," which must be identical to the key that Clare had secreted somewhere in Castle Halthorpe. Laying it down on his chest, he regarded her with sleepy wonderment. "You are a very remarkable woman."

Even in this dim candlelight, he could see the heat rise in her cheeks. She lifted the sheet of parchment on

which Hugh had transcribed the document he'd found
in Clare's chamber. "Don't you want to know what it
says?"

"By all means." He tucked an arm under his head
and yawned again. "Why don't you read it to me?"

" 'Tis a letter addressed to Clare." She cleared her
throat and began to read. " 'From Eleanor, Countess of
Poitou, Duchess of Aquitaine and Queen of—' "

Hugh bolted upright. "It's from the queen?"

Phillipa laughed like a little girl.

"Give me that!" Hugh yanked the letter out of her
hand and began reading. Phillipa set aside her other
pages and shifted so that she sat shoulder to shoulder
with him, reading along.

"God's bones," Hugh muttered after he'd read it
through a second time.

"Indeed."

The letter, dated a month ago, began by mentioning
a previous letter from Clare to Eleanor, in which Clare
promised that certain arrangements had been made and
that their victory would be swift and decisive—assur-
ances that the queen professed to find appallingly
indiscreet . . . *It is deemed treason simply to contemplate
such matters, yet you have written of them in unencrypted
French as if gossiping about your latest tedious little liaison. The cipher you were given before you left Poitiers
was meant to apply to your communications to me as
well as mine to you. That you did not understand this
greatly diminishes my confidence in you and your
brother.*

Eleanor went on to assert that she had been hesitant
right from the beginning to entrust so much responsibility in Clare and Aldous, given that they were both
"greasy little court rats" who liked nothing more than
to scheme and seduce and bluster about it afterward.
*But as regards the matter in which you are serving me at
present, rest assured that if you two cannot manage to
still your tongues on your own, they will be stilled for
you. Do not make the mistake of regarding this as an idle*

threat. I have installed at Castle Halthorpe an agent of my own, charged with safeguarding my interests against the ineptitude and imprudence of you and your brother. If it begins to look as if the situation there is becoming more than you can handle, you will be removed from the world and it will be handled for you.

"Eleanor has planted a spy here," Hugh said.

"So it seems."

Hugh rubbed his jaw. "One of Clare's guests?"

"It stands to reason. They all came here either from Poitiers, which is Eleanor's domain, or from Paris, which is that of her ally, King Louis. It could be anyone."

"Not anyone," Phillipa corrected. "If we're to believe all that about stilling their tongues and removing them from the world, then it's someone who's capable of cold-blooded murder. That's got to rule out . . . well, virtually everyone."

Hugh couldn't help chuckling at her naïveté. "No one is better at playing the innocent than a cold-blooded murderer. 'Tis impossible to point them out by demeanor alone. I say again, it could be anyone."

Phillipa chewed on her lip. "Turstin de Ver is an intimate of the queen's, is he not?"

"Turstin?" Could the genial old troubadour be Eleanor's mysterious agent? Of course he could. Anyone could. "There's also that priest, Nicolas Cappelanus. He came from King Louis's court in Paris—perhaps he was sent at Queen Eleanor's behest. There's Robert d'Ivri, Simon de Saint-Helene . . ."

Phillipa looked at him. "Raoul d'Argentan."

"Raoul? Nay—never."

"I thought you said it could be anyone."

" 'Tisn't Raoul."

"He seems very much under the thumb of his wife," Phillipa said, "and isn't she a confidante of Eleanor's daughter, Marie de Champagne? And we know he can kill—he was a soldier."

"Raoul is as gentle off the battlefield as he is ruthless on it. Even at Isabelle's bidding, I can't believe he'd—"

"What about Isabelle?" Phillipa asked, turning to face him. "Why can't it be a woman? After all, Eleanor has created an entire world in Poitiers that revolves around women."

Little wonder, Hugh reflected, after King Henry turned his back on their marriage—which had been a love match, after all, not a political arrangement—to form an alliance with another woman. Hugh's low opinion of marital infidelity had been formed at the age of seven when his father, finding his wife's labor with their second child to be wearisome, joined his mistress in London—a girl named Eglantine who was fourteen but looked about eleven. When he returned home a week later, Elizabeth of Halthorpe was in her grave and Hugh and his new sister were motherless. Hugh could not have been more sympathetic to Queen Eleanor's rage over her husband's betrayal, nor could he help being impressed with the magnitude of the revenge she sought; for if the rumors were true, she intended to strip him of the English crown and give it to her son. But treason was treason, and orders were orders. If he could thwart her, he would.

Phillipa was ticking Clare's female guests off on her fingers. "Then there's Marguerite, of course. We mustn't rule her out simply because she's such a good friend of Clare's."

Hugh shook his head. "She's too busy playing the evil temptress to take an interest in political intrigue."

"Aye," Phillipa said, "but she'd probably love having an excuse to kill. 'Twould be just another dark thrill to her, a new and higher form of sensual gratification."

"*Hmm . . .* you may be right about that." Hugh yawned again. "I'm too tired to sort this all out tonight." He scooted over on the bed to make room for her. "Why don't we get some sleep and think it through tomorrow?"

She yawned, too. "All right." After hiding her pages away in a secret compartment of the big iron-banded trunk Lord Richard had had made especially for her and visiting the garderobe, she blew out the candle and joined him in the small bed. She faced away from him as she always did, her body curled against his, where it fit perfectly. He draped a companionable arm around her, tucking her up close. The straw in the mattress crackled as they shifted and settled in together.

After Aldous moved to the chamber above the great hall, Clare had offered Hugh and Phillipa his former chamber, with its more luxurious furnishings and larger bed. Hugh had been game, but Phillipa had protested that she couldn't even look upon that bed without thinking about what had transpired there between Aldous and Marguerite. She had told Hugh how she'd found them that night after she'd engineered her little ruse to lure Marguerite to his room, and asked Hugh to explain what they had been doing, and why. Although sorely tempted to answer glibly, as he had when she'd questioned him about Aldous and Elthia, he managed instead to deliver something of a dissertation on sexual idiosyncracies, which she had absorbed with wide-eyed fascination. Some of the activities he'd described had repulsed her; others had seemed to intrigue her, which in turn had intrigued him, which was when he had concluded the conversation, reasoning that she'd learned enough—and that, given their present situation, perhaps it was best if they didn't talk too much about sex.

Sharing this small bed with Phillipa *was* frustrating, hence his feverish dreams of her, from which he often awoke with a ferocious cockstand and no way to ease it. Two nights ago, he'd awakened thrusting against her, which had not, thank God, seemed to rouse her from her sleep. The warmth of her delicate little body against his, her womanly scent, the way the silken strands of her hair sometimes tickled his face . . .

Sleeping with her like this, as if they were a contented old married couple, did have its trying moments. But it was also deeply satisfying in a way that Hugh wouldn't have anticipated, having never in his life spent the night in bed with a woman unless he'd had her first. Instead of sharing their bodies, Hugh and Phillipa shared their thoughts, their feelings, their observations of the day, talking late into the night as sleep overtook them.

Astoundingly, they actually had become friends—even if part of him still longed for them to be more.

"How did you come to be so knowledgeable about codes?" he asked her, his voice barely above a whisper; they always spoke softly in the dark.

" 'Twas a special interest of my uncle Lotulf's," she said, "a way to pass the time, to occupy his mind when he wasn't serving the bishop of Paris. King Louis's cipher secretary taught him about encryption, and he in turn taught Ada and me."

Hugh nodded. During their late-night conversations, she had told him all about her curious childhood on the Isle de Notre Dame, immersed in the rarified world of academia with no children for company save for her beloved twin sister. He had, however, dodged her inquiries about his own upbringing, the more miserable aspects of which he had never told anyone. Dwelling on past difficulties was pointless enough; why share them so that someone else must dwell on them as well?

"Ada and I found cryptography absolutely enthralling," Phillipa continued. " 'Twas a way to create our own secret languages, to communicate with each other in complete confidence. We soaked up every cipher Uncle Lotulf taught us, then invented some of our own. We were obsessed with codes from about the age of six."

"Six?" That seemed awfully young to be immersed in such an analytical pursuit.

"Well, we started out with the most elemental ciphers—mirror-image writing, transposing letters, simple alphabet substitutions, grouping words together or separating them into blocks . . . Then we figured out how to apply mathematical patterns to create a secret message within a seemingly innocent message. We came up with several methods of assigning number values to characters, and then there were spiral ciphers, compass ciphers, map ciphers . . ."

"Map ciphers?"

"That's where you draw a seemingly ordinary map, except the clusters of trees or mountains actually spell out a message. One can do the same thing with any sort of picture."

Hugh was laughing softly.

"What's so funny?" she asked.

" 'Tisn't really funny, just . . ." He nuzzled her hair, which always smelled faintly of lavender, and tightened his arm around her. "I'm very pleased to have gotten to know you. You really are a most singular woman."

She lapsed into silence.

She was more than singular; she was extraordinary. Yesterday morning, when she'd told him he could stop worrying about whether he'd impregnated her the night of his arrival, he'd been weak with relief. Phillipa had professed to feel the same, but there'd been something in her eyes, a certain wistfulness, as if part of her were disappointed. Was it possible, he'd wondered, that the self-sufficient, learned Phillipa de Paris felt the same innate longing for motherhood that other women felt? That she clearly did made her seem even more remarkable in his eyes, more complex and surprising.

Wanting to hear her voice again, Hugh said, "I take it you and Ada eventually lost your interest in ciphers."

"Not at all. Even now, our letters to each other are always encoded. We invent the most complicated code we can, and the recipient must decipher it in order to read the letter."

"I'm curious. If Canon Lotulf knew so much about codes, why didn't he encrypt his letters to you, especially the ones about the plot to dethrone King Henry?"

He'd been afraid she might react badly to his introducing the subject of those letters, but she seemed to have set aside her ire over that, for she merely chuckled and said, "If you think *I'm* a creature of the mind, you should meet Uncle Lotulf. He's the quintessential academic, always walking about with his nose in a book and no notion of what's going on around him. To him, cryptography is naught but an amusement for the intellect. 'Twould never occur to him to apply it to any practical application."

"When I met you," he said, "I thought you were much the same."

With a little huff of laughter, she said, "I was. It's changed me, being with you, being of the world like this. I do feel like a butterfly that's broken out of its cocoon." She threaded her fingers through his, making his chest ache with a longing that had nothing to do with sex and everything to do with this strange new intimacy of the heart and mind. "Thank you."

He kissed her hair, the only part of her he ever touched his lips to anymore, thinking how gratifying it was to know that she cared for him—so gratifying that he was almost tempted to strip away the armor around his own heart and hold it out to her as she'd held hers out to him.

Almost.

Chapter 17

"Methinks," intoned Clare from her thronelike chair on the dais at the north end of Halthorpe Castle's great hall, "that I am prepared to render a judgment in the matter that has been so eloquently argued before me this evening."

Clare's face was a chalky mask in the yellowish torch-light, her tightly laced gown the color of dried blood. On her gauntleted left fist sat her favorite hawk, the kestrel Salome, wearing a ruby-studded leather hood fes-tooned with a jaunty tuft of red-dyed feathers.

Hugh, standing in the shadows at the south end of the hall, looked toward his friend Raoul d'Argentan, sitting with his wife Isabelle among the audience that had en-dured tonight's interminable court of love. During the eight days that Hugh had been at Halthorpe Castle, Clare had staged four of these travesties. Normally Raoul, who had as little patience for them as Hugh had, would slip away early in the proceedings to join Hugh for a summer evening's stroll along the river that mean-dered through Halthorpe, during which they'd reminisce about their years as mercenaries while passing the wine-skin back and forth—although Hugh never had more than a cup's worth of wine, having cut sharply back on it after his drunken ravishment of Phillipa the night he arrived here.

Raoul, although he normally disdained Clare's courts of love, had had reason to stay and listen tonight, for the subject under consideration had been him—specifically, whether he'd had the right to punch Robert d'Ivri in the nose yesterday evening for having kissed Isabelle on the mouth rather than the cheek at the conclusion of the dance of the chaplet.

Isabelle, through her advocate, Marguerite du Roche, had argued that Raoul had acted barbarically and with no regard for her feelings; indeed, he had humiliated her before all who'd witnessed his savage display. Raoul, through Turstin de Ver, had maintained that his jealousy was, in fact, proof of his deep and abiding love for Isabelle, and that his actions, although uncalled-for, were forgivable in that context.

Hugh, who'd seen it all yesterday—Isabelle's shameless flirtations with Robert, no doubt calculated to torment her husband, and Robert's lingering kiss on the mouth, during which he had, in fact, caressed her bottom—felt that Raoul had, if anything, been too restrained in his reaction. Hugh would have taken the man outside and cracked a few ribs, perhaps reshaped his nose for him. In fact, his "friendship" with Phillipa notwithstanding, every time he glanced over to find Aldous holding her hand, as he was doing now, or whispering in her ear, as he had done all evening, Hugh's hands twitched with the urge to do that and more. This drive to stake a claim and punish interlopers was, as Marguerite had correctly pointed out in her arguments tonight, a uniquely male urge—primal and brutish—but it was an undeniable force of nature, and as such, undeserving of reprimand unless it was taken too far.

Turstin, standing and facing the dais along with Marguerite, bowed deeply toward his patroness. "I eagerly await your judgment, *midons*."

"And I, as well," said Marguerite, dressed tonight in a gleaming yellow tunic perforated with dozens of round openings to display the transparent kirtle beneath. "Perhaps, when the gentleman in question is forced to confront your righteous censure, he will come to understand that civilized men do not snarl and snap at each other like hounds fighting over a bitch in heat. Indeed, by rights, 'tis the bitch who should do the choosing, is it not?''

Marguerite turned her stinging gaze on Raoul, sparking much laughter from those who knew about her infamous List of Twenty, and that Raoul had had the temerity to rebuff her when she'd set her sights on him. Even Isabelle laughed, although Hugh wondered how she would have felt had Raoul capitulated to Marguerite. Although the couples who aired their grievances before courts of love usually did so without revealing their identities, there was no possibility of anonymity in this case, since nearly every guest at Halthorpe had witnessed the punch in question.

"Is it possible," Marguerite asked, still spearing Raoul with her merciless gaze, "that the gentleman's truculence is due not so much to jealousy as to frustration with—and shame over—his own amorous inadequacies?"

There came a buzz of interest from the audience as Marguerite hunkered down, preparing to pounce. Raoul looked around in pink-faced confusion, clearly unprepared for this tactic. Hugh cursed under his breath, wondering whether to intervene.

"For it is my experience," Marguerite continued, "that a man who is a true lover of women, who desires them and knows how to satisfy them, doesn't feel as threatened by other men as does a man who doubts not only his ability to please women, but his very interest in them . . ."

She was drowned out by a chorus of hoots, laughter, and applause. Raoul, who got it now, sprang up from his bench, crimson-faced, and looked around in wild mortification. Hugh stepped forward, but stilled when he realized it was too late. In the wake of his public humiliation at Marguerite's hands, Raoul wrenched himself away from Isabelle, who tried vainly to grasp his tunic, and stalked out of the hall, to jeers and guffaws.

Hugh turned to follow him when something caught his eye—the door to the corner stairwell opening and Istagio emerging from the cellar, flushed and sweating as always. Orlando had already come upstairs and gone out to the kitchen for some late supper. Hugh knew, because he and Phillipa had made a covert study of their routine, that whichever of the Italians was last out of the cellar at night would immediately fetch Clare, who locked the door to the stairwell with one of her many keys.

Closing the door behind him, Istagio looked toward Clare on the dais—only to have his attention instantly snagged by the maid Edmee walking toward the assembled guests with a tray of sweetmeats in each hand. He called to her, raking damp hair off his face; she saw him and adopted a look of weary disinterest. Seemingly unperturbed, he sprinted heavily after her and snatched at her skirt. "Edmee . . . you and me take walk, yes?"

Hugh looked toward Raoul, storming out through the front entrance, then toward Clare, holding forth from her throne to much laughter, then toward Istagio, beseeching Edmee as he leered at her breasts . . . and finally toward the unlocked cellar door.

Do it. But quickly.

On swift, silent feet, Hugh crept along the perimeter of the hall to the door, which he opened to a slow grind of rusty iron hinges, and slipped through, closing it carefully behind him. He sprinted down the narrow stone stairwell, lit by a single torch on a wall bracket, only to find a second door at the bottom.

"Please be unlocked," he muttered, before he noticed that there wasn't even a keyhole on the door. He turned the handle; the door opened.

So did the door at the top of the stairs; Hugh heard those rusty hinges groan. "Hugh?" It was Clare's voice.

Shit. Hugh whipped the door open and peered in as her footsteps descended the stairs, knowing this might be his only chance to see the laboratory where Orlando and Istagio spent their days and most of their nights, doing whatever it was they did that produced those intermittent thunderclaps.

It was black as pitch in there, save for the faint glow of banked coals in a wall hearth, the air stifling hot and poisoned with a rotten-egg stink. By the meager light from the stairwell torch, Hugh could make out what looked like a worktable cluttered with flasks and tools, and on the far end of it something round and with the dull gleam of iron. A helmet? No, it was too large.

A bell? *Istagio . . . he make the bells.*

Except it was too round to be a bell. What the devil . . .

"Ah, that *was* you I saw coming down here." Clare squeezed past Hugh to pull the door closed, her cloying scent mingling with the resinous fumes from the torch to make the gorge rise in his throat. She still held that fancily hooded hawk on her fist. "Doing a bit of exploring, are you?"

"I suppose you could say that." *Look her in the eye,* he thought when he caught himself averting his gaze. *Don't give yourself away.* "I was just a bit curious as to what's down here."

She fiddled with her keys, which Phillipa had told him was an indication of nervousness. "If it's those noises you're wondering about, they're just barrels of wine—"

"Yes, I know. As I said, I was just curious. I'm a bit restless, if you must know. I'm afraid I'm not too keen on those courts of love."

"You're restless?" Her tone changed abruptly, becoming overtly flirtatious. "I could do something about that, if you'd let me."

"I'm certain you could," he said with a smile that he hoped didn't look too forced.

"Then why won't you let me?" There was an edge to the question, a brittleness.

"Ah. Well . . ."

"It's been over a week since you came to Halthorpe," she said, moving toward him.

He backed up against the wall—against the wall, for pity's sake, which was precisely what he had chided Phillipa about after their initial encounter that night in Oxford.

"Has it really been that long?" he asked, thinking she

looked remarkably like a two-day-old corpse this close up. "I've been having such a—"

"Why haven't you fucked me yet?"

Ah, the splendor of courtly love. "There hasn't really been a convenient—"

"I shove my tits in your face at every possible opportunity. You always seem to have an excuse. Don't you find me attractive?"

This was a treacherous arena. Hugh couldn't afford to snub her, lest she cast him out of Halthorpe Castle, along with Phillipa. The only reason Clare had defied Aldous and kept him around this long was her assumption that he would eventually break down and tup her. Now he knew how Phillipa felt, having to string Aldous along when the thought of bedding him filled her with revulsion.

"I find you immensely attractive," he claimed, straining to make eye contact while not wincing at the dead-white skin, the harsh smears of rouge. *Bloody hell, it's a wig,* he thought when it became too unnerving to stare at her face and he started staring at her hair instead. *God knows what's under it.*

"Then, why," she demanded, each word snapping off like a dead twig, "won't, you, take, me, to, bed?"

"I . . ."

"It doesn't even have to be a bed." She smiled that whore's smile of hers. "You could have me against the wall."

"Ah. Enchanting though that prospect—"

"Or bend me over right here." She took a step forward, pressing her bosom to his chest as Salome squawked and fussed; her right hand began gathering up his tunic. "I rather like the idea of you mounting me from behind. You could take me hard and fast, just like a real stallion."

"Won't that disturb Salome?"

"She's used to it."

He seized her hand as it began crawling up his thigh. "Clare . . ."

"It's been twenty years since I've had it from a real man. The last time was your father, the night of my wedding. He came into my chamber as I was awaiting the boy I'd married, and locked the door and—"

"I have the pox," Hugh blurted out, recalling that night with Phillipa in Aldous's stable. *I'll tell him you have the pox and I don't want to catch it.* At the time, he'd been outraged, but now . . . "The thing is, I wouldn't want you to catch it."

"Don't worry." She smiled conspiratorially. "I have it, too."

When, he wondered, had she been planning on telling him? "I'll tell you the truth, then," he said with feigned sobriety. "I'm . . ." *Mother of God . . .* "I'm incapable of performing."

She stared at him with those flat black eyes of hers. "Nay . . ."

"It's true, it's . . . it's because of the pox." *Yes! Of course!* "The pox has made me—"

"Marvelous."

"What?"

"I do so love a challenge."

That was Hugh's cross to bear of late, women who loved challenges. "But you don't understand. I can't—"

"Of course you can. All you need is a little inspiration— something I feel certain I can provide."

"But—"

She pressed a finger to his lips, murmuring, "My chamber. Tonight. Don't knock. Don't speak. Just join me in my bed and let us surrender ourselves to each other."

I know! Phillipa had said. *I'll tell him you prefer men . . .* Hugh opened his mouth, but the words just would not come out.

"Tonight," Clare whispered.

Hugh let out a long, ragged sigh. "Tonight."

Chapter 18

"He says he can't perform in bed," Clare told her brother. Tonight it was she who stood in the shadows at the south end of the great hall, along with Aldous, watching Hugh and that wife of his dance an intricate and ritualistic *galliard* along with the rest of her guests, while Turstin sang and plucked at the *mandore* lying across his lap.

"Verily?" Aldous looked like a little boy at Christmastide. "Does that mean he can't get it up at all, or he can't—"

"How would I know?" She plucked a shred of raw hen flesh out of the bowl she'd bullied Aldous into holding and dangled it in front of the unhooded Salome, who clung to her gloved left fist. The bird snatched the meat out of her hand and devoured it. "He promised to come to my chamber last night and then never showed up. That was after I'd found him snooping in the cellar. He claimed he was just curious, and I believed him. I'd wanted to believe him. But now I'm not so—"

"If he can't get it up at all," Aldous mused, "then God knows how long it's been since she's had any. She's probably seething with suppressed desires. She'll be a real vixen in bed if I can just—"

"I know it's a struggle, Aldous," Clare said wearily, "but do try and concentrate on something other than your cock for one damned minute, will you?"

"Perhaps I'd be able to," he snapped, "if you'd send Hugh of Wexford back where he came from so I could finally take a poke at his bloody wife!"

" 'Twas my understanding that Marguerite is seeing to your needs in the meantime."

Aldous grimaced. " 'Tisn't the same. Half the time she doesn't even let me . . ." Reddening, he looked away.

"God, you are pathetic." She fed another tidbit to Salome. "All right, since you seem incapable of sorting through this on your own, I'll spell it out for you. Hugh's behavior is making me suspicious. For one thing, he's put off tupping me for more than a week now while feeding me a series of increasingly implausible excuses."

"You mean you don't think he's really impotent?"

"If he is, it's a recent development. According to the kitchen wenches in Poitiers, he could go all night, and he made them scream like banshees. Ah yes, and so well endowed was he that it was like being 'impaled on a war club.' "

Aldous's face fell; he swore colorfully.

"But it was last night, when I realized he wasn't going to come to me," Clare said, "that I started thinking about the way he'd darted down into the cellar, looking around as if he didn't want to be seen. And then, when I took him back up to the hall and locked the door at the top of the stairs, he stared at the key as if it were the holy grail."

Aldous frowned. "I don't understand."

"Of course you don't, because you are, despite your patina of refinement, a drooling lackwit." Salome screamed for more meat; Clare fed it to her. "It's possible that Hugh's motives for being here are not entirely pure. He might, in fact, have been sent here to spy on us."

Aldous blinked. "Do you mean you think he's the queen's agent?"

Clare rolled her eyes. "No, Aldous. The queen's agent, whoever he is, is here simply to keep an eye on us and make sure we don't say or do anything to jeopardize her rebellion. Which wouldn't have been necessary if you didn't have such a reputation for imprudence and dim-wittedness."

"*Me*! You're the one who wrote her an unencrypted letter!"

Clare closed her eyes briefly, summoning the composure not to rake her nails across her brother's face. "As I was saying, the queen's agent is merely here to observe us."

"And to dispatch us to our Maker if we displease him."

"By being indiscreet or losing control of the situation here. But that's not going to happen, is it, Aldous?"

He pulled a face. "I'm not a child, Clare."

"Then why do you cry when you're spanked?"

He gaped at her, a tide of purple staining his face.

"Marguerite and I share everything," Clare said with a smile as she chose another scrap of meat from the bowl. Well, almost everything. Marguerite had never asked what was going on in the cellar and Clare, loath to incur the queen's wrath by compromising the secrecy of Orlando's work, had never volunteered the information. "I'll find out who the queen's agent is eventually," Clare said with confidence. "I've been making inquiries among our guests, and I've narrowed down the possibilities to a handful of people with connections to Eleanor. Once we've identified him, we can make sure he observes us only at our most circumspect and competent. That means you will only do and say in his presence what I tell you to do and say, is that understood?"

Aldous opened his mouth—probably to point out again that he was not a child—but seemed to think better of it.

"In any event," Clare continued, "the queen's agent would have no reason to sneak into the cellar. Presumably he already knows what's going on down there. But an agent for someone else, say King Henry, might very well want to—"

"King Henry! You don't think Hugh is working for—"

"I don't know. But I mean to find out."

"How?"

Clare regarded him balefully. "The less you know

about any of this, the better. I'm sorry you've gotten as deeply involved as you have. Suffice it to say I've taken certain measures aimed at misdirecting . . ." She trailed off, watching Hugh bow to Phillipa as the *galliard* concluded, whereupon he led her toward a table. Marguerite intercepted them and spoke to Hugh, telling him, presumably, what Clare had asked her to tell him—that his friend Raoul d'Argentan, who had kept to his chamber since bolting from the court of love last night, needed to speak to him on a matter of grave urgency, and that he would meet him in the buttery.

Even from across this cavernous hall, Clare could read Hugh's lips as he said, "The buttery?"

Marguerite pointed toward the door in the corner that led to the service rooms. Hugh said something to Phillipa, touching her arm, then turned and walked in that direction.

"Excellent." Clare transferred Salome to a linen-wrapped hawk perch jutting out of the wall nearby and tugged off her gauntlet, handing it to a bewildered Aldous. She smoothed down her low-cut, plum-colored tunic and patted her wig. "Now I shall find out just how eager he is to get into that cellar."

"What are you going to do?" Aldous asked.

Clare glanced heavenward in exasperation. "I'm going to maintain control of our end of things and thereby keep us from getting our throats cut in our sleep by Eleanor's agent. Look after Salome."

"But . . ."

Without a backward glance, Clare strode across the great hall, through the corner doorway, and down the service corridor until she came to the open door of the buttery. Hugh was in there, scowling as he perused the casks of wine and ale stacked around the perimeter of the windowless little storage room, lit by a brass lantern dangling overhead. He was excruciatingly handsome tonight in a silver-trimmed black tunic, his hair pulled off his face, that deliciously phallic infidel dagger sheathed on his hip.

"Clare," he said warily when she stepped into the buttery. "I'm . . . waiting for someone."

"You're waiting for me." She closed the door and leaned back against it. "I had Marguerite tell you it was Raoul who wanted to see you, because I was afraid you wouldn't come if you knew it was I who was summoning you."

"If you're wondering why I didn't come to your chamber last night—"

"I know why you didn't come. I don't excite your desire."

"That's not true, Clare." But he looked down as he said it, the lying cur—the contemptible, arrogant blackguard. If Clare was good enough for William of Wexford, she was damn well good enough for his son.

"Then why didn't you come?" she asked.

"I got drunk and passed out."

"You've used that excuse before."

"I get drunk a great deal."

"Funny," she said, "I haven't seen you in your cups since the first night you were here."

"I do most of my drinking late at night, after everyone's retired."

"Well, you're not drunk now." She skimmed her hands down over her breasts, eyeing him seductively. His gaze lingered on the cluster of keys at the end of the gold chain around her neck. "It cuts me to the quick, the way you keep putting me off. Last night, when you didn't come, I decided there was no way to salvage my pride except to ask you and your wife to leave Halthorpe."

Alarm flickered in his eyes.

"But then I thought perhaps I should give you one last chance to make it up to me. And that's when I arranged to have you meet me here." Her gown laced up the front by means of a satin cord. Without wresting her gaze from him, she tugged open the bow in which it was tied.

"Clare, I really don't think I can do this," he said.

"Beautiful though you are, it's been a very long time since I've been able to rouse to a woman."

"The women who failed to rouse you weren't as creative as I am." She slid off her many bracelets and tossed them on top of a nearby wine cask. "There are things a woman can do, clever little tricks that could bring a dead man to full attention—things that priggish little wife of yours could never conceive of, much less bring herself to do. Shall I try a few of them out on you?"

He held his hands up. "I really . . ."

"There's some almond oil in the pantry," she said, pulling off her key chain, along with her necklaces, and setting them next to the bracelets. She saw his gaze home in on the keys. "You wouldn't believe what a little oil and a lot of imagination can accomplish. Shall I go fetch some while you undress?" she asked, reaching for the handle of the door.

After a moment's hesitation, he said, "I don't suppose it could hurt to try."

"Not unless you want it to." Tossing him a wicked little grin, she left, closing the door behind her.

Clare stood on the other side of the door, listening for sounds from within, but it was a thick door and she could hear nothing. She waited several minutes anyway, and was about to go back in when she remembered about the almond oil. *May as well make this look good.* She fetched the flask of oil from the pantry and headed back toward the buttery, only to encounter Hugh as he was leaving.

"Where are you going?" she asked. "I thought you were taking off your things so I could . . ." She jiggled the flask.

"I just remembered," he said, his gaze darting away from her, "I told Phillipa I'd be right back to dance the *tourdoin* with her. She'll come looking for me soon. 'Twould hardly do for her to find us . . ." He gave her that too-charming lopsided grin of his and shrugged his big shoulders. Bastard.

"Perhaps she could join us," Clare suggested coyly.

He shook his head. "Nay, she . . . she would never . . ."

"Yes, of course she wouldn't, poor little prude. What a shame, just when things seemed to be working out."

"Indeed. Perhaps some other time."

"Why don't I just take this"—she caressed the flask suggestively—"up to my bedchamber, and perhaps some night when you haven't drunk yourself into a stupor, you can pay me a visit and let me open up my little box of tricks."

"I can think of nothing more enticing." With a cursory little bow, he turned and made his way back to the great hall.

Clare reentered the buttery and stood over the wine cask, inspecting her collection of household keys, which normally numbered thirteen and now numbered twelve. The large, distinctively ornate brass key that fit the lock at the top of the cellar stairs was gone.

Just as she had expected.

Phillipa, holding a glass-covered lantern to stave off the midnight darkness of the great hall, held her breath as Hugh inserted the big brass key into the lock on the cellar door and turned it. There came a muted click. He grasped the door handle and pulled slowly, opening it an inch.

She released her breath in a grateful rush and smiled at Hugh. He smiled back. Nodding toward the handful of house servants asleep in the rushes at the other end of the hall, she put a finger to her lips; he nodded.

Hugh slipped the key into the rolled-up sleeve of his shirt. They had arranged with one of the kitchen maids to reattach it to Clare's chain after she brought up her mistress's breakfast tray in the morning but before she awoke her—for a price, of course.

Phillipa handed Hugh the jar of kitchen grease they'd absconded with, which he smeared over the door's rusty iron hinges before opening it all the way. There came only the faintest of creaks, which did not disturb the sleeping servants.

Slipping through the door and closing it behind them, they padded down the narrow stairwell on bare feet, Phillipa lifting the skirts of her wrapper and night shift well off the stone steps, lest she trip and rouse the entire castle. At the bottom of the stairs there was, as Hugh had told her, a second door, this one *sans* lock. He opened it and they stepped through, into a wall of reeking heat.

"That smell is sulphur." Phillipa held the lantern high as they scanned the undercroft, a long, narrow chamber of damp rock, the front part of which, unsurprisingly, appeared to have been fitted out as a laboratory. The flickering lamplight eerily illuminated a long table scattered with thick glass flasks, vials, mortars, tools of various types—tongs, sieves, spoons, scoops, chisels, hammers—a press of some sort, an anvil, a stack of books, some odd little cups with spouts sticking out of them, and a number of covered earthen vessels.

"There was that round iron thing on this table last night," Hugh said. "That thing I said looked like a helmet at first, remember? 'Tisn't here anymore."

Jutting out from the wall behind the table was a high, hooded stone hearth on which an iron cauldron and a number of clay and metal crucibles rested on a rack over dimly glowing coals. Tongs and pokers hung on one side of this fireplace, which had been altered to hold extra fuel and fitted out with a leather-and-wood bellows to feed air to the flames.

"They've made it into a furnace," Hugh observed.

More earthen pots—dozens of them—sat on shelves and workbenches against the walls. On the floor near the makeshift furnace sat sacks of various fuels for it: charcoal, peat, and dried dung. Off to the side were devices that Hugh identified as a pole lathe and a rotary grindstone, although Phillipa wasn't too clear on their purpose.

"What's that?" Phillipa asked, aiming the lantern's

wavering corona of light at a tall, tapering clay vessel mounted over a sort of brazier and connected to another vessel by means of a copper tube.

"I have no idea. I can't begin to imagine what any of this—" He broke off abruptly and pointed to a spot in the middle of the floor. "Shine the light over there."

Phillipa did as he asked, staring incredulously at what she saw. Scratched into the floor of packed earth was a large circle containing eight spokes radiating from a central point, at the tip of each of which a mysterious symbol had been inscribed and a candle placed. In the hub stood a tall, ornate mortar filled with some sort of powder.

Hugh and Phillipa exchanged a look, and then his gaze shifted above her, toward the ceiling. "What the devil . . . ?"

Turning, she raised her lantern, causing its light to shift and dance over dozens of writhing serpents dangling from the rafters.

She squealed, almost dropping the lantern.

"They're dead." Coming up behind her, Hugh wrapped his arms around her waist, his chin resting comfortably on top of her head. With a chuckle, he said, "I never would have thought to hear Phillipa de Paris screeching like a schoolgirl over a bunch of dried snakes."

"What are they for?" she asked, her heart still tripping in her chest.

"What is any of this for?" Releasing her with a reassuring pat, Hugh approached the long table and picked up the book on top of the stack. "*Turba Philosophorum.* Says it's translated from the Arabic."

"I'm not familiar with it." Leaning over one of the workbenches, Phillipa lifted the top from an earthen pot, revealing an unidentifiable inky liquid. Another was filled with crumbly yellow sulphur, another with willow charcoal and another . . . "Ugh!" She quickly recovered it, wrinkling her nose. At Hugh's questioning look, she said, "Urine, and none too fresh."

"Hmph." He squinted at the title of another book. "*De Compositione Alchemiae* by Robert of Chester."

She shrugged. "Never heard of it. Or him." Bracing herself, she opened the largest of the clay pots, then tilted it to display the powder within to Hugh.

"I think that's saltpeter," he said. "The infidels call it 'Chinese snow.' This"—he swirled a small container he'd just opened—"is quicksilver. I've seen it in Italy."

Phillipa looked around in mystification. They had assumed Orlando's work would be of some benefit to Queen Eleanor in her revolt against the king; otherwise why was it so shrouded in secrecy? Indeed, why had he and Istagio been brought here at all?

"Perhaps they're developing some sort of new poison," Hugh suggested.

They both looked toward the talisman inscribed on the floor, and then at each other.

"What's this?" Phillipa crossed to the opposite wall, against which stood an empty cage of finely wrought grillwork, the type of cage valuables were kept in. "It looks new. Whatever they're working on, they expect the results to be worth something."

"Let's see what's back here," Hugh said, heading toward the far end of the long chamber, beyond the massive stone support columns.

Phillipa followed him into the vast and unnerving darkness, her lantern held high. They passed a deep hole lined with stone. She peered into it; a drip of water rang in its depths. "A well? Down here?"

Hugh nodded. "Lots of castles have wells in the cellar so that there's a source of fresh water in the event of a siege."

"Ow!" Phillipa hopped on one foot, the other smarting.

Hugh spun around and came to her. "Are you all right, love?"

Love . . . "I stepped on something. Something small and hard."

He massaged the sole of her foot as he looked around.

"Here it is." Plucking something off the earthen floor, he stood and held it close to the lantern.

"What's that?" Phillipa asked as Hugh rolled the little iron ball around in his palm.

He shrugged. "I've seen children play a game with little balls of stone or clay. Perhaps this is naught but a game piece."

"What's it doing down here?"

Hugh shook his head. "The more I see, the more perplexed I am." He tucked the little ball into his sleeve and took her hand, urging her to continue toward the rear of the vast chamber. "Is that a door in the corner?" It was, but all they found behind it was a garderobe. On the wall nearby was a rack that Hugh told her had probably held instruments of punishment at one time. He pointed to the ceiling. "Aim your light right there, on that beam."

A pulley had been attached to the beam, she saw.

"They would tie someone's arms behind his back and hang him up high," he said, "possibly weighted with rocks, then drop him, dislocating his—"

"Yes, I think I get the idea," she said.

"Come, let's finish this. It's hot as blazes down here."

It was—sweat prickled Phillipa's scalp and trickled beneath her nightclothes—but she felt chilled to the marrow by what her lantern illuminated next. "Hugh, my God, what's that? Is that for . . ."

"For torture, aye."

It was a massive iron chair fitted with leather straps and shackles, the whole thing blanketed with a thick layer of dust.

"I've never seen one of these outside of the Rhineland," Hugh said. "We'd find them in the cellars of castles we seized. Frederick Barbarossa was very keen on torture. Even petty thieves would get the rack, or be strapped into this thing, to get them to confess." He pointed to a blackened depression in the dirt floor beneath the chair. "A fire would be built underneath—"

"Oh, how awful."

" 'Twas meant to be awful. I've never known a man to be tortured who didn't eventually crack."

"How can people do such things to other people? Is there no spark of human compassion in their hearts? Even if a man is your enemy, he's still a man."

"Those who have that spark of compassion assume it's in everyone," Hugh said grimly. " 'Twould astound you if you knew what seemingly ordinary people are capable of doing to others—and not just to their enemies."

The unaccustomed gravity of his tone made Phillipa wonder if he weren't speaking from personal experience, but before she could formulate an inquiry along those lines, he pointed to a device on the wall next to the chair and said, "Ah, look, a sachentage. You don't see many of these."

Phillipa shone her lantern on a small, dusty iron frame bolted at right angles into the wall of rock. In the center of this frame, connected to it by chains, hung two hinged halves of an iron collar lined with spikes.

"The idea here," Hugh said, fitting the two halves of the collar together, "is to force the prisoner to stand interminably, which prevents him from sitting or lying down, or from getting any sleep—if he dozes off, the spikes will wake him up quick enough. If one's jailers are particularly merciless or determined to break one down, they withhold food and water, as well. A man can't last more than a few days without water, and death by thirst is a painful way to go."

Phillipa shuddered, imagining the agony of being locked into such a device day after day. "I would tell them whatever they wanted to know immediately," she said. "I could never bear up under such punishment."

"You'd be surprised what you can bear if you only approach it the right way," Hugh said thoughtfully as he turned the cruel iron collar over in his hands, leaving fingerprints in the dust. "Pain can be transcended. The trick is to rise above it, as if you were floating in the air, watching it happen to someone else."

Phillipa's gaze lit on the ugly, pinched wound where his right thumb had once been. *He placed his hand on the block as calmly as you please . . . Didn't make a sound when the thumb came off . . .*

"Hugh," she asked quietly, "how did you get those scars on your back?"

His eyes grew opaque as he contemplated the sachentage. " 'Twas a long time ago. I scarcely remember."

"Hugh . . ."

"We've seen all there is to see down here." He dropped the collar and took her hand. "Come. Let's go to bed."

Much later, as they lay together in the dark, snugged up front to back, waiting for the veil of sleep to float down over them, Phillipa whispered, "I know you don't want to talk about it, and I shouldn't press the issue, but I can't stop wondering . . ." She drew in an unsteady breath. "I think it's because my feelings have gotten so tangled up with you." This was the first time she'd mentioned her feelings for him since they'd agreed to be friends, although they consumed her every waking thought. "I'll only ask this once, and you needn't answer if you really don't want to, but . . . why were you flogged, Hugh?"

The silence was so deep and lingering that Phillipa concluded he must have fallen asleep. She closed her eyes on a sigh, thinking she really ought to get some sleep herself.

" 'Twas because I cried for my mother." His voice was so scratchy-soft she wondered if she'd imagined it, but then she felt his arm tighten around her and she realized she hadn't.

"I don't understand," she murmured.

His chest expanded against her back; his breath ruffled her hair. "My mother died of childbed fever after Joanna was born. I'd loved her so much. She was . . ." Phillipa felt his head shake slowly. "She was my mother.

I was seven. She was everything to me. I couldn't stop crying."

"Of course not." She grasped his hand. "You were a child."

"My sire wanted me to be a man. He said I was weak, that I needed better command over my emotions if I was to become the greatest knight in Christendom. He told me he hadn't shed a single tear over my mother, and was proud of it. I pointed out that he'd been tupping his whore when my mother died, in pain and delirium, crying out his name, and that I despised him and hoped to God I grew up to be nothing like him. I told him to send away Regnaud, the master at arms who'd been training me in the arts of war, because I didn't want to be a knight anymore—I'd rather be brought up in a monastery and trained for the priesthood."

So stunned was Phillipa that he would disclose so much that she was loath to speak, lest she discourage him from continuing.

"My father was . . . displeased," Hugh said with a harsh little laugh. "I don't think anyone had defied him in a very long time, if ever. Regnaud had been chafing at the bit for some time to discipline me with his . . . not a whip, exactly. 'Twas a steel-tipped thong meant to open the flesh, not just leave welts."

Phillipa closed her eyes, praying for the strength to listen to this.

"Regnaud thought I needed toughening up. After my tears and defiance, my father agreed. He said he loved me too much to let me wallow in my weakness—that a sapling needed to feel the bite of the pruning knife if it was to grow up straight and strong. He gave Regnaud permission to tie me to a post and give me a half-a-dozen lashes. He said I would thank him someday."

"Oh, Hugh." Phillipa tried to turn around, so as to embrace him, but he tucked her more firmly against him, as if he didn't want to face her as he recounted these melancholy events.

"I cried, of course," Hugh said. "I was only seven,

and it was excruciating. My father told Regnaud to give me six more lashes for having cried. He said I ought to take it like a man, without so much as flinching. After that, he gave Regnaud a free hand with the whip, with standing instructions to double the lashes if I showed any reaction."

"That's when you learned how to . . . rise above the pain, wasn't it?"

"Aye. 'Twas almost as if I would hover over myself, watching the whip tear into me, and feeling it . . . but in another realm, where I could keep myself apart from the worst of it. It's difficult to describe."

"No, you're . . . you're doing fine. It's hard for me to understand, though, what kept you at Wexford until you were eighteen. Weren't you tempted to leave before that?"

"Aye, long before that. But there was Joanna to think about. She was a willful little thing, and always earning our sire's wrath."

"He didn't have her whipped, did he?"

"Nay, but he beat her from time to time, after locking me in the cellar so I couldn't stop him. I told him I'd kill him if he ever hurt her, and that I didn't care if they hanged me for it or not. I think he believed me, because he never beat her too badly. When she was eleven, he sent her to London to serve the wife of Baron Gilbert de Montfichet. I was dubbed shortly thereafter."

"And because Joanna didn't need you around for protection anymore, you felt free to leave Wexford and turn mercenary."

"That's right. And I promised myself I would never again be crushed beneath the wheels of anyone else's expectations of me—that I would go my own way, unencumbered by any demands but my own."

Phillipa nodded, understanding at last the forces that made him so fiercely autonomous and self-contained. "Yes," she said soberly. "I would have done the very same thing."

Chapter 19

"I have an announcement to make," Clare informed her guests at the conclusion of supper the next evening—another open-air repast in the outer bailey, not in deference to any holiday this time, but to a wave of brutal July heat. "Tomorrow morning at dawn, I'll be leaving to visit an old and dear friend . . ."

Murmurs of protest arose. Aldous, Phillipa noted, seemed as surprised by the news of his sister's impending departure as did everyone else.

"No, no, you mustn't think I'm abandoning you," she said with a cool little smile. "My friend lives just to the south of London. I'll only be gone a few days . . ."

Istagio, loitering near the drawbridge to the inner bailey, got that lascivious glitter in his eye that could only mean one thing—he'd spied the object of his unrequited lust, Edmee. Tracking his gaze, Phillipa saw the maid emerging from the cookhouse with two jugs of wine. The corpulent Italian hurried toward her and blocked her path as she walked toward the tables; she paused, looking beyond him with an expression of listless forbearance. He pointed toward the gatehouse; according to Edmee, he was forever trying to talk her into walking with him along the river. She shook her head no, indicating the jugs she held and nodding toward the tables. He whispered into her ear, glancing around as if wary of being overheard, and opened the leather case slung across his chest to show her something. She stared unblinkingly at whatever it was for several long seconds, then handed her jugs to a passing maidservant and let Istagio take her hand and escort her across the bailey.

Also observing this exchange was Orlando, sitting across from Phillipa, who caught Istagio's eye and gave him a furious little shake of the head—curious, since Orlando always seemed so imperturbable. Istagio waved his hand dismissively as he led Edmee toward the gatehouse. His expression grim, Orlando braced his hands on the table as if to rise, but hesitated when he realized Clare was still holding forth; it wouldn't do to bolt from the table while his hostess was speaking. He fiddled with the ties of his felt cap, stealing furtive glances toward the couple until they disappeared through the gatehouse.

". . . and so I trust everyone will continue to enjoy my hospitality even though I won't be here," Clare was saying. "While I'm gone, I entrust my brother with the keys to Halthorpe Castle"—these she removed from around her own neck and draped around his—"as well as responsibility for the comfort and happiness of my guests. Should you need anything while I'm gone, just ask Aldous."

As soon as Clare took her seat, Orlando leapt up from his bench and darted toward the gatehouse, nearly tripping on the hem of his long tunic. Capturing Phillipa's gaze, Hugh cocked his head toward the departing metaphysician and raised his eyebrows.

He was right; this was the perfect opportunity for them to question Orlando about the things they'd seen in the cellar last night—alone, Castle Halthorpe being a place where privacy was at a premium. They rose together from the table, to the consternation of Aldous, sitting next to Phillipa, who grabbed the tapering sleeve of her blue satin tunic to ask in a terse whisper where she was going—with *him*.

"Just for a walk along the river," she said, prying his fingers from her sleeve. "I'll be back before the sun sets, and then you and I can go inside and have a nice game of backgammon in a quiet corner." Aldous preferred backgammon to chess, which she suspected he didn't understand well enough to play.

He sighed grumpily and raised his wine cup to his mouth.

By the time Hugh and Phillipa had made it through the gatehouse and across the moat, Orlando was well ahead of them, holding his tunic up off the grass as he scurried down a grassy, tree-studded embankment toward the patch of woods that hid the river from view. Hugh took Phillipa's hand and they sprinted after the Italian, calling out, "*Signore* Orlando! Wait!"

Orlando paused, looking from his pursuers to the path through the woods that led to the river, and back again.

"Good evening, Orlando," greeted Hugh as they approached him. "Mind if we have a word with you?"

"I . . . er . . ."

"Just for a moment," Phillipa put in. "We want to ask you about something."

"Er . . . perhaps later," said Orlando, edging toward the path.

Hugh said, "It has to do with the cellar."

Orlando stilled, his gaze snapping to them.

"We were down there last night," said Phillipa. "And we have some questions about your . . . experiments."

Nodding limply, the Italian crossed to a tree stump nearby and sat, wiping his damp brow on his tunic sleeve. "*Sì* . . . I thought you would."

Hugh and Phillipa exchanged a look. Why would he have anticipated their curiosity? Had he found out they were in the cellar last night?

"We saw some things," Phillipa said, "that were most perplexing. You've always put me off when I've tried to ask you what you're doing down there, but now I simply must know."

"Is just *esperimento*," Orlando replied. "With the *dissoluzione e coagulazione*."

"Dissolution and coagulation, the two essential forces of nature," Phillipa said, recalling Orlando's famous treatise of several years ago.

"Sì!" Orlando perked up, as he always did when he discussed matters of metaphysic with Phillipa. "I heat the *zolfo*—what you call sulphur—and the *mercurio,* the quicksilver, and . . . how you say . . . distill them. I break them down and bring them together. Is very noble work."

"I'm sure it is." Hugh rubbed his jaw. "The, uh . . . the snakes gave us pause."

"Ah. Yes, well, I need the organic *materiale* as well. Is very complicated."

"And the talisman scratched into the floor?" Phillipa asked.

"Talis . . . ah, the *magico cerchio.* Sì, is part of it. Is *very* complicated."

"We're very intelligent," Hugh said. "Explain it to us, won't you?"

"Is very hard to explain," Orlando said. "Many people, they don't understand. Other *scienziati,* other metaphysicians, they say is sorcery, this *alchemia.* But is science, very old science of the Cosmos. You have heard, perhaps, of the search for the philosopher's stone?"

"The philosopher's stone!" Phillipa exclaimed. "You're not one of those 'sons of Hermes' who are trying to turn lead into gold, are you?"

Orlando grimaced. "Is very small part of the whole. Very, very small part. We search also for the Elixer of Life, and for the Alkabest, which will dissolve any substance . . ."

He went on to expound on the origins and practice of this "Hermetic philosophy," which, as far as Phillipa could tell, was an attempt to rediscover forgotten secrets of nature by conducting experiments from ancient Eastern texts. The alchemists' premise seemed to be that all elements of nature, even minerals, contained a life force, with sulphur representing the active pole and quicksilver the passive. The disintegration and reformation of these two opposing primordial forces, Orlando told them, was akin to the coming together of man and woman in sexual congress.

This discourse left Phillipa more mystified than ever. If Orlando's research into this mystical Eastern pseudo-science was intended to turn the tide for Queen Eleanor, it did not seem like much of a threat. And why was Orlando suddenly so willing—even eager—to reveal what he'd been so tight-lipped about before?

"The active principle," Orlando continued excitedly, "it is *sole,* and the passive, it is *luna.* Think of the sun as man, and the moon as woman. Very much separate, very much apart. But bring them together . . ." With a smile, he gestured toward Hugh and Phillipa, still holding hands as they stood before him. "From the chaos of nature is formed something new, something altogether wondrous. Is *magico,* no?"

Hugh, seeming discomfited, released Phillipa's hand to rake his fingers through his hair. "That's . . . fascinating, Orlando, but there are still some things I don't understand. Why did you come all the way to England to conduct your experiments? Surely it would have been simpler to remain in Rome, where you presumably have your own laboratory, your own equipment."

Orlando shook his head forlornly. "My *laboratorio,* it burn down."

"Oh, dear," Phillipa said. "From one of your experiments?"

He nodded glumly. "And my *assistente,* he die." Orlando executed a somber sign of the cross. "Is much bad feeling for Orlando then, very much scorn. They say is dangerous, my work, as well as foolish. After the fire, I have no place to work, and nothing that I need. The *materiale,* it is very . . . what is the word? Cost very much *monete.*"

"Expensive," Phillipa supplied.

"*Sì,* the *mercurio* most especially. Very 'spensive. The lady Clare, she has much *monete,* and much big heart, no?"

"Er . . ." Phillipa's gaze darted toward Hugh, who appeared to be biting his lip.

"She bring me here to finish my work where there is

no one to laugh at Orlando, no one to say I am not man of learning but sorcerer. And she buy much that I need. Without her, I could not do the work of my heart. She is very great lady."

Phillipa was about to ask if there was anything Clare expected in return for this bounty when there came a loud *crack,* as of a tree being cleaved by lightning, although the sky was clear. It was so startling that Phillipa jumped, the air leaving her lungs in a shrill little outcry.

Hugh gave her that crooked smile of his. "I rather like this new squealing of yours."

"Orlando?" Phillipa said as the Italian leapt up off his stump and began running.

Hugh grabbed Phillipa's hand again and together they followed Orlando into the woods, catching up with him as the narrow path opened up onto the craggy riverbank. About fifty yards downriver stood two figures with their backs to them—Istagio leaning over a flat-topped boulder, striking a fire-iron against a flint, and Edmee watching him from a distance. When the flint sparked, producing a faint glow from whatever it was he was lighting, Istagio hurriedly backed up to where Edmee stood, both of them covering their ears.

"Istagio!" Orlando yelled something in Italian as there came another sudden *crack,* accompanied by a flash of white light from the top of the boulder. Shreds of something sprayed in every direction. Phillipa's ears rang.

Orlando scurried up to Istagio, berating him in furious Italian. He and Istagio both seemed to be talking with their hands as much as with their mouths. Orlando yanked Istagio's leather case away from him, causing its contents—a number of light-colored little cylindrical objects—to spew out, scattering in the tall grass.

Still castigating Istagio, Orlando fell to his knees and began searching through the grass for the little cylinders. Hugh loped over to him in order to help; together they gathered them up and returned them to the leather bag.

Edmee turned and walked back toward the path as Orlando continued to rebuke Istagio. When the maid passed Phillipa, she caught her eye and looked toward the heavens; Phillipa smiled and shook her head.

Hugh came up to Phillipa then, grabbed her arm, and led her to the path as well. When they were several yards into the woods, he paused, reached into the kid purse hanging from his belt, and withdrew one of the cylinders.

"You took one!" Phillipa exclaimed.

"It seemed like the thing to do." He turned the little object over in her hands. It was a tube made of parchment, tied off at both ends; from one end there protruded an inch or so of cord.

Unsheathing his *jambiya*, Hugh slit the tube lengthwise, revealing its contents—a fine black powder. He emptied some of the powder into his palm; it glittered in the semidarkness of the woods.

"What is that stuff?" Phillipa asked. Whatever it was seemed to have a very violent reaction to flame. She'd never seen anything like it.

"I think I know," Hugh said as he studied the powder. "In the Levant, I met an Englishman, an Augustinian friar, whose mission it was to spread Christendom to the Orient. He'd been farther east in his travels than any European I've ever met, all the way to China. He told me once of a children's toy that would pop when lit. Perhaps . . ."

Istagio came bulling past them, herded along the path by Orlando, still ranting furiously. The word "stupid," Phillipa realized, was recognizable in any language.

Hugh grabbed Orlando's sleeve as he passed. "One moment, if you would."

Orlando continued his diatribe as Istagio disappeared down the path, although he switched to English. "I tell him so many time! Is . . . how you say, *segreto*, our work!"

"Secret," Hugh translated.

"*Sì*, is not for showing off to . . ." Orlando trailed off, staring at the slit-open packet of black powder that Hugh held out to him.

"Is this what you were making when you burned down your laboratory in Rome?" Hugh asked.

Orlando sighed pensively. "The lady Clare, she will be very much angry if she know you see this thing."

"So this is where your alchemical experiments have led," Phillipa said. "This is why you were brought to Halthorpe."

"Were you promised a laboratory and equipment," Hugh asked, "as long as you agreed to reproduce the Chinese powder?"

"Are you developing some sort of weapon?" Phillipa asked. "Is that how you're paying Clare back for—"

"*Prego!*" Orlando spread his hands beseechingly. "You have see too much already. I will be in very much *difficoltà* if I speak to you of my work."

"You mean this part of your work," Phillipa said. "Clare knows we've been snooping around. She wanted to mislead us, didn't she? She told you to tell us about the alchemy—but not that you were using it to make the black powder."

"And she made you hide all evidence of it yesterday," Hugh said, "knowing I would steal the key to the cellar if the opportunity presented itself." He chuckled humorlessly. "And I tumbled right into her trap."

"*Prego,* I beg of you!" Orlando implored. "I am making *volta di segretezza.*"

"Vow of secrecy," Hugh said.

"It will go very badly for me if she find out I tell you about the . . ." He nodded toward the parchment packet in Hugh's hand.

"But you didn't tell us," Hugh said.

"Yes, but . . . you know."

Hugh shrugged. "Not through any fault of yours. Phillipa and I would have no reason to speak of this to Clare . . . unless you did first."

Orlando's eyes lit with comprehension: Hugh and Phillipa would keep their mouths shut if he would—and all of them would be spared Clare's wrath. The Italian nodded. "Is agreed. We keep each other's *segreto,* yes?"

"Yes, but . . ." Phillipa touched his arm. "Orlando, you know you shouldn't be doing this work."

He looked taken aback that she would say such a thing. "Is good work. Is great challenge to the mind."

Just like Uncle Lotulf, Orlando embraced the intellectual pursuit while ignoring its practical application. "But think of all the harm that could come of it."

Orlando shook his head vigorously. "All knowledge is good. All learning is worthy."

"I've always thought so," Phillipa murmured. "Now I'm not so sure."

Phillipa swam out of a fitful sleep that night to the realization that it was, if anything, even hotter than when they had retired. The air felt thick; her night shift clung damply to her.

What had awakened her this time? she wondered, and then it came to her. Hugh, sleeping behind her with his arm around her, as usual, had stirred; perhaps it was his restlessness that had roused her. She was about to speak to him when he moved again, his hips flexing slowly, pressing and releasing. She felt the tension in his flanks, the hard column of his sex grazing the small of her back. She was stunned; he hadn't attempted any intimacies since his first night at Halthorpe, when he'd told her they shouldn't be together like that anymore.

He moved again, another lingering, sinuous thrust.

"Hugh?" she whispered.

His hand twitched; he sucked in a breath. He'd been asleep, she realized; she'd awakened him. He went very still for a moment, and then his breath left him in a long, tremulous exhalation. "Sorry, I . . . I was dreaming."

He lifted his arm from her and moved back so that he wasn't in contact with her—not easy in this narrow bed. She heard the straw in the mattress crackle as he shifted his position.

She sat up and gathered her sweat-dampened hair off her neck, thinking she should have braided it before bed, given the heat. Hugh was lying on his back, his left leg bent at the knee, his right arm draped over his eyes. Tonight, for the first time, he had dispensed with his shirt and gone to bed in naught but his underdrawers, probably because of the heat, but possibly also because, having revealed to Phillipa how he came by the scars on his back, he felt less inclined to hide them.

Moonlight filtered through the arrow slit closest to the bed, painting a streak of iridescence across Hugh's glistening body—the hard-packed planes of his chest, the taut ridges of his belly. Bands of muscle defined his long arms, his powerful legs. He was the quintessential male animal, lethally strong, achingly beautiful.

Phillipa rose from bed. "Would you like a drink of water?"

He shook his head without uncovering his eyes.

She poured a cup of water from the ewer on the wash stand and drank it, then filled the basin, dampened a washrag, and bathed her face and the back of her neck.

Her night shift stuck to her, an oppressive weight in the heat. She pulled it away from her skin, thinking how delicious it would be to peel it off and sleep without a stitch on. Odd; she'd never slept in the nude before, never even wanted to, no matter how warm the night. Now, imagining it, she wondered why not. The linen sheets would feel soft and cool against her bare skin, the straw beneath just slightly prickly. If a stray breeze crept through the arrow slits, it would caress her like a lover's breath.

She looked over at Hugh, still lying in the same position. Even with his upraised leg, she could see the rigid shape beneath his drawers.

Think of the sun as man, and the moon as woman, Orlando had said. *Very much separate, very much apart. But bring them together . . . is magico, no?*

It *had* been magic, making love to him that first time—although, if she had it to do over again, she would have let him undress her. *A thousand times I've imagined what you look like without your clothes on,* he'd told her. *Every night, I dream of holding you naked in my arms.*

Was that what he'd been dreaming about just now?

Phillipa sought out her moonlit reflection in the looking glass tacked over the wash stand. A butterfly smiled back at her.

Without looking in Hugh's direction, lest she lose her nerve, Phillipa pulled her shift over her head and hung it on a peg. She would have expected to feel painfully exposed, standing naked in the same room with a man, even Hugh; instead, she felt an exhilarating sense of rightness.

A film of perspiration clung to her. Wringing out the washrag, she skimmed it over her throat and along each arm. She dipped it in the basin again and squeezed it over her chest, her nipples puckering as the water trickled in rivulets down her breasts and belly and legs. Dropping the cloth back in the basin, she gathered up her hair and plaited it in a single braid, securing it with the leather thong Hugh had tossed onto the wash stand after untying it from his own hair. She turned toward the bed.

He was watching her, still lying on his back, his right arm curved over his head, his chest rising and falling as if he'd just raced up a hill. His eyes were luminous in the shaft of moonlight that played over his face, his expression that of a man who'd just seen a statue of an angel spread its wings and rise into the heavens.

His gaze was riveted on her as she came toward him and sat on the edge of the bed. She trailed a feathery caress down his cheek.

He closed his eyes, his throat moving. "This isn't wise, love."

She lowered her mouth to his. "It isn't supposed to be."

Early morning sunlight was gleaming through the arrow slits by the time Hugh and Phillipa uncoupled for the third time, drenched and sated, their chests heaving. Phillipa's body hummed like the strings of a lute that had been played all night, making the most sublime and joyous music imaginable.

Lying on his back next to Phillipa, Hugh lifted her hand to his mouth and kissed it, his own hand still slightly unsteady. "God, Phillipa," he whispered.

When she'd taken off her shift and come to bed, and he'd told her it wasn't wise, she had worried, for a moment, that it had been a mistake. But the touch of her lips against his had seemed to galvanize him. He'd banded his arms around her, pulled her close, kissed her with such raw hunger that she'd felt as if her heart were going to burst.

She'd reached down to untie his drawers, her fingers grazing his straining flesh as they fumbled with the task; he'd growled, arched his back. He yanked at the drawstring, snapping it, kicked the drawers off, and rolled onto her, crushing her into the mattress. That first time had been hard and furious, two beings thrashing together in a violent struggle to fuse into one.

The second time had been slow, so slow, a dreamlike dance of two sweat-slicked bodies. He'd touched and kissed her everywhere, his caresses rhythmic, deep, the heat of his mouth intoxicating . . . and she'd done the same to him, until they were both trembling and moaning, quivering on the edge. She'd felt as if she were filled with glittering Chinese powder, and Hugh was the flame. When he lunged into her, she exploded. He drove her to a second paroxysm before surrendering with a roar to his own fierce pleasure.

After that, they curled up front-to-back and fell asleep—at least, Phillipa did, only to awaken at dawn to the slippery glide of his fingertips on her throat and chest, her breasts, her belly, the slick heat between her legs. He'd pressed into her from behind, rocking them both to delirious fulfillment.

Now, gazing at the ceiling rafters as she lay side-by-side with him on the damp, rumpled sheet, her hand in his, Phillipa knew with absolute certainty that her heart, her soul, her body, would forever belong to one man and one man only—Hugh of Wexford.

"I love you, Hugh," she said quietly.

He squeezed her hand and held it to his lightly furred chest. She felt the swift, erratic thudding of his heart.

"We shouldn't have done this." His voice sounded as if it had been scraped raw.

She turned her head to look at him. "Does it frighten you so much, to be loved?"

"You think you love me." He met her gaze, his eyes all-too-transparent in the morning sunlight. "You don't feel what you think you feel."

"I know what I feel. And I think I know what you feel, too."

He looked back at the ceiling, but not before she saw something grim and bleak chase the warmth from his eyes. "This *was* a mistake—I knew it from the beginning."

"I remember," she said. "You told me you didn't want to be the man a woman couldn't bear to look at the next day when she realized it really was just about sex."

"That's right." He let go of her hand, clawed his limp hair off his face.

"But I am looking at you, Hugh. Because it wasn't just about sex."

"Wasn't it?"

"No. It was about *us*."

"There isn't an 'us.'" He sat up, his elbows braced on his updrawn knees, the heels of his palms grinding against his forehead. "There can never be an 'us.' Christ, Phillipa, one of us needs to be strong. Can't you see that?"

What she could see, horribly ugly and real in the light of day, was the network of scars on his back—a decade's worth of anguish that he had endured by retreating from it.

She sat up and laid a hand on his shoulder. "You're good at being strong, Hugh. You can rise above anything, even your feelings for me. But you needn't. You shouldn't."

"Those feelings—if I had them—would be my ruin. And yours."

"Perhaps they'd be our salvation. Why should we have to be strong alone when we can be twice as strong together?"

"It doesn't work that way, Phillipa. We'd be only half as strong if we tethered ourselves together. We'd be dependent on each other, subject to each other's whims and demands—and therefore weaker and more vulnerable. You're so young, so sheltered, so untouched by the world's miseries."

She nodded, conceding the point. "I only wish you were, too."

Footsteps raced down the corridor outside the bedchamber, followed by the frenzied pounding of a fist on the door. "Milady! Sir Hugh! Are you awake?"

"Edmee?" Phillipa said. "What the devil . . ."

"It's Istagio. He's . . ." Edmee broke off in a choking little sob. "Jesus have mercy. He's dead."

Chapter 20

Hugh smelled it as they climbed the stairs that led to the second level of the north wing, where Istagio's bedchamber was located. The stench of death was unmistakable.

"Wait, love." *Damn, why can't I stop calling her "love"?* He reached for Phillipa, in front of him on the narrow stone stairwell, closing his hand around her waist. Edmee, ahead of them, continued on. "Why don't you wait downstairs? This is likely to be pretty unpleasant."

"I've seen dead bodies, Hugh." She looked absurdly pretty in the pink linen kirtle she'd thrown on hurriedly after Edmee's summons, her face framed by disheveled wisps of hair that had sprung free from her braid during their long night of lovemaking.

"But with this heat and all . . ."

"I'm fine—really." Her mouth quirked. "Of course, if *you'd* prefer to wait downstairs . . ."

With a smirk, he prodded her up the stairs. "Come on, let's get this over with."

They heard Orlando's piteous lament as they emerged from the stairwell; the Italian, still in his long night shirt and sleeping cap, was among a group of guests and servants gathered at this end of the corridor. According to Edmee, it was Orlando who had discovered Istagio's body in bed when he'd knocked on his bedchamber door to awaken him this morning. "God forgive me for how I speak to him last night. I call him bad names, I tell him he is fool. And now he is gone and I can never take it back . . ."

"Orlando." Phillipa embraced him. "I'm so sorry. But you mustn't blame yourself for the things you said last night."

"She's right." Hugh patted Orlando on the back. "He provoked you. You're only human."

Phillipa spent a few minutes comforting Orlando and then asked which room was Istagio's, so that she and Hugh could pay their respects.

Edmee pointed to an open door at the far end of the corridor.

Turstin de Ver removed the scented handkerchief from his face to say, "Nicolas Capellanus is in there now, giving him Last Rites."

"Is too late," Orlando moaned. "He's already dead. Now he never be at rest."

"Even those who die unshriven can benefit from Last Rites," said Hugh, who hoped this was true, having known many good men who'd lain dead on the battle-field for hours or even days before the sacrament of Extreme Unction could be administered to them.

Phillipa touched Hugh's arm and nodded toward Istagio's room. "Shall we?"

"Here." Turstin handed Phillipa his perfumed handkerchief. "If you're going down there, you'll need this. The windows are open, but it doesn't help much."

The smell became so staggering as they approached the door to Istagio's chamber that it was all Hugh could do to put one foot in front of the other. He closed his mouth and covered his nose with his hand, but it didn't help. The fetid odor crawled in through his nostrils to settle, thick and rank, in the back of his throat.

They arrived at the open doorway to find Father Nicolas standing beside a narrow, four-post bed in his white surplice and stole, a cloth tied around his lower face, pulling a sheet up over Istagio's head. He nodded at Hugh, then corked a little vial and slipped it into a satchel on the floor.

"She shouldn't do that," Father Nicolas told Hugh when Phillipa took hold of the sheet to pull it back. It was telling, Hugh thought, that the priest directed the comment to him rather than to Phillipa, as if his disdain for women ran so deep that he wouldn't even lower himself to censure one directly.

"Why not?" Phillipa asked.

Maintaining eye contact with Hugh, Nicolas said, " 'Tisn't a pretty sight."

"I would hardly expect it to be." Phillipa drew the sheet back slowly, partially uncovering Istagio's remains, which were nothing short of monstrous. His body, already obese, had distended grotesquely in the heat. The poor man stared sightlessly at the ceiling with half-open eyes, his mouth agape, his face swollen and discolored. Hugh and Phillipa both crossed themselves.

With the hand that wasn't holding the handkerchief to her nose, Phillipa gently tilted Istagio's head back to examine his neck. "I wish my sister Ada were here. She'd know what to look for."

"Is this the way you found him?" Hugh asked the priest.

"Aye."

"His arms were crossed over his chest like this?" Phillipa inquired.

Father Nicolas untied the cloth from around his face and handed it to Hugh on his way to the door. "Here. There's some aromatic oil on it."

Hugh took the cloth gratefully and pressed it to his nose. "Did you cross his arms, Father?"

"He is just as I found him." From the doorway, the priest scowled as Phillipa uncovered the lower half of Istagio's naked body. "Has she no shame?"

"We're just trying to determine why he died," Hugh said.

"He died because the Lord chose to take him. That is as much as any of us needs to know." Father Nicolas turned and left.

"How long do you suppose he's been dead?" Phillipa asked.

"All night."

"You seem very sure of yourself." She lifted one of Istagio's arms.

"I've seen bodies left unattended in every sort of climate and condition you can imagine." Too damned many of them. "I know the rate at which they putrefy in damp heat like this."

"So he was killed yesterday evening, then?"

"He *died* yesterday evening—before matins, I would say. It could have been from natural causes, though. I don't see any wounds on him, and unless I'm missing something, there are no obvious signs of strangulation."

"Look at this." Phillipa turned Istagio's bloated hand from side to side.

"And . . . what, precisely, am I looking at?"

"These marks here. They're hard to see, but—"

"Ah. Yes."

"He's got them on both wrists." She moved down to peer at Istagio's feet. "And on his ankles, too."

"Mother of God." They turned to find Aldous standing in the doorway, a hand clamped over his mouth, his horrified gaze riveted on Istagio's corpse. He had obviously just arisen from bed, given his wayward hair and his attire—a rumpled shirt over underdrawers. Clare's keys were visible as a lump beneath the shirt.

"Aldous," Hugh asked, "is Clare still here?"

"Nay. She . . ." The deacon closed his eyes; his sweat-sheened face was as pale as candle wax. "She left before dawn."

Hugh started to ask when she was expected to return, but Aldous lurched away, keys jangling, a panicked moan rising from him. Presently there came the sounds of violent retching.

Hugh rubbed his jaw. "Clare would have been furious if she'd found out about Istagio's little demonstration at the river yesterday evening, after all the trouble she's gone through to keep their activities a secret."

"Aye," said Phillipa, "but do you think she could actually murder someone in cold blood?"

Hugh shook his head. "Nay, I can't see it."

"What about Aldous?"

"He hasn't got the stones for it. Besides, listen to him out there. He'd not be reacting like that if he'd been the instrument of Istagio's death."

"It must have been the queen's agent trying to silence Istagio before he did even more damage." Phillipa sighed and returned her attention to the corpse. "Help me to turn him over, would you?"

They inspected the body at nauseating length, but without uncovering any additional signs of violence. "What do you think?" Hugh asked.

"I think we should speak with Orlando."

They found the metaphysician in his chamber on the floor below, fully dressed now, but gazing listlessly out the window as he sat on the edge of his bed, his face drawn, his eyes red-rimmed.

"We need to know how you found Istagio this morning," Phillipa told him. "*Exactly* how you found him."

"I find him dead." Orlando executed a quavering sign of the cross. "He die in his sleep."

"Did you touch his body at all?" Hugh asked, thinking about those crossed arms.

Orlando shook his head. "I leave him as I find him. He die in his sleep."

Phillipa glanced at Hugh as she sat next to Orlando, clasping one of his hands. "You're trying to protect him, aren't you? You're worried about his reputation, about what people will think if they know how you found him."

Orlando shook his head, his eyes wetly glazed. "I know Istagio since he is little boy. Is good people, his *famiglia*. They no want him to leave Roma, but I say . . ." His shoulders shook; tears trickled down his face. "I say I take care of him . . ."

"You did take care of him," Phillipa said. "You did

the best you could, but how could you have known we
have a murderer among us?"

"No! Istagio die in his—"

"You're trying to protect his memory," Phillipa said,
"when you should be helping us to figure out who did
this to him. Tell us the truth—Istagio was tied up when
you found him, wasn't he?"

Orlando buried his face in his hands, murmuring to
himself in his own tongue.

Phillipa put an arm around his shoulder. "You untied
him so he wouldn't be found that way, didn't you?"

He nodded. "It was so . . . undignify. He would be
shame for people to see him like that."

Hugh thought it best not to mention that, in life, Istagio was hardly a paragon of dignity. "Were his hands
and feet bound to the bedposts?"

"*Sì.*" Reaching under the bed, Orlando produced a
tangle of black silk stockings. "With these. And the . . .
how you say . . . *cuscino* . . ."

"Pillow," Hugh supplied.

"It was on top of his face."

"Oh." Phillipa shook her head. "Poor Istagio."

Orlando leaned down to fumble beneath the bed
again.

"What are you looking for?" Hugh asked.

"This." The Italian brought out a whip of the type
known as a "cat" for the scratchlike marks its many
lashes left on flesh. "I find it on the floor next to his
bed."

Phillipa did not look surprised to see it.

Marguerite du Roche's bedchamber was at the top of
Halthorpe Castle's north turret, the door to which was just
down the corridor. Given that the woman had very likely
committed a rather gruesome murder the night before,
Hugh insisted that Phillipa and Orlando wait at the bottom
of the tower while he confronted Marguerite alone.

Phillipa knew better than to object. Hugh was, after
all, a trained, experienced soldier. If the situation be-

came dangerous, she and Orlando would only get in the way.

Hugh opened the tower door and climbed three steps of the winding stairwell that coiled through the ancient stone tower, then paused, frowning.

"What is it?" Phillipa asked.

"Don't you smell it?"

She stepped into the stairwell and breathed in; so did Orlando.

"Oh, my God," she whispered. It was the same smell they had encountered as they'd approached Istagio's room; it was the smell of death.

Hugh sprinted up the stairs, not protesting when Phillipa and Orlando followed him. He hesitated on the landing at the top of the stairs, where the odor was most pronounced, then slowly opened the door.

The room was dusky, the window shutters being latched tight. A mammoth, curtained bed stood against one wall; God knew how they'd gotten the mattress up those stairs. Against the opposite wall was one of those slanted writing desks with an attached chair, such as a monk would sit at in his scriptorium. Marguerite, clad in a crimson silk wrapper, was slumped over the desk facing away from them, her hair draping her like a flaming waterfall.

Hugh circled the desk and lifted the hair off her face, then closed his eyes and let it fall back. He crossed himself as he straightened up. Phillipa and Orlando followed suit.

"I don't think she's been dead as long as Istagio," Hugh said. "Look here—she wrote something." He slid a sheet of parchment from beneath Marguerite's hand, the fingers of which were still curled stiffly around a raven's quill. There was an open clay jar of ink on the flat upper edge of the writing desk, alongside an empty silver wine cup.

Hugh unshuttered the window above the desk, flooding the chamber with sunlight. His eyes widened slightly as he studied the sheet of parchment, and then he handed it to Phillipa. There were three short lines of words neatly inked in the middle of the page—in Hebrew.

"It's gibberish—" Hugh said.

Phillipa looked up to meet Hugh's sober gaze and share in the same unspoken conclusion—that Marguerite must have been Queen Eleanor's agent, or else how could she have known the queen's cipher?

Turning, she surveyed the chamber, which was small but lavishly appointed, with fine silken hangings adorning the stone walls and bed curtains of purple brocade. A dozen or more luxurious gowns hung from hooks in the wall. Scores of little vials and pots cluttered the wash stand, and the gilt-framed looking glass tacked above it was the largest Phillipa had ever seen. Crossing to the little table next to the bed, she peered into the ewer that sat there, finding it half-filled with wine; cloves and cinnamon sticks floated on the surface of the ruby liquid, but the smell of death overpowered their scent.

Hugh rubbed his jaw. "You did say that murder would be just another thrill to Marguerite, a new form of gratification."

Orlando said, "What means this . . . grati . . . gratifi . . ." He shook his head as if to clear it. "Why she do this to Istagio? He never hurt nobody."

"It's . . . complicated," said Phillipa, pulling the stopper out of a little blue glass vial she'd found lying on its side next to the ewer. "There's much that we don't understand, either."

"Such as why she's dead." Hugh lifted Marguerite's hair again to look upon her face, his expression grim. "She presumably killed Istagio, but who killed her? And how?"

"Look at this." Phillipa tilted the vial, spilling a little pile of white crystalline powder into her palm.

The two men came closer to examine the powder. Orlando sniffed it. "Is smell too bad in here to tell if there is odor." He dipped a fingertip into it and touched it lightly to his tongue; Hugh followed suit.

"No taste," Hugh said.

Orlando nodded. *"Arsenico."*

"Arsenic?" Hugh spat into the rushes.

"Arsenic, *sì.* White arsenic. Don't worry, that little won't harm you."

"This is arsenic?" Phillipa rubbed a bit of the granular powder between her thumb and fingers. It looked so innocuous.

Orlando nodded. "The *minerale* from the ground, it has the golden color and the very strong taste. But the great Saracen alchemist Jábir ibn Hâyyan, he roast the *minerale,* thinking maybe it is the key to the philosopher's stone. Instead, he make the white arsenic. Is most dangerous poison. It mix up good in hot liquid—no color, no smell, no taste. Very powerful—kill very much fast."

"Spiced wine is served hot," Phillipa said.

Hugh handed the sheet of parchment to Phillipa. "Take a look at this. There are seven words here, but two of them are repeated twice. Is it some sort of verse, do you suppose?"

Because of the easily recognizable word pattern, it took Phillipa less than a minute, even without having the key to refer to, to decipher what appeared to be Marguerite du Roche's departing message to the world. "Well, I'll be . . ."

"What does it say?" Hugh asked.

" '*Mea culpa, mea culpa, mea maxima culpa.*' "

"Through my fault, through my fault," Hugh murmured, repeating the familiar litany of contrition in the common tongue, "through my most grievous fault."

"Perhaps," Phillipa said thoughtfully, "she did not find murder so gratifying after all."

It was much later that morning, nearly nones, when Hugh opened the door of the bedchamber he shared with Phillipa to find her sitting in a big wooden bathtub pouring a bucket of lavender-scented water over her head.

"Oh, sorry." He started to back out through the door.
"I'll just—"

"Don't be silly." With a smile, she set the empty
bucket aside and skimmed the wet hair off her face;
water droplets trembled on her bare breasts. "Why
shouldn't you stay?"

Why shouldn't he, indeed, after last night? Still, he
felt a low hum of unease. It should please him that she
could bathe in front of him without a hint of self-
consciousness. How often had he dreamed of seeing her
just like this, exquisitely naked and smiling at him with
the intimacy of a lover?

But that was just it, he realized. It was that very intimacy that discomfited him. He'd felt it all morning, a
nagging disquiet that he couldn't shake despite the appalling discovery of two bodies in Halthorpe Castle and
the conclusions they'd been forced to draw—that Marguerite, in her capacity as the queen's agent, had murdered Istagio for his indiscretion, only to find herself so
overwhelmed with guilt that she took her own life.

Phillipa stood up in the tub, water sluicing off her
elegant little body like quicksilver. "Would you hand me
that towel?"

Hugh lifted the sheet of soft linen from the back of a
chair and gave it to her, then turned away and crossed
to one of the arrow slits. Through it he saw Raoul and
Isabelle d'Argentan standing near the gate to the outer
bailey, engaged in a heated quarrel. No, not a quarrel,
of course not; Raoul would never quarrel with his beloved wife. Instead, she seemed to be berating him,
while he stood there like a whipped dog and took it. A
handful of onlookers snickered openly.

After that humiliating court of love three days ago,
Hugh had finally asked Raoul how he could tolerate Isabelle's treatment of him, and wasn't he ever tempted to
pick up and leave, perhaps petition for an annulment of
his marriage. Raoul had maintained that Hugh was only
seeing it from an outsider's perspective, that he loved

Isabelle and she him, but that it had become complicated, terribly complicated.

To which Hugh had replied that love tends to do that. *Does it frighten you so much, to be loved?*

Indeed, it frightened him a great deal.

Water splashed softly, followed by the muted snap of rushes; Phillipa must be stepping out of the tub. "Have the bodies been seen to?"

Without turning around, Hugh said, "Aye. Orlando has arranged for Istagio to be buried in the chapel graveyard. But Father Nicolas has refused to let Marguerite be laid to rest there. He said suicide is too grave a sin to reward with interment in consecrated ground. He ordered her body taken into the woods and exposed."

Phillipa whispered something he couldn't make out.

"Unfortunately," Hugh said, "after he made that announcement, Orlando declared that it was just as well, because a murderess ought not to be buried with decent people."

"Oh, no," Phillipa moaned. They had wanted to keep the circumstances of Istagio's death a secret, given the sensitive political issues involved. "But we'd asked him not to say anything about—"

"He was distraught and not thinking. He apologized to me afterward."

"Did many people hear him?"

"Aye. You should have seen the color drain from Aldous's face. I thought he was going to keel over."

"No doubt he was contemplating all the times Marguerite might have pressed a pillow over *his* face after she'd gotten him . . . how did she put it that time? . . . all trussed up like a roasted swan."

Isabelle was swatting at Raoul now, driving him back toward the castle entrance. Hugh knew what the altercation was about. Raoul had been anxious to leave Halthorpe ever since the court of love, but his wife had refused. He had redoubled his efforts to talk her into it after this morning's gruesome discoveries, but Isabelle, like the rest of Clare's guests, seemed to view the murder-suicide as just another tantalizing scandal for their amusement. Why should they leave now, she had demanded of her husband at breakfast, just when things had gotten so terribly exciting?

"Would you lace me up?"

Hugh turned to find Phillipa approaching him in a white linen kirtle, holding her damp hair in a knot on her head. She turned and he saw that the garment was open down the back, the cord that secured it strung slackly through the bottom few eyelets. He hesitated, feeling strangely taken aback. Over the years he must have laced up a hundred kirtles, but it had never felt quite the same as it did now, like a domestic task, something one might ask of a husband.

"Edmee normally does this for me," Phillipa said over her shoulder, "but at this time of the day she's needed to help serve dinner."

Hugh tugged the cord tight in its bottom eyelets, snugging the kirtle around Phillipa's small hips and slender little waist, then began threading it through the rest of the eyelets. His fingertips brushed her back as he worked; her skin was like satin over the delicate little bones of her spine, warm from her bath and redolent of lavender. He loved to touch her.

He loved it too much.

"Did you have a chance to ask Orlando what's really going on in the cellar?" she asked.

"Aye, but he's more close-mouthed than ever, after what happened to Istagio. I don't think he truly realized what he'd gotten himself involved in. Now that Istagio's been murdered for his folly, Orlando is determined to keep mum."

"But the person who killed Istagio is dead," Phillipa pointed out. "Shouldn't that make Orlando feel safer about talking?"

"Theoretically, yes, but he's not taking any chances. In truth, he's so upset about Istagio that he's not really thinking logically. In any event, I couldn't talk him into opening up."

"Perhaps I'll have better luck," Phillipa said.

"I doubt it." Having woven the cord through all the eyelets, Hugh pulled it tight, causing the kirtle to conform to Phillipa's feminine slopes and curves as if it had been sewn onto her. "Orlando seemed adamant about keeping his counsel. Said he wished he'd never heard of the black powder."

"So do I, now that I've seen what it can do—especially in the hands of someone like Orlando. Dried snakes and talismans notwithstanding, he's a brilliant man. If it's his objective to create some devastating new weapon for Queen Eleanor, he will do it."

"And it *could* be devastating, indeed," Hugh said as he tied the cord into a bow. "If the queen were to equip her soldiers with weapons that burst apart like those Chinese toys, her revolt would be victorious within days."

Phillipa turned to face him, releasing her hair, which fell in an inky tangle down her back. "Are you sure?" she asked as she retrieved her big oxhorn comb from the wash stand and sat on the edge of the bed to comb out the wet snarls. "King Henry has at his disposal thousands of the most seasoned archers and crossbowmen in Europe. Not to mention swordsmen, like you, and then there are his siege engines, and—"

"I daresay none of that will matter if the queen gets her hands on whatever it is Orlando is cooking up in that cellar. Swords and arrows and maces and the like— weapons that pierce and crush—require skill to wield effectively, skill and nerve. It takes some ballocks to . . . pardon me."

"That's all right." Phillipa smiled as she plucked at a particularly stubborn knot. Hugh resisted the urge to take the comb from her and perform the task himself. It would be reminiscent of that first night they'd made love, when he had brushed her hair to relax her—too reminiscent. Would that he had had the strength to walk away when she had asked him, so sweetly and shyly, to take her innocence. Would that he had never placed his heart in her hands, because taking it back was going to be the most agonizing thing he'd ever done.

Pacing restlessly away from her, he said, "It takes some grit to walk up to a man and run him through with your steel, especially if he's armed as well. And it takes a fighting force of vast numbers to overwhelm one's enemy with such weapons, because they take down one soldier at a time. A weapon that explodes, if it's powerful enough, could kill scores of men at once, shatter curtain walls, destroy castles . . ."

"Merciful God," Phillipa whispered.

"God is not always in a merciful humor," Hugh said. "I've seen the results when He's feeling vindictive. The aftermath of battle is an ugly sight. I can't imagine how much more hellish it would be if one side had weapons of such brutality that can be so easily employed."

"We've got to stop that from happening."

Hugh turned toward Phillipa to find her sitting with her comb clutched in her lap, her eyes wide with distress.

" 'Tis our mission to do so," he reminded her.

"I don't just mean in order to stop the queen's rebellion, but because no army should have such horrible power at its disposal."

Hugh sighed and leaned back against the wall. "You should know better than most that knowledge can't be curtailed forever, even destructive knowledge—especially destructive knowledge. The Church has tried to outlaw the use of crossbows against Christians, but with little success. Rest assured, this black powder will eventually be produced in Europe, and terrible weapons made from it, and warfare will never be the same. Nothing we do now can prevent that from happening. But we just might forestall the inevitable by keeping such weapons out of the hands of Eleanor of Aquitaine—and in the process, we'll ensure that the duly crowned king of the English remains on his throne."

She rose from the bed. "Now that we're fairly certain of what's going on in the cellar, isn't our work here essentially done? If King Henry finds out about the black powder, won't that be enough for him to move against the queen?"

"Unfortunately, no. Remember our meeting with Lord Richard? He stressed that the king needs 'solid, unimpeachable evidence' if he's to take the queen into custody. His position with his subjects and allies is rocky right now. He can't afford to jeopardize what little support he's got by incarcerating a wife he's already publicly wronged just because we're 'fairly certain' of what's going on in the cellar of Castle Halthorpe."

"Solid evidence . . ." Phillipa murmured. "What about that letter from Queen Eleanor to Clare? She implied that they're hatching treason. Isn't that enough to—"

"Nay, we need more than implications, and she can always claim that the letter is a fake. The king needs unquestionable proof that she's preparing to go to war against him, something he can show people."

"You kept that little parchment packet of black powder. Isn't that enough to—"

"Nay, 'tis but a toy, a curiosity from a distant land. We've got to get our hands on one of Orlando's weapons and spirit it out of here. That's the only way we can prove what the queen is up to."

Phillipa sat down again and tugged the comb through her hair, but with an air of distraction as she sorted through their situation. "Marguerite was evidently the queen's agent, and she's dead, so that simplifies things and affords us a measure of safety. But we've still got Aldous to deal with, and Clare, when she returns."

"They're harmless, the both of them. They haven't got the stomach for killing."

"Even if their very lives are at stake? Treason is punishable by burning, isn't it?"

"Depends on one's rank and the nature of the disloyalty. More often than not, traitors are simply hanged, although sometimes they're cut down before they've choked to death so that they can be disemboweled, quartered, and beheaded."

Phillipa whispered something and crossed herself.

"If the king is disposed toward mercy for some reason," Hugh continued, "they might simply be confined under armed guard. Certainly that will be the queen's fate, if she's found guilty of conspiring against her husband. He wouldn't dare execute her, not after the outcry over Becket's death, and especially after betraying her so openly with Rosamund Clifford."

Phillipa worried her lower lip between her teeth, making her look like a sagacious little girl. Hugh closed his eyes and rubbed his forehead, wishing she didn't affect him the way she did.

"We've got to get back into the cellar," she said. "If there are weapons to be found, that's where they'll be."

"Aldous has the keys now." Hugh rubbed his chin. "I might be able to steal them from him. If I were to sneak into his bedchamber tonight while he's asleep—"

"It won't work."

"I can be as quiet as a ghost when I need to be."

"I know that, but it won't help you. He sleeps with those keys on. Remember? He had them under his shirt this morning. You could never get them off without waking him."

"Ah." Hugh raked a hand through his hair. "No, I don't suppose I could. Then perhaps . . . I don't know, perhaps you could talk him into . . ." Hugh shrugged. "You're so clever at this sort of thing. You think of something."

"I've got to admit," she said as she drew the comb through her now-smooth hair, "I'm at a loss this time."

He crossed his arms, grinning. "You mean you're admitting defeat? You? I never thought I'd see it happen."

"If that's meant to be a challenge that I'm supposed to rise to, I'm afraid I'll have to disappoint you. There's only one way I can think of to get those keys from Aldous."

She regarded him with quiet gravity, the comb in her lap, compelling him with her gaze to understand what she meant.

"Nay," he said automatically, pushing away from the wall.

Her eyebrows quirked. "You used to tell me it was the only way."

"And you used to tell me that there were more ways to get what one wants from a man than to barter one's body for it."

"Obviously, I was wrong, or I would already have succeeded, wouldn't I?"

He shook his head vehemently, wishing to God she wasn't right. "We'll think of something . . ."

"I already have," she said with exasperating calm. "Tonight, I'll go to Aldous's chamber and let him seduce me—"

"Jesu . . ."

"But I'll tell him the keys are getting in the way, as undoubtedly they would, and I'll ask him to remove them. Then, after he's asleep, I'll simply take them, let myself into the cellar, and—"

"I don't like it."

"Do you think I do?" She rose and returned the comb to its place on the wash stand. "It's the only way, Hugh. You know it."

He did. But . . . "Could you really do it? Could you give yourself to him, after . . ." His gaze lit on the bed, their narrow little bed with its humble straw mattress and blissful memories.

"Why shouldn't I?" she asked softly, her back to him as she stood at the wash stand, fiddling with her toiletries. "Just this morning you told me that what had transpired between us last night was just about sex, and that there would never be an 'us.' You said any feelings we might have for each other would be our ruin. So tell me, please, why I shouldn't sleep with Aldous Ewing for the good of the realm."

From where he stood, Hugh could see Phillipa's image in the little steel looking glass nailed to the stone wall over the wash stand. Her reflection was distorted, hazy . . . yet he could make out the look in her eyes, a look by now all too familiar to him, the look of a small, shrewd creature intent on outwitting its foe.

He realized then what she was trying to do. She wasn't at all prepared to sleep with Aldous Ewing; most likely she had no intention of doing so. Her purpose was to force Hugh to confront his feelings for her, to beg her not to.

Part of him ached to capitulate to her, just as he had that night in Southwark when she'd asked him to be the first, just as he had last night when she'd come to him naked and irresistible in the dreamy moonlight.

He should have been strong from the beginning, he should have risen above his hunger for her, his torment of longing. He should have resisted her, knowing what would come of it, knowing that he cared too much and should keep his distance. Instead, he'd let himself get ensnared in a morass of feelings he couldn't control. And now . . .

Now he had the chance to make it right. By claiming she was ready to sleep with Aldous, Phillipa was unwittingly giving him the opportunity to do what he should have done long ago. He'd lacked the strength then.

He must summon it now.

Turning to face an arrow slit, he braced his hands on either side of it. "All right, then," he said woodenly. "I'll return to Eastingham today."

"What?" The rushes behind him rustled. "You're . . . you're leaving?"

He closed his eyes, his jaw clenched, willing himself to say what had to be said, to do what had to be done. "As far as Aldous is concerned, the only reason you haven't bedded him yet is because I've been here. Therefore I must leave Halthorpe if you are to . . . carry out your plan."

There came a long moment of silence, and then she said, "Perhaps . . . perhaps you're right. Perhaps I *can* figure out some other way to get those keys from—"

"Nay." He swung around to face her, determined to allow her no retreat from what she had wrought. "You were right when you said it was the only way. And it is—make no mistake. Whether you meant it or not when you said you were willing to sleep with Aldous, the fact is, it's our only hope for gaining access to those keys. You've got to do it, and that means I've got to leave. I'll go to Eastingham."

"Hugh." She took a step toward him, imploring him with those big, liquid-brown eyes. "Please don't leave. I won't feel safe here without you, not after everything that's happened."

"Marguerite was the only real threat. You said yourself that her death makes things much simpler and safer."

"Aye, but there's still Aldous and Clare."

"They're all bluster and no backbone. They're incapable of doing you any harm."

"I'm not so sure of that."

"I am."

"Hugh." She came toward him, but he sidestepped her. Snatching his satchel up off the floor, he threw it on the bed. Swiftly he plucked his clothes off their hooks and stuffed them inside.

Hugh tossed his razor, whetstone, and comb into the satchel. "If you find yourself in some sort of fix, Raoul will help you. He's a good man with the sword, and trustworthy."

"Hugh, please stay. Please." She grabbed the sleeve of his tunic.

He shrugged her off as he lifted his wineskin from its hook and looped it over his chest. With his back to her, he said, "There's naught to be gained by my staying, and much to lose."

In a small, unsteady voice she said, "Hugh, I love you. I didn't mean what I said before. I can't sleep with Aldous. Please, Hugh . . ."

Gritting his teeth, Hugh latched his satchel with abrupt movements. *Be strong. Rise above it . . .* "You can and you should. Perhaps tupping Aldous will take some of the mystery out of sex and help you to stop mooning over me."

Hugh turned to find her staring at him, looking very small and utterly stricken, her arms wrapped around herself. As he watched, a shimmer of tears pooled in her eyes.

Before they could spill over, he stalked to the door, whipped it open, and left.

Chapter 21

Aldous was dressing for supper the next evening—substituting a tunic of gleaming black Florentine silk for the Sicilian wool he'd worn during the day—when a knock came at his bedchamber door. "Come."

It was his sister's maid, that sturdy, straw-haired peasant with the Poitevan accent. "The lady Clare's askin' for you in her chamber, Master Aldous."

Hunching down slightly to peer into the silver looking glass on the wall, Aldous adjusted his satin skullcap and primped the thick, dark hair that was his secret pride. "She's back already?"

"Aye—dismounted out front and went directly to her chamber. Asked for some wine and that bird of hers. And you, sire."

It had been just yesterday morning that Clare had left for her visit with some "old and dear friend," taking along two of King Louis's men as an escort and saying she'd be gone a few days. Why had she returned so soon? "She's only just arrived, then?" Aldous asked, curious as to whether she'd been informed yet of the extraordinary events of yesterday.

"Yes, master."

Yes, master . . . Two of Aldous's very favorite words, especially when spoken by a comely serving wench. Turning, he eyed this one a bit more thoroughly than he had in the past, wondering why he hadn't thrown her skirts up yet—for on those occasions when Marguerite had simply untied him and walked away after seeing to her own pleasure, leaving him aching with lust, it had been his practice to seek out the nearest maidservant for relief.

He shivered, thinking about Marguerite and what she could have done to him had she been so inclined. With a mental effort, he swept aside the image of Istagio's bloated, reeking corpse and returned his attention to the wench standing in front of him.

"What's your name again?" He inspected her up and down, noting with interest her substantial bosom and broad hips. He actually grew a little stiff, thinking about stripping that kirtle off and getting a good look at her.

"Edmee, sire."

"Edmee." She had big hands—big, capable hands. He rather liked that. But there was something about the breadth of her shoulders and the squareness of her jaw that displeased him. And then there were her eyes, small and squinty, like those of some ratlike little forest creature.

Still, there were those tits. Aldous was on the verge of telling her to open up her kirtle so he could get a look at them when he remembered Phillipa.

And smiled.

Phillipa, so pale and lovely, so exasperatingly unattainable; Phillipa, whom he'd been wild to bed for seven long years, who had inflamed him deliberately in Paris only to turn her back to him again and again, taunting him, beguiling him, driving him to the quivering edge of madness in his desire for her . . .

Tonight, she would at last be his.

He'd sought her out in her chamber yesterday afternoon—which he felt safe in doing after seeing her husband saddle up and ride off—to ask why she hadn't been at dinner, only to find her sitting wanly on her bed, her eyes puffy and red-rimmed. She and Hugh had suffered a serious falling-out, she'd told him; Hugh was gone and would not be returning. Aldous hadn't been able to erase the grin of anticipation from his face even as he took her in his arms and comforted her, offering gentle words of solace while his mind's eye conjured up images of her prostrating herself naked before him, offering herself in complete abject submission.

What I wouldn't give for the chance to make amends for how I acted toward you in Paris, she had once said.

Aldous's liaison with Marguerite had awakened in him an appreciation for the erotic potential of punishment. How would it feel, he'd wondered, to take the whip hand himself? Imagining Phillipa bound and vulnerable and completely at his mercy had aroused him intensely. So inflamed by the possibilities was he that he'd begged her to come to his chamber that night.

Distraught, Phillipa had begged off, saying her heart wouldn't be in it. Aldous, loath to admit that he was far more desirous of her body than her heart, had expressed his complete understanding. He'd waited this long, he'd told her; he could wait one more night.

And that meant that she would be his tonight.

Now fully erect beneath his clerical robes, Aldous gave the maidservant another swift perusal, his gaze lingering on those plump, red little lips. The temptation to order her onto her knees was almost irresistible. It wouldn't take long, given the state he was in; he wouldn't leave Clare waiting more than a minute or two.

But no, best not to dampen his lust before tonight. The randier he was when he took Phillipa to bed, the better the tupping. There would be plenty of opportunity to have a go at this Edmee when Phillipa's luster had worn off a bit, perhaps in a few days.

"If I may be dismissed," Edmee said, "I'm needed to help put dinner on the—"

"Go." Gesturing her away with a wave of his hand, Aldous left and made his way to his sister's chamber.

He found the door open, and Clare, dressed in a dusty brown riding tunic with that blasted hawk on her fist, pacing back and forth with a grim determination that instantly gave him pause.

"Shut the door," she bit out.

Aldous did so. She yanked the window shutters closed, plunging the chamber into semidarkness.

"He's a spy."

"I beg your—"

"Hugh of Wexford, or Oxford, or whatever the bloody hell he's calling himself these days—he's a spy! He's King Henry's goddamned spy!"

"You can't be—"

"I knew it. I *knew* it!" Her eyes were wide and fixed, showing the whites all around the irises. Salome pumped against her restraints, but Clare didn't seem to notice. "From the moment I saw him slither down into the cellar that night, I *knew* something wasn't right with that conniving whoreson. So I paid a little visit to his father."

"William of Wexford? You went to Wexford Castle?" Aldous sought out the ewer of wine on the table next to Clare's bed and poured himself a cup. "Ah, yes, Hugh and Phillipa had been visiting with him before they came to Southwark to stay with—"

"Lies!" She wheeled on him abruptly; Salome screamed. "Lord William told me hasn't seen his son in years. They've been estranged since Hugh was eighteen years old and left Wexford to turn mercenary. William didn't even know Hugh was married."

"They lied?" Aldous downed his wine and poured himself another.

"Yes, Aldous," Clare said, her frantic tone giving way to weary disgust at having to explain things to him, as usual. "They lied about having visited Lord William in order to trick you into asking them to stay with you, which I don't imagine was all that difficult, given how utterly witless you can be in the presence of a perky pair of tits. They lied about being in sympathy with Queen Eleanor, they lied—"

"Are you sure?" Aldous asked, finding it inconceivable that Phillipa could have looked him in the eye and spoken untruths.

"*He* lied," Clare said, transferring Salome to one of several freestanding hawk perches set up around the room. "According to Lord William, all he knows about Hugh's recent activities is what he's heard from Richard

Strongbow, with whom he has a passing acquaintance. Apparently, Strongbow was so impressed with Hugh's valor during the Irish campaign that he recommended his services to Richard de Luci."

"King Henry's justiciar?"

"The same."

"What kind of services?"

"Lord William seems to think he's just some sort of armed retainer, but it couldn't be more obvious that he was sent here to ferret out information about the queen's rebellion."

"And . . . Phillipa?"

"What about Phillipa?"

"Is she a spy, too?"

Clare snorted scornfully as she yanked off her gauntlet. "That absurd, overeducated little prig? Honestly, Aldous."

"But she herself told me that they'd visited Wexford—"

"If she went along with some of Hugh's fabrications, well, that's the sort of things wives do as a matter of course. But I'll wager she knows naught of his work for Richard de Luci—such work requires the utmost secrecy, even from one's own wife. No doubt he would have left her at home, as he did when he went to Poitiers—which, of course, was just another spying mission—but she was needed this time to serve as unwitting bait. He dangled her in front of you, your cock sprang up, and here we are."

"Did Lord William ask you why you were cutting your trip so short?"

"Nay." Clare sat heavily on her huge bed, its curtains tied back to reveal mounds of silken pillows in shades of plum, scarlet, and bloodred. Morosely she said, "He was probably glad to see me go."

Aldous frowned. "I thought you and he were . . ."

"That was twenty years ago." From her purse she withdrew a little ivory case and flipped it open, examining her image in the looking glass it held. Stroking her cheeks, her jowls, she said softly, "Time doesn't weigh on a man the way it weighs on a woman. Sixty years old, and William of Wexford is still the handsomest man I've ever seen. He looks much like his son—tall and lean, with that bearing of easy authority to him—but with a rapacious glint in his eye that's always made my heart quicken."

"So I take it you and he didn't . . ."

"Not for want of trying on my part." She snapped the mirror closed and leaned back against the pillows, gazing at nothing. "He got married last month to this dewy little twelve-year-old Blanchefleur. The girl's mother took one look at me and kept an eagle eye on him. Still, he could have sneaked away and come to me if he'd wanted to. But he didn't."

Never had Aldous heard his sister sound so melancholic. He almost felt sorry for her—until she sat up and growled, "It's all your fault, you driveling fool, you and that greedy little piglet that hangs between your legs!"

Aldous choked on his wine. "Greedy little piglet?"

"That"—she pointed a trembling finger at his groin— "is what got us into this fix! If you hadn't been so blinded by lust for the Brilliant Little By-blow, if you hadn't welcomed her and that duplicitous knave she's married to into your home . . . and *mine*—"

"I seem to recall your harboring a fair measure of lust yourself for the 'duplicitous knave,' " Aldous observed. "In fact, you refused to send him away when I begged you to."

"This is *not*," she snarled, "a good time to try and get clever, Aldous. We have a problem to deal with now, a very serious problem. If the queen's agent finds that we've welcomed the king's spy to Halthorpe and given him virtually free run of the castle—"

"Clare . . ." Aldous interrupted, realizing she didn't know about Marguerite.

Tossing her looking glass aside, Clare got to her feet and resumed her rigid pacing. "Once I suspected who Hugh really was, I should have had King Louis's men take care of him and bury him in the woods. 'Twas a mistake to simply have Orlando hide his weapons and let Hugh steal the key to the cellar. I'd just wanted to put Hugh off the scent in case he *was* working for the king, and before the queen's agent caught wind of what he was—"

"Clare, I think you should know—"

"But now I realize it would have been far better to have turned him over to Louis's thugs the moment I saw him sneak down into that cellar. It's what I should have done then—and what I intend to do now. Queen Eleanor will find out, of course, but it needn't go badly for us—in fact, it might even raise us in her esteem, knowing that we had the bastard instantly dispatched once we found out for sure that he was working for the king. Yes . . . yes . . ." Clare paused, her eyes glittering with newfound hope. "Eleanor doesn't think we can 'handle the situation' here—that's how she put it in her letter, that's why she sent her agent to keep an eye on us. But if we prove that we *can* handle—"

"Eleanor's agent is dead," Hugh interjected.

Clare stared at him, raised an eyebrow as if to say, *Go on.*

He licked his lips nervously. " 'Twas Marguerite who was spying on us for the queen, Clare. Yesterday morning—"

"*Marguerite?* Impossible!"

"Yesterday morning we found her dead. She'd poisoned herself after killing Istagio. Apparently she'd never killed anyone before, and she found she couldn't live with—"

"I . . . I don't understand. I was almost certain the queen's agent was . . ." Clare lowered herself onto a trunk against the wall, her eyes glazed. " 'Twas Marguerite? Why would she have killed Istagio?"

"He must have compromised the secrecy of their work, let something slip. You know how he is." Aldous crossed himself, envisioning the monstrous corpse that had once been Istagio. "How he was."

"Dear God." Clare shook her head. "It doesn't make sense, though. Marguerite never gave a fig for politics, and she didn't even like Eleanor. And . . . and she was my closest friend in the world. I can't imagine her spying on me. It can't be true."

"I find it as incredible as you do, but what other conclusion can we draw? Look at it this way—at least she's dead now, so we know neither of *us* will be smothered in our beds."

Clare winced and crossed herself. "We will still incur Eleanor's wrath if we don't deal with Hugh of Wexford. Not only that, but we could end up being exposed as traitors. Do you know how King Henry punishes traitors, Aldous? The best we could expect, the very best, would be imprisonment for the rest of our lives. We might even end up tied to stakes and—"

"Jesu!" Aldous tossed back the rest of his wine and poured himself another cup. Once, in France, he'd seen a heretic burned. He'd gone to watch out of curiosity and ended up vomiting his guts up as the poor bastard writhed and screamed, the charred flesh bubbling and peeling from his bones. "What do we have to do?"

"We have to eliminate Hugh of Wexford as soon as possible. God knows what he's found out, especially if Istagio *was* indiscreet." Clare muttered a foul oath. "You don't suppose Hugh has managed to pass any information on to his superiors, do you? Has he sent any letters out?"

Aldous swore to himself as he remembered watching Hugh ride over the drawbridge yesterday. "Er . . . Clare . . ."

She stood and began pacing again. "We'll have to find out how much he's learned and whether he's shared it with anyone. I'll leave it to Louis's men how they want to handle it. They're a bloodthirsty pack of mongrels—they'll get it out of him." She smiled. "They could strip him down and cook him for a while on that iron chair downstairs—that might do the trick. Then, after he's talked, he can be taken out to the woods and—"

"Clare, Hugh left yesterday."

She ceased her pacing and stared at him in the keenly focused way that reminded him of her damned bird. "And when, precisely, were you planning on telling me this?"

Aldous fortified himself with a gulp of wine. "He and Phillipa had some sort of row, a bad one. He's gone— for good, she says."

"You don't," she said tightly, "by any chance, know where he went."

"Nay."

Clare closed her eyes and stood absolutely still for so long that Aldous began to wonder if it was possible for someone to die standing up.

"Clare?" he began tentatively. "I . . . I'm sorry. I would have mentioned it sooner, but—"

"Do shut up, Aldous," she said without opening her eyes, and then she lapsed into silence once more.

Aldous sat on the edge of her bed and sipped the rest of his wine slowly.

At long last she opened her eyes and looked at him. "Here is what we're going to do."

Chapter 22

"Have you ever wondered what's going on in the cellar?" Aldous whispered in Phillipa's ear toward the conclusion of supper that evening.

Phillipa paused with her spoonful of rose pudding halfway to her mouth and glanced at the deacon, who had stuck to her like a leech since Hugh's departure yesterday—and tonight, God help her, he expected her to come to his chamber for their long-anticipated tryst. It remained to be seen how she would maneuver her way out of it; she'd exhausted every excuse she could think of, and she was still so emotionally ravaged by Hugh's departure yesterday that she couldn't think straight. "The cellar?" she said carefully. "What do you mean?"

"You know—those booming noises." Aldous looked about as he sipped his wine, as if wary of being overheard by their tablemates. "There've been quite a lot of them today, in particular."

"Your sister told me those sounds were produced by barrels of wine falling over."

Aldous cast her a skeptical look. "If it had happened only once or twice, I might believe that, even though it doesn't much sound like barrels falling over."

Phillipa swallowed her pudding thoughtfully. "You must know what's going on down there. After all, you escorted Orlando and Istagio here." She declined to mention that he had also transported two cartloads of mysterious cargo here from Paris, under armed guard, for he would wonder how she'd come to know this.

He shrugged. "Clare enlists me for various errands, but she only tells me as much as she thinks I need to know. I asked her once to let me into the cellar, but she refused—said I wouldn't understand it, as if I were a child. Really got my hackles up, I can tell you. But now, with her off visiting that friend of hers, and me in charge of the keys . . ." He patted the lump on his chest where Clare's keys hung under his tunic, then leaned closer, sliding an arm around her waist; it felt like one of those serpents she'd heard about that kills its prey by squeezing it to death. "What do you say?" he murmured seductively, "Care to do a little exploring with me?"

Phillipa bought a moment by eating some more of the pudding, which tasted far too strangely floral for her taste. "Edmee told me Clare came back a little while ago."

"Oh." Aldous, looking suddenly ill at ease, removed his arm from her waist. "Really? She's back? Hmm, I wonder why she didn't come down to supper."

"Fatigued from her journey, I should think."

"Yes, indeed. That must be it. Yes." Aldous drained his wine cup. "So, uh . . . she'll be asking for her keys back this evening, then. If we want to see what's in the cellar, our only chance is to go now."

Phillipa ate a little more of her pudding, stirring this remarkable new development around in her mind. Her mandate at this juncture was to get into that cellar, whatever it took. Aldous's offer to show it to her in an apparent attempt to ingratiate himself with her was therefore timely and fortuitous—almost too fortuitous, and she couldn't ignore the whisper of foreboding that tightened her scalp. For him to make this offer after weeks of dodging her subtlest inquiries about the conspiracy against King Henry naturally roused her suspicions. But if, as he now professed, Clare had merely been employing him as an errand boy while keeping him in the dark about that conspiracy, it did not seem strange at all. Was it possible that Phillipa had mistaken Aldous's ignorance for circumspection?

"Of course, Orlando is down there," Aldous pointed out, adding imperiously, "But that's of no import. I can deal with one old Italian."

Ah, yes, Orlando. After taking yesterday off from his work, he had spent all of today in the cellar, and had not yet emerged from it. It put Phillipa at ease a bit, knowing she would not be alone in that secluded, windowless undercroft with Aldous. And then there was the fact that her only other alternative for gaining access to the cellar was to bed Aldous and steal the keys from him.

What a fool she'd been to tell Hugh that she was willing to do just that. Had she really thought he would be so horrified by that prospect that he would reveal the deeply buried feelings he'd been denying all this time? Were there any feelings to reveal, or had she been deluding herself, finding his assertion that it was all about sex just too painful to accept?

In any event, she had mishandled things—badly—and now Hugh was gone. When he left yesterday, it was as if a piece of her soul had been torn right out of her, leaving her wounded in a way that couldn't be seen, but was nonetheless agonizing. The devastating sense of loss had receded little since then. Comporting herself as if naught were amiss, when inside she still howled with pain, was the hardest thing she'd ever had to do.

"Well?" Aldous prodded, rising from the bench and reaching for her hand. "Shall we go exploring?"

She set down her spoon, stood, and put her hand in his. "Let's go."

At the door to the cellar stairs, Aldous pulled the chain of keys from beneath his tunic, chose the large, ornate brass one, and turned it in the lock. He preceded her down the torch-lit stairwell and swung open the door at the bottom. Phillipa followed him into Orlando's laboratory, now brightly lit by hanging lanterns, and not nearly as warm and fetid as when she and Hugh had stolen down there to investigate. In fact, it felt as cool and damp as in any undercroft; the reason became clear when she glanced at the makeshift furnace and saw that the fire had been allowed to go out.

"Good evening," Aldous said.

Orlando, standing over his worktable, looked up in surprise. "Master Aldous . . . Lady Phillipa." He looked at her and raised his eyebrows slightly, clearly mystified that Aldous should have brought her there after he, Orlando, had been sworn to secrecy about his work.

Glancing around curiously, Aldous said, "I thought we'd look around a bit, if it's all right with you."

"Er . . . if the lady Clare were to find out . . ."

"My sister asked me to bring the lady Phillipa down here, show her what you've been working on."

"Is true?" Orlando asked Phillipa.

Weighing her distaste at lying to her friend against the need to gather evidence to stop the queen's revolt, Phillipa said, "It's true."

"*Buono.* I am please for to show you my work."

Aldous stepped up to the worktable, on which were laid out a number of strange cast-iron devices shaped like tubes, each with a different sort of handle on the end. Scattered about on the table were scores of little iron balls like that which she and Hugh had found on the cellar floor the night they'd sneaked down here to investigate. "What have we here?" Aldous asked.

"These are the *armi della mano,* to be held in the hand," Orlando said. Pointing over Phillipa's shoulder, he said, "Those are the throwing weapons, the *bombe.*"

The cage, which had been empty when she had explored the cellar with Hugh, now contained about a dozen enclosed iron vessels of various shapes and sizes, mostly round, with lengths of cord emerging from them—as menacing in her eyes as a cluster of dragon's eggs.

"How do those work?" Phillipa asked.

"Is very simple," Orlando said, setting down the *arma* and funnel he held. "The more, how you say, *solido* the vessel that hold the powder, the more *violento* the reaction. In China, they put it in the *bambù* tube, or sometime the iron *globi*. Istagio"—he glumly crossed himself—"he make for me in his bell foundry many different shape so that I may see which one work best. I fill each *bomba* with a powder made from the *salnitro,* what you call the Chinese snow . . ."

"Saltpeter," Phillipa said.

"*Sì,* and the *zolfo* and the *carbone di legna.*" Orlando swept his hand toward the pots filled with sulphur and charcoal. "And then Istagio, he close them up good. The *fusibili* . . . how you say, the . . . wick?"

"Those long cords?"

"*Sì,* the cords I soak in the *alcool,* the fluid from the distill, along with a little *salnitro*. Is burn very slow, very steady, until the cord burn down and the fire meet the powder. Then . . ." He spread his hands, fingers extended. "Very loud boom."

"Are those the sounds we've been hearing from down here?" she asked. From the corner of her eye she saw Aldous puttering among the devices on the worktable, the *armi della mano*.

Orlando saw him, too, and swatted at the deacon's hands. "No touch, please, no touch! I load them all for the test. Is very much danger to handle. Some of them, because of the shape, is very powerful but go boom very easy. My *assistente* in Roma, he is test one and it burst apart in his hand and kill him. And then the straw on the floor, it catch on fire, and whoosh! No more *laboratorio.*"

"Ah." Aldous backed away from the table. "Well, then."

"Those sounds you hear," Orlando told Phillipa, "they come from when I test the *armi*. The *bombe*"—he nodded toward the cage—"those I cannot test. Is much too *violento,* I think, much too danger to test indoor. I will take outdoor when I am ready."

Phillipa saw the chain and padlock securing the cage and realized that stealing a *bomba* would present quite a challenge. The hand weapons, however, in addition to being accessible, could conceivably be secreted on one's person. She glanced down at her tunic of pink shot silk, wondering if its folds were deep enough to conceal an *arma della mano*.

Approaching the table, she asked Orlando, "Are these filled with the black powder, too?"

"How did you know it was black?" asked Aldous.

"Er . . ."

Orlando came to her rescue, lifting the top from a green-glazed clay pot to display the glittering black granules within. "She see it."

"But that was covered."

"Not when you first come in."

"Really? I don't recall——"

"The *arma*," Orlando interrupted, "it need the black powder to work, but only a little. Too much, and *boom*."

There seemed to be entirely too many opportunities, Phillipa reflected, for inadvertent *booms*.

Gesturing to the tidy row of weapons on the table, Orlando said, "I have load all these for testing with the powder and iron ball. The hole in the top, here, that is where the hot wire go in." He picked up an *arma* and turned to a small tabletop brazier on which a shallow pan scattered with short pieces of red-hot wire sat over glowing coals. With a pair of tongs, he plucked up a length of wire and held it close to, but not touching, the hole. "When the wire touch the powder . . ."

"Boom," Phillipa said.

Orlando nodded. "And the ball, it come flying out at very high rate of speed, so fast you cannot see. Make very big hole in flesh. The pig and the . . . *capra* . . . how you say, goat, they die very much fast."

Phillipa winced. "You test these on live animals?"

"Just once. The lady Clare, she insist—she wanta see what happen to living thing when the little ball go in. But now I just shoot the balls into the well."

"And those are the sounds we hear," she said.

"*Sì*. Is good weapon, do very much harm, but is one big problem. It only shoot once and then must load the powder and the ball all over again. The crossbow reload much quicker. Same with the longbow and the shortbow. I am work on a solution."

"Fascinating, no?"

Phillipa wheeled around to find Clare standing in the doorway, dressed with unaccustomed utility in a plain brown riding tunic.

Aldous didn't so much as blink at his sister's appearance, Phillipa noted. It was as if he'd been expecting her.

A cold alertness gripped Phillipa. *Keep your wits about you,* she cautioned herself.

"Would you like to try it?" Clare asked Phillipa as she strode into the cellar.

"Try . . ."

"Shooting one of Orlando's *armi.*" Clare took the weapon from Orlando and hefted it in her hand. "I come down here and do it myself from time to time. It's really quite exciting in a curious sort of way."

"I . . . I don't think—"

"I'd like to try!" Aldous said.

Clare directed a look of languid contempt toward her brother. "Perhaps later, Aldous. I want Phillipa to feel for herself the incredible power and potential of these weapons."

She went to hand the device to Phillipa, but Orlando grabbed her arm. "Not that one, my lady. Is one of the type that sometime make bad *esplosione.* To test this one, I must ignite with the slow *fusibile* and stay much far away in case it burst apart."

"Ah." Clare handed the weapon back to Orlando. "That wouldn't do. We don't want anything untoward happening to our dear Phillipa, do we? Which one would be safe for her to shoot?"

Orlando chose another *arma* and held it out to Phillipa, handle first. "You wanta try?" he asked, evidently oblivious to the ominous undercurrent sparked by Clare's arrival.

Phillipa accepted the weapon with some trepidation, wrapping her fingers around the handle, which was anvil-

shaped, rather like that of Hugh's Turkish dagger. It felt
cold and heavy in her hand. "What do I . . ."

"Here." Orlando handed her the tongs that held the
still-glowing wire, and led her to the well in the middle
of the cellar's earthen floor. Aldous and Clare followed.
The torture devices on the far wall, Phillipa noted,
looked no more benign clearly illuminated by lamplight
than they had in the dark three nights ago—if anything,
they were even more starkly menacing.

"Hold the *arma* like so," Orlando said, "pointing
down into the well. Then you just stick the wire in the
touch-hole, like so, and . . ."

"Boom," Phillipa said thinly. The well was deep, so
extraordinarily deep that she couldn't see the bottom. It
seemed to descend into the very bowels of the earth.

"Brace yourself," Clare warned. "That thing kicks like
a mule when it fires."

"*I'll* brace you," said Aldous as he positioned himself
behind her, his arms around her waist. His sister rolled
her eyes at the gesture.

"Hold on tight to the *arma,*" Orlando instructed. "I
no want you for to drop it down the well."

"I'll do my best." Phillipa drew in a steadying breath,
held it, and slid the wire into the hole as Clare and
Orlando put their fingers in their ears.

The weapon bucked in her hand, throwing her back
hard against Aldous, its roar echoing off the walls of the
well like rolling thunder. Following a quick flash from
the open end of the *arma* there came a gust of acrid
smoke that hung in the air.

Orlando took the weapon and tongs from her and
smiled, as if she'd done well.

Through the ringing in her ears, Phillipa heard Clare
snicker. " 'Twas worth all that trouble just to hear Lady
By-blow squeal like a little girl."

Had she? Recalling Hugh's teasing words—*I rather
like this new squealing of yours*—Phillipa felt a rush of
longing for him so keen it pained her physically, in the
chest.

As her hearing returned in full, Phillipa realized that
Clare was telling Orlando that he'd worked long enough
today, and that he should go upstairs and get some supper. "In fact," she said as she led him toward the door,
"given that you've spent every single day down here
since coming to Halthorpe, perhaps you'd like to take a
few days off. Rest a bit . . . get over what happened to
poor Istagio . . ."

"*Grazie,* my lady," said Orlando, "but my melancho-
lia, it get smaller when I work. Is why I come down here
today, to make the bad feeling go away."

"There are other ways to ease one's grief, Orlando.
You've been working far too hard. A few days' respite—
a week, perhaps—will serve you well, I think."

"But—"

"But I really think it would be best," she purred as
she guided him out the door. "In fact, I insist. *Buona
notte,* Orlando."

"I'll go up with him," said Phillipa, but she'd taken
only one step toward the door before Aldous's arms
snaked around her from behind, over her own arms, effectively restraining her.

"Not quite yet," he murmured into her ear, holding
her far too snugly against him.

Her heart rattled in her chest. She struggled against
him, but to no avail, and with her arms immobilized like
this, she couldn't reach her eating knife in its little
sheath on her girdle.

*If you find yourself in some sort of fix, Raoul will help
you.* Phillipa opened her mouth to call a plea to Orlando—*Tell Raoul I'm in trouble!*—but Aldous clamped
a hand over her mouth, hard.

Clare *tsked* as she closed the door behind the departing Orlando. "So eager to leave already? We have
another, even more instructive demonstration in store
for you." Indicating the array of *armi* with a sweep of
her hand, she asked her brother, "These are all loaded?"

"That's what Orlando said," Aldous replied. "He was
preparing them for testing."

"How exceedingly convenient." Clare glided a be-ringed hand over the row of weapons as if choosing a pair of slippers to wear. "This one, I think. I've fired it before, so I can be fairly sure it won't blow up in my face." With the *arma* in one hand and the tongs in the other, she turned to the brazier to pluck a hot wire off the pan. "You may remove your hand from her mouth now, Aldous."

The moment he did so, Phillipa filled her lungs with air and screamed, "Help me! Somebody—Raoul! I'm in the cellar!"

"They can't hear you," Clare said as she sauntered toward Phillipa. "The only thing anyone can hear from down here is the occasional *esplosione*. One more will draw no notice whatsoever."

Clare pressed the open end of her weapon against the side of Phillipa's head. When Phillipa flinched, wresting her head to the side, Clare seized the single, ribbon-wrapped braid that hung down Phillipa's back and yanked her head upright. "You may tie her hands now, Aldous. I know how you've been looking forward to this part."

From somewhere on his person, Aldous produced a tasseled satin cord, such as draperies are tied back with. Gripping her wrists behind her, he looped the cord tightly around them and tied it off.

"I heard Orlando tell you about the goat and the pig," Clare said. "He let me do the shooting. 'Twas a . . . deeply rousing experience, holding this"—she pushed the iron shaft hard against Phillipa's temple—"to the head of a living thing and sliding this"—she held the hot wire in front of Phillipa's eyes—"into its little hole."

Aldous wrapped his arms around her again, his breath hot and swift on her hair. She felt against her back the hard lump of the keys he still wore around his chest, and farther down, against her bound hands, a different and more sinister pressure, one that chilled her given that she was essentially at his mercy.

"The effect of firing one of these into a living creature

is really quite remarkable," Clare said as she brought
the glowing wire toward the touch-hole. "You can feel
the flesh burst open, hear bone explode even over the
beast's death scream. It drops instantly, of course, con-
vulses a bit, and then goes very still. The pig's brains
ended up on the far wall. With the goat, the head came
entirely off."

Phillipa closed her eyes, took a deep breath. *Keep
your wits. Panic is your worst enemy.*

"We haven't tested it on a human yet," Clare said.
" 'Tis an oversight that would be easy enough to
remedy."

They're harmless, the both of them, Hugh had said of
Clare and Aldous. *They haven't got the stomach for killing.* Was that true, or were they, indeed, capable of murder if enough was at stake?

"After you."

Phillipa opened her eyes to find Clare gesturing with
her weapon toward the rear of the undercroft, where the
iron chair and sachentage were bolted side-by-side to
the wall. Shaking her head, Phillipa squirmed against
Aldous's arms. "Nay . . ."

Clare stood to the side, swinging the *arma* back so
that it was aimed at Phillipa's head. "Aldous." She
cocked her head toward the rear wall.

With a viselike hand around Phillipa's neck, Aldous
pushed her forward until she stood, panting with dread,
in front of the terrible engines of punishment.

Summoning her wits, Phillipa asked, in as steady a
voice as she could manage, "Why are you doing this?
I've done you no harm." Having no idea how much they
knew or had surmised, it would be best for the time
being, she reasoned, to feign complete innocence.

" 'Tis one of life's more sobering truths," Clare said,
"that people seldom truly deserve the bad things that
happen to them. We are perfectly well aware that you've
done us no harm. That is not, however, true of your
husband." Leveling the *arma* at Phillipa's head, she said,
"Aldous, get her into position."

Aldous shoved her toward the sachentage.

God, no, Phillipa thought as he pushed her head down under the small iron frame jutting out from the wall. He pried open the hinged collar that hung from the frame by chains, displaying its cruel, inward-facing spikes, and closed it around her throat. Thankfully, the spikes barely grazed her, probably because her neck was more slender than that of the men this instrument was designed for. Because of her short stature, however, the collar, even hanging at its lowest point, dug into her jaw, tilting her head upward slightly.

"Lock it," Clare ordered her brother. "It's the little iron key with the square top."

Don't panic, don't panic . . . Phillipa repeated to herself as her heart thudded wildly and trickles of sweat crawled beneath her tunic and kirtle. "Think about what you're doing, Aldous," she entreated as he twisted the key in the collar's lock.

"I am." With an all-too-intimate smile, he lowered his head to her. "You've never looked lovelier to me."

Phillipa instinctively whipped her head to the side when his lips touched hers, only to cry out in pain as the spikes bit into the side of her neck.

"You foolish little thing." Aldous, his expression solicitous, touched a finger to the wound. "You've made yourself bleed." He licked the fingertip, his troubled gaze meeting hers. "You must be more careful. We're not trying to hurt you, my dear. We just need to secure your cooperation in a matter of grave consequence."

"What sort of cooperation?"

Lowering her weapon now that Phillipa was immobilized, Clare said, "Your husband left Halthorpe yesterday, and we don't know where he's gone. We assume you do. We need you to write to him and convince him to return."

Phillipa swallowed against the hard, cold collar. "Wh-why?"

"Let's just say that we have enemies, and we've recently discovered that your husband is working for them."

They know.

Aldous said, "We realize you have no idea he's been spying for—"

"That's enough, Aldous!" Clare snapped. "If you tell her too much, we'll be forced to have her dispatched as well as him, and I know you've got plans for her."

"D-dispatched?"

"Not you," Clare assured her. "Just your husband."

Phillipa went to shake her head, wincing at the pressure of the spikes. "You wouldn't. You haven't got it in you."

"Perhaps not, but those Frankish brutes hanging about the barracks have it in them not only to send Hugh of Wexford to his maker, but to extract from him beforehand certain information of a sensitive and critical nature." Clare's gaze lit on the malevolent iron chair with room beneath for a fire.

No . . . Phillipa ransacked her mind for a way out of this, for Hugh's sake. "What information do you want?" she asked, thinking she might be able to come up with something plausible enough to appease them without actually revealing anything damaging to the king. "Perhaps I can tell you what you need to know."

Clare shook her head. "You know naught of these matters."

"What if I did? What if *I* were the spy and 'twas Hugh who knew nothing? You haven't considered that possibility because I'm a woman, but—"

Clare cut her off with a harsh burst of laughter. "You're not the one I caught sneaking down here in an effort to unearth our secrets. And you're not the one who was sent to Poitiers a year and a half ago to spy on the queen. I'd like to say I admire your inclination toward self-sacrifice, but the truth is, I find it pathetic."

"Especially given the way Hugh has misused and debased you." Aldous lightly stroked her upturned face. "I don't know what you two quarreled about yesterday,

but I know he left you in tears. He's never loved you—
you told me so yourself. And all this time he's been
lying to you, deceiving you, keeping his true vocation a
secret from you even as he exploited you to gain access
to me."

With a gentleness that made Phillipa shiver, Aldous
brushed sweat-dampened tendrils of hair off her face.
"He's used you, Phillipa, regarded you with utter contempt, even as I've ached to make you mine. After he's
gone and we're together, I'll treat you like a princess.
I'll install you in a splendid house in Southwark so you
can be close to me. You'll have servants and jewels and
fine gowns, finer than anything he ever gave you. You'll
want for nothing." Lowering his mouth to hers, he murmured, "You're the one, Phillipa, the only one."

He kissed her. She pressed her lips tight against the
sluglike insinuation of his tongue.

"Write to your husband and tell me where to have
the letter sent," Clare said. "Once he's back at Halthorpe and in our custody, I will release you into Aldous's keeping with the understanding that no harm will
come to you as long as you never speak of this to anyone. When asked what became of your late husband,
you are to say he drowned in the Thames and that his
body was never recovered."

"Nay," Phillipa said. "Never."

Aldous, looking genuinely astounded, said, "After
what he's done to you? We could be *together,* Phillipa,
just you and I. Think about it!"

It was far too revolting a prospect to contemplate.
"Do with me what you will," she said, "but I have no
intention of summoning Hugh back here to be tortured
and killed."

"What we will do to you," Clare informed her icily,
"is simply to leave you right where you are, locked into
this device day and night, with no respite—although I
suppose I'll have to come down from time to time to let
you use the garderobe. There are esthetic considerations,
after all. But other than that, you'll be forced to stand

without relief, which I understand can become fairly painful of its own accord. You'll get no sleep, no food, and no water, until you consent to write a letter to Hugh, which I will dictate to you word for word."

"I'm not writing any letter," Phillipa said, "so you may as well kill me right now."

"We haven't got it in us, remember?" Clare sneered. "Of course, if I wanted you dead, I suppose I could enlist the Frankish soldiers for that purpose. They would embrace the task with a fair measure of enthusiasm, I'm sure, especially if I were to give them free rein to disport themselves with you before putting you out of your—"

"Clare, no!" Aldous grabbed her arm. "You said I could have her. You *said*—"

"Unhand me, you simpering dunce!" Clare demanded as she wrenched her arm from her brother. "I'm just making conversation, for pity's sake. If I wanted her dead, she'd be dead already. I'd much rather leave her in this thing until she breaks down and does our bidding. Or perishes slowly and in agony," she added with a malignant little smile in Phillipa's direction. "It's really up to you, my dear. I doubt it would take more than a week for you to succumb to thirst, but 'twill be the longest week you've ever endured."

"Phillipa, for God's sake, write the letter," Aldous pleaded. "I can't bear to think of you destroying yourself this way—especially for the likes of him." He closed his hands around her waist, skimmed them upward until they were snugged up against the undersides of her breasts. "You're ravishing in pink. This tunic, it's the one you were wearing that afternoon when I first saw you on London Bridge. That was no accident, you know. Hugh brought you there hoping I'd run into you, knowing that if I saw you again, I would do anything to have you."

Leaning over, he whispered in her ear, "You look so beautiful like this, so exquisitely helpless. I could take you right here." He lowered his hands, closing them around her hips, which he drew toward him so that she could feel how hard he was beneath his diaconal robes. "Perhaps tonight, when everyone's asleep, I'll come down here and—"

"Not tonight, Aldous." Clare, who had evidently heard her brother's heated whispers, pulled the chain of keys over his head and looped it around her own neck. " 'Twould be prudent, I think, to hold such a visit in reserve. Perhaps in a day or two, if the lady Phillipa continues to refuse to write the letter, I'll give you the key to the cellar door. But only to the door, so you can get down here, not to the sachentage—I don't want to risk letting her escape. If you want her, you'll have to have her standing up."

Dear God, Phillipa thought. *She's not even human.*

"Say good-bye, Aldous," Clare instructed as she turned and strolled toward the door. "I can't bear it down here for another moment."

Aldous spent a few moments fondling the captive Phillipa and whispering into her ear the things he would do to her when his sister deigned to give him the key to the door at the top of the stairs. Clare, meanwhile, laid the *arma* on the worktable and extinguished all but one of the lanterns, leaving the laboratory area dimly illuminated but plunging Phillipa's end of the undercroft into deep and horrible darkness.

Brother and sister paused in the doorway before departing, Clare to inform her that she would return around matins in case Phillipa needed the privy, and Aldous to blow her a goodnight kiss.

Chapter 23

Pain can be transcended. The trick is to rise above it, as if you were floating in the air, watching it happen to someone else.

Hugh whispered his counsel over and over in Phillipa's mind, a never-ending litany of comfort and strength that had sustained her for . . .

How long had it been since they'd locked her into this fiendish thing? How many days had she stood here in unchanging semidarkness willing herself not to feel the crushing pain in her legs and back, her neck and shoulders and jaw, the grinding hunger in her belly, the consuming thirst that sucked at her and sucked at her, driving her to the edge of madness and back again . . . to rise above the constant agony that had sunk deep, deep into her bones?

Without seeing the sun rise and set, without being privy to the daily rhythms of the world around her, Phillipa found herself at a loss to judge the passage of time. In the beginning, she had tried to count Clare's periodic visits to the cellar, during which Phillipa would be briefly freed from the sachentage in order to be escorted with an *arma* at her back to the corner garderobe. She had become only minimally adept at using the privy with her hands tied behind her back, but that was of little import now, since she rarely needed it anymore.

Indeed, Clare's visits seemed to have tapered off, although they hadn't been very regular to begin with, as if to thwart Phillipa in her efforts to track time. And, of course, whenever Phillipa asked her how long she'd been down there, or if it was day or night, Clare would merely tell her that she could find out soon enough for herself— if only she would write the letter to Hugh.

She craved sleep with a desperation that maddened her, literally. The struggle to keep her head upright so as not to fall victim to the collar's spikes, along with the strain of having her hands bound behind her, made her neck and shoulders burn with pain. Her mind swam in and out of delirium as it searched for a reprieve from this waking hell. Phillipa yearned for the blessed oblivion of sleep even as she fought it, denied it, refused it. All too often she drifted off despite her best efforts, only to awaken to the bite of the spikes and her own cry of pain.

Once, she did not awaken immediately. She dreamed instead—or was it a hallucination; she'd been having them, too—of a horned devil with a chain of keys around its neck and a mouthful of long, sharp teeth, who took her head in its mouth and bit down, hard, around her neck. It sank its teeth into her slowly, inexorably, in an effort to sever her head from her body and eat it.

She'd jolted awake with her head having fallen sideways, the spikes on that side puncturing her skin like the imagined monster's teeth.

Little wonder her imagination had conjured up a devil, for if this wasn't Hell on Earth, what was? To intensify her torment, Clare had set a jug of water on the floor near her feet where, despite the darkness in this part of the cellar, Phillipa could see it well enough if she looked down—which she tried not to do, so as not to add to her anguish, but still she knew it was there.

The water was but a tangible token of the taunting and abuse that Clare seemed to delight in, her favorite threat being that she would give Aldous the key to the cellar unless Phillipa agreed right then to write the letter. Every time the door opened and Phillipa recognized her visitor as Clare, she whispered a few words of gratitude; she had uttered many such prayers and supplications during this hellish confinement. Although disinclined

toward piety in the past, Phillipa had discovered that
suffering did, just as Uncle Lotulf had always said, bring
one closer to God.

She thanked God most earnestly every time she saw
that it was Clare and not her brother who had stolen
down to see her. What was it Clare had said . . . *Perhaps
in a day or two . . . You'll have to have her standing
up . . .*

But it must have been more than a day or two since
they'd locked her into this thing—mustn't it?—and still
Aldous had not come. And for that she was grateful
beyond measure. Her rational mind—still nominally
functional—told her that, whatever Aldous did to her, it
would be naught compared to the other torments she
was enduring. But logic was of little comfort in this dank
underworld of fear and pain. The idea of his using her
that way, making a sordid mockery of what she had
shared with Hugh, distressed her even more than the
terrible thirst and the ache in her bones and the interminable sleeplessness.

Phillipa's memories of making love to Hugh—those
charmed intervals when it was just the two of them, becoming one—were touchstones of solace and sanity in
this endless nightmare, regardless of Hugh's dismissal of
their lovemaking as being just about sex, and her feelings for him as naive fancies. He might or might not be
deluding himself about what had transpired between
them; he could not delude her.

If she closed her eyes and thought hard enough, she
was *there* with him, transported in his embrace, rising
above this worldly anguish, drifting high over it, separate
and apart from it, watching it happen to someone else
entirely, free of pain, of worry, of her very body . . .

The door squeaked.

Phillipa opened her eyes to find her head slumped to
the side. She straightened it, flinching when she felt the
spikes withdraw.

She squinted toward the shadow passing through the
door, silhouetted as always by the single horn lantern

that burned over the furnace. Her stomach clenched
when she saw that the figure was taller than Clare, the
shoulders thicker.

"God, no," she whispered desperately. "Please, God,
I beg of you. There's only so much—"

"My lady?" It was a woman's voice; Phillipa recognized the rustic Poitevan accent.

Trembling with relief, Phillipa said, "Edmee? Is that
you?" Her voice emerged raw and grating from her
parched mouth.

"Milady, where . . . ?" Edmee paused to stare in turn
at the work table with its array of *arma* and the *bombe*
in the cage. "Jesus have mercy," she muttered, crossing
herself. "Where are you, milady?" she called out, peering toward Phillipa's unlit end of the undercroft.

"Here . . . back here, in the dark. Bring the lantern."

Unhooking the lantern from its chain, Edmee came
slowly toward her, stepping warily around the talisman
etched into the floor and the unfathomably deep well,
her small eyes widening in horror when she saw Phillipa
in the sachentage. "My God, milady, what . . . what on
earth . . . did . . . did Lady Clare do this to you?"

Phillipa tried to nod, but the spikes prevented that.
"Aye."

"Why, for pity's sake?"

"She found something out about . . . about my husband," Phillipa said hoarsely. Mindful that Edmee had
served at the Poitiers court and would naturally harbor
loyalties toward Queen Eleanor, she thought it best not
to volunteer too much. "And now she knows he's her
enemy, and she wants him dead, and . . ." She licked
her cracked lips. "Please . . . there's a jug on the floor.
I haven't had water in . . . how long have I been down
here?"

"Well, let me think . . ." Looking around for someplace to put the lantern, Edmee spied the iron chair and
crossed herself. Setting the lantern on the floor, she
lifted the jug and held it to her mistress's mouth. Phillipa
drank greedily, not caring that some of it spilled down

her chin, or that her stomach tightened painfully as soon as the water hit it.

" 'Twas four nights ago," Edmee said, "that I went to your chamber to get you ready for bed and you wasn't there. The next mornin', Lady Clare told everyone you'd left Halthorpe. I thought it was strange that you hadn't said good-bye to me. Even stranger that you'd left all your clothes and things in your room."

Phillipa paused in her drinking to rasp, "Four nights ago . . . and what time of day is it now?"

"Early mornin', milady. The chapel bells haven't even rung prime yet. So that's three full days you've been down here, and four nights." Edmee tilted the jug to Phillipa's mouth again. "I didn't know what to make of you bein' gone till it dawned on me that Master Orlando, he wasn't comin' down here no more. I asked him why, and he says how Lady Clare told him he was to stay away from here, even after he told her he wanted to get back to his work. And then I remembered how you was always askin' about them sounds from down here, how you didn't never credit that business about the wine barrels."

Phillipa turned her head away from the jug. "That's enough," she said breathlessly; talking was less painful now that her throat was dampened. "Thank you. Would you mind untying my hands?"

"Oh, you poor thing. Of course!" Reaching behind Phillipa to fumble with the cord wrapped around her wrists, Edmee said, "First thing this mornin', I asked Lady Clare if she wouldn't like a nice bath. The moment she'd settled in to soak, I took them keys of hers—that's the only time she ever takes them off, when she's bathin'—and I come down here and—"

"You've got her keys?" For the first time, Phillipa noticed the chain around Edmee's neck, with the cluster of keys on the end. Rubbing her wrists, sore from the friction of the cord they'd been tied with, she said, "Oh, Edmee, I don't believe it! Good for you!"

"I excused myself and run down here quick as a rabbit. I haven't got long, though. Her ladyship's still in her bath, and she's expectin' me back right a—"

"You can get me out of this!" Phillipa exclaimed. "The collar unlocks with one of those keys—the small iron one with a square top."

Edmee sorted through the keys on the chain, her frown deepening. "A square top?"

"Aye—I saw it," Phillipa said, growing uneasy. "It's very little."

Edmee squatted next to the lantern, scrutinizing the keys by its yellowish light. Shaking her head, she said, "I'm sorry, milady, it isn't here. Would she have taken it off for some reason?"

Phillipa groaned. She had assumed that, when Clare was ready to let Aldous come down here, she would take the key to the cellar off the chain and give it to him. But perhaps, worried that he would misplace it, she'd removed the key to the sachentage instead, so that she could give him the entire chain without risking Phillipa's escape.

That meant it wouldn't be long before Aldous paid her his visit—all the more impetus to secure her freedom.

"Listen to me, Edmee. Hugh said if I ever needed help, I should go to Raoul d'Argentan. I want you to find him and tell him what's happened. He might be able to get the key from Clare, or perhaps . . . perhaps there's something else he can—"

"He's gone, milady."

"Gone?"

"Aye, yesterday he upped and rode away, leavin' that shrewish little wife of his behind. I heard her sayin' as how it was all Sir Hugh's fault, for tellin' him he should get their marriage annulled, which is what he's aimin' to do."

"Oh. Oh, no . . ." Phillipa couldn't deny that Raoul had made the right decision, under the circumstances, but why couldn't he have waited one more day?

"There's no one else," she said despairingly. "No one else I can rely on . . . except you."

"Tell me what to do," Edmee said, "and I'll do it. I can't bear to see you like this, milady."

"Did you see those devices back there on the table? And the others, in the cage? You did—I saw you looking at them."

"Aye—what the devil are they?"

"Awful new weapons of terrible power. They have a black powder in them that explodes when it gets hot. The ones in the cage—what Orlando calls *bombe*—they burst apart like those little parchment tubes Istagio showed you, but with far more violence. They can destroy whole buildings, kill scores of people at once."

"My word." Edmee turned to look back toward the laboratory end of the cellar, now shrouded in darkness.

"The hand weapons on the table," Phillipa continued, "what Orlando calls his *armi della mano,* they shoot little iron balls very fast when a hot wire is stuck in the hole on top. It doesn't sound very dangerous, but one shot can be deadly. I want you to take one of the *armi,* the one next to the brazier." It was the one Clare held on her when she came down here, so Phillipa was confident that it wouldn't explode when fired. "There are tongs next to the brazier for handling the hot wire. Take it upstairs to Lady Clare's chamber and aim it at her and demand the key to the sachentage. It's good that she's in her bath, because she'll feel all the more vulnerable and more likely to—"

"Oh, God, milady, ask anything else of me," Edmee pleaded, wringing her big hands. "Taking them keys was one thing. I can't go up there and aim that thing at Lady Clare and . . . and even if I did, she'd see it in my eyes that I could never shoot it at her."

"Edmee, I'm begging you. I need you. Please."

"I can't, milady. Please—ask me anything else, *anything,* and I'll do it!"

Phillipa sorted through the possibilities, or tried to,

but she was so exhausted, so traumatized. "Without the key, I can't get out of here. I'll never get out of here."

"If only Sir Hugh was here. He'd get you out of that thing."

"Thank God he's *not* here. They'd light a fire under that"—Phillipa looked toward the iron chair—"and strap him into it until he told them whatever it is they want to find out. He once told me he'd never known a man to be tortured who didn't eventually talk. And then they'd kill him. I'd rather die here like this than have that happen to him."

She *was* going to die here, Phillipa realized with a sense of numb inevitability. There didn't seem to be any way to prevent it, other than luring Hugh back here, and that wasn't an option. She would give up her life, but not without one last effort to avert another ruinous civil war.

"Do you know how to ride a horse, Edmee?" Phillipa asked.

"If it's anything like ridin' a mule, I can manage well enough."

"Fritzi's a tame little mare—you'll manage fine. You'll find her in the next to last stall on the right in the stable. Tell the stableboy to saddle him up for your mistress . . ."

"Unca Hugh sad?"

Hugh smiled down at his niece, happily ensconced on his lap at the dinner table. It was the first time he'd smiled since his arrival at Eastingham four days ago, and it was a herculean effort. "No, Nelly," he said, "I'm fine, just tired."

"Don't lie to her, Hugh," said Joanna, sitting next to him. "She's got eyes and ears, just like the rest of us."

"That's right." Graeham reached across the table to refill Hugh's wine cup. "I've never seen you so melancholic. I've never seen you melancholic at all."

"I'm just tired," Hugh said testily.

"You don't get tired," Joanna observed with a

crooked smile as she cut up a slab of stag meat for little Hugh.

"Everyone gets tired," he retorted.

"When was the last time you were well and truly fatigued?" she challenged. "I mean, tired enough to take to your bed and sleep like a stone?"

It was when he and Phillipa had been staying at Aldous's house in Southwark, Hugh reflected, thinking about those nights he'd ridden to the point of exhaustion in an effort to forget how desperately he wanted her. If he could only have her once, he'd thought, then his ravenous hunger would be appeased and he would be free of her spell.

What a fool he'd been. He would never be free of her, never. For the rest of his life, whenever he inhaled the scent of lavender, or heard girlish, high-pitched laughter, or touched something achingly soft, like his niece's cheek, it would remind him of Phillipa.

And it would hurt. It was not the type of hurt he could rise above; it was too much a part of him, too insidious. He would hurt for the rest of his life because he had turned away from her, because he had stabbed her with his words, cruel words meant to harden her heart to him, and walked away, not looking back.

'Twas for the best, he told himself for the hundredth time. Perhaps someday he would believe it.

"Sir Hugh."

Hugh blinked and looked up to find Joanna's elderly cook addressing him. "Yes, Aethelwyne?"

"There's a woman come 'round back askin' for ye. Says she rode all the way from Halthorpe. I said I'd fetch ye." Aethelwyne turned and walked stiffly away.

Hugh's first thought was of Phillipa, but if she had come to Eastingham, she would have made her entrance through the front door; servants and villeins came in through the back.

"Made a new conquest among the serving wenches at Castle Halthorpe?" Graeham asked with a knowing smile. "Can't say as I'm surprised."

Hugh kissed Nell's silky hair and handed her to her mother. "Let me go see what this is about."

Out back, sitting in the harsh midday sun on the stone fence enclosing the kitchen garden, he found the thick-boned Poitevan wench who had served Phillipa at Castle Halthorpe. "Edmee," he said, bewildered. "What are you doing here?"

"Oh, sir . . ." Edmee rose, clutching the skirt of her humble brown kirtle. "The lady Phillipa sent me. She sent me with a message, but . . ."

"But?"

Edmee's brow furrowed. "First the message, just as she told me to deliver it." She took a deep breath. "She says as how you should ride to West Minster and ask . . . Lord Robert?"

"Lord Richard," Hugh supplied.

"Aye, that's it—Lord Richard. You're to ask Lord Richard to send as many armed men as he can spare to Halthorpe Castle right away, because she's seen what Master Orlando's been inventing in the cellar and it's got to be stopped. It's weapons, Sir Hugh—terrible weapons. I saw them."

"Yes, but if Clare and Aldous see the detachment of soldiers approaching, they'll destroy or hide these weapons before we can—"

"Nay, she said to tell you they can't get to them because I've got the only key to the cellar." Edmee pulled a chain from beneath her kirtle; it was Clare's chain of household keys.

"God's bones! How'd she manage to get that away from Clare?"

"I'm the one who managed it," Edmee said proudly.

"Well done," he praised, and held his hand out. "Give the keys to me, then, and I'll set out for West Minster as soon as I can get my horse saddled up."

She shook her head grimly, her hand fisted around the keys. "That's not the whole message, sire. She said I was to tell you that you yourself are to stay well away from Halthorpe Castle. 'Twould be riskin' your life to go anywhere near it. I'm to tell you they're on to you, and that the Frankish soldiers will torture you in that horrible chair and kill you if you come anywhere near there.''

"Indeed.'' Hugh rubbed his chin, studying Edmee with interest as she chewed her lip and wrung her hands. "Why did Lady Phillipa send you? Why didn't she come herself?''

"She'd be furious if she knew I was tellin' you all of it. She said under no circumstances was I to let you know—''

"Out with it.''

Edmee drew in a breath and exhaled shakily. "That . . . *thing* in the cellar next to the iron chair, that iron collar thing''—she wrapped her hands around her throat in illustration—"with the spikes . . .''

"The sachentage?'' *No. Please, God . . .*

Edmee nodded. "She's been in that for three days and four—''

"*Jesu!*'' Hugh clawed his hands through his hair. "Christ! Why didn't you come to me before—''

"I didn't know till this morning,'' Edmee said, looking very distraught. "Please, sire, I didn't know! They've had her in that thing, Lady Clare and Master Aldous, since the day after you left Halthorpe. They're on to you, like I said. They told her they'd let her go free if she wrote to you and got you to come back, but she won't do it, 'cause she knows what they'll do to you if you show your face there.''

Hugh groaned and sank his head in his hands. *Phillipa, Phillipa . . .*

"Perhaps I shouldn't have told you, but if you could see her . . .'' Edmee made a tremulous sign of the cross. "I can't bear to let her waste away like that and not do anything to stop it.''

"Are they letting her have water?''

"Nay.''

Hugh swore rawly.

"I gave her a little this morning, but she's . . .'' Edmee looked down. "She's not doin' too well, sire. I can't imagine she'll last another two days. And I think she knows it."

It would take longer than that for Lord Richard to mount an effective assault of Halthorpe Castle, given how many soldiers would be defending it. Phillipa knew that, because they'd discussed the military particulars. She knew she would be dead by the time Lord Richard's men got there.

But Hugh would be alive, and safe. Which had, of course, been Phillipa's objective when she'd ordered Edmee not to tell him of her plight. She'd chosen to die in agony so that he might live, despite the way they'd parted, despite the hurtful things he'd said in response to her earnest, heartbreaking declaration of love . . . *Perhaps tupping Aldous will take some of the mystery out of sex and help you to stop mooning over me.*

Hugh cursed himself in a roar that scattered the sparrows chattering on the stone fence.

This was his doing. He'd abandoned Phillipa, left her to her own devices, a defenseless woman, after smugly assuring her that Clare and Aldous were harmless— something he'd wanted to believe, so he'd convinced himself of it—simply because he couldn't handle the feelings she'd spawned in him. He couldn't rise above them, so he'd ridden away, resigning her to her fate.

That she should make the ultimate sacrifice for him after all that . . .

Hugh scrubbed his hands over his face. *Dear God, what have I done?*

"Hugh?" Feeling a hand on his shoulder, Hugh turned to find Graeham behind him. "Was that you I heard bellowing like a bear out here?"

"It's Phillipa. She's . . ." Hugh raked a shaky hand through his hair. "She's in trouble. Edmee, if I went back to Halthorpe with you, do you think you could spirit me down into the cellar without my being seen?"

"You'd have to dress so you wouldn't be recognized right off," she said. "In a laborer's clothes, maybe, with that hair covered. And you'd have to ride something other than that stallion of yours."

"That's not a problem."

"What can I do?" asked Graeham, sober now, a soldier ready for battle.

"Get some men together, as many as you can, and follow me to Halthorpe as soon as possible."

"Consider it done."

"Oh, and Graeham? Good men, and well armed. I'm hoping to slip in quietly and handle this without any trouble, but if I can't get Phillipa out of there by myself, I'm going to need some muscle at my back." Gravely he added, "This time, I'm not leaving without her."

Chapter 24

The door squeaked.

Phillipa started, moaned at a pain in her neck, looked around her. Where was she?

Oh, God, the cellar.

The sachentage . . .

Someone was entering through the door. Clare? No, it couldn't be Clare, because Edmee had kept the keys when she went to Eastingham to warn Hugh to stay away from here. By now, Clare would be beside herself, having found both her keys and her maid missing.

Phillipa grabbed onto the sachentage's iron frame to help support herself, grateful that her hands were now free. She couldn't make out the identity of her visitor because that end of the cellar was now immersed in darkness—the lantern was on the floor near her, where Edmee had left it—but the shadowy figure was tall, much taller than Edmee, and broad of shoulder.

Please don't let it be Aldous, please . . .

But of course it couldn't be Aldous, because without the keys, he had no way of gaining access to the cellar.

"Phillipa?" It sounded like Hugh. She must be imagining things; she'd been doing that a lot.

Someone else came through the door and closed it behind him. *Her,* Phillipa realized, when she saw that this person was wearing a skirt. Edmee?

The man who came toward her out of the darkness wasn't Hugh. He had on rough homespun trousers and a tattered woollen mantle—peasant garb.

"Who . . . who's there?" Phillipa asked, her voice raspy again; she'd had no water since Edmee had left.

Her visitor paused at the well and lowered his hood, revealing a head of flaxen hair and a stricken expression. "Oh, God, Phillipa . . ."

"Hugh . . . no . . ." What was he doing here? Why had Edmee brought him? "You shouldn't be here. You must go. Now!"

"Phillipa . . ." He started toward her again, taking long strides. "How could I—"

"Please, Hugh! Leave now! Louis's men will kill you."

"No, they won't," said Edmee from behind him.

Hugh turned toward the maid, striding into the lamplight with her arms extended stiffly before her, holding something in Hugh's direction . . .

"*No!*" Phillipa screamed as a flash emerged from the *arma* in Edmee's hand, accompanied by a thunderclap and a cloud of smoke.

Hugh jerked backward, landing with a thud on the earthen floor, his forehead a burst of crimson. He groaned once, rolled his head to the side, and went horribly still.

Edmee stumbled backward, but stayed on her feet. Regarding Hugh's limp form, she said, "Louis's men won't have the chance."

"*No!*" Phillipa wailed, rage and grief roiling inside her, stinging her eyes. "Oh, my God, Hugh! *Hugh! Hugh!*"

He didn't move. With his face turned away from her, she couldn't see the wound, but the earthen floor on that side was dark with blood.

Clutching the iron frame with white-knuckled fists, Phillipa screamed Hugh's name, over and over until it wasn't his name anymore, just raw, wrenching sobs. Her cries of anguish filled the undercroft; hot tears streamed down her face, her throat.

Edmee strolled closer to Phillipa, studying the *arma* in the corona of lamplight that surrounded her. "Remarkable."

"Oh, God, Edmee," Phillipa choked out through her tears, "Oh, God, how could you? Why *would* you?"

"You haven't figured it out yet? And you're supposed to be so clever." Edmee's voice had changed, its coarse Poitevan inflections replaced by the refined speech patterns of proper Norman French. "I suppose your confinement may have affected the workings of your mind. But no, even before, there were things you missed, conclusions you drew because I led you to them . . . like your conclusion, on the basis of four black stockings and a whip, that it was Marguerite du Roche who executed that blundering oaf Istagio."

"Oh, God," Phillipa sobbed. " 'Twas you all along."

It was Edmee—or whatever her name really was, for she was no Poitevan peasant—whom Queen Eleanor had sent to Halthorpe Castle to ensure that discretion would be observed, control maintained. " 'Twas you. How . . ."

" 'Twas an ague that kept Clare's maid from returning to England with her," Edmee said, "but perhaps not quite an innocent one. I've found that small, frequent doses of wolfsbane produce a very credible lingering illness, complete with chills, fluxes, and a gradual wasting away of the body—which left her position vacant and ready for me to step into. What more perfect vantage point with which to monitor Clare's activities than as her personal maid?"

Phillipa closed her eyes against the nightmare of Hugh's lifeless body, and saw it all . . . Edmee lurking in the background all these weeks, watching and listening, seeing everything with those shrewd little eyes . . . Edmee allowing Istagio to seduce her after he'd made the terrible mistake of trying to impress her by igniting those packets of black powder. He would have been surprised but intrigued when she tied him up and produced the whip, bewildered when she lowered the pillow over his face.

Suspicion would naturally fall on Marguerite, her proclivities being well known and the stockings and whip being hers. It would have been a simple matter to see to the rest of it . . . a late-night ewer of warm spiced wine laced with arsenic, a litany of penance in the queen's code . . .

And Hugh. *Hugh, forgive me. I should have known, I should have puzzled it out sooner.*

"You wanted us to think the queen's agent was dead so we'd let down our guard," Phillipa said.

"I wanted *Clare* to think the queen's agent was dead," Edmee corrected, "because she'd gotten too inquisitive as to who that agent might be. I could tell she was beginning to suspect me, and the queen had instructed me to maintain my disguise at all cost. As for your husband, 'twas only this morning that I came to realize he was in the king's employ. And you as well, I take it. A workmanlike job, I must admit." With a glance toward Hugh's inert form, she added, "Not quite workmanlike enough, of course . . ."

"Burn in hell," Phillipa rasped, fresh tears welling in her eyes, clutching at her throat. *Hugh . . . oh, Hugh . . .*

Edmee smiled, the light from the lantern on the floor casting her face into sharp upward shadows, producing an eerily demonic countenance. "Not all hells are fiery, as you should know after four days in that thing." Slipping the *arma* and tongs under her girdle, she sorted through the keys hanging around her neck until she located the little iron one with the square top, which she removed. "Why, look what I've found."

"You . . . you had it all along," Phillipa said.

"Let's see . . . what to do with it?" Edmee tossed the key in the air, catching it in her big fist. "I know!" Pivoting, she walked back to the well and held the key over it. "How deep do you suppose this is? Let's see if we can tell by how long it takes to hear a splash."

"Edmee, listen to—"

She dropped the key.

Phillipa hitched in a breath.

Presently there came a faint, muted splash as the key hit the water and sank to the bottom of the well.

Edmee let out a long, impressed whistle as she peered

into the well. "Forty feet, I'd say, till the water starts—maybe more, and that's straight down. Can't imagine how they dug it."

Phillipa closed her eyes. That was it, then. She would never be free of this sachentage. She would die here.

Perhaps it's just as well, she thought. Without Hugh, she would be empty, forever incomplete.

"You understand why I couldn't possibly let you live," Edmee said, her voice farther away now. Opening her eyes, Phillipa saw Edmee hold a taper to the coals in the brazier, then light the lantern that hung over Orlando's worktable. " 'Twould be most injudicious, after all the effort the queen has put into developing these new weapons, to leave alive anyone who knows of them and cannot be trusted to keep his counsel. That includes not only you and your husband, but Orlando and—"

"No, not Orlando," Phillipa said. "Please—he's just a gentle old—"

"And, of course," Edmee continued implaccably, "Clare and Aldous, who know far too much for people who have a hard time keeping their mouths shut. They've proven themselves naught but liabilities to the queen's cause."

"Surely even you have your limit as to how many people you can bring yourself to kill."

"If I do, I haven't reached it yet. Dispatching large numbers at once can get a bit awkward, though." She regarded the contents of the cage thoughtfully. "How do those work? Do you happen to know?"

"I have no idea," Phillipa lied.

Crossing to the door, Edmee said, "I know someone who does."

"Where . . . where are you going?"

"Don't worry, I'll be right back," Edmee said as she closed the door behind her. "I can imagine how lonely it would get down here"—she glanced at Hugh—"with only one's dead husband for company."

Phillipa cursed Edmee at the top of her lungs as she departed, only to collapse into wracking sobs once she

was gone. "Hugh . . . oh, God, Hugh . . ." If only he
hadn't come. She could have borne this so much better,
perhaps even with a little dignity, if only he had been
spared.

When Edmee returned, not long afterward, it was in
the company of Orlando. Phillipa screamed at him as he
entered the cellar ahead of Edmee, warning him to flee,
but he just blinked at her in astonishment across the
length of the lamplit cellar.

"Lady Phillipa! *Il Dio mio!* What happen to you?"

Edmee smirked. "A bit of ill fortune. Happens to all
of us from time to time." Edmee closed the door and
chose an *arma* from the table. Withdrawing the tongs
from her girdle, she lifted one of the glowing wires from
the pan on the brazier.

"Orlando, run!" Phillipa cried.

"If you're going to run," Edmee said, leveling the
weapon at his head, "please be so kind as to run in this
direction." She nudged him toward Phillipa's side of the
cellar. "Otherwise I'll be forced to put a hole in your
head, and as you can see"—she nodded toward Hugh—
"the results can be most debilitating."

Orlando muttered a prayer as they passed Hugh. "Is
he dead?"

"If he's not," Edmee said, "he will be soon enough.
Sit there." She pointed to the iron chair.

Orlando shook his head and tried to back away from
it, but Edmee shoved him forward with the *arma*. "Don't
worry, I'm not planning on cooking you—unless you're
particularly uncooperative, and then I make no
promises."

With a weighty sigh, Orlando seated himself in the
chair and obeyed her when she ordered him to lay his
left forearm on the arm of the chair and buckle it down.
Setting her weapon down briefly, she secured his right
arm.

And then she aimed the *arma* at Phillipa's head. "This
is how this conversation will take place, *Signore* Orlando. I will ask questions and you will answer them in

a direct and straightforward manner, or else Lady Phillipa will experience a sudden, crushing headache. Am I understood?"

"*Sì.*"

"Don't tell her anything, Orlando!" Phillipa said. "It doesn't matter if she kills me—she's going to kill us all, anyway."

"Those things in the cage," Edmee said, as if Phillipa hadn't even spoken. "Those . . . *bombe,* is that what you call them?"

"*Sì.* From the Latin *bombus*—mean much loud noise."

"How appropriate. Is it true that they're powerful enough to destroy buildings?"

"Depend on how big is the building and how many *bombe*—"

"Say, this building," she said. "Castle Halthorpe. Could the *bombe* in that cage destroy—"

"Don't answer her, Orlando!" Phillipa cried.

Edmee held the hot wire just a hairsbreadth from the touch-hole. Nodding toward Hugh, she said, "I think I've shown that I'm more than willing to shoot one of these into a person's skull. So just tell me the truth, Orlando. If all of those *bombe* were ignited at once, what would happen?"

Grudgingly, Orlando said, "The building break apart, and probably is much big fire."

"Fire?" Edmee smiled slowly. "Fire would be good. Fire would be excellent, in fact. If Halthorpe Castle were to burn to the ground, killing everyone inside, who could say how it had started once there was nothing left but smoldering ruins?"

"*Everyone?*" Phillipa asked. "You would kill every soul in this castle just to take four lives?"

"If you think those people upstairs have souls, then you haven't been paying very much attention these past few weeks." Edmee turned to Orlando. "Do the *bombe* work like those little parchment packets? One sets fire to the cord and waits for it to burn down?"

"*Sì,*" Orlando said on a sigh.

"Will I have long enough to get out of the castle and get as far as, say, the outer bailey before they erupt?"

He nodded. "Is very long *fusibili*. You be much far away before the boom."

"Thank you, *signore*," said Edmee as she strode back toward the other side of the cellar. "You've been most accommodating. Ah—one more thing. Where might I find that extraordinary black powder of yours?"

"In the green pot on the table."

Edmee laid the *arma* and tongs on the table, emptied the purse hanging on her girdle of its few coins and filled it with powder from the green pot. Crossing to the cage, she fumbled with the keys until she found the one that unlocked it. When she held the taper to the hot coals, Phillipa said, "Edmee, don't do this. No cause is worth the death of all these innocent people."

"Innocent?" Edmee sneered. "You really haven't been paying attention, have you?" Oblivious to Phillipa's continued pleading, she squatted down at the cage and lit the ends of the long, trailing cords, one after the other. They burned steadily, but so slowly that it was obvious Edmee would be far beyond Halthorpe Castle's curtain walls before they exploded.

She relocked the cage so the burning cords couldn't be tampered with, then carried the keys to the well with Phillipa begging her to rethink this.

"*No!*" Phillipa screamed when she tossed them in. "How can you do this? What kind of monster are you?"

"The best kind," Edmee said with a smile. "The kind who can pass for human." To Orlando she said, "If it's any comfort to you, your inventions will live on. Those *bombe* should be simple enough to reproduce, and I'll take this"—she picked up the *arma* she had set down—"as a prototype so that more can be made in its image—"

He sat forward, shaking his head. "No . . ."

"No?" Edmee's eyebrows rose. "After all the years you spent developing these weapons, I can't imagine you'd want the world to lose the knowledge of how to make them."

Neither could Phillipa when she recalled how Orlando had rationalized his work for Clare . . . *All knowledge is good. All learning is worthy.*

"I no wanta lose the knowledge," Orlando said, "but that is not the *arma della mano* from which to make others. Is one of the type that make *esplosione* when the hot wire go in."

Phillipa groaned in dismay, wishing desperately that Orlando had not volunteered this piece of information. Would that the only surviving *arma* would destroy itself the first time it was fired!

Edmee laid the weapon back down with the others. "Which ones are safe to shoot?" she asked.

"That one on the end," Orlando said. "The one with the curved handle."

Edmee hefted this larger weapon, weighing it in her hand.

"You will need to know how to make the black powder," Orlando said. "The *armi* and the *bombe*, they are just useless piece of iron without the powder."

"For pity's sake, Orlando," Phillipa moaned.

"I have some as a sample." Edmee patted her bulging purse.

He shook his head. "Cannot be reproduce that easy from sample, or would not have take Orlando so many year."

With a quick glance at the *bombe*, the *fusibili* of which appeared to be burning down slowly enough, Edmee said, "Very well, then. How do you make it? What goes in it?"

To Phillipa's surprise, Orlando smiled. "I say you will need to know. I not say I will tell you."

Phillipa almost laughed. It seemed he had come to the conclusion that all knowledge was not, after all, worth preserving.

After a moment's incredulous pause, Edmee grabbed the tongs and plucked a hot wire out of its pan. Stalking toward them, her *arma* aimed toward Phillipa, she said, "You *will* tell me, and now!"

"She gonna die anyway." Turning to Phillipa, he said, "Sorry, but is true."

"Quite," Phillipa agreed. "Don't tell her a thing."

Edmee, a red tide of anger crawling up her throat, swung the weapon toward Orlando's legs. "How do you suppose it would feel to have a leg blown off? And then, if you don't talk, I'll get another one of these and blow off the other one. And then—"

"*Sì,* I am understand the idea," Orlando said with a shrug. "Is all right with me. The longer it take you, the more likely you get caught in the *esplosione.*"

With panic in her eyes, Edmee turned to check on the *fusibili,* which had burned down about a quarter of their length. Spinning back around toward Orlando, she leveled the gun at his right leg. "Tell me now, or I swear I'll shoot, and then you'll not be so cocky, I'll wager."

"Will be interesting to see." Turning to Phillipa, he said, "What you think? I still be cocky or no?"

Edmee bared her teeth, snarled, "You stupid old bastard," and shoved the wire into the touch-hole.

There came a roar as the weapon erupted in her hand, followed by a second, more violent blast as the black powder in her purse exploded.

For a long moment, Phillipa could hear nothing but the dull, incessant ringing in her ears, see nothing but the caustic black smoke that hung in the air, stinging her eyes, tickling her throat.

As the smoke dissipated, she saw, through its haze, that Edmee had been hurled backward, into one of the massive stone columns that supported the undercroft. Her body, blackened and bloodied, lay slumped against the column like a rag doll that had been tossed carelessly aside. The gaping wound in her belly was awful to behold, and all that was left of the *arma* she'd fired were a few twisted shards of iron scattered about the cellar.

Orlando was coughing.

"You tricked her," Phillipa said, impressed. "You had her put down one of the good weapons and take one of the—"

There came a low, ragged groan. Could Edmee still be alive? Phillipa wondered, and then she realized the sound hadn't come from Edmee. It had come from . . . *Oh, God.* "Hugh! Hugh!" The explosion must have roused him. Relief washed through Phillipa. "Hugh! Thank God, Hugh, you *are* alive. Orlando, he's alive!"

"Hugh, wake up!" Orlando commanded as Phillipa offered a tearful prayer of thanks. He was alive! She felt drunk with relief.

Hugh stirred, but he did not awaken, despite Orlando's exhortations.

"Hugh!" Orlando cried. "Open your eyes, *now*!" Phillipa echoed Orlando's pleas. If Hugh came to, he could save not only himself and Orlando, but the other occupants of the castle, before the *bombe* detonated.

Orlando jerked his arms against the leather straps that restrained him, swearing in Italian. Phillipa extended an arm toward the straps, thinking perhaps she might be able to unbuckle them, but her reach was too short by an inch or two.

"My eating knife!" Unsheathing the sharp little knife, Phillipa held it by its tip and extended it handle-first toward Orlando. "Take this! Use it to cut the straps."

Orlando could just barely reach the end of the ivory knife handle. When he took it, it almost slipped from his fingers, but he kept his grip, carefully reversing the direction of the blade so that he could slide it under the strap around his wrist and saw away at the leather.

Hugh groaned again. Phillipa looked toward the cage to see that the *fisibili* had burned about halfway down. "Hurry, Orlando!"

"*Fatto!*" Orlando exclaimed as the strap split open. "Is done!" Hurriedly he unbuckled his left arm. Rising from the chair, he strode purposefully toward the other end of the cellar.

"Orlando, where are you going? Don't leave yet! Take Hugh with you!"

"I no leave," he said as he sorted frantically through the flasks and vials on his worktable. "I am look for

something to . . . ah!" Holding up a small blue glass
vial, Orlando went straight to Hugh and knelt next to
him. He uncapped the vial and held it to Hugh's nose.
"If he *can* wake up, this will—"

Hugh growled as if in disgust and rolled to the side.

"Is work," said Orlando as he leaned over Hugh, waving the vial back and forth under his nose. "His wound,
is not so bad. It bleed very much, but is no big hole.
The little iron ball, I think it just graze the skull, not
go in."

"Open your eyes, Hugh!" Phillipa cried out. "Please!"

With a bellow, Hugh opened his eyes and swatted the
vial away. "God's bones . . ."

"Hugh!" Phillipa exclaimed. "Oh, thank God. Hugh,
get up! Get up!"

Hugh looked around blearily. On seeing Edmee's
body, he muttered, "Jesu . . ." An angry gash, matted
with hair, sliced through one side of his forehead, and
his face on that side was sticky with blood. He touched
his wound and winced. When his gaze lit on Phillipa, he
moaned her name and clambered shakily to his feet.

"You've got to get out of here, Hugh," she said as he
staggered toward her.

"What? Nay—not without you." He framed her face
in his hands. "Not this time."

"Hugh, you don't understand. Edmee, she . . ." Phillipa shook her head in frustration; there was no time to
explain everything. "Look behind you, at that cage.
Those things inside, they're like the Chinese weapons
you told me about, the ones that are filled with black
powder. Those cords are burning, and when the fire
reaches the black powder, this entire castle is going to
explode and burn."

Hugh tugged at the iron collar around Phillipa's neck.
"I've got to get you out of this."

Phillipa shook her head wildly. "The key is gone,
Hugh—it's at the bottom of that well, along with the
key to the cage. You've got to get out of here, you and

Orlando, and make everyone leave the castle. We haven't got much time!"

"Orlando, you go," Hugh said. "Get everyone out of here. Tell them to run. Get them as far away from the castle as—"

"You, too, Hugh!" Phillipa clutched at his mantle. "Go now, while you still can."

"I told you," he said quietly, capturing her gaze with his incandescent eyes. "I'm not leaving you." Ignoring her frantic entreaties, he turned to Orlando and said, "Hurry."

Orlando stood in front of Phillipa, his eyes glimmering, and took her hand. "When first *bomba* ignite, it will set off the others. Will be very big *esplosione*." Gravely he added, "You be very quick to die. Not suffer."

"Thank you, Orlando."

"Andare con il Dio." He lifted her fingers to his lips; she felt a wet trickle on the back of her hand.

Straightening up, Orlando executed a solemn sign of the cross, gripped Hugh on the shoulder, and left.

"Hugh, you've got to go with him," Phillipa pleaded, her chin quivering. "I'm begging you. Hugh, please!"

He was fiddling with the lock, his forehead furrowed. "I might be able to pick this. I need something sharp and narrow. Where's your eating knife?" he asked, noting the empty sheath on her girdle.

"There"—she pointed to the floor, where the knife had fallen after Orlando was through with it—"but, please, Hugh—"

"Shh. Hold still." Hugh slid the tip of the knife into the keyhole and jiggled it, staring at it as if he could open the lock by sheer force of will. He worked the knife in every direction, pulling on the collar, but it didn't budge.

" 'Tisn't working, Hugh."

He sighed and tossed the knife onto the iron chair, then closed his hands around her head and kissed her, very tenderly. "I'm not leaving, Phillipa."

Her tears overflowed. "Oh, Hugh, please. I want you to live."

"I don't want to," he said softly, touching his forehead to hers. "Not without you."

She looked into his eyes, so close, so fathomless, and was astounded to find them glazed with tears.

"I love you, Phillipa," he said, his voice damp and raw, stroking her hair with trembling hands. "I'm sorry I couldn't tell you before. I'm sorry I was so stubborn, so . . ." He shook his head, a tear meandering through the blood on his cheek. " 'Twas wrong to pretend I didn't feel what I felt. I was mad to throw you at Aldous, to abandon you as I did. This"—he yanked at the cruel iron collar—"is my fault, my fault entirely, and I'm staying with you no matter what happens."

"Hugh, I love you, too, and that's why I want you to get out of here." A glance toward the cage revealed that only a few inches of unburned *fusibili* remained. "*Please,* Hugh, those things are going to explode at any—"

"Don't look at them." Gripping her head, he compelled her to meet his gaze. "Look at *me.*" He kissed her deeply, his tears mingling with hers, his arms banding around her. She felt him shaking and realized he was as terrified as she, yet still he refused to leave her. "Think about me and how much I love you," he whispered against her lips. "Think about us."

"Think about *yourself. Please,* Hugh, those things are *filled* with black powder. They'll destroy this castle with you in it."

Hugh looked at her as if she'd said something remarkable. "Yes . . ."

"What . . . ?"

"If a lot of black powder could destroy a castle, perhaps a little—a very small amount—could destroy a lock." He looked at the collar and then at her.

Phillipa's gaze lit on a misshapen scrap of iron on the floor—a remnant of the *arma* that had exploded when Edmee lit it. "It could work," she murmured.

"It could also injure you," Hugh said. "Badly. I'm not sure how much to use, and—"

"Do it."

"Are you—"

"Yes. *Now,* before it's too late."

Hugh sprinted to the other side of the cellar, scooped some black powder into a funnel and lit the taper.

Phillipa looked at the cage, murmuring a prayer when she saw that the *fusibili* had burned almost all the way down. "We don't have long, Hugh. Hurry!"

A moment later, he was back, handing her the taper. "Hold this." Tilting the funnel at an angle to the lock, he poured a few grains of black powder into the keyhole. "I'm going to start with just a little," he said, setting the funnel aside and taking the taper. "Turn your face away—that's right. I'll shield you as well as I can with my hand."

"Hugh, I don't want you to hurt your—"

"There's no time to argue." Hugh took the taper from her and aimed its lit end at the lock, while holding his right hand over her face to protect it. Turning his own face away, he said, "Close your eyes. Ready?"

"I'm ready."

Lightning cracked in Phillipa's skull, deafening her and snatching her feet out from under her. She was dimly aware of a searing pain on the side of her neck, and a spinning sensation, as if the world were whirling in the wrong direction.

That groan, did it come from her?

Strong arms banded around her. She felt strangely weightless, and opened her eyes to find Hugh carrying her through the cellar—running, because the *bombe* would explode at any second, but laboriously, because her weight was slowing him down.

"Put me down," she implored him. "I can run, put me down!"

He set her on her wobbly legs, seized her around the waist and half-dragged her up the stairs, through the deserted great hall—*They got out . . . they got out in time*—out the front entrance and down the steps.

They sprinted over the flagstone courtyard hand-in-hand, across the close-cropped grass surrounding the castle toward the gate to the outer bailey, Phillipa's legs numb, her lungs burning—

A sudden concussion lifted her off her feet, pitched her forward. She felt the roar more than heard it, and then another and another and another, a deafening reverberation that shook the very earth beneath them.

Finding herself facedown on the grass, she started to rise, but something pressed her down—Hugh's body as he threw himself on top of her, shielding her from the continued force of the blast and the debris raining down on them.

As the cataclysmic rumble subsided, Phillipa became aware of a voice in her ear, Hugh's voice, talking to her, softly and earnestly.

". . . forever," he was saying. "Always, love. I'll always be there for you, always. I'll never leave you again."

Epilogue

June 1173, London

A butterfly flew in through the window.

Phillipa looked up from the communiqué she was en-
ciphering to watch the dainty white creature flitter out
of the sky as if transported on a ray of morning sunshine.
It alighted for a moment on her inkhorn, as if in greet-
ing, before setting off on a roundabout exploration of
her library, which took up the entire top floor of the
Thames Street town house she had called home for some
ten months now.

The butterfly meandered lazily past the books shelved
floor-to-ceiling on the windowless north wall, setting
down briefly on a stack that had overflowed onto the
floor, as if pondering the volume on top—a surprisingly
good life of St. Catharine by the nun Clemence, which
Phillipa had just finished.

With a tremble of its fragile wings, the butterfly arose
once more to drift curiously among the items scattered
on the corner table: a stack of correspondence weighed
down with Phillipa's jewel-encrusted dagger in its sheath;
an iron candelabra; her old tooled leather document
case, in which Aristotle's *Logica Nova* and *Logica Vetus*
still nestled cozily; more books, of course; and a silver
tray bearing the remains of her breakfast—a half-eaten
squire's loaf and a few crumbs of the sharp yellow
cheese she couldn't get enough of lately.

From the table, the butterfly wandered over to the
cabinet in the opposite corner, which could be locked

but stood open at present to reveal a number of rather more arcane items: cipher keys, some devised by Phillipa and some which she'd divined by decoding intercepted dispatches; two different kinds of invisible ink, one invented by her sister Ada; blank seals, wax, ribbons, cords, and other implements for resealing letters without revealing that they'd been tampered with; magnifying glasses that fit over the eyes; frequency tables for every language in which sensitive correspondence might possibly be conducted; parchment of all different weights and qualities from every type of animal utilized for that purpose; razor-sharp pen knives for scraping words off parchment without leaving a trace; and various other matériel employed by Phillipa in her capacity as cipher secretary to Henry Plantagenet, King of the English.

Victorious in thwarting the revolt against him, King Henry had punished his wife with confinement of the most liberal sort at Salisbury and his sons with formal censure. As for Queen Eleanor's hapless co-conspirators Aldous Ewing and Clare of Halthorpe, they were apprehended by Graeham Fox and his men while fleeing the burning rubble of Halthorpe Castle, whereupon Richard de Luci tried them for treason and imprisoned them indefinitely in adjoining cells in the Tower of London. It was said by the guards there that their bickering never ceased.

Watching the butterfly's circuitous journey, Phillipa fancied that she could feel the beating of its tiny wings in her very womb. She rested a hand absently on her rounded belly, starting when she felt it again, whispery ripples against her palm.

"Hugh!" she called toward the door that led downstairs. "Hugh, come quick!"

Footsteps pounded up the stairs, followed by Hugh bolting into the room as he yanked a shirt down over his head. "Are you all right? Is it . . ." His anxious gaze lit on her stomach. "Is anything—"

"Nothing's wrong," Phillipa said with an indulgent

smile. "I just wanted you to feel this. Give me your hand."

Hugh knelt in front of her, his hair a tousled golden riot, his eyes luminous as glass in the morning sun, and held out a tentative hand—his good left hand, the right, in addition to being thumbless, having been further mangled last summer when he blew that iron collar off her neck with the black powder. *Better to make an already ugly hand even uglier,* he told her whenever she bemoaned his sacrifice for her, *than to have ruined that extraordinary face.*

That wasn't his only souvenir of their mission, for the little iron ball that grazed his skull that afternoon had left in its wake a long, narrow scar on one side of his forehead, from his hairline to his eyebrow. Of course, he professed to view his new disfigurements as blessings. *The Sheriff of London shouldn't be too pretty,* he liked to say.

Phillipa took his hand and placed it on her belly, where she had felt the soft thumps of tiny feet from within. "Wait," she whispered. "You'll feel it—"

Hugh gasped in astonishment when the baby kicked again, and laughed delightedly. "God's bones!" He put both hands on her then, caressing her stomach with an expression of awe. When he looked up at her, his eyes were wet. "It's a baby."

"That's what I've been telling you," she murmured as she lowered her mouth to his. He curled his hands around her head as they kissed, sweetly and lingeringly.

A memory came to Phillipa then—her standing in the twilit orchard at Eastingham, filled with wistful fascination as she watched Graeham touching Joanna's belly as Hugh was now touching hers. Graeham had laughed, and then they'd kissed.

Knowing naught of the world, Phillipa had reflected at the time that some women were meant for marriage and children, some for different things. If she had been told then that, less than a year later, she would be married to the likes of Hugh of Wexford and awaiting the birth of their first child, she would have been utterly incredulous.

And yet here she was with Hugh's babe frolicking in her belly, and his arms around her, and never in her life had she felt such peace and fulfillment. As Orlando Storzi had put it following their nuptial mass last August, she and Hugh were living validation of the alchemical principle that two opposites can unite to create something altogether new and extraordinary.

The little white butterfly cavorted around the embracing couple as if in celebration, and then it flew out the same window through which it had entered, dancing out over the thatched and tiled rooftops of London, into the bright warm sun and the infinite blue sky, into the light, into the heat . . .

Into the world.

Coming in 2001
by Patricia Ryan

Pure and Simple

A New, Contemporary Romance
from Signet

"Jaclyn Reding is a rising romance star!"
—Catherine Coulter

JACLYN REDING

❏WHITE KNIGHT   0-451-19852-2/$5.99

Fleeing the cold, cruel knight she was forced to marry, an unhappy bride takes refuge in a remote castle—and finds a chance at true love with her mysterious husband....

❏WHITE MAGIC   0-451-40855-1/$5.99

❏ STEALING HEAVEN   0-451-40649-4/$5.99

❏ WHITE HEATHER   0-451-40650-8/$5.99